Rogue Blades Presents

DEMONS
A CLASH OF STEEL ANTHOLOGY

As Conceived by Armand Rosamilia

Rogue Blades
ENTERTAINMENT

Edited by Jason M Waltz
Milwaukee, WI

Published by
Rogue Blades Entertainment
4068 S 60 Street, Suite 401
Milwaukee, Wisconsin 53220
USA
www.roguebladesentertainment.com

Cover Artist: Johnney Perkins
Interior Graphics: M.D. Jackson
Back Cover Text provided by: Brian Dolton, Sandro G. Felcher, Rob Mancebo, Nicholas
Ozment, Barbara Tarbox, Bill Ward, and TW Williams

This is a work of fiction. All the characters, places and events portrayed in this anthology are either fictitious or used fictitiously.

Rogue Blades Presents
Demons: A Clash of Steel Anthology
Copyright © 2010 Rogue Blades Entertainment
ISBN-13: 978-0-9820536-4-5 (paper)
ISBN-13: 978-0-9820536-5-2 (electronic)
Library of Congress Control Number: 2009925849

First Edition: June 2010
Printed and Bound in The United States of America
0 9 8 7 6 5 4 3 2 1

Find out more about the contributing authors and artists at the RBE website.

The following stories originally appeared in *Clash of Steel: Demon* edited by Armand Rosamilia and published by Carnifex Press, copyright © September 2006, and are reprinted here by permission of the authors:

"Zeerembuk" by Steve Goble, copyright © 2006
"Azieran: Bound by Virtue" by Christopher Heath, copyright © 2006
"Joenna's Ax" by Elaine Isaak, copyright © 2006
"Into Shards" by Murray J.D. Leeder, copyright © 2006
"Demon Heart" by Bryan Lindenberger, copyright © 2006
"Blood Ties" by Trista Robichaud, copyright © 2006
"Mistaken Identity" by Robert J. Santa, copyright © 2006
"The Vengeance of Tibor" by Ron Shiflet, copyright © 2006
"Toxic" by Steven L. Shrewsbury, copyright © 2006
"The Beast of Lyoness" by Christopher Stires, copyright © 2006
"The Lesser: A Swords of the Daemor Tale" by Patrick Thomas, copyright © 2006
"Son of the Rock" by Laura J. Underwood, copyright © 2006

Rogue Blades Entertainment
Putting the Sword back into Swordplay; the Hero back into Heroics!

ACKNOWLEDGMENTS

It is with great delight that I am finally able to present this title to you!

Demons: A Clash of Steel has journeyed hard to reach publication. I and every reader and supporter of exciting action adventure speculative fiction owe the artists and authors found herein a debt of gratitude for their patience and perseverance throughout its long production. I guarantee that the stories contained here are worth the wait.

It was a sorry day indeed when Carnifex Press was forced to close its doors, prematurely bringing an end to the Clash of Steel series. Or so I thought. In a flash of inspiration, I contacted Armand Rosamilia and made a proposal: Allow Rogue Blades Entertainment to adopt the series, and RBE would swear to carry on its fine tradition of hard-hitting steel-centric sword and sorcery tales. He accepted. Here now is the result of that agreement, the first title of a procurement definitely to the gain of RBE.

The following tales cover most every imaginable demonic entity, from diabolical evil to mischievous imp...to perverse mortal. They equally cover almost every type of heroic character there is, from stalwart champion to willing sacrifice to the person present at a particular moment to meet a threat. There are serious tales and comedic; there are double-crosses and twisted, turning conniving fiends immortal and not; there are dark gods, powerful devils, and dangerous mortals. There are tales from new writers to seasoned veterans; first-time tales to further adventures in running series. Every tale possess at least one demon, just as every tale ends in victory...though not always for humanity. There is a tale here for every taste, and particularly tasty treats for more than a few.

My thanks again to everyone who has contributed to this title, to everyone who has helped kick off this first book in the rejuvenated Clash of Steel series. From my girls three to creator Rosamilia to artists Perkins and Jackson to every author to those who partook in the back text contest to every reader. Without each of you this title would not be what it is—a damn fine read.

Jason

Milwaukee, WI
USA

OTHER RBE ANTHOLOGIES

Clash of Steel

(Coming Titles)
Assassins
Reluctant Heroes
Sea Dogs

Heroic Adventure

Return of the Sword
Rage of the Behemoth

(Coming Titles)
Roar of the Crowd

Challenge!

(Coming Titles)
Discovery

ARTISTS

Cover ~ Johnney Perkins

Johnney W. Perkins is an avid fan of Fantasy, Horror, and Science Fiction. He has made his living as an artist for the better part of twenty years, working commercially for one of the nation's leading tourist attractions, and working with the Walt Disney Company on theme and design. Johnney has worked in the SF/F/H genres for more than fifteen of those years, and truly loves what he does. He feels blessed to be able to make a living producing and creating visions for others to imagine along with him. Find more of Johnney's work at www.myspace.com/jperkins24 and at www.fantasyartists.org/Gal30_Johnney_Perkins.asp.

Transitions ~ M.D. Jackson

M.D. Jackson has been an artist since he could first hold a pencil. He has been a designer and an illustrator for many, many years. His work has appeared in *Art Scene International Magazine, ImagineFX Magazine, A Fly in Amber, Abandoned Towers, Flashing Swords, Outer Reaches Magazine, Realms Magazine* and on the covers of various anthologies from Pulpwork Press and Rage Machine Books among others. Much of his work is digital, mostly using Corel Painter and Photoshop. Happily he is also handy with an ink pen and, of course, that old tested and true technology of the HB pencil and a scrap of paper. Visit his gallery at http://community.imaginefx.com/fxpose/mdjacksons_portfolio/default.aspx or his blog at www.mdjacksonart.blogspot.com/.

CONTENTS

CLASH OF STEEL: A FOREWORD

When you think of a great Fantasy story, what comes to mind? Warriors battling wizards and dragons, castles and piles of gold, fair maidens and battling nations...good versus evil. What could be more evil than a Demon in Fantasy? That's what I wanted to find out when the original call for Carnifex Press' *Clash of Steel: Demon* went out. I wanted to see if Fantasy writers could step up and write something original, with the focus in their short story being on a Demon.

My initial worry was that all of the stories would be the same, focusing on a giant red-haired, flame-throwing Balrog rip-off destroying a city before our puny stone-throwing hero managed to toss one into its weak spot and save the day...Wow, was I wrong! The stories were so diverse that I sometimes found myself reading them not as an editor but as a Fantasy reader, and I'd have to go back and start over with my editor hat firmly in place.

In the original collection and in this new update on the theme you're going to find a diverse array of Demons and Devils and Pure Evil, battling such a variety of Heroes...of the dozens and dozens of stories submitted, the very best choice cuts were culled, and the collection speaks for itself.

When Carnifex Press closed and the original collection went out of print I was resigned to the fact that, while sales had been decent, these great stories and the idea for them would live on only sporadically if the stories were re-sold or if the idea sparked further stories for some of the authors. When Jason M. Waltz, a big fan of the original and a bigger fan of the Clash of Steel series, swooped in, I was ecstatic.

Jason brings such a love of Fantasy to the game that you can't help wanting to work with him, to promote his releases and to know that he's behind a project one hundred percent. With his focus I have no doubt that the second time around for the Clash of Steel series and for *Demon* will be bigger than ever, because Jason knows what a great Fantasy story is, and he is able to pull a few gems from that slush pile and bind them as one.

I'm also excited to see the returning stories that appeared in the first collection, and they happen to be some of my favorites. Tales from Christopher Stires, Laura J. Underwood, Bryan Lindenberger, Ron Shiflet, Steve Goble and so many more...but I'm also amazed at the newer stories that really tie this collection up nicely.

I'm proud to have been a part of Clash of Steel and proud to have handed over the reins to Jason, who is doing the series justice. I look forward to the next collection!

Armand

Armand Rosamilia
Florida, USA

Armand Rosamilia
is a native New Jersey boy currently living in Florida, where he chases his
loving children, bothers his fiance' Kim, and watches the Boston Red Sox
devoutly. He's had several short stories published recently, and his urban
horror novella "Death Metal" was released by Sam's Dot Publishing in 2009.

THE MAN WITH THE WEBBED THROAT

by Steve Moody

He knew what reaction to expect from the townsfolk as his dragging feet kicked up tiny dust clouds on their streets of dirt. Strangers were rare; few people had reason to seek out the remote town and he wasn't one of the infrequent merchants who arrived every few months to trade fancy fabrics and other luxury items. His clothes were not merchant robes, but tough, dark leather, and the sword at his side was wrapped in a scabbard of dirty rags. Black hair kept short at the front and back, longer on the sides, framed an unshaven and scowling face.

A few people were curious enough to leave their houses and gawk at him, but he saw that most watched from windows, no doubt wondering what his business could be. None of them were close enough to notice the dots of red left behind in each footprint, nor could they hear the *pit-pat* of droplets falling upon his left boot from the hidden gut wound. He squinted upward at the sun, revealing a spider web tattooed across his throat. Then he came to a halt, and turned to face the building on his left.

A ramshackle spire twisted from the top of the wooden roof, its iron sculpture of a woman's smiling face attached by worn ropes; this was the closest the town had to a church. The tallest structure for miles around, it was in as much disrepair as the others; not neglected through spite, but apathy. He headed for the big, open double doors (the windows had shutters over them), and clumsily made his way up the six steps of wood, each with a tenet of the faith carved into it. The spatters of blood coming from his body fell heaviest on the step marked "A Fight You Cannot Win Is The Noblest Fight Of All."

Two rows of empty seats were on each side of the gloomy, narrow hall. At the far end of the church stood a granite statue of a forlorn child staring upward—the Orphan, abandoned and alone in a world that needed to be faced and fought against. Behind the statue were scattered paltry offerings: clay pots full of old leftovers, torn clothes, split shoes and so on. He looked at the offerings scornfully, and anger flashed in his eyes. The place stank of dust.

3

"Hello, who's that?" croaked a weak voice from a small side door. The stranger turned and saw an old man in mud-colored robes walking toward him, caution—not age—slowing his steps.

"My name is Cauzier," the stranger said with no sign of friendliness.

"I am Father Maltillay, the local priest. Can I help you?"

"No." Cauzier lowered his gaze and his tone became tinged with regret. "No, you cannot."

"I see by your tattoo that you are of the Brethren. What brings a holy warrior out here, so far from battle?"

"I brought the battle with me."

"What? I don't understand." Maltillay sat on a wooden bench close to the warrior.

"Understanding is overrated." Cauzier said. "It often leads to sorrow."

The old man frowned and shook his head. "It is understanding that puts us above the animals in the field. So teaches the Orphan." He gestured to the statue.

"The Orphan has led me down a path I would sooner have avoided," Cauzier stated, then grimaced.

"Are you hurt?" asked Maltillay. "Goodness! You're bleeding!" He stood, but Cauzier held up a halting hand.

"Don't fuss. It's a fatal wound father; I'm dying." As if to prove his point a drop of blood hit the floor, mingling with the dust.

"We have a doctor in the town, perhaps he—"

"No doctors!" snapped Cauzier. "I'm dying and there's the end of it. Too late for me, now." He looked at the statue again. "Too late for all of us."

"You speak in riddles; ominous riddles. Please sit, and maybe we can clarify things."

Cauzier sighed and sat next to the priest, who shuffled aside. "To explain the situation to you I will have to reveal some secrets; not that it matters now. The first thing you should know is that within our Order there is a secret chapter that guards our interests. Only an elite cabal knows of its existence, though there have always been rumors."

"I have heard bits and pieces," said Maltillay with a shrug.

"This secret chapter protects a scripture written by the Orphan himself; they are prophesies that have never been wrong since they were written over a thousand years ago."

"You are serious?"

"Indeed. The prophesies have foretold many wars, deaths and births; all of which came to pass as predicted."

"Then the Orphan is truly great!" said the priest, almost yelling in excitement.

"I was taken from the orphanage as a child and raised by the order's clergy, as I am sure were you," said Cauzier.

"Of course." Maltillay smiled fondly. "A fine upbringing."

"However, I was often kept separate from the other initiates," continued Cauzier. "I was being trained for something special. When they had taught me all a holy warrior needed to know, and more besides, I was brought before the inner cabal and had my destiny explained to me."

"What an honor that must have been!"

"I thought so. At first." Cauzier ran a trembling hand through his hair. "They showed me the prophesies, and to my everlasting horror I was featured in them! The Orphan had described me perfectly, and wrote that I was the chosen one, with the birthmark to prove it." Cauzier raised his trouser leg to reveal a red, dagger-shaped birthmark on his right ankle. "There could be no doubt."

"The 'chosen one'?" Maltillay frowned. "What chosen one?"

"According to the prophesies, it is my destiny to save the world from extinction." Cauzier said this as simple fact. Maltillay gave a snorting laugh, then stopped as soon as Cauzier glared at him.

"You are jesting with me, surely," said the priest.

"I am not one for jesting."

"No, I do not suppose you are." Maltillay noted the warrior's grim expression. "So, what was supposed to destroy the world?"

"A demon unlike anything you can imagine. Powerful enough to kill every living thing on the planet. It would escape from the wailing abyss, after killing the angels who act as its gaol wardens, and set about extinguishing all life."

"And how would you defeat such a thing?" Maltillay was getting caught up in the tale, despite his skepticism.

"It was written in the Orphan's prophesies that I would be endowed with all the strength and fortitude I would need, simply by virtue of being the chosen one. When the priests told me, I was understandably shocked.

"They told me not to worry; that the scripture confirmed I would be victorious. They left me alone to peruse the tome, so that I would be convinced of my future."

Cauzier looked again at the statue of the Orphan; his eyes were dark and cold. "Yes, I read the future, about the tremendous battle that awaited me against an almost unkillable foe. I felt no fear, for there in black and white, by the Orphan's own infallible hand, was the proof that I would vanquish the demon, and save humanity."

"If what you say really is true then we cannot allow you to just sit here and bleed to death." Maltillay took hold of Cauzier's elbow. The warrior shrugged him off.

"I will finish what I have to say," he snarled. "The Orphan teaches that we are all flies in Death's web; I fear not the spider." He briefly touched his web tattoo. "Alone with the prophesies, I found out not only the future, but also the past. The Orphan had predicted my birth and told of my parents' death from the plague; deaths that could have been avoided had they had medicine available to them."

"Such is the way of the Orphan," said Maltillay, sadly.

"The prophesies told much of my past, including things I never knew. I had a sister, who like me was only a few months old when we were orphaned. I had no memory of her, and she was sent to a separate institute. The village she went to was attacked by pirates when she was about ten years old. She died when they burned down the orphanage. Until I read about her in the prophesies, I was never aware of her existence."

"You have been blighted by tragedy, it would appear." The priest nodded. "Such is often the way for those with great destinies to fulfill."

Cauzier got up and made his way, with obvious discomfort, to the statue of the Orphan. It was life-size so he towered over it, looking down at a mop of hair cut from stone. "Everyone suffers tragedy," Cauzier said, "but some of it can be prevented."

"Fate is fate," said Maltillay. "You seem to have accepted yours."

Cauzier sat back down and the blood under his clothes made a squelching sound; his breath did not come easily, and he appeared in desperate need of sleep.

"Have I?"

"Listen my friend," said the priest. "I will be honest and say that I don't believe all you have told me. But, assuming for a moment it is true, we have to get you help; if you truly are the so-called chosen one, you have to stay alive to save the world."

Cauzier closed his eyes. "I make my own choices."

"But if the prophesy says you'll fight the demon, that's what you have to do."

"I have already confronted the demon, several hours ago."

"You have? Ah, hence the wounds," the priest said, excited. "You must tell me what happened."

"I arrived at the appointed place, at the appointed time." Cauzier's voice weakened. "A small lake, just a few miles from here…it turned to boiling blood as I watched, and from it stepped the creature, straight from hell and with the screams of dying angels echoing behind it. Man-sized, yet I could not deny the aura of power about it. Red scales adorned its seething skin, and barbed horns writhed and twisted from its broad face. Without boast, no other man would dare face this monstrosity, let alone fight. But I had the power of my faith and stood my ground."

"You are a brave man, Cauzier," complimented the priest.

"It stood before me, the ground under its feet rotting by the second. The demon grinned, and birds fell dead from the sky. Strength, holy strength, coursed through me; as the agent of destruction charged I knew that I and I alone had the power to save this world." Cauzier panted for breath.

"And?"

"And I chose not to," said the warrior.

"I'm begging your pardon?"

"I chose not to save the world." Cauzier's words were a struggle now, and the wooden bench was slick with blood.

"You've lost me," said Maltillay—yet the queasy echo of his words revealed his alarm.

"Don't you see?" Cauzier asked through clenched teeth. "I've been nothing more than a puppet my whole life. The priests, they could have prevented so much suffering by using the prophesies. They could have helped my parents, my sister; they could have stopped wars, warned of famines. But instead they let everything play out as written in the scripture."

"There is no arguing with fate, I suppose."

"Well, there is!" Cauzier made fists. "I let the demon inflict a mortal wound that is soon to claim me."

"Why? Why would you do such a thing?"

"To prove them wrong. To show that I don't have to follow their prophesies. To show that we do have free will."

"By letting the world be destroyed?"

"Mankind will finally be free." Cauzier coughed, and a line of red ran from the corner of his thin-lipped mouth.

"This is preposterous!" protested Maltillay. "I won't hear it!"

"The freedom will be brief, and end horribly, but it will still be freedom." Cauzier spat a gobbet of blood onto the floor.

"I fear that walking in the sun too long has deranged you. You're mad, we must get you help."

Cauzier slid from the seat onto the dusty ground. Maltillay knelt to help him up, but the holy warrior was a (nearly) dead weight. His eyes were closed and he looked almost at peace. As the priest tried to lift him, a wolf-like howl sounded in the distance.

"It is here," whispered Cauzier, opening his eyes.

"What is?"

"The demon. It has caught up with me. The town will be destroyed. I'd suggest you flee, but that won't save you." Cauzier made no effort to stand. The howling grew louder, more high pitched, more crazed.

"You're making this up! You must be!" The priest tugged at Cauzier's arm, but could not lift him.

The manic screeching rose in volume, the droning, buzzing undertone to it like nothing the priest had heard before. Its effect upon him was evident and immediate; convulsions gripped his stomach and he gagged as the unnatural bellow drew closer.

"Stand up," Maltillay implored. "If there is something out there, we must face it."

"I already have," replied Cauzier, "and the fate of the world is sealed."

"Stand up, damn you!" Something about the howling grated upon Maltillay's senses and sent him into a panic. His skin paled and he started weeping and shivering. The rectangle of sunlight shining onto the floor from the door vanished. Darkness rose in its place, as if night had instantly fallen.

The howling stopped, leaving an expectant silence that was just as bad— an assassin's silence, the quiet in which foul deeds took place. A stench filled the air, the rancid, sour odor of a rotting illness. "Please get up," Maltillay whispered.

Cauzier closed his eyes again. He heard the priest whimper as the doorway shattered, and scream as splinters of wood stabbed into their flesh. He felt no pain. Maltillay screamed again, and Cauzier heard the demon snatch the priest from his feet and hurl him across the room like a toy. A soft squishing sound and a brief gurgle followed. A slim smile spread over the holy warrior's pale face.

As the world began to end, and his life along with it, Cauzier knew he had made the right decision.

Steve Moody
*lives like any other writer. Between working in an office and sleeping, he tries
to cram the writing of speculative fiction into his schedule.*

IMPRISONED

by Carl Walmsley

It was the color of an old bruise or jaundiced skin——a sickly yellow smoke that congealed beneath the ceiling. Vordecai gagged, unable to breathe until the last threads had left his mouth. His twitching lips were flecked with saliva, and a smell like child's vomit hung in the air. He raised a hand from where he lay upon the floor, only for the cloud to drift away. He had not the strength to follow it. A window shattered as a fist of smoke scythed through it and, despite the wind and snow that gusted in, the cloud twirled and slid through the opening and was gone in moments.

Vordecia did not know how long he lay there. The edges of shattered glass had frosted and fresh snow coated the cabin floor when the door was forced wide and an anxious figure knelt beside him.

"One of them is free," Vordecai breathed.

In and out of consciousness he moved, like a bobbing man in a stormy sea. He perceived the snow of Heleck's streets, grimly lit by gargoyle-lanterns in the dead of night. He felt the snow crunch and shift beneath his feet. He heard a door slam, and felt the cold press of floorboards on his cheek. Muttering and cursing, his own unintelligible words were the last thing he heard before the darkness took him.

"Stay here until I return. If anyone finds you, they will not understand what is happening." Vordecai listened to the words as if in a dream. They made little sense.

"Try to discover which of them escaped."

There was the sound of a door closing.

Vordecai's senses pieced together his surroundings as if assembling a puzzle. He lay, staring up at a broad, vaulted ceiling creating the unnerving sensation of being high above the belly of a boat. Rows of benches lay on either side of him. At the far end of the room was a high alter, over which stood a leering effigy, wings spread, mouth wide. It was Heleck's chapel.

"Baliol?" Vordecia's words tasted sour, and his mouth was dry.

The crystal windows revealed darkness beyond. The wind ranged itself against heavy arched doors, making them rattle in their frame. All else was silent. His bondsman was gone.

It was an effort to stand.

Vordecai's head pounded, as it had in the days when his only concern had been getting home after a full day of drinking. He sagged against a bench, breathing slowly and deeply.

He had been taken completely by surprise. This was supposed to have been a simple excursion to collect vital supplies. He had chosen Heleck because it was such a nothing of a town—a remnant of the days when the passes through the mountain were watched. Yet something here had enabled one of the imprisoned to overcome his defenses. He needed to find out what.

He quieted his mind, ignoring the fatigue and aches that plagued his frame. He searched within, treading carefully before the cages and gazing warily at what lay inside the arcane prison that had been forged in his soul.

One door—the lock blackened and torn—was open wide. Even the memory of the creature within made him shudder. He checked, but knew already that the cell was empty.

Aware of his inward eye, the other beasts—formless demons and malevolent spirits—gnashed and pounded at their prison walls. Vordecai opened his eyes, allowing the screams to fade.

"It's Antininus," he said aloud.

The doors to the chapel were flung wide. Four men strode purposefully in, the foremost with his sword drawn. "Who are you?" he demanded.

Vordecai ignored his question, scanning the building for a means of escape. He had no wish to fight these men.

The lead swordsman gestured one of his cohort before the only window large enough to jump through.

Vordecia sighed and spread his hands. "I am just a pilgrim. If you wish me to leave, I will do so."

"I don't think so. There's been a murder tonight—stranger. Now lay down your weapon."

Vordecai held out his sword, hilt first. As the lead man reached for it, he let it fall. The fellow leant forward and down—and the heel of Vordecai's boot connected with his skull. He ran, then, headlong toward the open doors. One of the men tried to bar his way, but Vordecai shouldered him aside. He was beneath the doorway—looking out at the snow-filled streets—when something clattered against his head. He landed face first in a drift and slid to a halt. By the time he rolled to his back two men stood over him, their swords drawn.

"You need to release me," Vordecai said, doing his best to remain calm.

The man he had kicked in the head—Heleck's sheriff as it turned out—glared at him through the bars. He had a bloodied rag shoved up one nostril, and his eye had already started to blacken.

"We haven't had a murder in twenty years. The night you turn up, we find a man cut to ribbons outside his home." He tossed the cell-key onto a table. "You're going nowhere."

Vordecai heard the beasts clamor within. Their perception of the world was imperfect, but they could feel his anguish—and they reveled in it. They knew that if he died, they would be released. They hoped that might happen here and now.

"It wasn't me, idiot!" Vordecai hissed, realizing too late that his captives were trying to goad him into anger.

The sheriff glowered at him. "I hope they stretch your neck."

"There's something out there in your town—something evil." Vordecai was desperate now and, though he knew that the sheriff was unlikely to believe such a fanciful tale, saw no option but to confide in him. "It needed to kill to restore its strength."

The woman who entered was wrapped in white furs, and had long dark hair. Her appearance was enough to cut short the sheriff's scornful reply. In fact, he moved to tend to her with such rapt enthusiasm that Vordecai wondered if she was his wife—or, more likely yet, a woman he wished were his wife.

"Caylin, what are you doing here?" asked the sheriff, doing his best to conceal the bloody rag before offering her a chair.

Ignoring the gesture, the woman moved toward the cell in the corner of the room. "Is this him?" she asked.

Vordecai was already stalking toward the back of the tiny room.

"Don't get too close, now. He's a real animal."

The woman made a small, vulnerable sound and stepped away. A little tentatively, the sheriff placed an arm around the woman and seemed pleasantly surprised when she enfolded herself in his embrace.

"Tell me what happened," she said quietly.

The sheriff hesitated, considering which details to include. "He killed Jendan Gaites. Right outside his house, most likely on his way back from the tavern."

"Did anyone see?" the woman asked.

The sheriff shook his head. "But this fellow's one of only two strangers in town tonight. And they both arrived together. We'll round the other one up soon enough."

"Is that all?" The woman tilted her head, peering up through strands of raven hair.

"I'll get the rest out of him when the time comes," said the sheriff confidently.

Vordecai felt it a moment too late—a pulse of evil, moving like a wave front across a calm pond. He sprang toward the bars in time to see the sheriff stagger back, fumbling at the cavity in his chest—reaching for the heart that was no longer there. The man flopped onto the chair he had pulled out for his murderer—and died there.

The woman licked blood from her fingers and tossed the heart onto the dead man's lap. "You couldn't tell it was me, could you? At least, not until it was too late."

Vordecai tried to reach between the bars to touch the woman. She swayed back, comfortably out of reach.

"I don't think so. Ten years rattling around inside your hollow soul is quite long enough." The woman began to wander about the room, lifting and examining various objects as though searching for something.

"There must be some very dark sorcery in this town," Antininus said, using the woman's lips. "Enough to help me escape—and then to conceal my presence from you." She paused to gaze at a map of the town resting on the dead sheriff's desk. "It's got you all muddled, hasn't it? I shall have to see if I can't give them a hand."

The woman pocketed the map and then strolled toward the door. "Good luck explaining the corpse." And she was gone.

The voices within roared and wailed, and hideous black laughter filled Vordecai's soul. He moved back from the bars and forced his mind to be still. It was several seconds before his thoughts cleared.

Beyond the cell, the sheriff's blood had pooled and spread, and his dead eyes were wide and staring. Twice, Vordecai threw himself at the door, confirming his suspicion that he would never batter his way out of the cell. His sword and scabbard hung from a nail on the far wall, and there was nothing in reach that might be of use. There was only one thing he could think to do, and he would have to be very, very careful.

Flat on his belly, Vordecai forced his shoulder against the bars and reached out to the circle of blood. The instant he made contact, he felt the connection form. Carefully, he willed open his *soul-cage*, allowed its presence to draw forth the dead man's spirit. It rose, spectral and hazy as early morning mist, taking form beside the corpse. The impression of a face appeared—as indistinct as a reflection in a troubled pool. Its expression was one of profound sadness.

Vordecai willed the door almost

shut: he had no wish to imprison this soul, merely to draw it forth.

The spirit coalesced, its features becoming more distinct. Its voice, when it spoke, was filled with woe. "Caylin? Why? I loved you."

"It was not Caylin."

The spirit gazed in horror at its dead form, then away toward the door through which the woman had left. Vordecai felt a tug as the spirit sought to leave.

"No." He opened the door a little wider. The spirit recoiled as though struck and turned to face him. "It was not Caylin," Vordecai repeated. "She is possessed. It is the evil thing I told you of that now controls her."

The sheriff's soul stared at him blankly, and then its features darkened. "You! You caused this! What did you do to her?"

"Nothing—"

"Liar!" As it raged, the spirit's features twisted as if its skull were pressing at its skin making it seem dead and rotten.

"Don't." Vordecai knew that he was losing him—knew that the sheriff's love and grief were too strong for him to respond rationally. For just an instant, he opened wide the door in his soul. It was enough. The spirit screamed as its phantasmal form was torn apart. A moment later, it re-formed but now hazy and more insubstantial.

"Do as I say and I will save Caylin. If not..."

There was fear in the spirit's eyes. It had seen a glimpse of the cage within which it might be locked—and of the pain involved in such imprisonment. It nodded meekly.

"You must re-enter your body."

The spirit gazed at its ruined husk.

"I will help you," Vordecai said, "but—it will hurt. You must ignore the pain. Think of Caylin. Think of your love for her."

The spirit nodded slowly.

"You need to get me the key to this cell."

The spirit seemed unsure, but moved over to its blood-soaked corpse. The two forms merged, the ghostly apparition sliding and coiling like smoke through the wound in the sheriff's chest. The body screamed—a real and fiendish sound—and fresh blood pumped from the wound. The heart, resting still in the corpse's lap began to pound frantically.

Vordecai channeled his will, forcing the spirit to remain within the brutalized flesh. He could feel it struggling to escape. "The key!" he hissed.

The corpse bucked and squirmed and then rose unsteadily to its feet. Vordecai felt his own chest pulse and burn with every step. Clumsy, blood-smeared fingers closed about the key, and then the mannequin-corpse staggered toward the cell. A few feet from the bars, its legs buckled and it fell. A wail emerged, not from corporeal lips, but those of the escaping spirit. It writhed away into the most distant corner of the room.

The pain in Vordecai's chest was gone. Prizing open the corpse's fingers, which lay only inches from the door, he retrieved the key. Then he reached out and closed the sheriff's eyes.

"Go now," he said, directing his words at the mist. "Be at peace." Within, he forced shut the door. At once, the mist began to fade and vanish like dew-haze in the rising sun.

All Vordecai could think about was whether he really would be able to save Caylin.

Heleck's former grandeur had not been entirely lost. It had once been a bastion town overseeing passage to the Regal States, and therefore an important place for trade and diplomacy. Against the purple sky the last of its watchtowers stood out like a black lance. Its strong walls had been hewn from the mountain and then topped with a domed parapet.

Even in the darkness there were signs of activity in Heleck. Lights blazed behind shuttered windows and more than once, Vordecai was forced to hide as bands of men came searching along the snowy streets. He had little doubt that they looked for him. This far south, and at this time of year, there were never more than a few hours of daylight. Judging by the position of the stars, Vordecai guessed that he had a few hours before the sun came up. He needed to complete his work before then.

The climb to the tower was not an easy one. Steps had been carved from the mountainside but these were coated in ice, and the assent to the parapet was only possible via a rusty iron ladder. Even through the gloves he had taken from the sheriff's office—along with his belongings—Vordecai felt the bitter cold of the chilled metal.

"It's the town doctor," a voice announced as Vordecai gained the last rung. It was a moment more before Baliol emerged from the shadows.

"Show me."

The two men stood at the battlements, peering down at the white rooftops hundreds of feet below. Near the centre of town was a large house with jagged, black slates poking through the snow. Roosting upon these were four monstrous carrion birds.

"Eaters of the dead," Baliol said, pointing at the birds. "There are scores of rooftops in Heleck, and yet every one of the feathered gluttons ends up there. If that's not a sign of witchery, I'll break my own blade."

Vordecai had known that Baliol would be here waiting for him. When first they had entered the town, they had agreed upon the tower as a refuge if things did not go according to plan. Besides being private, it offered a unique vantage point – one that had now proved its worth.

Baliol stepped away from the crenulations. "So, what happened at the chapel?"

Officially, Baliol was his protector and servant but Vordecai had never thought of him as anything less an equal. Listening now to his reproachful tone, he was reminded of the fact it could never had been any different. Succinctly, but fully, he set out the events that had lead him here.

"So, it's Antininus?" Baliol said afterward. "That makes sense. He's seduced and abetted sorcerers in the past. He must have fed on the power generated by whatever the doctor's been conjuring up."

"There's another thing," Vordecai said hesitantly. "The woman that Antininus has possessed. She isn't to be harmed."

Baliol raised an eyebrow, furrowing his bald pate. "That will be interesting."

"If I can touch her, I can pull him out."

"And you think he will just let her go?"

Both men knew the answer to that one. Antininus had been an especially cruel demon when they had first captured him. As a shapeless spirit trapped inside a *soulcage* for ten years he had become even more sadistic.

"We can try," Baliol said, heavily, "but if it comes to it, you're my priority—and the things imprisoned within you."

One of Baliol's great talents was that he always seemed to have the right tool for the job. Crouched now in the shadows beside the doctor's house, he produced a grappling iron and a length of knotted rope from inside his pack and cast it high up onto the roof. A precautionary tug, and he began to climb.

Ascending behind him, his view of the town broadening with each slippery step, Vordecai caught a glimpse of another search party moving through the streets. They would need to be quick—and, if at all possible, quiet.

Hidden amongst the sloping peaks of the doctor's oddly structured house was a flat expanse of roof. Upon this sat a solid, wooden table. Beneath a dusting of snow an oilcloth was visible, fastened to the base of each leg. A swelling indicated that something lay concealed beneath it.

Surefooted as a cat, Baliol moved across the tiles onto the open space. Across his back were several sheathed weapons, including his blessed blade. Vordecai had seen firsthand what this could do—even to demons and the waking dead. Brushing away the snow, Baliol began to lift the cloth.

"Leave that!" It took a moment to place the source of the voice. So white was the doctor's cloak that he seemed to emerge from nowhere. He snapped a look at each of the intruders and then raised a withered hand, crooked like a claw.

The shrieks of the roosting carrion birds gave way to the beating of wings. In moments they had taken to the air and like veiled assassins, their pitch feathers merging with the gloom, they dived and slashed with razor talons.

Vordecai felt a wing slap his face and the slice of beak or claw upon his neck. Tucking his legs, he allowed himself to slide down toward the flat rooftop where he landed in a heap. Baliol was instantly beside him, and in a cleaving arc the warrior cut one of birds from the air. It lay flapping and squawking in the snow, till its bones crunched beneath a heavy boot.

With his own weapon now in hand, Vordecai stood back to back with his companion and fought against their winged assailants. The night was filled with shrieking black feathers and swift steel that blazed in the starlight. Blood—hacked from man and bird—stained the snow, before the last of the raptors died on the end of Vordecai's sword.

"Who are you?" The doctor now stood beyond the table, clutching the sheet which he had hauled back. A black form, humanoid but misshapen, rested upon the wood.

"Whatever black sorcery you practice here, know that it is at an end." Vordecai's words were laced with ice. "Surrender yourself—or die here."

The doctor's face twisted with incomprehension and rage. He raised the same, stunted hand that Vordecai had seen before. Now, more clearly seen, it was apparent that a part of each finger had been lost. In these climes—it was almost certainly the result of frostbite.

"You have no authority over me!" snarled the doctor.

"A golem," said Vordecai, gesturing at the prostrate form. Its black limbs gleamed like burnt wood.

"Yes!" hissed the doctor. "Constructed from the frost-bitten flesh that this cursed snow has taken from the town's folk!" He extended his maimed hand, curling the stumps about the golem's arm and lifting it. "My fingers! Taken from me!" There was madness in his voice now, sharp as a chilled blade.

"What use is a doctor who cannot tend his patients? Yet if this works, I will have a way to bestow life upon dead flesh!"

Vordecai had heard enough: whatever insanity the doctor had planned was against all the laws of nature. "Baliol, subdue him."

The warrior had shifted his weight forward just enough that the bolt took him not in the throat but in the shoulder. Even so, the impact spun him from his feet and sent him crashing to the ground.

Caylin stood in the same small doorway through which the doctor had accessed the roof. Her expression showed mild annoyance that she had missed her mark. "Finish your spell, doctor," she said mildly.

For an instant the doctor stared in bewilderment at the newcomer. Then he raised his withered hand and began to chant.

Vordecai stepped over his wounded friend, into the path of the advancing woman. She dropped her crossbow and drew a slender blade.

"This body may not be strong," she said, lunging forward. "But I suspect you will be reluctant to destroy it."

Vordecai deflected a series of surprisingly swift attacks, aware that he had to do something to deter Antininus. With all the precision he could manage, he sliced at his adversary's leg, gashing Caylin's thigh. Her body staggered back,

Antininus' shock writ large on her features.

"I have a special cage for you, demon," whispered Vordecai, with a cold smile. "And that body won't save you from it."

There was a sound like a fish flapping around in the bottom of a boat. The golem was moving; its reanimated limbs thrashing against the wood. The doctor made a stunted fist with his ruined hand and then slumped to the floor. Antininus' eyes flashed, and he leapt from the melee. In desperation, Vordecai followed but, within a few paces, Caylin's form collapsed like a stringless puppet. Vordecai gripped her leg, searching for Antininus—but he was already gone.

Above the table—and the juddering assemblage of stitched, frost-bitten flesh—two ghostly shapes appeared. The doctor's face, daubed in smoke, drifted toward the golem. A wreath of spectral smoke spiraled around his form and squeezed it like a coiling snake. The doctor's spirit-cloud screamed silently and dispersed into tiny wisps. Antininus' shade slithered into the golem's mouth, which closed with a crunch.

As it rose from the table, Vordecai seized hold of the dead flesh—feeling its chill burn through his gloves. He flung wide the cage within his soul, but felt the doctor's spell—the magic used to re-animate this flesh—push against him.

The golem raised a black fist, crashed it against Vordecai's jaw.

Towering above his adversary's stunned form, Antinius stretched his limbs, becoming acquainted with this new-made host. The golem's voice was the rasp of a coffin lid drawn across frozen stone. "This will do…nicely." With leisurely precision, he raised a dead foot and ground his heal into Vordecai's nose. The brittle cartilage snapped and spread, tearing the skin and spewing blood.

The Antininus-golem smiled—atrophied sinews stretching gruesomely. "What to do with you," he mused. "A quick death hardly seems fitting."

Looking around, he espied the doctor's corpse and retrieved a medical blade from within the folds of his cloak. With creaking limbs, he knelt before his fallen captor. Rigor-mortised fingers prized open Vordecai's blood-smeared jaw. "You always did have too much to say for yourself. Now…open wide."

Antininus paused, blinking several times before gazing down at the steel tip protruding from his chest. It was withdrawn with a crackle of splintering bone.

"I loved him!" There was such fury in Caylin's voice that it was this—as much as the second thrust of her sword—that held Antininus in place. "And you used me to kill him!"

Desperately, Antininus raised a blackened arm, deflecting a further lunge. His skin split like leather beneath the sword's edge. Ignoring the woman's fevered screams, he seized the blade in his nerveless fingers and wrenched it from her grasp. The woman seemed ready to pursue the attack with her bare hands when Vordecai's voice drew her back.

He was on his feet now and had Baliol's blessed blade in his hand. "I promised the sheriff that I would keep you safe. Let me deal with this thing."

Caylin stepped away, shaking with grief and rage, and the Antininus-golem turned on Vordecai. "You think to kill me with a sword? You'll never get me out of this body!"

"Have it your way," said Vordecai—and unleashed such a sudden and terrible sweep of his blade that the golem's head fell from its shoulders and settled in the snow.

Black lips curled back over grey teeth as severed vocal chords flapped noiselessly. There was enough hate in Antininus' still twitching eyes to make any words unnecessary.

"You're sure he can't get out?"

"Not for a very long time—far longer than if he had remained inside me."

Metal grated against the ice and a shovelful of snow settled over the severed head. Vordecai continued until the ditch was filled—and blended seamlessly with the vast expanse of snow.

He could have drawn the spirit out; the doctor's magic was not strong enough to have denied his *soulcage* in-definitely, but this seemed more appropriate. Antininus had freed himself once. There was no sense in risking that a second time.

"I think the woman will recover," Baliol said, wincing as he disturbed his bandaged arm.

Vordecai nodded, hoisting the shovel onto his shoulder. He hoped so. It would not be easy to live with what she—or rather Antininus—had done. He was not sure whether his explanation had helped or just made her feel even more insane.

"What now?" Again Baliol groaned under the weight of his half of the supplies.

"We have prisoners to look after," said Vordecai, touching his chest. "And until word arrives to go in search of another, we keep as far away from civilization as we can. It's safer that way."

And with that he turned toward the cold, southern sun and began walking.

Carl Walmsley
has now found publication with Rogue Blades Entertainment for a second time. His first story—"Serpents Beneath the Ice" *in* Rage of the Behemoth—*was a finalist for the 2009 Harper's Pen Award. He is hoping to have his first novel published later this year.*

TOXIC

by Steven L. Shrewsbury

*"Truly, I recognize what wickedness I propose to do,
but stronger than all my afterthoughts is my rage,
rage that brings upon mortals the utmost evils."*
~ ANCIENT PROVERB

A heavy weight smashed into the wooden door of Noel's room, bursting the restraint bar inward. Head still groggy from too much ale, Noel bolted up from his stupor, dagger in hand. However, through the haze left by the dying candles, he found no threat in the sight that greeted him.

"Come and help us, outlander!" the portly man screamed, waving his arms in the smoky air. "I know that you just arrived in town late this night, but you may be our last hope."

Swinging his long legs out of the straw mattress, Noel kept the sharp dirk up as he barked, "By the ass of Wodan, Evzen, what do you want? I never asked for more towels, servitor."

Loping across the room with some difficulty, Evzen threw open the somewhat rotting shutters and pointed. "Look for yourself." He said, his flabby arms shaking. "There isn't much time." As Evzen caught his breath, Noel wondered if the fat man would drown in the sweat accumulating in his russet gypon. Evzen claimed, "Get your things and let's go!"

Still wary of the youthful, if obese intruder from the boarding house staff, Noel leaned toward the window. Brushing away locks of brown hair, Noel saw the distant, picturesque mountains of Avari thrusting skyward like grand teats. They stood proudly over the flat plain of Shynar outside the village of Oliverian. Though the moon was only partially visible, the scene outside was easily discerned. A pair of figures gave off radiance, emitting light as if they were the sun itself, while soldiers and people from the village of Oliverian scrambled away.

One of the glowing entities was a woman, Noel observed. Mystic or not, his blood rushed at her femme shape and manner. Tall, lithe, fair-haired, and bouncy, her outline made Noel gape, even if her sorceress ways gave off a Stygian bent. The fire, lurid lights and death dealing made her allegiance doubtless.

If anything, her gods had given her an overabundant bosom blessing—to the point of deformity, even at this distance. She walked with an arrogant gait, though, fluttering lustrous hands in the air, causing men at arms and fleeing women alike to plummet to the wilted autumn grasses. Many barking hounds fell with a whine, as lifeless as their masters. Noel thought he saw ashes or butterflies escaping from her hands as the people from Oliverian dropped around her. The sensual, gleaming body strutted toward the other luminescent figure. Noel blinked at the waiting figure's scarlet hue.

"What on Earth is going on?" he said, hardly able to articulate the words while struggling to pull up his breeches.

Evzen wiped perspiration from his eyes, and grabbed up Noel's bags. "We must get out!"

Noel blinked, and then squinted outside once more. He could see a six-pointed star shimmering on the ground, surrounding the reddish-hued being. It was then he perceived that while this entity looked male, it was not human. Reptilian eyes and raised spikes covered most of its hulking body, though fins not unlike those of a fish lined its shoulders. A corona of flame ringed its body, and raged within the star. The man-beast stared at the approaching woman. She waved at it, and bolts of flame erupted from the star, striking many of the soldiers in chain mail that had attempted to close upon her. The men fell to their knees, frozen in place as their skin boiled and seeped through the links of their chain mail.

Noel muttered, "What damnable living thing is that?"

The fat man chuckled in nervous terror as he shoved Noel's belongings at him. "I thought you could tell us."

Ignoring Evzen's strong body odor, Noel swiftly descended the dim stairway. They emerged from the side of the bordering house situated on the edge of the hamlet of Oliverian. Instead of fleeing into the series of small, single story thatch-roofed homes, Noel looked to his left. He watched several fighters drop their maces, cast off their baldrics and flee. Other armored men fell down hard and died, their bodies twitching out their last breaths before the woman and her fiend from beyond.

"Many thanks for waking me," Noel said to him, and turned to his right.

"Stop!" Evzen exclaimed, jowls trembling. "It is you who can save us! You must combat this sorcery at its core."

Laughter echoed on the plains of Shynar as the woman waved her now-blazing hands, causing more lines of fire to burst from the hexagram. She maneuvered them like whips, strafing the dead bodies. It was then that Noel's suspicions were confirmed: The sorceress sported three breasts of equal size.

Incredulous, Noel exclaimed, "What? What do you think I can do against that? Because I am a world traveler does not mean I know any special methods of fighting."

"I've heard of you," the man said as they ducked behind the tavern. More men in light armor and armed with long bows approached. They launched a barrage of arrows as soon as they were within range. Pursing her cherry red lips, the sorceress waved her arms and blew a kiss in their direction.

"That is comforting," Noel replied as the projectiles of the bowmen plummeted to the ground as they neared the woman and her radiant hostage. "Who is she and what does she want? That broad has a heck of a censer beside her!"

"She is the terrible sorceress Rajni Nanikub, and she seeks the scrolls of Elajac in the vaults under our town." Evzen paused and mumbled, "I never have seen a woman with three breasts. I wonder why that is?"

"Probably a supernumerary teat used to suckle the dark forces," Noel said. "Some workers in darkness hide such a deformity, but she wears it well."

Noel saw the bowmen try again and then witnessed Rajni bark orders at the being next to her. This creature gave Rajni a disdainful look, then vomited a spurt of bile out of the star. This phlegm rolled and took on mass, growing larger at each full turn.

"Damn, even the bowmen of Urak have failed." Noel said in surprise.

Whimpering, Evzen whispered, "When she learns the scrolls of Elajac are already stolen…"

"Why in the name of Donar would she want such things?" Noel spat, trying to keep his head down.

Breathing heavily, Evzen answered, "Some say if all of the fragments of the scrolls are united, they form a pattern that will give the reader great powers."

"Then they should stop telling tales like that," Noel remarked as he watched the glob in the dead grass start to form a spinal column.

"She will enslave us all to her evil will," Evzen assured him. "A life of evil labor under that taskmaster is unthinkable."

"If she can cage and control a demonic persona like that…damn, Evzen, you are mad if you think I can do anything against that. A woman who controls a demon!

"I'm just in town for the mint wine and the Asiatic dwarven whores, three for a gold piece as advertised." Noel almost laughed while peering through a line of stone idols by the tavern's hitching post. "I don't care if she does want the scrolls of Elajac of Jericho. She can use them for waste wiping for all I care! I'm so sacred now I couldn't use my manhood for an act of fake Rhahdomancy."

When the archers saw the ball of spit suddenly transform—sprouting a spine, scales and wings until becoming a man-sized dragon—they took flight.

"But you are a powerful wizard," Evzen begged, himself watching the dragon struggle to unfold its tiny wings.

Rajni cocked her head as if she heard the plump man, and hissed in a masculine voice, "Bring forth the challenger to me and let me be done with these petty fools or I will blight your land for a thousand years."

The diminutive dragon stared at them and peeled back its leather lips in a mocking grin. Rows of teeth parted and its fiery breath slammed into the side of the tavern. Noel and Evzen jumped to their feet and ran, dodging behind the line of granite icons that honored local and varied gods of the world.

Noel snarled at Evzen, "You stupid man. I am not a wizard. I am a bard and a comedian. The wizard was in the room next to me."

The stout man blinked. "Oh."

Rajni giggled. "Little wizard, I have divined the moment of your death and it is now. You shall die horribly."

"She's as funny as a tooth extraction with no booze," Noel said.

They were forced to scramble from their spot as the tiny dragon swiped its tail, reducing the statues to pebbles, and sending them to all fours with another blast of flame.

Evzen implored Noel, "Don't you have anything in that bag of yours?"

"I'm no magician or magus," Noel insisted with a hot tone, but reached into his bag all the same. "But that bastard is about on us, so anything is worth a try."

Shooting Rajni a glance and confirming that she was content to let her newly conjured beast fight this battle for her, Noel dug through his satchel. His right hand emerged with a tiny clay jar, a clear substance oozing from its lid. He reared back and flung the jar at the dragon.

Instinctively, the monster snapped at the container, crunching it to pieces within its heavy maw. The gluey contents splattered over its mouth, lips, and nostrils. The dragon took a few steps then staggered, the beginnings of a roar caught deep in its throat. It twisted its head back toward its demonic creator, but no other sound emerged from its constricted jaws.

Rajni looked puzzled while the demon beside her appeared amused. Smiling, its chest heaving, the demon said, "I can generate creatures for you, my rotten jailer, but I cannot teach them to fight."

Eyes afire and lips spraying spittle, she retorted, "Mind your mouth or you shall return to the abyss!"

While the dragon stomped and thrashed in confused circles, the demon said, "That may be better than serving a grimy wench like you. If I but had my hands free, I'd be on you in an instant. Once you possess the scrolls in Oliverian, you will hold the keys to controlling those in the abyss."

She grinned wolfishly. "And that will make me a goddess."

The demon nodded ruefully. "Or close to it."

The dragon's mouth puckered in like a fist, but no flames came out. Panic descended upon the beast, but it had taken only one step when suddenly it stretched flush to the ground and an inferno ejaculated out its backside. A stream of combustion flowed from beneath its tail as it fell to the dirt. It lay still, flames slowly ebbing from its lower quarters. Rajni could not hide her look of astonishment.

The demon laughed.

"What magic is this?" she hissed, hands curling into cruel talons.

Still short of breath, Evzen stammered, "Yeah, what magic was that?"

Noel replied, "Just a gift from magi, a balm for furious piles. I don't know how it sealed that thing's mouth, but luck was with me."

"Luck!" Rajni roared, her voice like a clap of thunder in an empty valley. "There is no such thing as luck!"

The demon snickered yet again as the dragon melted. "Chance or fate, though, may be the comrade of this modest bard."

"Does this young one realize what power I command?" she asked, but no one was certain whom she addressed. "Why, I could call forth any number of minions via the power of my dark servant. With but a word or desire I could send forth solar scarabs, berserker wasps, or feral harpies in numbers unimagined, soaked in poisonous ooze! However, in this case, this puny boy doesn't rate that much blood."

Rajni raised her hands and balls of flame started to cultivate there, sapped off the sulfurous nimbus of the demon beside her.

Evzen was up and jogging back toward the burning tavern, but Noel took up his bag and ran in the direction of the ruined idols. Ducking and dodging, he narrowly evaded the spheres of fire dropping around him. Rajni strode closer, moving away from her demon. Her fireballs grew smaller the further the separation grew.

Rajni paused and looked down into the dead faces of two of the men-at-arms who had died upon their knees. With a cackle, she clutched their heads between her smoking hands and split their skulls like rotten timber. When the pieces of skull had fallen away, the gray organs left erect pulsed purple under her touch. Inhaling and loosing her breath in a guttural roar, she puffed upon each brain until they had grown three times their size and sprouted four legs each. The sorceress continued on her path to Noel as her new creations pulled free from their former hosts.

Watching these monstrosities learn to walk on their fresh legs, Noel realized he had only moments before they—or the woman—were upon him. All of his dodges and shoulder rolls could only keep them at bay for so long. Landing beside the gooey remains of the dragon, he jammed a hand into his bag and produced a dark, spongy object.

The sight of this made Rajni pause, the rhythm of her triple breasts stopping with a bump. Noel stuck his latest find into the dragon's wet mass, then made a fist. With great speed, he side-armed the glob at the sorceress.

Rajni, stunned at his actions, let it slap across her face. A gelatinous mass spread over her eyes. She shrieked, turned and ran back toward her creature, who roared in laughter. Inadvertently, Rajni stomped on one of the brain creatures and it exploded in a puff of gray dust and lavender juice.

Evzen gaped at him, but before he could ask, Noel said, "Merkin. It was all that I had that was absorbent."

Gasping with laughter, the demon said, "Blinded by a crotch wig. This is an excellent day for your fine self."

With great curses to all, Rajni wiped her eyes free of the substance and started to hurl flame globes again. From deep within her bosom came chants and curses, raising a host of insects from the wastelands behind them. The second enlarged walking brain headed toward Noel.

The bard scooped handfuls of broken stone into his bag, dodging Rajni's fire and eyeing the cloud of bugs forming behind the two invaders.

"Bah, I am through with this maggot," Rajni snorted and spread her arms wide. "I call upon the Skum of the Earth to aide me!"

The outlines of humanoid forms started to appear in the weeds and dirt of the plain. Noel pulled his bag shut and muttered, "One shot." Then he dashed toward Rajni and her devil.

The demon watched Noel dodge the Skum creatures not yet free of their earthly bonds. It smiled when the bard planted his feet and swung his bag just as the crawling brain launched itself at him. Bag and brain collided and the creature stuck to it, legs convulsively digging in. Noel kept running forward.

Shaking its eerie visage in bemused appreciation, the demon said, "Stones he has, my dire jailer, and not just in his bag."

Rajni flared her nostrils, expelling mucus. "He is drunk or mad! Look at him?" She tossed her head back and snorted. "What can he hope to do?"

Her hilarity waxed greater as he Noel bounced off one of the lunging, grassy Skum. In her arrogance, she allowed him to close the distance between them. Finally, she commanded the demon to shield them. Both muscled arms of the demon went up and a faint yellow glow stretched across their bodies.

Noel drew his arm back and lobbed the bag, brain creature and all, through the air.

Rajni giggled, covering her mouth to suppress majestic laughter.

The weighted bag, traveling toward the demon, fell dismally short of the target...but never hit the shield... plummeting just shy of their position... hitting the drawn out edge of the six-pointed star. The brain creation splattered on impact and the heavy bag rolled.

The mystic line, now imperfect, was broken. The demon's eyes flared emerald green. Never looking at Noel, it immediately attacked Rajni, pulling her to itself in extravagant embrace. Its hug scorched the sorceress' minimal clothing from her willowy body.

The entwined figures rose into the sky, the demon laughing, and peeling Rajni like a banana. Strips of the sorceress' flesh fell to the dry grass to either side of the slack-jawed bard, and her screams pounded in his ears. The fiend vanished with a sudden clap of thunder, taking its skinless prey with it.

As the echo of their departure rolled across the sky, the shade of insects dispersed. Evzen emerged from his cover. He approached Noel and said, "Thank you so much."

Exhausted, Noel dropped to his backside and sucked air. He looked at the discarded strips of Rajni's flesh and sighed.

Evzen exclaimed, "That was just incredible! I cannot believe you even took them on."

"I'm the youngest of seventeen boys. One learns to fight back, if not to win every time out of the box."

Hands to his ample waist, the heavy youth clucked, "Damn, what a display of courage!"

Noel looked down at his still quaking fingers, and felt the gooseflesh on his skin ebb away, the bellow of the demon fading like outlying thunder. "Next time, get a wizard. I am just a damned joker."

"Tell me a joke!" Evzen requested with enthusiasm.

Slowly, Noel arose. "How do you keep a jackass in suspense?"

"How?" The fat man asked as Noel walked away.

Steven L. Shrewsbury lives, works and writes in Central Illinois. He enjoys football, books about history, guns, politics, mystery shows and good fiction. 365 of his short stories have been published in print or digital media. His novels Stronger than Death, Hawg, Tormentor, *and* Godforsaken *run from horror to historical fantasy. His collaboration with Nate Southard,* Bad Magick *from Bloodletting's Morningstar line, will be his first hardback release.*

AZIERAN: BOUND BY VIRTUE

by Christopher Heath

"Why have you summoned me?" The speaker was a demon.

Old Rah-noth paced about the magic circle formed by thirteen naked and dead, daisy-chained virgins. The mage did not deign to answer immediately, but busied himself with brushing away the sudden scent of brimstone from his nostrils. A thick-framed wizard of bald pate and owlish features, his head rested low on his shoulders; he slouched in his shambling gait. A branding iron was angled across his chest, its end glowing red-hot. He finally decided to answer the question.

"My enemy is bringing a dark force against me: one of your kin—a revenge demon. I have spied this through clairvoyance." The crack of thunder could be heard outside, and heavy raindrops splashing against the conical roof far overhead.

"How long ago?"

"Three days."

"Three days! The demon is likely bloated with Abyssal ichor by now, and too powerful to be laid low by my blade. Why have you waited so long to petition my aid?"

"It is difficult to find thirteen virgins of age during these times."

"No fault of your own, I presume?"

Rah-noth ignored such low-browed levity and eyed the risk demon with calculated expectations. Its form was humanoid, though two short horns rested atop its head, and red-scaled skin appeared beneath its tight, black leather armor. A golden, serpent-skin scabbard held a formidable blade of ivory hilt angled across his back. At his sides, two short staves of crimson wood—thundersticks from the Abyss, both holding a charge of brimstone at each end—hung by tethers.

"Step toward the edge of the circle," the diabolist commanded.

The demon stared intently at the grooved cement floor, canals of virgin blood forming his mystic prison. He sniffed the miasma and found the blood was wholesome unto the last drop. He strained to the edge of the circle, knowing he could not cross the pure, yet dead flesh.

"What do you offer for your part of the bargain, old man?" The question was asked with a menacing snarl.

Rah-noth responded immediately, in his curt, somber voice. "I offer only a keepsake; a demon amulet bearing your true name—that which has been my focus and allowed your summoning. If you succeed in defeating the revenge demon, an iscaris'ri, and aid in fighting my nemesis, Vathryn, then you will own the amulet, and your true name, Azrédien. You will be forever free from my summons."

Azrédien had to think little on the matter, though he did not fully trust the diabolist's words. His exotic and extra-sensory mind sought out possible avenues of the future, catching brief glimpses of what might and could transpire. He began to form a plan. "I accept your offer."

The old mage stabbed forth the branding iron, and a fount of steam exploded from the risk demon's forehead. Azrédien, the cambi'ri, howled in pain, showing vibrant fangs and spewing venomous froth which streamed down to etch the dead, pallid flesh at his feet.

Rah-noth quickly removed the brand, kept his distance, and allowed a moment for the vapors to clear. It pleased him to see the emblem fully burned above the brow of his summoned captive. He nodded solemnly, now knowing the demon could not attack him. Rah-noth dropped the branding iron to the floor, and huffed as he dragged the dead weight of a virgin to the side, opening the circle.

Azrédien moved cautiously from his confinement of flesh, bending over to smell the blonde virgin's hair, imbibing her natural fragrance and even taking time to remove a lock of her hair with the sharp of his nail. He raised the tress to his nose, smiling slightly, before placing it in a pocketed fold of his armor. Rah-noth shrugged. Demons had their fetishes, he supposed.

Azrédien noted the vast open tower that formed a cylinder until tapering at the shingled apex some forty feet overhead. An archway led to other areas of Rah-noth's keep. The demon let his gaze linger across the open expanse to where he noted a score of small kennels scarcely fit for dogs, thirteen with their doors open—obviously used to house the virgins in the days before their sacrifice. He noted the narrow, barred windows, and the lift latches which locked the doors. If a prisoner was locked in, the latch could be reached by a slender blade; that would be perfect.

"We haven't long," Rah'noth warned, handing Azrédien a black loaf housed in the chitinous shell of some gargantuan, rat-sized beetle.

The demon opened it, and found what he expected—a black, tar-like substance which barely held its shape. It was Abyssal ichor, the sustenance of his home plane, which would make him ever stronger when consumed upon this world. He devoured it with a voracious appetite, feeling vigorous as it slid down his throat, sorcerous powers waxing strong.

"More!" he demanded, but Rah-noth merely shook his head.

"I regret that is all I have to offer, but you are the more powerful demon of the two. We must both pray that your advantage holds."

"I do not pray."

Rah-noth shuddered beneath his robes. "I suppose not. Then may your luck hold, for both our sakes." The diabolist was now cradling a staff in hand, eyes rolling back in his head. "They are coming, through wind and rain, beneath moon and star. Power! I hear the power of evil pounding in their hearts. We will face them as we must, we will wrest that strength from them and claim it as our own!"

Azrédien remained skeptical at the suggestion of camaraderie, and the ambiguous promise of sharing power. "If you do not hold your own against Vathryn, and allow him to aid his demon against me, we are both doomed."

Rah-noth nodded, knowingly.

A sudden explosion filled the cylindrical chamber as timbers blasted down with shingles on the wing, flitting like a thousand crazed bats from a belfry. The storm vented its fury in full form, sheets of rain in windswept currents spiraling toward the flagstone floor. Azrédien squinted through the downpour and debris to see the hulking silhouette of an ape-like figure dropping toward him with incalculable speed. A slender wizard's figure levitated slowly downward, staff glowing with the bluish hue of mana, dispelling the tower's many wards against intruders.

The risk demon laughed in sinister fashion, as he was prone to do, and clutched his thundersticks tightly. The iscaris'ri, weighing nearly half-a-ton beneath its thick, black fur and measuring twelve feet in height, readied its ape-like claws, preparing to rip the red scale hide from his opponent. At the last instant the thundersticks lunged upward, their tips exploding against its furry shin and groin, sending the beast spiraling backward some twenty feet, slamming against the brick and mortar wall of the tower and caving in the section. Washes of blue and violet light scraped against each other as the wizards entered their duel, but the cambi'ri focused his attention on more personal matters.

Advancing against the ape-demon, Azrédien's eyes glowed a baleful emerald haze as he attempted to fog his enemy's mind. It shook its massive head from side to side, slinging spittle from a great grinning maw of razor-sharp teeth, its black fur bristling over corded muscle and fat as it crouched, ready to spring. But it did not spring; its leg spewed black blood, and its shredded groin still smoked from the wound. Azrédien noted the massive, swollen belly, gorged with what had to be Abyssal ichor, its power bolstered by the sustenance.

"You have been fed well, like a favored dog!" Azrédien spat through the tumultuous rains, letting the thundersticks fall and hang by their tethers. The ends of both sticks fumed with brimstone, their charges having been spent.

The iscaris'ri stretched its head forward and half-screamed, half-growled a ferocious challenge, its wounds healing instantly by supernatural means. Azrédien cringed to see how easily the creature mended itself. It finally sprang.

The attack came far more quickly than the risk demon thought possible, and the iscaris'ri closed before its enemy's sword could be fully drawn. The great ape maw closed on Azrédien's neck, tearing flesh asunder, ripping veins and arteries in a lethal gash, and sending black blood flowing freely into the cold. The cambi'ri dropped to the ground, his sword escaping his weak grasp. His hand clasped about the gaping wound, holding onto life for precious seconds. The risk demon turned to his inner, mystic strength.

His kind were known as risk demons because they could afford to take chances. An inherent power allowed the cambi'ri to distort time, over short stints, but was costly to their vitality. In essence, a risk demon could relive a moment of dire consequence, should it choose. In this instance, Azrédien chose well.

The iscaris'ri stretched its head forward and half-screamed, half-growled a ferocious challenge, its wounds healing instantly by supernatural means. Azrédien cringed to see how easily the creature mended itself. It finally sprang.

The risk demon had already drawn its sword of ivory hilt, exposing a deep scarlet, alien blade that glowed with an eldritch heat long retained from the legendry fires which forged it. Hot razor steel punctured the shoulder of the ape-like beast, and Azrédien deftly jerked his head to one side as the snapping maw came darting in, and the reverse end of a thunderstick was rammed into its mouth.

The explosion sundered the beast's jawbone and sent it reeling. Teeth scattered like tossed dice into the keening winds. Its lengthy tongue smoldered and hung limply from its mouth, chunks of flesh missing in haphazard fashion.

Azrédien advanced to deliver the killing blow, when a shock of lightning rattled his form, boiled his blood, and threw him across the room near the open kennel doors. He had ignored the wizards and their duel, much to his pain; Vathryn must have found the time to aid his beast. The risk demon could only hope that Rah-noth was not wholly defeated.

Slowly, Azrédien arose, relieved to see that his sword was still in hand and that old Rah-noth held his own as magical energies flashed back and forth chaotically between the wizards. The ape beast

stood, and began lumbering forth—in seconds it was at a full run, its mouth now fully repaired.

The risk demon sniffed out the kennel that once held the virgin whose lock of hair he still possessed in a fold of his armor. He moved in front of that small cell and braced himself, sword in one hand, and a reversed thunderstick—his last charge—poised to strike.

As the beast closed, Azrédien felt himself consumed by the impact of hard muscle and bone, smothered by a mass of fur. He was carried backward into the kennel even as his sword slipped into the creature's chest. The ape lay atop the risk demon as it thrashed about him in cramped quarters. The cambi'ri felt a claw rip through the leather armor of his shoulder and tear into his scaly hide.

The creature convulsed, the heated blade piercing through its chest, through its heart, and out its back. It reared back, clinging to life as it grabbed hold the weapon, a great paw blistering against the heated steel. The iscaris'ri forced the blade from the spurting wound. In moments, it would heal the bloody lesion.

Azrédien did not pause in wonderment at how this nether-beast defied a death that should have been instantaneous, but instead plunged the last charge of his thunderstick into the wound, slipping between the cracked breast bone and hitting upon the ragged, beating pulp of its slit heart. This time the explosion was muted by the containment of the creature's insides, but undeniably lethal. The ape's eyes lurched wide with surprise, but stilled suddenly by the cold vision of death. Its mouth remained open, its tongue lolling to one side as red smoke escaped.

The risk demon found solace in the fact that his enemy was slain, and so he prepared to aid Rah-noth in his conflict against Vathryn. The massive, furred form of the revenge demon blocked his path, and he began to move it aside. That's when he heard the old mage's voice outside the kennel, but could not see him.

Rah-noth looked inside the small, darkened chamber, covered in black blood and fur. He saw movement within, black leather, and knew that his risk demon still lived. "Azrédien, I have slain Vathryn, and see you have managed a clean kill as well. That is good for both of us. However, I must renege on my promise to pay you for your services. Your demon amulet was what caused this conflict in the first place, you see. I stole the amulet from Vathryn, who once had two and was going to begin building his empire by enlisting your aid and that of the iscaris'ri. Upon discovering my treachery, he immediately summoned the revenge demon in reprise. Fortunately, he wished to feed the beast to its full potential in preparation for this conflict, not realizing how troubling it truly is for me to summon you from the depths. Had he struck swiftly, he would have caught me without you, my little pawn. His miscalculation was very providential indeed.

"Now that they are out of the way, and you are bound to my summons, I will force you to serve me. Refuse, and there are rituals of commanding which are quite painful. I had the luxury of lies to influence your actions to kill the ape-demon, but in the future, agony will be the yoke which guides your path. Step forward, back into the magic circle, and I will return you to the depths of the Abyss until such time as I have need of you. Forever you are branded unto me, and forever you must serve."

As Azrédien listened to Rah-noth's speech, he silently cursed the mage for his deception, even half-expected as it was. The risk demon used his sword to slice open the iscaris'ri's abdomen, and all throughout the mage's revelations, he drank feverishly from the Abyssal ichor which spewed forth, having not been previously consumed by the ape demon's supernatural prowess. Azrédien felt the power surge through him, flowing like intoxicating wine and filling him with unbridled mystic strength. Never before had he partaken of so much ichor while on another plane, never before had he felt so indestructible. But he knew with the brand on his forehead, he could not harm, much less defeat, Rah-noth—not at this point in time.

Time distortion was best accomplished in small increments, where time and place could be measured in but fractions. To go back too far was to invite uncertainty and destruction. But with his system stoked by the black ichor of his native plane, Azrédien, true to his nature, would risk it all. This plan he had concocted by glimpsing through windows of time: learning that his enemy would be bloated with ichor, noting a virgin and her scent, taking a lock of her hair, ferreting out where she lay in the past nights. Now he would chance it all.

Azrédien held tightly to the lock of hair, a focus to aid in the ritual, and he lay exactly where he wished to be in the past. He called upon his inherent mystic abilities. Time and space rippled, the cambi'ri disappeared.

It was yesterday, before Azrédien

had even been summoned. He appeared in the kennel, now free of the imprint on his forehead, and lay next to a buxom blonde virgin. His eyes immediately glowed a deep emerald, and she instantly succumbed to his whim, fell victim to his lust. She would not remember.

Within the hour, the risk demon had escaped the kennel by lifting the latch with his sword blade, then fled from the keep without having been discovered. He could search out and kill old Rah-noth, he mused, but his amulet was likely well hidden. Azrédien laughed at the fact that he would be summoned, not from across the planes, but from across only a mere short distance of space. He would answer, and gladly.

"Why have you summoned me?" The speaker was a demon.

Old Rah-noth paced about the magic circle formed by what he believed to be thirteen naked and dead, daisy-chained virgins. The mage did not deign to answer immediately, for he pondered

what might cause the absence of brimstone, which he had expected to appear about the demon. A thick-framed wizard of bald pate and owlish features, his head rested low on his shoulders; he slouched in his shambling gait. A branding iron was angled across his chest, its end glowing red-hot.

Azrédien breathed in the scent of the blood, and found the mixture to be tainted. He spotted the naked, dead form of the woman who had recently been the object of his desire. As Rah-noth moved alongside her while he paced, Azrédien leapt forth, knowing that he was not bound by virtue. In the blink of an eye he unsheathed his blade and cleared the magic circle, then sheared the head from the mage in a swift stroke of steel. It took the risk demon mere moments to recover his amulet and flee into the night.

A short while later the tower roof was torn asunder, an ape creature and mage descending amid wind, rain, and debris. The wizard Vathryn cursed his enemy as a fool, instantly surmising the ritual of summoning had gone awry, as testified by Rah-noth's decapitated corpse. He searched futilely for the head and the demon amulet, but neither was ever found.

Christopher Heath lives in Indiana and has been writing fantasy for over a decade, either as a role-playing game designer under the official Dungeons and Dragons logo or producing short stories and novels for his Azieran fantasy world. These works have seen publication in over thirty venues, including professional pay rate sales to Kenzer and Company, Fantasist Enterprises, and Pitch-Black Books.

BODYGUARD OF THE DEAD

by C. L. Werner

The rain beat down in a steady shower of biting cold, each drop stabbing like a knife into the muddy streets. Little cataracts streamed from the tile roofs of the close-packed houses of the town, filling the night with an unrelenting cacophony of drips and splashes. Writhing fires struggled beneath their hooded shelters, striving to endure against the assault of rain and wind, trying to fend off the gloom with their fragile flames.

Sheltering within a little alcove set into the side of a stable, three ragged looking men cowered against the cold, their dirty hands closed tight about the fronts of their woolen *hanten*, pressing the padded coats close around their throats to keep out the chill. Lost in their own brooding thoughts, the men did not notice the stranger until he was illuminated beneath one of the paper lanterns suspended above the narrow street. At once, the men scrambled into action, leaping to their feet, fumbling for bamboo umbrellas leaning against the wall behind them. They began a mad dash down the muddy lane, unfurled umbrellas leaning against their shoulders. Two of the men relented as the third drew well ahead of them with a burst of speed. Sullenly, they closed their umbrellas and returned to the shelter of the stable to sulk and brood.

"Keep the rain off your head, master?" the third man asked as he ran toward the stranger. His words lost some of their eagerness as he came close and could make out the details of the traveler through the darkness and the rain. No merchant or tradesman, this one, but a grim warrior of forbidding aspect. He wore armor over his pantherish frame, two swords beneath the red sash that circled his waist; a slender *wakizashi* with a jeweled hilt of sapphires set in gold and a large *uchigatana* with a sandalwood sheath and a bone hilt.

The traveler turned his icy stare upon the ragged man with the umbrella, rain streaming from the iron *kabuto* on his head. "It is a coward who walks in the rain and fears to get wet," the samurai told the little man. The man bobbed his head in nervous agreement and started to make his way back to the stable.

31

The samurai lifted his hand, motioning for the fellow to stop. "Even a brave man does not like to sleep in the mud," he said. "You can perhaps point a tired samurai to an inn?"

"Oh yes, master!" the little man said, eagerness back in his voice. He jabbed a dripping finger down the muddy lane. "If you would follow this street to the third lamp and then turn to your left, five doors down you will see the House of the Red Tiger." The man studied the samurai again, stroking the stubble on his chin as he considered the stranger.

"It is not every traveler I would recommend to the House of the Red Tiger," he said. "Ishiro caters to a very rough sort. Yakuza and ronin, sometimes even worse rogues. But they would think twice about crossing a samurai."

The armored warrior gave the slightest nod of his head. He fished a coin from the belt beneath his sash and tossed it to the little man, who seized it with fawning appreciation.

Shintaro Oba did not wait to listen to the full measure of the man's gratitude. It had been a long, hard road to Ikuro and many leagues since he had last rested his head upon a pillow and his back upon a bed.

The House of the Red Tiger was aptly named. The façade of the lower floor was fronted by wooden latticework dyed a deep vermillion. The earthen walls of the upper floor likewise had a dark red pigment to them while the clay tiles that jutted from the sloping roof and lower awning had been painted a bright and vibrant crimson. Somehow, the wooden bars of the *mushikomado* windows of the upper floor created the impression of stripes like those of a tiger. Before the large round doorway through which goods would be brought into the inn, a pair of stone lions, snarling *shisa* with floppy ears and puff-ball tails, stood guard.

At the smaller entranceway beside the big door, that meant for patrons of the inn, a more practical sort of guardian stood watch, a hulking brute with arms as thick as jungle pythons and a girth that would have impressed the Imperial yokozuna, that king of sumo. His scarred face twisted in an ugly leer as he saw Oba approaching the building. The samurai scoffed at the brute's crude bravado, locking eyes with the guard until the thug turned aside.

Oba strode past the surly guard, leaving him in the cold and rain. A murmur of voices and harsh laughter crashed down around him as he slid the door open and stepped into the House of the Red Tiger. He found himself in a large common room, a long counter of painted bamboo running along two of its flanks, a small staircase coiling up to the floor above.

All about the common room, low wooden tables were scattered, heavy woolen mats set beside each. Around many of the tables, little knots of humanity talked and laughed but mostly drank from the thin clay pots a brace of harried-looking girls raced to refill. Oba's eyes hardened as he took in the measure of the lounging men, a single glance telling him that here indeed was a place of ruffians and sell-swords.

"What is your pleasure, master?" The question came from the weasel-faced man standing behind the counter, his countenance made even uglier by the deep furrows gouged into his cheek and continuing up though the crudely stitched pit of a missing eye. There was a predatory gleam in the eye remaining to the innkeeper and a cunning turn to the smile that pulled at his scarred cheek, none of the deference or respect a samurai might expect from a commoner in his voice.

"Sake," Oba told him, making it sound like a demand, not a request. The innkeeper didn't move. Instead his finger tapped impatiently on the countertop. Oba gave the man a cold stare.

Ishiro grinned and pointed at his wrecked face. "Do you know how I got this?" he asked.

"Sake," Oba repeated, ignoring both impertinence and question.

"I was entertained by a samurai's wife and her perfume soaked into my skin," Ishiro said. "When I returned home, my pet didn't recognize my smell." A slight motion of the innkeeper's hand and an ugly face leapt up from behind the counter, scaly claws pressing into the bamboo as the creature supported its raised body.

Oba gave only a slight glance at the massive, wedge-shaped head, the black eyes and broad mouth. The ryuki was a formidable animal, a giant lizard from the jungle islands of Po. They could be trained, after a fashion, and sometimes were used by merchants and nobles for protection. Oba had seen what an angry ryuki could do. Ishiro had been lucky to escape with half a face.

"Sake," Oba told Ishiro, setting a steel coin on the counter. "And one for the quiet fellow flicking his tongue at me. Just in case he still has a bad taste in his mouth."

Ishiro snatched the coin up with a scowl. Another motion of his hand and the ryuki dropped back down onto the floor behind the counter. The innkeeper drew a clay pot from the low cabinet and set it on the counter beside the samurai.

"Forgive any impertinence," a soft, dignified voice spoke at Oba's shoulder. The samurai turned to find himself staring down at a young boy, not older than his tenth winter. The youth had a shaved head and wore the yellow *samue* robes of a monk. Despite his age, there was an aloof dignity about his lean features and expressive eyes. "My master would welcome you at his table, if you would prefer not to drink among reptiles."

Oba retrieved the clay pot as Ishiro set it down and stepped away from the counter, following the child monk across the crowded room. He noted with keen interest the way hardened ashigaru and tattooed yakuza shifted themselves out of the boy's path. He would not have imagined such a sinister grouping to show such deference to a monk, much less a mere child. Such men commonly had little use for the gods and even less for those who served them.

The boy led Oba to a short table set in the shadow of the stairway to the upper floor. The samurai could only dimly make out the figure of a man seated behind the table. There was a large bowl of tea set before the man and Oba had the impression he was leaning over the steaming vessel to inhale its pungent vapor. The child monk bowed deeply as he approached the table, then shuffled to the end not lost in shadow and seated himself on a wool cushion.

Oba gave the hidden man only the tersest nod by way of respect, uncertain of either his station or his identity. It would not do for a samurai to lose face before a simple peasant or scheming gambler. Warily, he shifted the heavy sword from beneath his sash and sat down opposite his unknown host. Resting across his lap, the sheathed uchigatana was eloquent in its silent menace.

Instead of speaking, the man in the shadows leaned down over the table. Oba heard the rustle of robes, the soft scrape of brush bristles against paper. After a moment, the unseen man pushed the paper across to the seated child monk.

Oba leaned back in alarm as he saw the man's hand emerge briefly into the light. The hand was brown and withered, more like a fleshless claw than anything human, the skin dry and gnarled. It was only a fleeting glance, but the impression was of something eerie and unnatural. Oba shivered with unease, wondering what horrible disease could ravage a man's body in such a way. Now he understood why even the villains who crowded the inn gave this table and its occupant such distance.

"You are Shintaro Oba," the child monk said in his soft, level tone. The words were not his own, he was reading from the paper that the withered claw had given him. "Last vassal of Lord Sekigahara Katakura, whose lands and subjects were destroyed by Shogun Yoshinaga. The sword you carry is named *Koumakiri*, commonly known as the demon sword of Sekigahara."

Oba scowled as he heard the boy read off his history with all the emotion of a dead carp. The death of his master, the horrible fate that had claimed him after death, were things he could not accept with the cold fatalism of a monk. He was a samurai, the last of the Sekigahara clan, and to him had been entrusted the duty of redeeming his lord's spirit from the demon that claimed it when he died without an heir to assume the sinister debt that was the clan's legacy.

Oba lifted his hand, motioning for the boy to stop reading. "You know who I am, but who are you? Why have you sought me out and how did you find me? There are a hundred villages I might have tarried in. Only by following me could you know I would be in Ikuro."

The man in the shadows ignored the threat in Oba's voice. Again, the soft rasp of paint brush upon paper, again the withered claw pushing a message to the monk.

"You were not followed," the boy read. "It was by divination that your path was revealed to me and the place where it might cross my own was made known. I am Kambei-kai, once Tsukamoto Kambei. The boy is Kinchi-san, my voice and my eyes. I have sought you out, Shintaro Oba, because I need your help."

A thin smile spread over Oba's face and he shook his head. "I do not work for yakuza and do not help men who hide in shadows."

More sounds of brush against paper. This time, however, when the claw pressed the message to Kinchi-san, it did not retreat back into the darkness. Instead, the man in the shadows leaned into the light. Color drained from Oba's face, his expression filling with awe.

Kambei-kai, the man in the darkness, was not a man at all. True, he wore the flowing robes of a priest's *jo-e* and there was a tall *tate-eboshi* cap upon his head, long silken flaps draping down across his shoulders, but it was no human thing that wore the rich garments of gilded thread. At least nothing that could still be called human. The grisly claws were matched by a face that had shriveled into a brown skull, covered by the thinnest layer of skin and devoid of flesh. The nasal cavity gaped above a lipless gash of mouth and only emptiness stared out from the eye sockets.

Kambei-kai, through poison and deprivation, through spiritual purity and balance, had transcended the mortal coil.

He had shed his humanity to become something greater, something even the most base villain in Ikoru regarded as holy and inviolate. Kambei-kai had become a living mummy—a *sokushinbutsu*—a physical manifestation of divine power and the endurance of the soul beyond the tyranny of death.

Oba had not bowed before Kambei-kai before. He did so now, bending in half, all but touching his forehead to the floor, a gesture normally reserved only for emperors and shoguns. The mummy leaned back into the shadows, waving his claw at Kinchi-san to continue.

"Exactly one hundred years have passed since the oni Ushitora was banished from the world," the monk read as a stunned Oba resumed his seat at the table. "I was the priest who banished Ushitora and ended his outrages against the peasants of Koya Prefecture. A demon may only ever be banished from the world by the same man once. It must languish beyond the gate of kimon for one hundred years and a day before it may seek to re-enter our world.

"Normally, a man will end his days long before the demon he has banished may return," Kinchi-san continued, "but I succeeded in my quest to become sokushinbutsu. I have endured past my mortal days and now the time of Ushitora's return is at hand."

"You fear the oni's revenge?" Oba asked.

The answer, it seemed, had been anticipated by the sokushinbutsu. Kinchi-san skipped ahead and read from the paper in his hand. "Ushitora is a mighty demon and knows I have survived. For a century he has been able to fight his way to the threshold; when the hour of the rat falls, he will be able to pass through the kimon gate. He will seek his revenge. My powers have grown great since transcending the flesh, but I am powerless to oppose a demon I have already banished once."

Oba fingered his pot of sake. With a quick motion, he sent the stinging rice wine down his throat. "I have fought demons before and am no stranger to the brutality of oni. I will kill this Ushitora for you."

Kambei-kai handed another message to his attendant. "This Ushitora is not the demon you seek; it is not the one that has claimed the spirit of Sekigahara Katamura. Destroying the oni will not help you in your quest."

The samurai sat bolt upright as he heard the monk read the words. "You know the demon I hunt?"

Again, the question had been foreseen. Kinchi-san shook his head, mirroring the motion of his master in the shadows. "To learn the name of a demon, one must ask other demons and their every word is twisted with lies. There is no reward I can offer you for fighting Ushitora."

Oba smiled and lifted his hand. "The honor of defending Kambei-kai is reward enough," he told the mummified priest. "But why choose this place to confront the oni?"

Kambei-kai handed another message to Kinchi-san. "Ushitora is cunning. Once I tricked him into entering the sanctity of a temple where he would be weakened. He would not be so arrogant again. If I secluded myself in some wild place, he would be wary and suspicious of a trap. But by staying here, among men, I may deceive him into believing I have forgotten him. It saddens me to put other lives in jeopardy; that is why I chose the House of the Red Tiger as my battlefield. The men here are rogues and murderers; they would be the first to admit the world would be a better place without them. If a sacrifice must be made, let it come from those whose loss may do some good."

The samurai sat in concentration as he weighed the mummy's words. He could feel the despair behind Kambei-kai's plan, the sorrow that he must risk other lives to preserve his own existence. On a pragmatic level, Oba agreed with the plan. The lives of thieves and gamblers were a small price to pay to preserve a sokushinbutsu.

There were perhaps only a few dozen of the undead holy men in all of Mu-Thulan and most of them confined themselves to their temples, locked in endless cycles of meditation. Those who did wander among men worked much good and showed no distinction between the lowest peasant and the highest noble in bestowing their mystical aid. The ravages of disease and drought could be broken by the blessing of a sokushinbutsu, demons could be banished and restless ghosts exorcised by their divine grace. No, there was little question that whatever the sacrifice, it would be worth it. If it cost even his own life, Oba was ready to accept even that grim possibility.

Oba turned and studied the large room around him, this time examining it with an eye toward strategy and defense. He did not like the openness of the inn, the sprawl of its tables. It did not allow the open ground a warrior needed to fight efficiently, yet at the same time it offered nothing by way of concealment.

The samurai nodded as he reached a decision. He turned back to face Kambei-kai and his attendant. "You must retire to the upper floor. When the oni comes, I will face him. If I fall, though it cost me my very soul, I will cry out warning to you with my dying breath."

The sokushinbutsu rose and shuffled out from behind the table, leaning on Kinchi-san for support and guidance. Both mummy and monk bowed before Oba, a gesture more expressive of their gratitude than any words could be. Oba watched them climb the stairs, then turned to take up position at their base. *Koumakiri* was stuffed once more beneath the red sash, the samurai's hand resting upon its handle of bone, a handle that had been carved from the horn of another oni by the lords of Sekigahara long ago.

With the retreat of Kambei-kai, a shroud seemed to lift from the patrons of the inn. Laughter became more boisterous, conversation rose to a dull roar. Several tattooed gamblers even initiated a game of oicho-kabu, seeking to part the drunken sell-swords from whatever money remained in their purses. Oba watched the activities with wariness, knowing that few ronin were ever as drunk as they seemed and few yakuza games as honest as they looked. Many a villain had been cut down because of such a volatile mixture.

The noise of the crowd made it difficult for Oba to hear the distant tolling of a temple bell. Once he became aware of the sound, he focused his full attention upon it, cursing the noise around him as it drowned out the notes. He could not be certain how many times the bell had been struck, nor how late the hour had grown. He was uncertain if it was the hour of the rat or that of the boar.

His answer came when a ghastly shriek rolled through the inn from the landing outside. The wooden door exploded in a spray of splinters as the hulking body of the guard was flung through it like a rag doll. The bruiser smashed against the floor, leaving behind a trail of blood as he slid across it to crash in a tangle of mangled flesh against one of the tables.

Deep, raucous laughter boomed like thunder from the darkness. Drunken men sobered instantly as they heard the sound, faces flush with sake turned pale, fingers probed beneath kimonos for hidden knives and hands closed about the hilts of swords and staves. Every eye in the room was turned to the broken wreckage of the door, watching as the wind sent the ruined portal trembling in its frame. Rain poured in from the rent, mixing with the blood of the slaughtered bouncer on the floor.

A bolt of lightning crashed outside, illuminating the street with a bluish glare. Nothing could be seen in that brief glimpse. Some of the ashigaru and yakuza laughed in nervous relief.

Suddenly the large door used to transport rice and wine into the inn shuddered as a tremendous force smashed against it. A second impact and the heavy oak panel collapsed, smashing down against the counter. Monstrous laughter again rumbled through the room.

An immense shape stomped across the fallen door, its weight causing the panel to flatten the end of the counter upon which it was leaning. Huge and savage, it stood easily twice the height of a man, with arms grotesquely swollen by thick cords of muscle. Its skin was a deep crimson and rough like leather. It wore only a brief tiger-skin loincloth about its waist, its only other adornment being strings of human finger bones jangling about its ankles. Its face was a nightmarish mix of man and beast, its sharp nose and flaring nostrils crouched above a mouth distorted by lion-like fangs. A rough mane of black hair rolled from the demon's scalp, clinging to the roots of two enormous spiral horns.

Ushitora's blazing yellow eyes glared at the terrified rabble staring at him. The oni hefted the gigantic kanabo clenched in his claws, blood still dripping from the iron club.

"Whoreson maggots," the demon's voice rumbled. "Slink home and have your wives lick the fear off your nethers or Ushitora will tear them from your carrion and feed them to the rats!"

The oni's obscene threat echoed from the rafters, and his voice became even louder as he strode across the shattered door. "Fly, cringing cowards, unless you would see your children boiled in their mothers' milk and their carcasses splashed in the street for the dogs to drink!"

The violence of Ushitora's voice excited the dull aggression of Ishiro's ryuki. The huge lizard launched itself at the oni, springing on the demon in one long leap that carried it from behind the counter to the ogre's shoulder. The ryuki's sharp claws sank into the meat of Ushitora's arm, its snapping jaws tearing at the demon's neck.

Grunting in surprise, Ushitora closed his fist around the lizard's head, ignoring the teeth that bit into his palm. The oni's face tightened into a scowl as he clenched his hand into a fist. There was a dull cracking noise, then a hideously liquid pop. Without breaking stride, Ushitora ripped the ryuki from his bleeding arm and threw the twitching body on the floor, its head a pulpy mess of broken bone and mutilated flesh. The ogre paused as he stepped across the reptile, his heavy stone sandals breaking its bones. He swung his malignant gaze across the room, his blazing eyes burning into each man's horrified stare.

"Are you still here, dung-chewing swine?" the ogre demanded, a hungry smile causing him to display still more of his leonine fangs.

The threat was too much for the rabble in the room. Gamblers and mercenaries fell over each other in a mad scramble to press through the rear door of the inn. Several howled in pain as those in back tried to cut their way through those in front. The ogre bellowed in amusement. Displaying a speed that belied his giant bulk, the oni charged into the rear of the struggling mass. A gambler went down, smashed into the floor by the downward sweep of the kanabo. The iron club struck him in the skull, driving him into the floor like a bloody nail.

An ashigaru turned, slashing at Ushitora with a frantic wave of his sword. The oni caught his arm in a monstrous fist and ripped it from its socket with a brutal wrenching motion. The mercenary fell in a screaming heap, clutching desperately at his bleeding shoulder, unable to stop the cascade of blood spurting from the severed arteries. Ushitora laughed at the dying man, then stuffed the dismembered arm into his fanged maw.

Other men, in their desperation, flung themselves at the oni. One was smashed into the wall of the inn, pressed into the wood panels by the powerful impact of the iron club. Another was pitched to the floor by the crushing fist of the oni, wailing in wretchedness as the ogre's huge sandal came stomping down on him, slowly breaking his ribs as Ushitora gradually brought his weight to bear on the helpless man. A third managed to stab the demon in the knee with his katana before the oni crushed his face with a backhanded sweep of his club. The mutilated ronin crawled away, shrieking as he tried to push his eyes back into his shattered visage.

The ogre's laughter roared like a volcano through the wrecked inn, spurring the last men through the door. "The same and worse for any who think they would fight Ushitora the Destroyer!" the oni shouted after them. "Tell the other worms their village lives only until Ushitora tires of it! Tell them if they want to beg aid from Tsukomoto Kambei, they must dig his bones from Ushitora's shit!" The oni brought his kanabo crashing down, gouging a deep crater in the floor, then shifted his eyes to the ceiling overhead. He could sense his enemy above, cowering like a rabbit in its hole. This time their contest would end differently. A century waiting beyond the kimon gate had given him many ideas about what he would do to the exorcist priest.

As Ushitora turned toward the stairs, the ogre blinked in surprise. A lone man stood before the steps, an armored samurai who stood as silent and still as a statue. The oni smiled, lips pulling back from his bloody fangs.

"A hero," the demon chuckled. "How amusing. Do you think you can stop Ushitora all by yourself, little bastard? I'll feed your liver to the crows and your ass to the eels!"

Ushitora began to march toward the stairs. As he advanced, Oba quickly drew his sword from its sheath. The oni paused as he saw the huge sword and noted its sinister handle. He could feel the murderous aura of the weapon like icy fingers against his leathery hide.

"*Koumakiri*," the oni growled.

"I am Shintaro Oba, of Clan Sekigahara," the samurai said, matching the ogre"s baleful gaze. "I protect Kambei-kai. You will not work your vengeance upon him."

The oni's eyes narrowed with hate, his face becoming impossibly more savage. "So the sniveling pray-spitter became a walking corpse, did he? He will wish he had not cheated his grave when Ushitora finds him!" Ushitora's knuckles cracked as he tightened his hold upon the iron club. "Stand aside, yapping cur, and Ushitora will let you play soldier somewhere else."

Oba shook his head, keeping his steely gaze focused upon the oni. "I will not make you the same offer, demon. I have seen your evil, and will not allow it to endure."

Ushitora's face darkened with rage as he heard the bold confidence in the samurai's voice. "You carry a sword with the horn of an oni as its hilt and think it makes you a demon slayer? What have you fought? A few kappa, perhaps a goblin or some starveling yokai?" The ogre grunted scornfully. "It needs more spine than that to face an oni. Ushitora doubts you have enough spleen for the fight. Maybe Ushitora will pull out your belly and look!"

There was no warning when the ogre struck. During his tirade, the demon had slowly inched his way closer, edging nearer to the stair and the samurai. Now,

with a final lunge, Ushitora brought his gigantic kanabo crashing down. Splinters sprayed from the floor as the oni pulverized the bottom step, the iron club sinking into the crawlspace beneath the inn. But wood and empty air were all he caught with his attack.

Oba swung around the descending club, lashing out at Ushitora with his sword. The uchigatana tore through the oni's hand, slicing deep into the leathery flesh. Fingers leapt from the wound, foul stinking blood spraying behind them. The oni roared in pain, rearing back, fumbling to pull his club from the crater in the floor.

The samurai slashed at the demon again, the keen edge of the uchigatana cutting through the oni's leg just below the knee, all but severing the limb from his body. Stagnant black blood boiled up from the wound, sizzling as it slopped against the wooden floor. Oba swung back around as Ushitora brought his iron club flashing down toward him.

The kanabo never struck, nor did Oba's rising sword meet its downward sweep. In turning to face the awful threat of the club, Oba had exposed himself to the ogre's fist. He had forgotten the childhood witticism that likened an oni with a club to the most excessive of overkill. Ushitora's fist smashed into the samurai with the force of an avalanche.

Oba was lifted from the ground, and flung across the room. His armored body crashed against the already weakened front wall, breaking through it with bone-jarring force. Cold rain pelted him as he tumbled into the street to lie in a twisted heap in the muddy gutter.

Ushitora lumbered from the inn, dragging his maimed leg behind him, struggling to keep his balance as he lifted his kanabo and smashed a wider opening in the wall. The oni's malignant face glowered at the injured samurai. The demon chuckled darkly as he saw *Koumakiri* lying in the street. Ushitora limped into the rain, positioning himself between the samurai and his sword.

"You've pissed me off more than Kambei-kai," the oni growled. "For that Ushitora will stuff your own feet down your throat before Ushitora rips your head off and spits down the hole!" The demon laughed as he watched the samurai painfully roll onto his side so he could stare up at the hulking ogre. "Not so tough without your fancy sword, are you, little bastard?"

The oni's leering smile vanished as Oba suddenly uncoiled, springing at Ushitora like a striking cobra. The little jeweled wakizashi sank into the ogre's foot, stabbing through flesh and sandal to pin it to the street. The demon reared back in shock and pain, howling. Oba seized the demon's distraction, diving between his legs, throwing his body in a long slide through the mud. When he finished his dive, the horn handle of *Koumakiri* was again in his hand.

The raging Ushitora turned on the samurai, driving his iron club in a bludgeoning strike. Oba did not fall away from the attack, instead rolling beneath it. His sword slashed out as he landed in a crouch at the oni's feet. Ushitora's pained howl became an agonized wail as Oba's sword cut through the demon's belly and spilled his steaming guts into the street.

The oni bared his fangs, gnashing at Oba as he slumped to his knees. The heavy kanabo fell from the ogre's weakened grip, its weight sinking it deep into the mud.

Oba glared back at the spiteful demon. With a single fluid motion, he brought his sword slicing across the oni's neck. An instant the ogre continued to glower back at him, then Ushi-tora's head slipped from the severed stump and splashed into the mud, the oni's carcass dropping down beside it.

The samurai sagged to his knees, almost falling down beside the dead oni. As the rush of battle drained out of him, Oba could feel the full impact of his injuries, the bruises and breaks he had forced himself to ignore while the ogre loomed over him. It was an effort just to replace *Koumakiri* in its sheath, a struggle just to hold himself straight and keep his face from the mud.

A cold hand closed upon his shoulder and suddenly Oba felt a warm sensation of strength course through his body. He raised his eyes, not surprised to see the skeletal face of Kambei-kai. The sokushinbutsu stood over him for only a moment, letting some of his mystical energies flow into the samurai, restoring some small measure of his endurance. Before the mummy allowed his attendant to lead him away, he pressed a scroll into Oba's hand.

The samurai quickly unrolled the message. The words Kambei-kai had written restored him even more fully than his eldritch magic. The sokushinbutsu apologized for deceiving Oba, but warned that if the samurai had fought Ushitora with any thought of personal gain or reward in his mind he would have lacked the purity of purpose to defeat the oni. Kambei-kai promised to use his knowledge of divination to aid Oba in his search, that in one year, the mummy would return to Ikuro and share with him whatever he had been able to discover.

Oba slowly rolled the scroll tight and stuffed it beneath his sash beside

Koumakiri. He turned and watched the figures of Kambei-kai and Kinchi-san as they slowly faded into the darkness and the rain. He bowed in gratitude to the sokushinbutsu, and this time the samurai did not balk at pressing his face to the ground.

C. L. Werner
is the author of fourteen novels published by the Black Library and numerous short stories set in the grim Old World of Warhammer. He is also lead background writer for Darkson Designs' AE-WWII setting, a retro sci-fi tabletop wargame that evokes an alternate history of WWII where robots and werewolves take the battlefield alongside Army Rangers and the Waffen SS. His first Shintaro Oba story appeared in Rage of the Behemoth *from Rogue Blades Entertainment. Visit www.vermintime.com/ for more of his work.*

KRON DARKBOW

by Ty Johnston

Thunk!

It's as oil on canvas as the big stupid one, Benny, turns in his chair. It takes him a moment or two to understand what's happened. Leon is dead; the shaft of my arrow sticks from between his ribs. The gold coins in his hand rest on the edge of his fingers. They are about to fall. The slightest breath will drop them.

I speak from the darkness.

"Brelvis."

Benny does something smart for the first time in his life and reaches for the spiked club on the table. With it he might stand a chance against me. A chance of hurting me, at least.

"Who are youse?" he asks with that stupid Swamps accent I hate so much. It reminds me of my childhood.

No answer from my corner. Instead I cautiously move to my right, behind another old crate. You would think thugs could pick someplace less obvious than an abandoned warehouse near the Docks as a hideout.

The candle on the table flutters.

"Look, whosoever you is, we can work somethin' out, right? I mean, there's at least seven or six gold pieces here. We could do even split."

I crouch and wait. Time is my ally. It builds fear.

Benny doesn't know his enemy. He doesn't know where I am. He doesn't know how I'm armed or even if I'm human. He doesn't know a damn thing except that his buddy Leon is going to start stinking up the place in a few more hours.

Unfortunately for Benny, I know too much about him.

"C'mon, man. We can work somethin' out!" He's getting angry. Fear can do that to some men. Especially big stupid ones.

A pair of daggers slide from the inside of my right boot.

"Alright. Have it your own way then, mister mystery. I'll just sit here and—"

The first dagger is in his shoulder to the hilt before I'm halfway to him. He screams and swings the club blindly. I go in low and slash up.

43

The club drops to the ground along with a few drops of big and stupid's blood. He catches a glimpse of my black form and lashes out with his good hand. I stay low and dive forward, putting everything into my legs. He tumbles. I kick out, intentionally knocking over the table. The candlelight dies.

Benny huffs and puffs. He's not used to fighting. He's accustomed to using his size and strength to get his way. He stands and fumbles backward in the dark.

I sit and hold my breath.

"C'mon, you!" Benny screams, "I got yer number! You ain't nothin'! Nothin'! Youse hear me, noth—"

"Hush."

The second dagger flies like a hawk. *Thunk.*

Now Benny can't feel anything below his left elbow. Poor Benny.

He spins and thrashes. He's lost in the dark. Again, he can't see his enemy. Unfortunately I can't see him real well either. But he's making more noise than a bunch of drunken Hiponese priests losing their virginity.

"Where is he, Benny?" I say barely above a whisper. "Where is Brelvis?"

Benny is still stupid. He kicks some more, hoping to hit an enemy he can't see.

"Come on, Benny," I say softly. "It'll go easier on you if you tell me now."

He stops thrashing. This time he's the one holding his breath. His head turns. He's sounding me out, trying to locate me through my voice and movements. Maybe Benny's a little smarter than I've given him credit for.

Enough of this.

My sword is unsheathed soundlessly. Benny takes a step to his right. I take a step to my left. He spins in my direction.

He knows where I am.

It won't do him any good.

"So, did they tell you?"

It's the fat, rich one that asks the question. He's always the one who asks the questions. No one else ever speaks. Just him.

"Leon is dead," I say. "Benny opened up, but only after I prodded him a little."

The fat, rich one smiles. I know how mice must feel when cornered by the cat.

"Good, good. Then you know where Brelvis is located?"

"Yes," I say.

"Find him. Return my object. If Brelvis lives, bring him to me. If he dies, so much the luck."

I nod curtly to the five robbed individuals, then I turn to leave. I have no more time for these of the Magic College. I have work to do. They are paying me for results.

A small-time magician by the name of Brelvis decided a week ago that he wanted to go big time. So he stole a glamoured item, one white egg, from his benefactor, Romule. Brelvis then disappeared. Unfortunately for Brelvis, Romule hired the best there is at hunting people.

Me. Kron Darkbow.

Personally, I have nothing against Brelvis, though I can't say I care much for Romule. But Romule is paying the bills. And Brelvis...

Ah, Brelvis. Low-born gutter slime. That's about the best I can say for him. The world won't miss him once he's gone.

I exit the gray halls of the Magic College and head back to the Swamps.

It is day now but night will follow soon enough. My time.

The magician is a little smaller than what I expected. Almost mousy. Definitely not a fighter. That long, yellowish robe he wears can't be much protection either; in fact, it would hamper his movements.

The five goons with Brelvis are another story. There's another one like Benny, big and stupid. The Swamps must breed them. This one carries an axe. A big axe. The other four characters are fairly nondescript. Little larger than average builds. Leather armor. One type of sword or another. They appear to have some training but not much. Nothing special. Nothing I can't handle.

From the windowsill of another warehouse, I hear it all.

"What d'you mean?" the big dumb one asks.

"I'm just saying all our troubles are over now that we've got this," Brelvis states, holding up the object I seek, the egg, "Now we don't have to take crap off anybody. And we're not going to have to do any work either. Just the threat of using the egg would be enough to drive off other wizards."

I ponder this for a second. Romule wouldn't tell me what powers the egg held. I'll just have to hit Brelvis before he can use the item. I lean back in the darkness.

"So what does this egg do? What's so special about it?" one of the nondescripts asks.

I put an arrow to my bow.

"It contains two souls," the wizard says. "One is the spirit of a demon. The other that of a girl."

I aim.

"So, there's a little girl in dat thing?"

I aim a little longer.

"Yes."

I launch.

At the wizard's hand. The hand holding the egg.

There's a cry and a splash of blood.

The egg goes flying.

"For Ashal's sake, don't let it crack!" Brelvis screams through his pain.

The rest of the goon squad goes fumbling forward. The big one catches the egg. It's not broken. I'm not sure whether that's good or bad.

The big one looks up.

I'm two stories away in a window. It's a moonless night. There's not much light in here except for several torches the goons put up. I'm dressed in all-black leather. Even the buckles of my clothing have been painted black. There's not a chance he sees me.

But I see him.

And I'm the one with the bow.

I let another arrow fly. This one is aimed at the big guy. It hits him in the shoulder. He grunts, returns the egg to Brelvis, then rips my arrow from his shoulder.

He didn't even wince.

I could be in trouble.

The rest of the mob finally come to their senses and dive for cover. Brelvis backs behind a support beam. The big stupid one just stands there in the middle of the room.

"If them little arrows is the best you can do, I'm gonna gut you and hang you out to ripen," the big stupid one says.

I put away my bow.

This guy wants to play tough.

I can play tough.

From the folds of my cloak I produce a small, gray ball. It's made of hard clay, at least on the outside. It's called a grenado. You throw them at people you don't like.

I love these things.

Big and stupid is waiting on me to make the next move. "C'mon mister, I ain't got all days," he says.

"Too bad, because I do," I say, throwing the grenado.

Big and stupid is suddenly on fire and it must hurt a lot since he lets go of his axe and starts screaming. He falls over and begins rolling on the ground, but it won't do him any good. Grenado fire has a tendency to stick to the skin.

I drop twenty feet to land on a wooden crate. Out of the corner of my eye I spy Brelvis and the rest of his boys moving toward the exit door. My bow comes back out.

Big and stupid goes quiet and quits moving.

I ready an arrow.

The goons are at the door. One of them opens it but Brelvis doesn't leave. Instead he turns to face the inside of the warehouse. I'm just about ready to shoot him when I hear something behind me. Something that sounds an awful lot like a sword slicing through air.

I instinctively drop and kick back with my right leg. I catch a glimpse of metal flying over my head and feel something soft connect with my foot. I look behind me and see one of the wizard's goons bending over and holding his stomach.

I glance back in Brelvis's direction. It's almost too late when I realize he's casting a spell.

Flames erupt around me as I roll backwards off the crate. I grab the goon I kicked and hold him in front of me. Anything for a shield.

We fall ten feet and land hard on the dirt floor. My shield is dead. He took the brunt of the blast. I'm not in the best of shape, but I've been worse. A little heat never killed anyone.

I stand and wipe soot from my clothes. I'm going to need a new cloak. And a new bow.

Between my grenado and the wizard's flame spell, the building is burning fast. It'll last at least until I make my escape, which I do expediently by heading for the door.

Brelvis and the last three goons are waiting for me outside.

"Somehow I knew you'd survive that," the wizard says.

I don't use time on words. I wade into them while drawing my sword.

I kick the closest one in the groin. He falls to the ground screaming. The one on my right swings his sword at me but it's blocked. The third one stabs and misses.

Brelvis starts mumbling. Damn spells.

I kill the foe on my left, my weak side. The one on my right backs away. He's wary of me now. And he knows his boss is about to do something.

I take advantage of the opening and dive forward. Straight at the magician.

There's a sputter of sparks and I smell smoke but nothing seriously bad happens to me as I tackle Brelvis. He falls to the ground and grunts.

I rise and stand over him with my sword pointing at his chest.

"Call off your dogs or you die now," I say.

He gives me a whimpering look but says nothing.

I can hear the last two goons moving toward me, measuring their chances. The one I kicked must have recovered.

I step on the wizard's injured hand,

the one I hit earlier. The one containing the egg.

"Oh please, gods, no! Don't do——AAAAAAAAAHHHHHHHHHH!"

I push the sword just enough to draw blood.

"Back off! Back off! Give him some room!"

My boot is removed from his hand and I pull my sword back. Just a little.

"Tell them to leave," I say. "I'm not here for them."

Brelvis looks as if he's going to hesitate, but he can see my eyes. He knows I'm good enough to kill him and finish the others.

"Do it," he says. "Leave us alone. Don't come back."

The last two goons shuffle off with backward glances. They'll remember what I look like. They'll know me if we meet again. I'll kill them if that day comes.

"Now, we're going to have a short chat," I say. "I want to know about the egg."

Brelvis sputters for a moment. He's frightened. It's understandable. He thinks I'm going to kill him. Maybe I will.

"What…what do you want to know?" he asks.

"The basics. What does the egg do? How does it get its power? I heard you say it held two souls."

"Th-th-that's right," Brelvis begins. "Romule entranced his own daughter several years ago, then killed her ritually. He bound her soul and that of a demon within the egg."

I remove my blade from in front of his chest. "Do go on," I say.

Brelvis continues. "The girl wasn't old enough to be a magic user, but she would have been the most powerful of our age. Romule wanted her abilities for himself, so he crafted the egg to store her

essence. With the egg any wizardling can become one of the most powerful. The demon keeps the girl bound within the egg. Romule could bind a demon, but he couldn't bind the girl's soul because she was so powerful. The demon won't let the girl's soul escape. He's a creature of Hell that has been trapped, and what more could he want than his own personal soul to torture for all eternity."

I've heard enough.

I raise my sword and chop off the hand holding the egg.

Brelvis screams briefly then falls unconscious.

I pick up the egg and leave him. He might survive. Or he might not. It doesn't matter. Without the egg, he's no threat.

Besides, I have other matters to deal with.

I step slowly through the curtains into the main hall of the Magic College. It's still night. There are only candles to see by. Romule is waiting for me. This time he's alone. Good.

"I take it you have dealt with my problem," the fat, rich wizard says, stepping forward.

I remove the egg from beneath my now-tattered cloak and hold it up for him to see.

"Good, good. I'm glad of it," he says and points to a leather bag on a table near him. "There is your gold. Take it and leave the egg."

I cautiously step to the table and investigate my new wealth. It's enough to keep me preoccupied for several months.

Romule waits.

I turn to him.

"Is it true about the egg?" I ask. "Is it true about your daughter?"

He stiffens briefly, then smiles. "Not enough gold for you?" he asks.

It's all the answer I need.

"No, no. It's more than enough," I say and throw the egg at him.

Hard.

Hard enough to crack it.

And suddenly all hell breaks loose. Literally.

There is fire and smoke and brimstone and this huge thing with bat's wings and a dragon's head. It doesn't hesitate to go straight for Romule, its captor.

I throw a grenado, just to add another problem to Romule's soon-to-be-short life, and more flames erupt as the wizard gets off some sort of fire spell.

All the flames don't seem to bother the demon one bit. In fact, I think he's enjoying it.

I grab the bag of gold and start backing toward the exit. I'm not sure what the demon will do once it's finished with Romule. Hopefully, he won't go looking for another snack.

Smoke bellows up in front of me, but after a moment it clears enough for me to make out the curtains I came through earlier. I run toward them.

Then, above the roar of the demon and the screams from the wizard and the crackle of the flames, I hear another sound. Crying. As if from a child.

I halt my movements and take in my surroundings. I'm almost to the curtains. I'm almost out.

But a child is crying somewhere. It sounds like a little girl.

I do something stupid and return to the smoke and flames.

The cries sound ahead of me and to my left. Good. It's away from the wizard and the demon who are still battling.

I hear another sniffle and step through a wall of fire.

There's a girl, no more than six years of age, on her knees before me. Her hair is in tails and she's wearing a short, tattered tunic.

I extend an arm. "Come on, honey," I say. "Come on. It's all over. All the bad things are over. You're free now."

She looks up at me with tears in her eyes. Eyes that have seen far too much pain. More pain than any mortal, especially a child, should ever have to bear.

"Truly?" she whispers.

"Yes, dear," I say. "You're free. You may go where you wish. There is nothing holding you here now."

A smile crosses her lips.

"Thank you," she says and a wall of smoke blinds me.

When I can see again, the girl is gone.

I have little problem making my way back to the curtains. There's another scream from the wizard just before I leave. He's tougher than I thought. At least he's still alive. I don't think he will be for long.

Ty Johnston is the author of The Kobalos Trilogy, an epic fantasy series featuring his Kron Darkbow character. He is also an online content provider, a blogger, and a former newspaper journalist. When not busy reading or writing, he enjoys spending time with his wife, their beagle and two house rabbits.

THE VENGEANCE OF TIBOR

by Ron Shiflet

Tibor clutched his sword and stood shivering on the outer edge of the ruins. The pallid moon cast grotesque shadows among the broken masonry and it was easy for one to see things that were not there. Inhaling deeply, he crept forward as silently as possible, though he doubted that the demon he had come to slay was oblivious to his presence.

Dreams. The dreams have led me to this place and in this place I shall have my vengeance on the murderous bastard. Sweat formed on Tibor's shaven, tattooed head, running like the tears he had shed, down the strongly chiseled features of his face. Wiping it aside, he moved forward on sandaled feet, searching for the temple he had seen in dreams, the lair of the one he sought.

Something dark slithered from beneath a crumbling stone, disappearing into a thin crevasse before he could react. *These ruins crawl with loathsome creatures. I must clear my mind or risk falling victim to more mundane dangers.* Clearing his mind was a feat easier contemplated than accomplished. Memories of death and atrocity were too fresh to be cast so easily aside. They burned in his brain. His son, crucified and eviscerated before the eyes of his mother; and his wife, unspeakably abused and left barely alive to revoke him for his absence during the horror that had come upon them.

Tibor's entire village had been razed, its inhabitants tortured and slaughtered in an orgy of demoniacal bloodlust. He had been away, seeking a weapon to counter the horror that had recently descended on the South Plains of Ivanoor. Possessing the weapon had done no good, its procurement having come too late to save his family and the other doomed people of his village. Vengeance was all that remained so vengeance he swore, refusing to rest until it was exacted.

Staring into the mist-laden night, he inched forward, entering the outer edge of the ruins, searching for the temple of which he had heard and dreamed, and where his journey would end. He temporarily banished the images of horror from his mind and concentrated on traversing the rubble-strewn streets of ancient Ompala.

Klotus, also called Corpse-Maker, grinned maliciously, staring into the mirrored surface of the meditation pool. An enraged and grief-stricken fool sought for him within the abandoned city. A fool with visions of soul-cleansing and bloody retribution—but a fool nonetheless. He chuckled mirthlessly at the human's audacity while silently saluting his courage. *How many had there been?* Too many to remember over the course of uncountable years. *One always comes and one always dies. Has it not always been so?*

Turning from the pool, the demon strode across the dusty stone floor, his crimson eyes blazing in the tomb-like gloom. Having been spawned in the primordial chaos of Yutran's creation, he believed himself destined to preside over its eventual destruction. The humans, who appeared countless eons after his birth, were nothing to him but living objects of amusement and tools to alleviate the ennui that too often stole over him down the long course of time.

"They are amusing," he whispered, hoarsely. "Their flesh tears and punctures so easily, and their screams of torment and agonized pleadings are musical instruments that only I can play to full effect."

Klotus, sensing Tibor's presence in the crumbling city, smiled. *This one will be easy to dispense with. I'll destroy him with his own foolish sentimentality and love. That which drives him forward will bring about his destruction. Is that not ever the case?*

Striding on elephantine legs, he approached the massive throne of bones and paused. He had supped deeply on terror and despair and now felt the usual lethargy descend upon him as it always did in the aftermath of gluttonous feasting. It was the harbinger of sleep, a period when he was most vulnerable. Picking flesh

from between his teeth, he belched and smiled. *Even in sleep I am not without defenses. I shall use but a small part of my energy to destroy the arrogant interloper before he even reaches the temple.*

The Corpse-Maker eased his massive bulk onto the skeletal throne and sighed. His eyes rolled back in his head and a low rumble emanated from deep within his scaly chest. A greenish fog issued from his flaring nostrils, moving snake-like as it flowed along the floor of the temple chamber and into the winding, weed-choked streets of Ompala. Klotus closed his eyes, breathed heavily and began to dream.

Tibor made his way through the labyrinthine streets of the once great city, his thickly corded muscles aching from the punishment they had endured. Since leaving the mountain dwelling of the wise and holy shaman, he had traveled first to his doomed village and from there to the outskirts of fabled Ompala. Driven by grief and a consuming lust for vengeance, he vowed to remain awake until the blood-drenched blade at his side pierced the black heart of the murderous demon known as Klotus the Corpse-Maker.

He sighed, knowing that his soul was already damned for killing the ascetic shaman but had little regret if it meant that Klotus would be slain. He had been driven by the legends saying that only a blade drenched in blood from one of unsurpassed purity could harm a Chaos Demon. Any sacrifice was acceptable if it meant that the destroyer of his village and slayer of his loved ones would die. There would be time enough later to worry about his place in the next world if indeed such a place existed. He had his doubts but hoped for the sake of his family that it was true.

Clouds obscured the moon, causing him to squint as he moved further into the heart of the city. *The temple should be easy to find. Much of it still stands—at least in dreams and if the stories of the elders are true.* Arriving at a deep crevasse in the once bustling street, he stopped and caught his breath. The gap wasn't overly deep but fatigue had taken a toll on his body. Inhaling deeply, he stepped back a few paces then leaped forward, clearing the dark gulf by but a foot. He peered into the gloom and listened carefully, sure that he had heard a familiar noise.

A human in this place? Not likely. Not a time to lapse into madness either. Tibor warily clenched the hilt of the sheathed sword and crept forward, listening for a repetition of the sound. He followed the course of the street, stopping briefly where a section of the flat-stones veered away, leading into another part of the city. The ruins of a building still stood, its dark gaping doorway reminding him of a corpse's silent scream.

A child's cries startled him and sent chills up his spine. *What child would lurk in these ruins? Or has some diabolical fiend brought its prey back to its lair...*

A sense of dread crept over Tibor and he stepped toward the opening. Clearing his throat, he called, "Child, what are you doing in this place?"

The crying stopped, replaced by the sound of clumsy movement. Peering intently at the dark opening, he again cleared his throat. "Come into the light. I won't harm you."

A small figure entered the doorway and stopped. "Father?" asked the voice of a young boy. "Have you come for me?"

Tibor's guts clenched. Swaying, he struggled to banish the madness that descended over him. He stared at the small figure, gasping as the boy walked toward him. *Rhone? How can such a thing be? I burned your remains with those of the others.* The partially obscured moon emerged from behind the clouds and Tibor stared in wonder into the face of his son. *Could madness have come over me at the village? Did the sights and sounds unhinge me?* The boy ran to him, crying, "Father!"

Tibor dropped to his knees, enveloping the child in his strong embrace. "You're freezing," he said. "Let me warm you."

He smiled, feeling the boy lay his head against his chest. The smile transformed into a startled curse as sharp teeth ripped viciously at his neck, sending blood flowing down his broad chest. Pushing the boy away, he cursed himself for a fool and unsheathed the sword. The boy's face changed into something inhuman, spitting a hiss at Tibor as the sword cut through the air, connecting with such force that the target was all but cloven in half. Tibor trembled, staring at the thing that had briefly looked like his son. Flesh bubbled and melted away, changing into a green mist and drifting away on the nighttime breeze.

Shaken by the sudden attack, Tibor sat on a broken chunk of masonry and muttered. He checked his wound, relieved that no major artery had been severed. Still, he was losing blood and had nothing to staunch to wound. Walking to a large crack in the street, he dug a handful of damp soil free and packed it around the torn flesh as best he could. *Can't afford to lose blood...too weak already...*

Stumbling onward, he seethed at the demon's ploy in using his family against him. He reaffirmed his vow to destroy the creature, and gripped his sword as if the weapon tethered his very sanity. He moved steadily into the heart of the city, keeping a wary eye for hidden snares or demon-spawned assassins, eventually reaching the center of the once thriving metropolis.

Tibor approached the Fountains of Ahtaris, though water no longer rose majestically into the sky from their ingenious system of pipes and pumps. The structure was cracked and broken, its once shimmering pools now dry and clogged with the detritus of the years. He sat on a broken stone, resting only long enough to catch his breath. His eyelids were heavy and he knew that he could rest only a few minutes or risk falling asleep. Slowly rising, he headed onward, knowing that the temple-lair of Klotus—and confrontation with the demon—was not much further.

Groaning, he continued past destroyed booths and broken pottery once part of a busy bazaar. The red eyes of rats glinted in the darkness, but the rodents decided to wait for easier prey. *If only they knew.*

After what seemed an eternity, Tibor saw his destination. Much of the temple still stood, though he would need to traverse a great deal of rubble before reaching its entrance. He sheathed his sword, and picked his way through the debris, thankful that his quest was drawing to a close.

Mere yards from the gaping doorway, he stopped in shock. His wife Tamara stood before him, looking as beautiful as the day they had wed. "Tibor, my love! There is no need to go further."

Staring at her, his heart ached at the thought of her being used in such a manner by Klotus. Gripping the sword hilt, he smiled grimly. "I've been fooled once tonight by demonic trickery. Not again, thank you."

"It's not what you think," she answered. "I'm truly alive…an offering from the cowardly Klotus. He knows you are here to destroy him and I am his last hope. He will allow me to live if you turn around and leave this place."

"And if not?"

"Then I will perish again."

Seeing his beloved Tamara weakened his will, even as he told himself that her presence was a lie. Never had his love been so consuming as when they had been together and the thought of a reunion weighed heavily on his resolve. With tears in his eyes, he said, "And what of Rhone?"

"He is dead," she answered.

His jaw clenched in anger. "That is all you have to say about our son?"

"I can give you other sons," she answered, smiling.

"You bitch!" he yelled, drawing his sword.

"Don't be angry," she begged. "I long to live!"

"And perhaps you might have," he said, "were you truly my beloved."

"But I am!" she cried.

"No, you're not," he growled. "The woman I loved would be tearing at the eyes of Klotus this very moment for what he did to our son."

"No, you're wrong!"

"Stand aside or die," he answered.

The change in the figure's appearance was sudden. In seconds, it had transformed into a faceless, sword-wielding creature. It lunged forward, but Tibor easily parried its first attack, turning the sword aside—and falling on the loose rock.

Groaning in pain, he blocked a terrific overhead blow, meant to cleave his skull in two. Crab-like, he crawled backward until stopped by more rubble. His attacker moved forward and thrust fiercely, managing to scrape the ribs on Tibor's left side. Tibor responded with a thrust of his own, plunging the sword point into the chest of his faceless foe.

The figure began to disintegrate in the same manner as the one that had impersonated Rhone. Tibor staggered to his feet, pressing his hand to his side with a curse. *Got to move quickly...lost too much blood...won't last much longer...*

With a grimace, he staggered through the temple door.

Tibor entered the temple's inner chamber. The area had once been the holiest of sanctums, forbidden to all but the religion's high priests. The full moon—now directly overhead—cast its light through a gaping hole in the dome, dimly illuminating the chamber.

Through the gloom, Tibor spied Klotus seated upon a throne of bones, reputedly assembled from the priesthood who once served the temple's now forgotten deity.

The stench of death permeating the chamber intensified as Tibor approached. The demon appeared lifeless but Tibor knew better than to hope for such a thing. His blood ran cold as he gazed on the hideous features. Already nearing the point of collapse, nausea threatened to overwhelm him. Unsheathing the blood-stained sword, he strode forward—and froze in his tracks as Klotus opened his eyes and smiled.

Klotus, still in the semi-dormant state that followed his feasting, remained motionless. He glared at Tibor.

"Human...you have traveled a difficult path...for naught. The sword will avail you not. You can chop me into a thousand pieces and I will return to make you wish you had never been born."

"Try another threat," Tibor grunted. "I've already wished for that."

He raised the sword. "Will you not fight a warrior? Perhaps you are only a threat to women, children, old men and farmers."

Klotus hissed, struggling to overcome the lethargy that bound him to the chair. "Keep talking, human. Savor this moment and hold tight to it so that you will have something when I torment your soul for a thousand eternities!"

Tibor smiled grimly. "There will be no return."

"Wishful thinking, mortal."

"See the blade?" Tibor asked.

"It is useless," answered Klotus.

Continuing, Tibor said, "It once glittered blindingly in the sunlight but now it is stained."

Klotus stared at the blade, an unwelcome thought blossoming in his corrupt brain. "It's only blood," he said. "Easy enough to clean."

"Only blood?" asked Tibor, smiling. "The blade is coated with the blood of Ahn-Rhan Kotalla, acknowledged by all as the holiest of men."

"The holy man is dead?"

"Yes, demon," Tibor replied. "Do not mourn him. He died for a good cause."

"And what cause would that be?" Klotus asked, no longer disguising his sluggishness.

"Your death."

Klotus roared, his fetid breath nearly knocking Tibor aside with its potent stench. His eyes bulged until bleeding as he struggled to rise from the throne. His long, stained teeth snapped futilely and the foul and corrupt parasites beneath his mottled skin grew frenzied, causing his putrid flesh to bulge with their sudden activity. Tibor steadied himself, speaking a final time to Klotus. "The death I bring is easier than you deserve!"

Clenching his teeth, he twirled the sword expertly above his head, stopped suddenly, and thrust the point of the weapon into the demon's scaly chest. Klotus's scream shook the very foundations of the temple, sending loose brick and stone crashing to the floor of the chamber.

Tibor dodged the falling rubble, but refused to loosen his hold upon the sword. Choking clouds of powdery dust filled the room, and Klotus bucked and writhed upon his throne—yet Tibor would not free the sword. The demon hissed and swore a thousand deaths upon his attacker, yet struggle as he might, he remained immobilized by the sword impaling his body.

Tibor watched as huge blisters formed upon the demon. He flinched in horror as they swelled to the size of sheep's bladders and burst in sprays of corruption. Small spider-like creatures emerged from each of the foul lesions, scurrying down Klotus's body and along the floor before exploding in flames of weird colors.

Tibor finally relinquished his grip upon the sword and backed against the sanctum wall, determined to live long enough to witness the demon's demise. Staring in stunned amazement, he saw its body jerk and spasm as if controlled by some demented puppeteer. Seconds passed—seeming an eternity—and Tibor watched Klotus levitate from the macabre throne, swell, and burst into flames. The demon's yellow eyes turned crimson then exploded, sending bits of vile, gelatinous matter against the wall with sickening splats. Klotus emitted a final, ear-piercing scream—then melted into a fiery puddle of tarry goo.

Tibor, blood flowing from his throat and side, roared in triumph, then collapsed against a metal brazier. As life fled his body, he struggled to speak. "Tamara…Rhone…you are avenged…if only I could tell you…"

His breathing grew shallow and his vision began to dim. He was dying, but he no longer cared. Having nothing to live for, he welcomed the peace that death would bring. A soft glow emanating from the corner of the chamber drew his waning attention. "What?" he whispered.

Two figures approached, smiling. Tamara and Rhone knelt beside Tibor, infusing him with an indescribable warmth, and bringing tears to his eyes. Rising from the cold stone floor, he looked down at the useless and unimportant shell that his spirit had inhabited. Smiling in the combined embrace of his loved ones, Tibur allowed them to lead him from the ruined temple.

Ron Shiflet is a Texas writer and is the author of Looking For Darla: Stories of Mythos Noir by Elder Signs Press. His work has appeared in such anthologies as Frontier Cthulhu, Horrors Beyond 1 & 2 and Cold Flesh. His webpage is in need of an update but is www.freewebs.com/rshiflet/.

THE BEAST OF LYONESS

by Christopher Stires

"He's coming, Crusader," Fabiyan said.

The lad spoke the words in a rush to warn me. But I already knew. All was too still. The birds had fled their nests around the cold water well several minutes ago. The village dogs had run off. All was still and quiet except for my Appaloosa stomping its hooves and tugging anxiously at its tether. That and a sour dead-meat odor suddenly tingeing the air.

Even in sleep, I knew.

I sat up and opened my eyes, rubbing them awake. *Yes. Time to earn my champion pay.*

Standing, I looked up at a sky thick with gray clouds. It was shortly after dawn. Sunlight barely penetrated the clouds and darkness. Rain seemed certain before the day was done. But the Beast was oblivious of the weather. He was only eager to begin. Eager for his pint of blood.

Fabiyan handed me a mug of cool water. I rinsed my mouth then spit the liquid into the dirt.

Lyoness was a town in the Northern coastal provinces. Once it had been a rich, flourishing fishing community. The seamen of Lyoness were renowned from kingdom to frontier. At one time, King Harold would only allow Lyoness lobster and crab to be served at his court celebrations. At one time, the sea captains of the great port cities of Blackharbor and Ipau and Shoi-ming would only set sail if they had a Lyoness navigator aboard. Once, it was said, a Lyoness boat with the fearless Burian as pilot had sailed to the edge of the world and back.

But no more.

The good fortunes of Lyoness had ceased.

The village was now a ghost.

Thirteen autumn seasons had passed since the Beast had arrived in Lyoness. Most of the townspeople had fled to Quantero down the coast. During that time, fifteen village men and six hired champions had gone to battle the Beast. The Beast remained.

I had come to Quantero round about. I had been on the trail, riding from the Valley of Lies to the town of Zoya, near the border of the desolate Cimera Plains. While at a small way-station tavern, I heard rumors of a rectory in Quantero where Galen monks were meticulously translating Pre-Thurian scrolls. One scroll had the exact location of a gateway to Hell.

Immediately I changed my direction and headed for the Northern provinces and Quantero. It took me five weeks to reach my destination and, on the first day in the port city, I discovered that the rumor, like most repeated tales, was myth. There were no translated Pre-Thurian scrolls; there was no rectory of Galen monks. There was no map of a gateway to Hell.

I knew from the beginning that the odds of the rumor being even half true were against me. Still I had to try. Lenore, my beloved and loving Lenore, deserved no less.

I offered my extensive services to a landed gentry lady. The woman, a widow for two years, was skeptical of my motives and intentions. I do not blame her. Sweet-talking frauds and well-heeled cheats tend to bloom around a woman of means with no husband or family. She lowered her guard in my case. Accepted my offer. I do believe however that the day's labor had more to do with my Appaloosa's haggard appearance than my winning smile and quotes from the philosophers.

In my youth I would have bristled at this realization and my pride would not have allowed me continue. I am no longer young and burdened with righteous purpose. And pride does not fill the empty bellies of man or his animal companion.

Job accepted. Payment—a full bag of oats and two carrots for my horse and one plate of potato stew for myself.

I was mucking out my fifth stall when they entered the stable. Eight men with a dozen younger men and boys following them.

The three stable hands fled. Undoubtedly to tell their mistress that a mob had arrived for the drifter she had hired.

I continued raking out the stall. I hoped that the potato stew would be hot. Hot or cold I intended to savor it.

A muscular broad-chested man, his left arm missing from the bicep down, stepped away from the others. "You can't be the Crusader."

I did not reply. I worked.

"You're covered in dung and mud. You can't be."

A disappointed murmur hummed from the seven other men. The younger men and boys echoed their sentiment. I raked the pile to the center then scattered fresh straw across the stall. All except the man who had spoken turned away. He stared at me.

"The Crusader is the hero of Shankur and Herron," the man said. "He killed the necromancer of Camd'n Rin. You can't be the Crusader."

"All right," I responded, moving to the next stall.

"Look here," a small voice called.

The man and I turned. So did all the others.

A small, grime-cloaked lad of maybe ten years stood beside my long coat. He had pushed it aside to reveal my pistol.

The man pivoted toward me. "A revolver pistol," he said in awe. "It was designed by the great gunsmith of Shankur and there is none other like it. The smith gave it to the man who rescued his children from the Griffin Vampire. He gave it to the Crusader."

I eyed the lad unhappily.

He would not meet my gaze. Instead he covered the pistol with my coat as it had been.

"I am Vas," the man stated. "I am the grandson of Burian of Lyoness." He extended his hand.

"Patrick Novarro," I said, shaking his hand with my dung-covered one. "Please go. I have work to finish."

Vas remained. "We wish to retain your services. We need a man of your experience."

"I am not ronin or mercenary. You need to take your troubles to the King's magistrate."

"You have not heard our…proposal yet."

"Others have come to me as you have today. Others have insulted me."

Vas frowned. "Some men can make their words sound like poetry," he said. "I am not one of them. We need help. Two of the King's magistrates have told us they cannot aid us. Fourteen of our own people and six hired warriors have already been defeated." He gestured at his stub. "I survived my attempt. Barely."

"What makes you think I can help you?"

"You are protected by Satan's own oath."

I looked away. *Lenore. I will find you. I shall never relent.*

"You are perhaps the only one who can help us."

"Why do you say that?"

"Our 'troubles' are because of a de-mon. Please, sire. Please just listen to us."

No, I wanted to say. I have heard enough tales of misery and sorrow to last me well into eternity. No more.

Vas dropped to one knee. The others, even the grimy lad, followed his lead.

I stared at them.

A heaviness settled around my shoulders. I could hear Lenore whispering to me. *Give them a few minutes. Hear their story. Perhaps you can help. If not then walk way without apology.* I sighed. Very well, my love. You would be disappointed in me if I did not grant them an audience. That I will not allow.

"Tomorrow," I said. "I will meet with you tomorrow. Now I must finish my work."

"Thank you, sire," replied Vas.

They left. I returned to the mucking. The lady of the property appeared moments later with the trio of stable hands. She gave me a bag of oats for my Appaloosa then ordered me to leave. I went to sleep hungry that night.

My days with Lenore were the most favored of my short life. My bride loved me and I loved her. And it was more than enough. Then, one night, it ended.

A thief, after my purse, stabbed me in the heart. As I lay dying, no doctor or shaman able to save me, my beloved Lenore entered into covenant with Satan. My life for her soul and for me to live the rest of my years without harm from Satan or his disciples. Satan gazed upon my frail scholar's body, reviewed my unremarkable history, and agreed.

And so it was. I lived, and Lenore died and was taken to the fallen angel's palace on the River Styx. Lenore knew the warrior I would become. She knew the havoc I would cause among Hell's earthly minions. She is pleased. Satan has placed a bounty on me. So far no one has been able to circumvent his protection over me. Twice, however, they have come close. But I will not perish until I rescue Lenore. I will not perish until the archangels have cloaked her in their embracing wings.

I will not.

"The beast came thirteen years ago," Vas said the next day.

The entire village populous must have been at the clearing to meet with me. The elders and the children, the strong and the weak, the once well-to-do's and the never-had's. All it appeared.

"We believe the beast is a punishment," Vas continued. "We, the people of Lyoness, became too prideful and arrogant. We did not give proper thanks for our blessings and good fortune. We acted as if we were entitled to what we had and those with less were lazy and undeserving."

I chewed on a blade of straw, considering his words. "How do you know you brought this on yourselves? Perhaps a sorcerer, jealous of your town's success, brought forth this demon."

"We wish that were so, Crusader, but alas he is a demon of our own making."

"Tell me why you believe this."

"First, he has grown smaller since we have repented. He has not departed but he is definitely smaller in stature than when he first came."

I nodded. I knew they truly believed this to be so. Perhaps it was.

Vas massaged the end of his stub with his palm. "But most tellingly are the rules of challenge. Any person or persons may challenge him. They have choice of weapons. They are given first strike. He will only strike second. A third has never been needed."

"Tell me more. Leave out no detail."

Vas did. Other village men and women joined in. Thirteen years ago, the beast appeared from the mountains above Lyoness. He lived in a deep cavern but claimed the village as part of his domain. Said that the people within his domain would have to pay tribute or perish. The tribute would be gold and silver coins, wines and silks. He had a mammoth appetite and three-quarters of the Lyoness ocean harvest would go to him. The payment would also include a new bride each winter. Grigor was the first to challenge the beast. He was killed and his wife, the beautiful and vain Kisa, became his first bride.

They told me about each battle. The beast had survived sword, crossbow, and axe. He had endured musket and blunderbuss. Vas recounted his fight and how the beast had taken his arm and the life of his older brother. I was told about the three village men, friends since boyhood, who fought the beast together. They related how they had hired Haj of Babylon and Euphemia the Amazon. The beast had won each encounter.

It was always the same. The challenger attacked, the beast countered. Twenty-one challengers; twenty-one defeats. Twenty-one maids and maidens taken; twenty-one maids and maidens perished within a fortnight.

I examined the faces before me. They swore an oath to me. If they regained their village, they would work hard and live decent and pious lives. For the most part. No people were all good or all bad. But they would try to do right.

It was enough. Lenore would've appreciated their vow and sincerity.

"I'll face your beast," I said.

Several voices shouted at once that they would accompany me to Lyoness.

"We will all fight at your side if you wish," Vas stated.

"I believe you," I replied. "One, however, will be enough I think. More than that would create problems."

Vas straightened his broad shoulders. "Choose, Crusader. None, not man or woman, not youth or elder, will decline to assist you."

I nodded and scanned the crowd. Finally I saw the one I wanted to accompany me.

Vas turned and looked in the direction I was staring. "Are you sure that it is the young rat-catcher that you want?"

"Yes."

I would've sworn, at that moment, that the grimy lad who uncovered my revolver was going to faint. His name was Fabiyan I would find out later that morning. He was an orphan and he survived by catching rats for which the Quantero sheriff paid a halfpenny a piece bounty on.

"Very well," Vas said. "Now, before we shake hands on the deal, we must discuss your reward."

"I am expensive," I responded.

"We will not barter. We have agreed on this already. Name your price. If we cannot pay all you ask at this time, we will pay a yearly tariff until it is paid in full."

I knew what I desired. I could already picture the prize in my mind's eye. "Who is the best cook in your village?"

A bewildered expression crossed Vas's features. For a long moment he remained motionless and speechless. Then he turned toward the others. They conferred and deliberated. Then they debated and discussed some more. Finally, they reached a consensus. The people separated until a dark-haired, slender woman of perhaps forty years stood all-alone.

"Not I," she argued. "You are wrong. I am but a plain and unremarkable cook."

The others disagreed.

The modest woman looked at me. She was at a loss for words. It was obvious that she never knew the others felt this way.

I smiled at her. My empty stomach gurgled. "Can the lad and I have supper with you, m'lady?"

It was a magnificent meal.

"He's coming, Crusader," Fabiyan said.

I rose to my feet. Despite the moist chill in the morning air, I removed my long coat. I handed the coat and my revolver to the lad.

"Strap these to my horse," I said. "Then stay with the animal. Talk quietly to him. Keep him calm."

"What if—?" Fabiyan started the sentence. He did not finish. He let the two words hang heavy in the air.

I grinned. "If the beast wins, mount my horse and ride. Ride fast."

"Yes, m'lord."

As Fabiyan walked to the Appaloosa, I turned toward the winding road from the mountains.

The beast walked into eyesight. He was half-human and half-creature. Some would say he had sprung forth full-grown from a madman's nightmare. He moved in a crouch with his powerful hands smacking the ground and propelling him forward. If he stood upright, I guessed that he would be close to seven foot tall. He had no shield; he wore no armor. The muscles in his arms and legs were large and chiseled. His flesh was covered with dusk-colored scales that wiry bristles rose between. Even from a distance I could see that his eyes were dead black pools and a short curved tusk protruded from the peak of his forehead. Gray drool hung, web-like, across his wide bearded chin.

I was in trouble.

Battle scars crisscrossed his head, neck and torso. They gleamed in the morning dew as if golden badges of honor.

I understood without doubt or uncertainty that this beast was not Hell's spawn. He did not pledge allegiance to Satan. Man had created him and, for that, he wanted his revenge.

And I also knew that he could beat me. This beast could accomplish what Satan had been unable to do thus far. Still I could not run. I would help the people of Lyoness. Lenore would not be ashamed of me this day.

So I waited, unarmed.

The beast came nearer. He looked at me then glanced, dismissing instantly, at Fabiyan. He sniffed the air. He surveyed the homes and shops behind us.

He smiled, amusement touching the deep creases of his face. "So you are these people's new champion."

"Yes," I replied.

"And you think you can defeat me?"

"Maybe, maybe not."

The amusement vanished from his features. He was surprised. "A humble and modest champion," he said. "You are the first of that breed I have ever encountered. The others have all been bold and decisive warriors. Haj of Babylon stated exactly how he was going to quarter me. Euphemia the Amazon said she would

sup on my liver. The others made similar claims. Alas they were not warrior enough. Tell me what your name is, my shy and meek fellow?"

"Patrick Novarro."

Talons eased from his fingertips.

Behind me, the Appaloosa neighed and stomped its hooves.

"Are you the one called the Crusader?"

"Sometimes."

"Satan's oath will not protect you here. I will use your skull for a piss-pot."

From behind me, a pistol fired. The bullet whistled past my ear.

Dropping low, I pivoted around. The beast rose to full height. I was stunned. Fabiyan was clutching my revolver in his small hands. Bellowing, attempting to cock the hammer back, he rushed forward. His boy eyes were wide. Sweat drenched his tiny brow.

The beast roared.

As Fabiyan came even with me, I tripped him. He slammed hard into the dirt. The revolver skidded from his hands.

I looked up at the charging beast. "Not yet."

The beast sidestepped us.

I yanked the lad to his feet. "What is your task?"

"I-I-I…" he stammered.

I pulled him closer. Our noses nearly touched. "What task did I give you?"

Fabiyan inhaled deeply as he fought back the tears. I could feel his entire body trembling. It was all I could do not to hug him to my breast.

"Tell me, lad," I said flatly.

"Stay with the horse," he whispered.

"And?"

He was bewildered, speechless.

I frowned. "Tie my coat and revolver to the horse. Stay with him and keep him calm. Did you misunderstand the words I used?"

He shook his head. "No, sire."

"Then why are we standing here?"

"I-I-I thought…" He could not finish the sentence.

I sighed. I turned toward the beast. "My apologies," I said. "This was not of my planning. If you do not believe me and find me unworthy to fight, I understand. I will call off the challenge."

The beast chuckled. "The challenge remains."

"Thank you." I curled back toward the lad. "Defy me again and I'll give you to him."

"Appetizer," the beast said.

Fabiyan nodded. He understood.

I released him.

He grabbed my revolver and dashed back to the Appaloosa.

I rose. Looked at the beast. "Shall we get the formalities out of the way?"

The beast studied me curiously. "Formalities?"

"Yes," I responded. "I am the champion of the people of Lyoness. I, and I alone, have come here to challenge you. There is no one fighting with me." I looked at Fabiyan. "No lads or armies or anyone but me." I turned back to the beast. "I am alone and I will fight you alone. Do you accept these terms?"

"Oh, yes."

"Good. I understand that I am given first strike. Is this correct?"

The beast nodded. "With any weapon you choose."

"Why?" I asked. "Why do you give me first strike?"

"Because I am the best there is. No one can defeat me." He gestured at his scars. "These prove that fact."

I shook my head, concerned. "You may want to change that for this challenge. I could get lucky and you'd be defeated. I know you did that with all the others because I was told, but I won't hold you to that covenant."

"I do not need first strike to defeat you, Crusader."

"Very well. I want you to know, however, that if you suddenly decide to take first strike I will understand. Everyone has fears."

"I fear no man," he growled.

"Fabiyan," I called over my shoulder. "If he takes first strike, it does not change anything."

"It changes all, sire," Fabiyan answered. "If he takes first strike, he will no longer be who he was. First strike must be yours."

"No, I won't hold him to that pledge."

The beast bellowed. The anguished sound echoed off the houses and shops. He clenched his fists at his sides. Veins pulsed angrily on his neck.

"Understood," I said, relenting.

"Only you and I will fight and I have first strike." I glanced at Fabiyan. "He's a beast. He doesn't have to keep his word."

Suddenly, a mammoth shadow loomed over me, and hot breath seared my neck.

Fabiyan stood rigid beside the Appaloosa. He swallowed. "I-If he breaks his word in this matter then he's a common bully and murderer. He can claim he's the best there is but it will no longer be true."

"Fight me," he snarled in my ear.

I turned and stepped back. I studied him from head to toe, from left to right.

"Fight me, Crusader."

"Oh," I said. "Now I understand. That's how you win. There's a time limit on the first strike. The challenger rushes and makes a mistake in his haste."

The beast shook his head. "No. I want you to take your time. I want you to choose your weapon carefully. I want you to plan your attack. I await your convenience."

"All right," I agreed, extending my fist. "Oath."

The beast tapped my fist with his. "Oath."

I turned. I walked toward Fabiyan and the Appaloosa. "Mount up."

"Where are you going?" the beast asked.

Fabiyan scrambled onto the stallion.

"Fight me," he demanded.

"I have to pick my weapon," I responded. "I have to plan my attack. I'll return shortly."

"Fight me!"

I swung into the saddle with Fabiyan behind me. "I shall return in a day," I told the beast. "Maybe a fortnight. Maybe longer. Wait in your cavern until I return. Remember you took an oath to only fight me. I'll call when I'm ready."

Fabiyan's small hands clutched my belt.

"You did well, lad," I said quietly. "Just as we planned."

He whispered, "What will keep him in his cavern?"

"Pride and arrogance created him," I replied. "Those same sins will keep him waiting for me to return. You have your village back."

"He'll not attack again?"

"If the people of Lyoness repeat their sins, he will be released. If they attack him, he will be released. Be as good as you can and leave him alone. Make the others understand."

Fabiyan pressed his face against my back and nodded. He would tell the others. He would make them understand. The young rat-catcher had a new job; he had a new role in his society.

We rode down the trail toward Quantero and the awaiting people of Lyoness.

For miles, we heard his voice echoing across the landscape.

"Fight me! I am the best there is! I am undefeated! Fight me!"

As we came within eyesight of the port city, we noted that we heard the beast no more.

Christopher Stires has had two novels—Rebel Nation *and* The Inheritance—*published by Zumaya Publications, and a third*—To the Mountain of the Beast—*released by Carnifex Press. He has sold over 70 fiction short stories, nonfiction articles and review columns.*

FIFTEEN BREATHS

by Phil Emery

The wind whipped like a cat-o'-nine-tails in Halgorr's face. He could have sworn it was a sensible-malignant-banshee-thing. Even huddled in a sheltered niche on the crag face it sought him out. Halgorr cursed it under his frost-paled breath, sipped from his waterskin, and resumed his climb.

Inside fingerless fur-lined gloves Halgorr's hands bled as he grabbed at the icy rock, inching his way upward. He had climbed above the clouds two days ago—*Or was it three?*—and the summit of the pinnacle was not yet in sight. *Did it truly touch the stars; was at least that myth true?* His face flushed with anger at his drifting thoughts. His only concerns should be the elements. The rain that turned to hail, harrowing his flesh, lashing against him. The cold too, that froze his bones and turned his powerful limbs blue.

The wind still harried him, his thoughts no less than his body.

Kaelan.

The higher he climbed the more the sound seemed to weave itself into the shrill of the wind.

Kaelan.

Generations ago, lost generations ago, the sound had been carried down to the ground and fashioned into a name for the mountain. It meant 'dying breath' in the native tongue, because it had been carried only by those who had attempted to scale the peak and fallen. Those who turned back never heard the sound. Those who reached beyond the cloud and heard it returned with the word on their frost-ragged lips—plummeted with the myth heavy on them. It was said that it took fifteen breaths to fall from such a height. Some survived long enough to utter the word with the remains of their fifteenth.

Kaelan.

Kaelan.

Halgorr heard it again, sharper this time, sharper than ever. And felt it too. On his back. And saw it too, as his hands were ripped from the crag face and he began to fall. As he took his first breath.

63

Some philosophers say that in the moment a man knows his death is near, the breath he takes is his first. Halgorr knew. As he let it out he accepted it. It was not as if he had not expected it. It was one of the first myths he had seen broken in his life, broken on his first battlefield under all the slaughter—the young man's unspoken belief that he would never die.

He drew the second breath.

It was not as if he did not want to die.

The release of it coincided with the unsheathing of his blade. It vipered free, a long wicked wafer of gleam. Not bronze or even iron. Halgorr had won it in a game of chance with a sot of a grizzled seaman who had claimed it fashioned from the cooled spewings of one of the fabled fire pinnacles found on the other side of the world. Dark, brittle as ice, but lighter and far keener than any metal. Halgorr had carried it on every mountain he had climbed.

He swept it as he took in the third breath, but it cut only air.

Kaelan.

The movement and the wind made him tumble, and during the next two breaths his senses kaleidoscoped and his innards were a sickening havoc. When his plunging frame steadied he had ten breaths of life to come.

He would welcome the fifteenth. It took several more battlefields and the deaths of countless friends and strangers and sights markedly more atrocious to rend the myth—the falsehood that death was worth the fearing. Aye, fear it he had, and did even now. But that was no more than a trick of the heart. Not a reasoned feeling. Men's hearts still beat when no reason remained for them to do so. Still raced when disillusion should long since have leadened them into sluggish bitter

pace. The heart, Halgorr knew, was a bedlamite lump, shambling blood through the body whether it willed it or not.

The sixth breath was different.

Its taste in his mouth was different, and the taking of it too. Incredibly it took him a moment to recognize both, and to understand why a vapid blindness rushed upon his eyes. By that time, as his lungs were beginning their seventh drawing, he had fallen through the cloud he had hauled himself above on his ascent.

His sight returned and he saw again the reason for his fall. Or something like it. It flitted above him. Halgorr swung his sword again. With control this time. With skill this time. He had wielded this blade and others before it countless times. There was little difference now. A blade cut through air before anything else. This time Halgorr was a blade himself, piercing air for another eight breaths.

The sound was there too, even below the clouds, softer now. A breath itself.

Kaelan.

If Halgorr had not climbed higher and heard it in its wind-whetted crystalline keenness he would not have known it. Would have thought it just the wind. Not something woven into the wind. Not something cried. Mocking. Vicious. Something mouthed.

The sword stroke did nothing to cut the cry short or to slice pain through it. Still, there was a balance in his fall now that was not harmed by the action. He swung again. The blade stretched out with the eighth exhalation. This time it cleaved more than air.

It was the moment Halgorr truly believed in what his eyes had seen and his ears had heard. After losing so many beliefs in his life. After losing belief itself.

For the first time he believed the myth of Kaelan real. The myth was flesh. The myth was blood. He had let it.

Even if the blood was not blood as men knew it. It was red, aye, bright and deep, yet it did not splash or spurt. It flickered up out of the cut and…

Halgorr had travelled to the boundaries of the known world and beyond. He had listened to stories of mountains like Kaelan, pinnacles that reached sheer into infinity. How the most evil creatures in all the world, living and dead, made each their home. How when the gods lived and warred, the Frost Demon buried the Fire Demon in a tomb of stone and ice so high that it touched the very stars. That, they often said—whoever 'they' were, wherever they were—was how the Pinnacle of Kaelan and so many others came to be. And now he knew it was, at least in part, at least in part true. It was the treasure he and all the other myth-chasers had searched for, had scoured perilous caverns and jungles and deserts, dived beneath forbidden seas, dared tabooed ruins, and, aye, climbed pitiless mountains in search of.

The bodies that had been found at the base, with their frames caved in, some with stranger wounds, they could have testified to the truth if they had lived long enough to utter more than 'Kaelan.'

Civilized travelers from the mellow regions explained those injuries with rational theories, discoursed on the differences between myth and legend and fable, referred to the roots of the words, displayed a contempt for superstition they felt was expected from them. The local crofters had no such obligation. They drew their own meanings from the raked and ripped corpses, created their devils and beasts from hell. But those banes were poised between truth and imagination with nothing to tip that balance.

But Halgorr knew. There were several of the things above him now, swooping and harrying as he took the ninth breath. Halgorr twisted to deliver another strike with his gleaming sword, a thrust this time. It was a fragile weapon, aye, but these things were no different—lighter and swifter than air and their talons just as keen as the dark edges of his blade. One of the creatures thrust at the same time. Halgorr's lunge pierced nothing. Not so the talons.

The pain made him yank in and jab out the tenth and eleventh breaths quickly. He grinned. Almost laughed. Their shortness meant, if he survived to the ground, there would be more than fifteen. *Another myth torn.* But he still had the demons. *Aye. I'll call them that.*

Not that the delusion of good and evil had survived for him. He remembered a vast plain years ago where two armies faced each other—two bristling skittish lines of mail and sparthe and arbalest and halberd. Halgorr had been part of one. The paladin-kings of each side, together with their most learned councilors, had debated the histories of their reigns, recounted the deeds of their rules. It was a battleground of vainglory and slur. Of lies and half-truths brawling to establish which cause was the more righteous. Which good. Which evil. And when no victor could be decided—there was still mail and sparthe and arbalest and halberd.

And sword.

Halgorr swung his again. Dark mirrored flats flashing. The shadows of the demons spat at his eyes. The twelfth breath filled his chest.

The blade splintered on crag.

Kaelan.

The thewed wind, though not as savage as above the cloud, still tossed him about. Nearer the face than he'd realized. A moment after the sword shattered.

Still the demons harried, unwilling to leave him to take the last few breaths. *Perhaps a crofter might look up and see them? No.* The creatures were little more than wind themselves. Taloned wind. Fragile taloned wind. Even if someone did catch a glimpse it would be no more substantial than the rumors that would soon start to gather around his corpse like ghost scavengers.

Unless—

Kaelan.

One of the demons closed, clawing——not as to slash, to score, this time—to wound more deeply. Halgorr gripped the hilt of his lava-knapped sword with its remaining shiver of blade. A stub. Still wicked but no longer keen.

He snarled. Not fit for his intent.

...The Frost Demon burying the Fire Demon in a tomb of stone and ice...

In the same breath he dropped it. Let it fall not more swiftly than he. Ripped free his knife. A common bronze dirk that had levered into gaps in the crag, butchered birds nesting in crevices or jabbed sucking holes in their eggs, grubbed or sliced mouthfuls of tuber growing in the face. Its edge sharp.

Halgorr opened his shoulders. Drew in another breath.

The demon's talons entered him. Halgorr felt them dig deep. Felt sudden fire pierce his heart. He whipped the dirk.

Kaelan!

Pain rent from a demon's throat.

A long vicious nail deep in his body. Severed from an inhuman hand. *Real. Solid.* A shard of legend cut by honest whetted bronze, a piece of fire demon buried in his chest. A legacy. *For the local crofters. For the civilized cynical travelers. For those like me.* The ones with the same bereft wasp gnawing in their skulls. The ones with ashen souls searching the world for something neither death nor myth but both or something between the two.

The scant breaths left him were of no matter.

Phil Emery is a pale, if not quite albino, ghost in several machines. His ectoplasm, in the form of stories, plays, novels, poetry and journalism, has been finding its way into print or onto the stage since the seventies. He spends his time writing, thinking, and teaching writing. He wishes he could do the first more quickly, wishes he didn't do so much of the second, and wishes the third paid better. He has never liked heights, and has never needed to climb anything to find demons.

THE PACT

by Jonathan Green

Demons. The sky swarmed black with them—foul-begotten leathery bat-winged feral furies of corded muscle and stinking matted fur. Their shrieking cries rent the sky asunder and set the firmament in tumult. They hung there, wings flapping fitfully, waiting. Below them yawned the rift, like a great gangrenous wound on the face of the earth.

But the bird-like calls of the bat-winged demons no more set the nerves of the defenders on edge and turned the blood in their veins to ice water than did the ugly, conglomerated mass of misshapen blasphemies that awaited them across the no man's land of black earth, transformed into a sucking black quagmire by the sheer quantity of blood that had already been spilt, by man and demon alike.

Not since the days of the Time of the Harrowing in the age of the Winter King had such a hellish host been gathered together in one place. It was as if Hell had opened wide its jaws and vomited forth all its infernal hosts, that they might make the world anew in Hell's own image, at this place, at this time.

There were red-limbed clawing things, blasphemous creatures made in the shape of brutish war-hounds, their heads nothing but slavering fang-filled mouths, and many-legged insectile things—the foot soldiers of the hell-spawn. Behind them were ranged the elite guard, the demon knights, their armor and weapons tempered in the blood of the fallen, and behind them, swaying hulks of demon-flesh, wrought of fire, steel and the stuff of nightmares. Row upon row, thousand upon thousand, against all that remained of the realm's beleaguered defenders.

The air crackled at their unholy presence. Heaven hid its face behind a pall of dark clouds as the sky burned red, lit by the smoking pyres upon which those unfortunate enough to be taken alive by the horde had been cast, screaming; a demonstration of what those who did not die immediately in the next charge could expect in return.

Eyes narrowed, Leondegar Lightbearer stared at the massed ranks of the enemy ranged before them still a quarter of a mile away; watched as the hordes of hell snorted and pawed the ground impatiently. Sulfurous fumes rose from the rift behind them, covering the defiled land between the two armies in a jaundiced yellow haze, making the shifting demon forms appear even more indistinct, even more threatening.

"What are they doing?" Turquin hissed from his place beside the paladin.

"Waiting," came Leondegar's curt reply.

Over six feet tall, his body adorned with gleaming silver armor, his gold-blond hair swept back from a high forehead, the paladin cut an imposing figure on the battlefield. In the saddle of his barded warhorse he was terrible indeed to behold.

It took the acolyte a moment to find the courage to speak again, but speak he did. "But what are they waiting for? They could finish us, here and now. We couldn't survive another onslaught like the last."

"Silence your prattling tongue, worm!" Leondegar roared, turning on Turquin. "Speak like that again and I shall dispatch you to hell myself. To speak like that is to speak without hope and if we have no hope, then Aztragal—thrice-cursed be his unholy name—has already won!"

"I beg your forgiveness, master," the acolyte said, cowed, dropping to his knee and bowing his head.

Leondegar watched him for several long seconds, his steely gaze boring into the man. "You are forgiven," he growled at last. "But do not let it happen again."

"No, Master. Thank you, Master." Turquin's fingers clumsily made the sign of the cruciform sword over his breast. "It shall not happen again."

To face the wrath of Hell was one thing. To face the wrath of a Paladin of the Light was another thing entirely.

A faithful follower of the Light might face the wrath of Hell with his heart strong, his spirit true and his re-solve firm. But to face the wrath of Leon-degar, Chosen of the Shining One, was a prospect that no man wanted to entertain.

Leondegar returned to surveying the enemy host. The bat-winged demons beat time above the horde, the move-ment of their wings sending swirling eddies through the sulfur smoke and ash-clouds, but still they did not move to attack. A greater will was keeping their unnatural appetite for warm flesh in check.

"So what happens now, master?" the acolyte courageously enquired of the army's commander.

"I hereby call a council of war," Leondegar declared, his voice ringing loud and true over the serried ranks of the survivors of the demons' initial on-slaught. "To my pavilion."

"I do not think this is a battle we can win," the grizzled sergeant at arms said, even though it seemed to cause him phys-ical pain to do so.

"If you were any other man, Ca-dor..." Leondegar rumbled, a gauntleted hand moving to the hilt of his scabbard-ed long sword.

"I know, Leondegar, I know. And although it pains me greatly to say so, it is the truth. We are outnumbered ten to one at least and the men are weary—weary of battle, of this crusade, of death..." He left the thought hanging in the air between them. "They barely have the strength of mind or body to do more than keep hold of the weapons in their hands and remain on their feet."

"Then what do you suggest we do?" The Confessor's words were as sharp and to the point as his face. But what the priest might lack in bodily strength he more than made up for in the passion of the believer and holy ardor.

"Retreat."

"Retreat?" the Confessor railed. "If to fight the armies of Hell means to die in holy battle, then die in battle we shall, pure of purpose and shriven of our sins."

"And then what?" Cador's scared and age-lined face could be read like a map of a lifetime's worth of experience, set down in the heat of battle. "Leave Gloriana to the mercies of Aztragal and his hell-spawned kin?"

"No, old friend." Leondegar put a reassuring hand on the grizzled veteran's shoulder. Something like a smile creased his hard set mouth. "We will not leave Gloriana to the predations of the Thrice-Damned and his minions. We shall fight. Pelleas is right; our purpose is pure. We have nothing to fear from Aztragal, for we have our faith——we are strong in the knowledge that the light of truth shines bright upon our cause——and faith can conquer all."

"Perhaps there is another way, master," came a voice from the door of the paladin's pavilion.

"I hope you have good cause to interrupt a council of war, acolyte," Leondegar growled.

"Yes, master, but I think you should see this for yourself."

The demon emissary was a wizened, crow-like thing, its carrion bird features re-shaped into something more human and so, as a result, utterly inhuman. It leaned on a staff of twisted black wood that seemed to writhe within its taloned grasp, as if in pain.

The bird-thing stood at the centre of a wide circle, the plate-armored knights and halberd-bearing men-at-arms forming an impenetrable wall of battle-tarnished steel around it. As Leondegar approached, a break appeared within the shield wall to admit him, and closed again just as smoothly once he was through.

The creature bowed obsequiously, its iridescent robes fluttering in the cold breeze sowing over the battlefield, the breath of the wind rank like the last gasp of a dying man.

"My lord," it said in a high-pitched croaking voice.

Leondegar said nothing.

"Do I have the pleasure of speaking with the commander of this valiant host?"

There arose a commotion behind Leondegar as Pelleas reached the shield wall.

"Do not speak with the demon!" the Confessor shouted. "Remember your scripture! 'Thou shalt have no truck with demons. Thou shalt abhor the demon'!"

"You do," Leondegar intoned, watching the emissary with a grimace of obvious disgust set upon his noble features. "What is it you want?"

"I come with an offer from my lord, his most gracious and mighty majesty Aztragal of the Pit, Master of Demons, Lord of Battle, the princely Embodiment of Rage."

"Do not listen to it!" Pelleas shouted.

"And what is this offer?" Leondegar asked.

"My lord Aztragal, thrice-damned be his name, offers you an end to this conflict."

"And an end is what we shall have, when every last hell-spawned blasphemy has been banished back to the Pit for all eternity," the paladin declared.

"But at what cost to the lands of men,

my lord?" the emissary enquired.

For a moment Leondegar was silent.

"What are the terms of your offer?"

"Not mine, my lord, but my master's. My lord Aztragal, Champion of the Rift, Right Hand of Darkness, Lord of the Damned, offers to face you in battle alone. My lord Aztragal challenges you to single combat, upon the outcome of which shall rest the outcome of this battle. As they say, to the victor, the spoils."

"It is a demon-wrought trick," came the Confessor's voice again, brimful of holy fury. "They are weak, they know they cannot win. Our faith is like a shield wall to them. They cannot resist us. We should press home the advantage, while we still can!"

"The men can barely stand." Now it was Cador's turn to speak. "My lord Leondegar, if the fight is within you, if the strength of the Shining One blazes strong, accept the challenge!"

For a moment, no one said anything. The only sounds that disturbed Leondegar's contemplations were the deathly moaning of the wind and the rattle of arms and armor, as the soldiers waited uneasily for the paladin's response.

"A challenge has been made," Leondegar said at last. "I am a Paladin of the Light—a loyal servant of the Shining One. I cannot refuse it. But I have nothing to fear from Aztragal, for I have already sworn my soul to another."

"Then we have a compact, my lord? We have an agreement?" the demon-emissary simpered.

"We do."

"Do you swear it?"

"I so swear," Leondegar declared solemnly.

"Very good, my lord."

Without another word being spoken, but with a great blaring of hell-horns, the ranks of the demon host parted and from between the hulking hell-spawn came the palanquin of Aztragal.

Borne aloft upon his bier by four gigantic demon-ogres, Aztragal, Master of Demons, Lord of Battle, general of the armies of the Rift, approached upon his throne of bone. His red flesh, inhumanly muscled, rippled with oily iridescence. The demon general was clad in chained pieces of armored plate torn from the bodies of captured knights since thrown to the hungry flames of the bone-fires. Leondegar recognized the shield of Blazon of Terranch among the demon's trophies and a silent rage boiled within his breast.

Aztragal's bullish head—his near human face appearing small upon the bovine skull—was adorned with a pair of twisting horns that spread out on either side like a pair of mighty antlers. When he descended from his palanquin, a thousand damned souls sang blasphemous hymns of praise to his majesty and malevolence, and the ground smoked and blackened beneath his great hoofed feet.

The shield wall disbanded utterly now, the defenders of Gloriana re-ordering themselves into serried ranks behind their master and general to await the outcome of the battle and watch what they already knew would be a struggle of titanic proportions.

The two champions met upon the emptied plain of battle between their armies. The paladin, clad from head to toe in gleaming silver, his broadsword—as long as he was tall, and more than any other man could even hope to lift—held out before him. The demon, resplendent in a cloak of screaming souls, a war-axe as large as a plough hefted in its black-clawed fists.

To those watching from the front line of the paladin's army, it seemed as if the power of the Shining One blazed from within Leondegar. A halo of holy fire surrounded his unprotected head, while his challenger's body smoldered with sulfurous vapors, and its demon's eyes sparked with hellfire.

Aztragal stared down at the paladin still standing firm before the goat-legged demon lord and smiled. "Let battle commence," it rumbled in a thunderous voice that was, nonetheless, as rich and as sweet as milk and honey.

With a shout born of rage and holy ardor, the paladin drove his blade home, sparks flying from the ruptured armor plate as the sword sliced through it and into the demon's heart.

Blood as thick and black as tar welled from the fatal wound and more gouted from between Aztragal's clenched jaws. Against all odds, Leondegar, Chosen of the Shining One, had beaten the Lord of the Damned in single combat.

But as Leondegar stood atop the dying demon's immense corpse, his armored feet planted firmly on the demon's chest, Aztragal began to laugh.

For the first time since their titanic battle had begun, an expression of doubt seized Leondegar's steeled visage.

"Why do you laugh, demon?" he demanded. "I have bested you in battle. The defenders of the Light have won a mighty battle this day, by my hand. An oath was sworn. A pact was made. We

have won. Your demon host must now descend again into the rift. So, tell me, why do you laugh?"

"You swore an oath," Aztragal gargled in that same honeyed booming voice that resonated deep inside the paladin's bones. "You swore an oath to a demon. A pact was made. The moment you did that, your soul was already lost. You are mine paladin." The fiend lurched beneath Leondegar, its hellish strength suddenly returned, the shining blade pushed free of its demonic flesh.

With a great sweep of his one remaining taloned hand, Aztragal swept the knight aside. Leondegar landed in the blood-soaked soil of the battlefield, his great armored bulk sinking into the mud straight away.

"It is you who has lost," Aztragal said coolly, rising upon his iron-hard hooves again. Silhouetted against the tumult of the sky, the bat-winged furies swarming behind him, he raised his thirsting axe high.

Only now it was Leondegar who laughed. Confusion seized the demon's bullish features.

"You have no power over me, Aztragal," Leondegar said, his voice deeper than before, rippling with liquid mirth.

The demon lord hesitated.

"I told your emissary that I had nothing to fear from *you*," the fallen paladin spat. "My soul is already promised to another. I swore my soul to the Shining One long ago."

At these words, Leondegar's body became enveloped in a shimmering sphere of light so bright it forced the demonic horde to shield its eyes. Aztragal took a faltering step backward.

Within the blistering ball of light, the paladin's body began to swell and re-shape itself. The silvered plates parted, no longer able to contain the brilliance of the light bursting from within him. Nubs of bone forced their way through the seams of his armor from his shoulder blades, elongating until great dragon-like wings unfurled behind him. Where once upon his head there had been a thatch of golden hair, a crown of horns sprouted. With ugly snaps his leg bones buckled, re-forming themselves into great bestial hoofed limbs.

Leondegar Lightbearer, Chosen of the Shining One, Harbinger of the Morningstar, towered above the upstart Aztragal. He looked down upon the stunned Master of Demons and pointed the tip of his sword—held now in one hand with ease, the blade ablaze with a fierce, actinic light—at the demon lord's chest,.

"*You*, a mere Lord of the Pit, would challenge *me*, a Prince of Hell, Aztragal?" the Shining One asked, almost curiously, in a voice like liquid fire.

A grimace of horror creased the demon lord's face.

"You shall pay for your audacity with a thousand thousand torments," the demon prince declared. Raising his sword high, he threw back his horn-crowned head and bellowed his war-cry to the heavens, the sound of it, like the clamor of battle itself, loud enough to rent the sky asunder.

"To battle!"

Jonathan Green *is a freelance writer well known for his Fighting Fantasy range of adventure gamebooks, as well as his novels set within Games Workshop's worlds of Warhammer and Warhammer 40,000, which include the Black Templars duology* Crusade for Armageddon *and* Conquest of Armageddon. *He has written for such diverse properties as Sonic the Hedgehog, Doctor Who, Star Wars The Clone Wars, and Teenage Mutant Ninja Turtles. He is also the creator of the popular steampunk Pax Britannia line, published by Abaddon Books, and has an ever-increasing number of non-fiction books to his name. To keep up with what he is doing, visit www.jonathangreenauthor.blogspot.com/.*

BLOOD TIES

by Trista Robichaud

Moonstone walked heedless through the streets of the ancient city of Virgoth, bereft of guardians and sense. Medium of height, midnight-black of hair and gray-blue of eye, she bore a face and figure that rendered many in this city of harlots green with envy. Her fine cloak trailed unchecked in the dust of the road, stirring up whirlpools of crimson motes, and her long dark hair caught the sun's blaze around her face.

Moonstone sank upon a bench by a mossy, crumbling well near the herdsman's district. Coming to herself, she grimaced at the crumpled parchment in her fist. She started to smooth it out again when drunken laughter intruded; the sour smells of wine and manure mixed unpleasantly in her nose. Between her lowered lashes, she spied four leering drovers, wine jugs held suggestively, laughing and poking one another. The largest one—a raffish red cloth tying back long, greasy hair—wheezed through a disfigured nose and collection of pustule scars. His companions were notable only in their unkempt, unshaven glory, similar rough red armbands pledging apparent allegiance to wine and ordure.

"Lady, you're much too fine for that rough bench," the large man's nasal voice grated, and his cronies chuckled. "Wha...What d'ya say we find someplace more comfortable, enjoy a little drink, maybe a little party—"

"I'm with the Guild." Moonstone announced, her voice ugly and flat. *Stupid, stupid, stupid.* She fought rising uncertainty. Nasal waved a hand, and one of his friends grabbed her arm and wrestled her upright. The force of his breath made Moonstone's world swim.

"Now isn't that sweet," Nasal said with a syrupy whine. "We'll take you back to our Guildhall, and show you our initiation." Sour body odor combated the wine for dominance as Nasal waggled his eyebrows at her. Moonstone tried to silence the chattering demons in her mind, seeking the peace she needed to invoke sorcery. *Too many. I can't knock out so many—*

"Garth!" A woman's clarion voice silenced the would-be revelers. A tall woman caparisoned in the black leather corselet of a mercenary and coated in road dust from head to toe, strode toward them. Her green eyes flashed, and Nasal's cronies edged away uncertainly. The one gripping Moonstone shoved her aside and turned to face the new threat, still squeezing her arm.

The titaness stopped and put fists to hips. "You sold me a slow poisoned horse, you double-dealing son of a goat." Angry and imperious, she extended her hand.

Garth glanced at his friends. "C-C-Caveat emp-it-or," he stuttered, but set the wine jug down and fumbled at his belt. He bared his weapon and rinsed down the mercenary's tall boot. The acrid stench of urine filled the air as the drunkards laughed uproariously.

"You bastard." Panther-quick, she grabbed Garth by shirt-collar and belt-pouch and pitched him headlong into the well. A hollow bang of bucket against stone preceded the splash as Garth's band gaped at this turn of events. The woman's eyes caught the light in a cat-like glow as she turned to face them, smiling in anticipation.

The two unencumbered thugs bolted for parts beyond, while Moonstone stomped hard on the instep of the man still holding her and drove an elbow into his gut. She tore away as he doubled over in pain, gasping epithets that were brought up short by the mercenary's grip on his ear. He whimpered as a groan of pain rose from the well.

"Your beltpouch, cur, and I never want to see you or your gods-be friends again." The woman enunciated slowly, as if speaking to a very small child. With shaking fingers he undid a shirt pouch and passed it to her. She flung him aside and looked into it, and then hurled curses at his retreating form.

Moonstone smiled uncertainly at her savior. "Many thanks, kind lady. You saved me from near certain dishevelment, not to mention discomfort."

The mercenary blinked at Moonstone, as if seeing her for the first time, and paced angrily over to the well. She

sent a great arc of spit into its depths as the groaning echoed upward. "Bastard horse died on me on the road east of here. Took almost two days to walk back to deal with this bastard son of a goat."

"At least let me buy you dinner and a bath to repay you." Moonstone said. "I know the best bathhouse in the city."

"Tess," the woman said, as a sunny smile broke her harsh visage. Moonstone returned the introduction, and they both set off through the deepening gloom, leaving behind only the mournful wails of the damned soul behind them.

A fireplace blazed comfortably, its dancing shadows revealing and concealing a room full of books, herbs, cosmetics, and other oddments. The remains of a fine supper lay before them both on the small table by the fire, though much more adorned Moonstone's plate than Tess'. The mercenary's dark blonde hair, striped brilliant white by the sun, wound in damp tendrils around her tanned neck as she devoured her supper. Bathed and perfumed, Moonstone shared her story around bites of roll.

"Ionia is my half sister, by the woman my ne'er do well father married for her fortune. Unfortunately, she died at childbed, but she had the last laugh on Richart; in her family, inheritance goes by the female line. So, Ionia will inherit when she comes of age…"

"You speak rather casually of he who got you." Tess commented, hacking off a section of roast chicken with her dagger.

Moonstone's face tightened with anger. "Richart is a drunkard and a gambler, more often in debt than out. He sold me at fourteen to a dockside whorehouse to pay his debts. I was lucky when Ducat bought my contract not much later. Ducat still employs me, more as apothecary and midwife than entertainer." Moonstone grimly chewed. "My old nurse wrote me. That bastard sold my sister."

Tess snorted, carefully peeling roast meat from bone. "If she is to inherit, how can he sell her? How many winters has she seen?"

"Barely twelve. For half her dowry, Richart's marrying her off to Maurin. I'd strangle my father for selling anyone, much less Ia." Moonstone said.

"Mmmm, Maurin," Tess purred, regarding Moonstone archly across the table. "Would this be the same Maurin whose name be used to fright children into minding? The advisor of the Prince, said to bend demons to his will to defend hearth and Kingdom? Whose tower has no outer door, and whose riches grow with each telling?"

Moonstone gaped at her dinner guest, anger temporarily forgotten. "Aye and aye. How——"

"Not much to garrison duty but drinking and swapping tales. I suppose you intend to do something about that sister of yourn. For a chance inside that tower, I'll gladly help ye." She paused. "You be a magicker, aye?"

Moonstone hesitated, pale skin flushing. "Mage Guild won't take ex-whores, but I know a few tricks."

"You can tell me what's what, then. Shall we go?" Tess stood and offered Moonstone her hand to seal the bargain. Unused to barbarian directness, Moonstone shook Tess's hand with rising hope.

"Thank you. You'll have to let me pay you, of course."

"I will," Tess surveyed Moonstone's finery. "I know little about ladies of fashion, but you are certainly underdressed for this evening's affair."

Moonstone laughed in surprise, and they fell to planning.

The moon's pale crescent shone through the ring of warped and blasted trees surrounding Maurin's tower, silhouetting the massive marble cylinder in a way reminiscent of the paintings in the Golden Bower's main hall. Moonstone made herself remember her plans rather than contemplate the masculine assertion.

Ensconced in an alley, Moonstone held up a gloved hand, hoping Tess could see it. Moonstone couldn't hear where the cat-quiet mercenary stepped, and her breath caught short when she turned. Green eyes shone with moonlight, reflecting amused radiance from a mere few inches.

"What do you see, magicker?" Tess whispered, glancing at the bonelike ring.

"These are said to descend from the trees lining the pits of Nher'gull, each hosting a legion of flesh-eating insects. It is said they are linked to Maurin, and he feeds on the souls of whom they consume." She glanced at the trees with dread. Mothlike shapes fluttered between the trees with deceptive laziness. It was all very well to plot an assault on the tower, and another thing altogether to find herself facing it. She tried to take comfort in Tess' unimpressed regard for the eerie glade as the blonde mercenary peered upward.

Moonstone sighed and retrieved a covered wooden cage from the alley, while Tess watched with evident curiosity. She gave the contents a few good shakes, eliciting angry noises and shuffling from within. With a mental appeal to her Goddess, Moonstone uncovered the pigeons, opened the box, and threw it almost within the perimeter of the tree ring. The birds flew sleepily from their open prison, and as Moonstone had hoped, took to the nearby trees to settle ruffled feathers.

Within seconds, each pigeon was covered in a host of pale, skull marked wings. The birds tried to take flight, but hundreds of tiny jaws had fixed, and the pigeon's open wings only gave the moth-things better purchase. It was as the first drained husk hit the ground that Moonstone turned to Tess.

"I'll sprinkle this incense between one pair of trees." With a gesture, Moonstone indicated the pair in the tower's great shadow. "After the smoke fills the gap, we should have a few minutes for your rope. It will confuse those…things…and hopefully their appetite will be less for the moment. Quickly. Don't breathe in the smoke if you can help it."

Tess bowed. "After you." Moonstone lit a small packet of incense in the alley and then eased forward, holding her breath. A few more thumps indicated the moth-things were almost done feeding. The moon disappeared behind a cloud, and Moonstone swiftly scattered sacks of fragrant powder and ducked back into shelter. After a few panicked breaths, she dared to look. Save for a billowing incense cloud, there was no movement between the trees.

Tess, bow drawn, was off. With one fluid movement she notched and fired. The arrow sailed upward into darkness trailing a thin line back to the cobbles below. Tess wasted no time in sprinting for the tower's base, and Moonstone's lungs burned as she scurried between trees to catch up. The silent blonde barbarian was already scaling the wall. Moonstone gripped the line between sweaty fingers and murmured an arcane phrase. *I've never used this spell before…I hope it works!* She gingerly set one foot against the tower wall, then the other, and stood sideways easily. Surprised and happy, she ran up the shadowed side of the tower, using the line to guide her way.

Moonstone looked back once about halfway up the pale marble span. The incense cloud had drifted to surround several trees below, but their guardian insects drifted in lazy, drunken patterns, uncaring of the unusual activity above. Of the sacrificial pigeons, there was no sign. She shivered.

Moonstone and Tess made it to the top of the tower and paused for breath. They panted among short flowering pots and garden hedges, the lush blooms of which emitted strange perfume. A rustle, and Moonstone barely had time to draw breath.

Two furry, slavering creatures the size of angry hounds leapt upon her, knocking her flat. Moonstone rolled instinctively, stabbing with her boot dagger until one dropped away, taking her weapon with it. She fumbled for another and scrabbled backward, away from the other beast's pestilent teeth and evil red glare.

Moonstone grasped for purchase and found a clay flowerpot. She smashed it atop the creature's cranium as she finally worked her second dagger free. She stabbed the blinded and be-flowered beast until it ceased twitching.

A meaty *thud* cut off a high-pitched *scree* to her left, and Moonstone saw something hairy collapse at Tess' feet. *Rat? If rats grew above knee height.* She watched the mercenary dance sideways, parry and slash, dismembering the squealing rodent before sending its head arcing over the battlement into the street below. Tess whirled, seeking more foes, but the round tower garden appeared silent.

"I hate rats." Moonstone chattered, terror coming now that the danger was gone.

"Easy, girl, you did fine." Tess amusedly kicked the severed corpse under a bench. "Think you can get us inside yon door?" With relief, Moonstone turned to the stairwell. She took several deep breaths and regarded the handle-less door solemnly. Then Moonstone ran her fingers lightly along the intricate knotwork patterns until she found the catch. A few moments later, the two women stole downstairs, the door behind them swaying in the night's faint breeze.

Moonstone found herself longing for that breeze as they revolved ever downward through the velvety dark. Her small bluish light ball danced happily but illuminated little; the air was rank with dust and rot. Tess stopped abruptly and Moonstone plowed into her with a muffled curse.

"There's a landing..." Tess murmured.

Moonstone frowned and listened. She heard the faint hushed breath of a sleeper, but nothing more. "Someone sleeps. Can we pass?"

The barbarian's quick smile exposed her look of catlike mischief. She turned and moved silently down the stairs. Moonstone was hard pressed to do the same. However, as they came level with the landing a high female voice snarled out of the shadows.

"Who goes there? Light!" As bid, torchlight spilled from a doorway onto the stairs. Caught, Tess rushed the room weapon bared. Moonstone wondered at the woman's rash courage. She followed just in time to see Tess holding her sword to a child's collared throat, menacing a manacled prisoner.

"New hires of Maurin, seeking to impress? Do it, and save him the trouble. He dares not kill me himself, the old coward." The grimy girl's rags did not conceal her battered, barely pubescent body.

Tess released her, standing back like a wary animal. The girl sank back against the filthy cot near her, dragging fingers through matted, dirty locks. Her eyes glittered as she watched them, and she stuck out her tongue at Moonstone. It was forked.

Moonstone felt her grip on the situation slipping. "Who are you?"

"Hrrm, not an employee then? I'll bet *you* harbor no love for Maurin, either. I have nothing to lose by answering, so...I'm a demoness. Maurin made a bargain with some of my Lords for me to inhabit the corpse of one of his 'brides.'"

She regarded her own skinny arms with disdain. "At least I'm not rotting like his past experiments. I've been hidden away like an embarrassing secret while Maurin courts his newest conquest...if you can call it courting. He seems to think I'd corrupt an innocent he'd rather despoil his way." She shrugged, and kicked the sigil-laden chains. "I'd love to teach that rat bastard some proper respect, but a contract's a contract. To serve him as best I see fit, and do him no harm, for ten more years." A demonic, offhand voice sighed from pearly teeth as Tess sheathed her blade. "Bored now."

Moonstone felt ill. "The 'new conquest'...where is she?"

"Why?" Interest fired the demonic eyes, and she sat a little straighter. Tess stepped backward, giving Moonstone the floor. Moonstone nervously opted for the truth, warily eyeing the girl for demonic eruptions.

"She's my sister. This wedding, er, isn't her idea."

A raucous guffaw burst from the waif's throat and she nodded.

"And you want her return, eh? That would embarrass Maurin nicely...I love it." A flash of baby teeth in blood red lips, surrounded by grime. "I can tell you how to defeat him...if you'll help me in return." Stubby fingers steepled before her, the pale girl bestowed them both with a thoughtful look. "He can't be permanently harmed by mortal weapons, you know."

Tess snorted. "All mortal men bleed."

"Aye, but this one's enchanted. What do you say?"

Moonstone sighed. Dealing with a demon didn't seem like the best of ideas, but she wasn't sure that she had a choice.

"Sorcery." Tess spat. "What would you have us do?"

The waif—*No, the demon*—leaned forward and smiled as she gave her instructions. After a moment, even Tess

had to smile.

The stairs were dank and slick as they spiraled downward. A creeping eon later, they came to a landing with an ornate red door set into the stone. Gold inlays into the red paint showed several magical wardings; a moment's scrutiny told Moonstone that they were meant to contain rather than prevent ingress. Tess, unimpressed, strode forward to grasp the handle, but Moonstone surprised herself by grabbing Tess' arm gently and holding her back. "Let me," she said. Moonstone cut her finger on her dagger and painted a ruby line in the golden patterns, and the door faded from view as if it had never been. Tess snorted in surprise.

The bower within was shrouded in a spider's worth of silk, but contained little cheer. A wardrobe and a few empty bookshelves adorned one wall, windows and spinning wheel the second, and a massive curtained bed the third. The walls were coated in massive hangings depicting heroic deeds of yesteryear. The faded images were bright only with embroidered gore. The room appeared lifeless.

"Ionia?" Moonstone whispered as she approached the massive posts. Tess close on her heels. Rumpled silk sheets, rank with sex and musk, lay tousled and empty upon the bed. Moonstone checked underneath and found nothing. Tess dangled something glittery before her kneeling form. Upon inspection, a golden chain was cuffed to one of the bedposts, its other end leading off toward the wardrobe. Moonstone tugged experimentally, and was greeted by a whimper.

Moonstone was suddenly furious, the deep lava of her anger rising unbidden to fill her vision with blood. She marched up to the wardrobe and threw the doors open.

A figure burrowed further under the spilling heap of fine fabrics with a frantic gasp. Moonstone could just see the end of a raven braid peeking out from the pile, adorned with a large pink bow. The velvets emitted a sobbing sound. Moonstone's anger evaporated as she bent to gently uncover the form. It was a much taller Ionia, dressed in a lacy child's nightgown that was far too short. Her arms and legs were braceleted with purple and green bruises.

"It's okay honey, Magwen's here..."

Moonstone winced at the sound of her old name, but the girl look up, violet-blue eyes wide in a pale, pretty face. She threw herself into Moonstone's arms, sobbing now in relief rather than terror. Tess idly pocketed something and then began exploring the pile of finery, ignoring the girl completely.

"Magwen...you've got to get me out of here before he comes back. I don't want to be his wife anymore. I never did. You got to get me out while I can still remember *me*." Her eyes welled with tears as she beseeched her sister, her high cheekbones smeared with snot. "Please!"

Ionia suddenly went rigid, and then began to struggle against Moonstone's comforting embrace. To Moonstone's surprise, Tess dived under the bed as Moonstone let go of her sister. Ionia settled her dress, wiped her face, and neatened the dark tendrils of her hair carefully, then walked over to the bed and sat at its foot. It was only then Moonstone heard heavy booted feet exit the stairwell.

"You look...familiar." A baritone drawled behind her. "I must insist on introductions before I kill you."

Moonstone interposed herself between Ionia and the tall, black-bearded figure before her, concentrating on a shielding spell. "No matter what the solicitors say, my sister isn't old enough to marry. I've come to take her home."

"Her father gave her, the priest sealed us. Honored sister, I must insist you leave at once." Lightning crackled from his hands and revealed her shield, scorching the expensive rug. A burnt smell permeated the air.

"Perhaps you might interest me after all. I have *many* uses for mageborn." Maurin leered. Gesturing, he sent eldritch blue mist wafting in Moonstone's direction, blurring the silken bower. She sat heavily on the bed next to smiling Ionia. Maurin advanced, sneering in anticipation.

Moonstone struggled against the fog in her mind and cast again, desperately willing Maurin to freeze in place, but he brushed her spell casually away. Moonstone watched, horrified, as Ionia lay back upon the bed and spread herself invitingly. Moonstone fought to move her limbs, her lips, anything to stop the repulsive scene of Maurin at his marriage bed. Ignoring Ionia, Maurin placed one heavy hand on Moonstone's shirt and ripped downward violently as he pushed her to the sheets. Moonstone wanted to gag at the crusty, musky smell as she felt her body moving to Maurin's commands.

It was then that Tess erupted from beneath the bed, a wet scarf tied around her nose and mouth. Maurin straightened and stood rigid as her sword made a shining arc that took his head off. The flesh parted without blood spray and the head rolled across the room. The body fell forward with a thump. Moonstone found herself able to move again, shoving Maurin onto the floor with extreme disgust. Ionia sat up, rubbing her eyes as Tess neatly sliced both hands from the body. Still no blood pooled upon the floor. Moonstone retrieved the head, holding it aloft by the hair. It made loose clucks of protest while the body's arms and hands continued to twitch.

"Try to concentrate now, sorcerer." Tess spat with satisfaction. Maurin stared at Tess as she looted his trunk, and Moonstone shook his head up and down to regain his attention.

"Thank you for your hospitality, but we'll be going," she said with a razor-edged smile. "You won't be lonely…there's someone who has missed you dearly. Really, you *must* catch up with her."

The demoness sashayed into the room and smiled a razored smile of her own. She had apparently found a bathing pool, for the moonlight glimmered across her mother-naked flesh, and her wet hair clung to her shoulders. She might have been a Temple Moon Maiden but for the infernal fires behind her eyes. Moonstone tossed the demoness Maurin's head and she caught it handily.

"Don't worry, Maurin dear," the demoness cooed. "Ceinwen will take care of you, protect you, and entertain you! After all, it's in my contract." She laughed, a girlish laugh that harrowed Moonstone's spine. The hands and trunk thumped the floor in panic.

Ceinwen glanced up at Tess and Moonstone. "Take what you like for your trouble, but do me a favor—hide one of those hands for me. Ta!" Ceinwen strutted out of the room, taking the head with her. Maurin's trunk staggered to its feet and followed clumsily. Tess thoughtfully juggled a snared hand as she watched them go.

Ionia plaintively interrupted. "Can we go now?"

Tess searched a fair number of rooms in the tower keep, claiming that she had to hide the hand well, but soon enough they were down the rope and on their way. The moth-things did not venture from their trees, as if stunned at their master's fate. The alleys held no surprises, but it was still false dawn as the weary band made it back to the bathhouse's rear entrance. To Moonstone's surprise, the Golden Bower's owner was waiting for them at the door. Smiling, he bade them follow.

Ducat, clad in a tall, curled wig, golden corset with full skirt, painted, primped, and otherwise ready for society, swished ahead of them. As Moonstone followed him down the hall to his office, she reflected she was still unconvinced as to his true gender. Whatever the case, Ducat preferred to remain an enigma, beautiful and dashing by turns.

"Ducat, I can explain…"

He (*She?*) waved her to silence and settled into a chair, arranging the skirts carefully.

"Tourmaline told me about your letter. I take it your mission was a success? Who are your friends?" Ducat inquired in a smooth tenor. Moonstone made introductions all around.

Ducat rose fluidly and knelt before Ionia, smiling. "I am glad to hear you're all right. Would you care to stay with your sister for a while? We could use another set of hands in the apothecary, or serving the lords and ladies at their gaming tables." Ionia nodded, too relieved to speak.

"Everyone who works for me gets a new name, so you can leave your old life behind. You'd like that, wouldn't you?" Violet eyes were wide as Ducat held her chin and examined her face. "You're certainly a lovely child." Ducat addressed Moonstone. "Take Iolite and let her get settled in the empty room next to yours. I'm sure you have a lot of catching up to do. I'll arrange the particulars with you later."

Moonstone was speechless with relief and gratitude. She turned to Tess. "You're welcome to stay with me 'till you're back on your feet," she said, uncertain if the barbarian would accept charity.

Tess laughed. "My feet are tired enough to rest a few days. Besides, we had a bargain." Tess shook her stuffed pack with a broad wink, then grinned and turned to Ducat. "Nice place you've got here."

Ducat curtsied. "We try, fair tigress. I'll have your story for a glass of wine, if you're willing. I've yet to meet a soldier who doesn't enjoy wetting her whistle." Ducat winked broadly at the smiling Tess.

The newly-christened Iolite swayed on her feet. "Go on, I'll catch up," Tess shooed, and the two sisters staggered off in search of their beds. The last thing Moonstone heard before she turned the corner was Tess saying to Ducat:

"I've come into possession of something you just might find interesting. Tell me, in your line of work, could you use an extra hand?"

Trista Robichaud
dedicates this story to Robert E. Howard, Marion Zimmer Bradley,
Mercedes Lackey, and her prolific writerly husband, Daniel R. Robichaud.
She lives in San Antonio, Texas with Daniel, who convinced her to step
away from the lab bench for awhile to write the kind of sword-and-sorcery
fantasy fiction she loves. In her professional life, she has a Ph.D. In
Biochemistry and is a full time researcher on cancer and protein chemistry.
You may find Trista on the web as a volunteer at Allexperts.com in the
Chemistry/Biochemistry category, and on Twitter as hntrpyanfar.

ZEEREMBUK

by Steve Goble

He ranted, snapped at the air, shredded a log with his nails—and envisioned peeling a wizard.

Then Zeerembuk took a deep breath. With a long, taloned finger he plucked muck from his scaly head; his other hand flicked aside a huge carp that flopped in his lap.

"Again," he muttered to the darkness of night. "The world of men." He growled quietly as the dank odors of fish and decaying leaves grew in his nostrils.

How many times through the long eons had he been dragged from his cozy, fiery domain to bow to some wizened mortal's idiotic whims? It was ever the same—"Make her love me," or "Eat my enemies" or "Gold, gold, gold, gold, gold!"

One moment, Zeerembuk had been playing with his three delighted demon-lings as they clambered on his back and swung from his tail. The next, he was sitting in distressingly cold mud and foul, stagnant water.

Zeerembuk stood, dripping green slime that clung to his scales. *The wizard who did this shall die*. It was the same thought he always had when summoned. But this time it was different. This time, he might actually be able to fulfill that desire. His mouth filled with warm saliva at the prospect.

Something in the wizard's summoning spell had gone awry, and instead of being imprisoned in the familiar blue chalk circle and shackled by a binding geas, Zeerembuk was here—in a smelly creek.

And, thus removed from the summoner's commanding presence, he was not magically bound. Zeerembuk could do anything he wanted—and he wanted to feast on wizard bones.

But first, he had to find his foe. An amateur summoner, most likely, reading some text he scarcely comprehended. That happened often now, unlike the early dealings between mankind and demons. Back then, illiterate men had merely prayed and begged for demonic help. It fed demonic egos to grant men their petty wishes; godhood was fun. The distance—prayers and boons crossed the void between planes, but demons did not—kept things civil.

But once men learned real sorcery, they started summoning. With binding words they made Zeerembuk and his kind reveal secrets and teach magics and perform miracles of vengeance. And once men had learned to write and share their knowledge with one another...

Now any idiot could try his hand at summoning. And so they did; Zeerembuk and his kind were repeatedly wrenched away from demonic tranquility at the beckoning of these power-mad mortals. Zeerembuk seethed as he recalled all the times he'd been forced into servitude. Many times he had dreamt of crossing that void on his own, and avenging himself on some mage who'd made a slave of him.

He crushed a log beneath his gigantic foot with a snap and a great splash of water and muck. A night heron tore into the air with a screech, and Zeerembuk ended the annoying shrill cry with a tongue that lashed forth like a whip to entangle the bird. He pulled it into his jaws, crunched it and spat feathers. He imagined it was the wizard between his teeth—then suddenly realized he was bound after all, by necessity if not by spells.

Zeerembuk was trapped here in the world of men. He would remain trapped unless he could find the wizard whose mispronunciation of a vital phrase or unwise burning of tainted ambergris had botched the summoning. To break the summoning spell and return home, Zeerembuk had to achieve the summoner's task.

No matter how compelling the thought, Zeerembuk would never go home if he ate the fool summoner. Zeerembuk tried to swallow the rage that could be his undoing.

Zeerembuk splashed to the bank, uprooted some saplings to clear his path and eventually found a road. It wound through a forest, giving him no real clue as to where he was. Over the centuries he had been pressed into service in Cathay, in Ultima Thule, in Mesopotamia. This lonely forest road could be in any of those places, or in any of a thousand others. He knew he was not in Atlantis, of course; he'd achieved the task the Atlanteans had set him, but after their binding spell had proved ineffective, he'd washed his hands of *those* bastards most thoroughly.

A scream ripped the night, and he turned all three eyes toward it. A blond girl, the kind usually offered him, though thin and perhaps a bit too stringy, gibbered at him. She fled, screeching incomprehensibly in some thrice-damned language that sounded vaguely Teutonic.

Zeerembuk followed her with strides longer than she was tall. She would be running for protection, and protection meant stone walls and—he hoped—the wizard.

Protection also meant armed men, and Zeerembuk rounded a bend in the road to find four of them charging toward him. They brandished their preposterous spears as the girl shrieked behind them. Zeerembuk halted, spread his hands wide with palms up and figured he'd give civil discourse a chance.

No such luck.

"I will skin you, red monster from hell!" The tallest man yelled as he charged forth. "I am mighty Sagurt! I will mount your head on my chieftain's wall!" Whatever language this was, Zeerembuk had heard it before. He understood it, though it was a far cry from the slithery, sinuous speech of demonkind.

"I am...unconcerned," Zeerembuk said, deeply annoyed.

The one who spoke carried no shield,

but he wore mail over broad shoulders, and his bright blue eyes carried a gleam the others lacked. The swift man's thrust would have skewered Zeerembuk's belly, had it not been deflected by a sweep of claws harder than the spear's steel-banded haft. The brave warrior charged squarely into Zeerembuk's gaping maw, and head and shoulders came off in a warm gush and a rain of broken mail. The demon chewed and spat chain mail as the others halted and stood with shaking knees behind their round wooden shields.

Zeerembuk willed himself to calm down. He wanted to speak, to explain his business and prevent more bloodshed that might escalate and end in the wizard's death—and his own eternal entrapment. But a chain ring was caught on his tooth, and his mouth was full of leather armor and bone. By the time he'd swallowed, they were on him, and all chance of negotiation was lost.

Their heads did not quite reach his shoulders unless he stooped, and he was broader than all of them if they stood abreast. But they had courage. They surrounded him, shouting encouragement to one another and calling him every foul thing that came to their minds.

A keen spear tip scraped his arm, and they battered him with their shields. *Idiots!* Zeerembuk snarled. With jabbing claws, sweeping tail and a lasso-trick of his lengthy tongue, he ended it quickly and messily—and stomped one of the blond heads deep into the road for good measure.

Once the clatter of battle ended, he heard the girl's screams somewhere ahead on the road. Zeerembuk cursed. Calm down, he reminded himself. *Don't get riled. Don't eat the misbegotten miscreant who brought you here...*

He chanted to himself softly: *Find the wizard, do what he asks, go home.*

Zeerembuk chased after the girl and found a clearing around a stone fortress with a single tall tower. The girl, presumably, had vanished across the drawbridge that was rising with groans and creaks. The fortress had been built to house an army and keep out barbarians, but that was no matter for Zeerembuk. He knew where he was now, for he'd been in this place before.

And he knew now the summoner was no amateur with a dusty tome fresh-stolen from who knows where. The summoner was Utvaard—presumptuous, lecherous, devious Utvaard—who had sought power to repel someone he called Romans. Utvaard had called upon Zeerembuk many, many times, and the demon had played a role in wresting this very fortress from its Roman builders.

How had that expert conjurer Utvaard fouled things so as to leave me sitting in a creek? Old age? Perhaps. A dotard's tongue might easily trip over many passages of a complicated spell, and by now Utvaard had to be ancient, as men go.

Zeerembuk spied the well-remembered tower where Utvaard stirred his potions and sprinkled his sparkling dusts. The tower was Utvaard's own, erected after the barbarians had swept the fortress clean of Romans. Its chief feature was an eastward-facing window large enough to allow Utvaard to work while viewing the rising stars so vital to his magic. The heavy shutters were flung wide open, and Zeerembuk could hear the wizard's curses spilling out of that high window, along with light from the conjurer's fire.

The window was beyond reach of invaders, but not beyond Zeerembuk's reach. The demon leapt across the moat even as thrown spears nicked his thick scales. The spears stung like gnats, but could not hurt him. He gained the top of the wall in another bound, and ripped in half the swine who sought to hamstring him with a hand ax. Zeerembuk flung the fool's shield like a discus, breaking the neck of another barbaric attacker and giving pause to the wild-looking men who followed.

Zeerembuk flung and kicked the warrior's bloody parts into the moat, and leapt again as a hurled torch bounced off his shoulder with a sizzle that left a black smear on his hide. Anger welled up from springs of long-pent resentment, and he roared: "Utvaaaaaaaaaaaaard!"

It was a long leap, though, and before his talons clutched the window sill he'd had time to remember his predicament, and his silent mantra. *Don't eat Utvaard, don't eat Utvaard, don't eat...*

Zeerembuk hurled himself through the wide window with a mighty tug, and his trio of eyes caught quick impressions. A blond girl, bound and gagged, with a delicious aroma and more meat than the girl on the road...a blazing hearth, tossing blue sparks that popped loudly, like distant war drums...chalked symbols on the floor, where Utvaard had meant to imprison him...a large leather-bound book, on a podium next to the table where the girl squirmed...and hoary old Utvaard muttering, one hand wiggling fingers and the other holding a bright dagger and drawing circles in the air.

Zeerembuk crouched and fought to cool the rage inside him. "Don't eat Utvaard," he whispered. "Give him what he wants and go home."

The wizard was startled into silence, but only for a moment. Utvaard glared over a beard of bleached white and pointed with the dagger toward his cabalistic floor scrawlings. "Doltish slave! Into your circle, demon! Where in all the hells have you—"

Zeerembuk bared fangs and growled deeply. *Who was this imperious slavemaster to crack a whip at him?*

Startled, Utvaard aimed the dagger at Zeerembuk's breast. Blue lightning sizzled from the blade and seared the air, and Zeerembuk averted disaster only by lifting the table as a shield. That maneuver dumped the sacrificial girl into a heap on the flagstones.

The demon hurled his table-shield at Utvaard; it sailed over the mage's head and shattered in a shower of splinters. The hurtling mass toppled shelves where skulls peered and clay pots burst in explosions of steaming red and blue fluids. Then Zeerembuk let loose a hell-bolt of his own, but Utvaard's magical protections made the lightning fizzle and vanish with a hiss.

Utvaard lifted the dagger and hurled another bolt that singed Zeerembuk's shoulder. The demon decided to take away the wizard's advantage; with a great leap, Zeerembuk pounced and lifted the sorcerer into the air.

Utvaard stabbed, and the silver blade cut deeper than any ordinary blade or spear tip ever could. It burned in Zeerembuk's shoulder like a hell-torch, and it kindled the demon's rage.

Zeerembuk chomped. He rended. He squashed. He smashed the wizard's head against a wall, tossed a leg into the hearth, twisted the neck and swallowed the snowy-haired skull. Tables overturned, books flew, acids boiled on the stone floor and bubbled as they oozed over the blue chalk circle. Zeerembuk unleashed eons of pent up hostility, and made Utvaard the embodiment of every wizard who had ever enslaved a demon.

It took a long while to vent such demonic rage.

Sated at last and his massive chest heaving, Zeerembuk halted and looked upon the red ruin with a smile. A smile that vanished once he realized what he'd done. Zeerembuk grasped the short horns at his temples and looked about at the slaughter. For a moment's revenge, he'd sealed himself forever away from his home and his little demonlings!

The girl shook, catatonic, and blood drops rolled in crooked trails down her frock. Zeerembuk thought to free her, for she was no less Utvaard's victim than himself. But footsteps echoed beyond the oak door where Utvaard's intestines draped on the knob, and the clangor of weapons grew louder with each heartbeat.

Men pounded on the door. Zeerembuk snarled. Let them come; he would kill them all. He had nothing better to do. He sprang toward the door, inhaling the man-stench and licking his sharp teeth. But he stepped on some object that slid in Utvaard's gore, and he toppled in a heap against the door. He hissed, and blinked his three eyes against splinters that rained upon him with each thunk of an ax on the far side of the door. Snarling, he looked to see what had tripped him up. He saw a volume of parchments bound with leather, with a bloody demon print on the cover. Utvaard's book.

Zeerembuk rose to his knees, crawled to the book and turned its pages as the door finally broke under the relentless ax. He quickly read enough to know what the book contained.

The demon howled and jumped, clutching the tome to his breast as heavy spears whizzed by his ears and chipped the stones framing the window. He landed atop the wall and vaulted across the moat. Angry cries and more spears followed him.

The book would not send him home; only accomplishing Utvaard's task could have broken the summoning spell. But the book would serve Zeerembuk well in this world that held him like a trap.

Zeerembuk was not one of those demons who could foretell the future, but as he ran laughing through the woods he could see a glimpse of it. He would use this book to summon a demon himself, and then another, and then another.

It might take a hundred years—even a thousand or more—to mount a sufficient conquering force...*But what was time to a demon?*

With the proper touches, this world could be made into a proper demonic home. Utvaard had summoned but one demon; Zeerembuk would bring them *all*.

Steve Goble
is a journalist living in Ohio. His short fiction and poetry have appeared in venues ranging from Flashing Swords *and* All Possible Worlds *to anthologies from Ricasso Press and Rogue Blades Entertainment. One of his short stories—"The Gods-Forsaken World" from* GrendelSong # 2—*was an honorable mention in* The Year's Best Fantasy and Horror 2008, *edited by Ellen Datlow, Kelly Link and Gavin J. Grant. For more, visit www.stevegoble.com.*

THE FEARSOME HUNGER

by Rob Mancebo

As Death marched down the seaward road he met a vile beast.
They matched each other fist-to-claw to see which one would feast.
~ from the Celtic Tale of Death.

Cadeyrn Mac Ansa trod the eyelash mountain trail carefully with his great shield slung across his back and his spear as a hiking staff. The Pannonian forest, painted in a garish medley of bright fall colors, spread throughout the valley far below him. He was weary and footsore, yet the trail stretched further and further up into the mountains. There was no rest in sight.

He hesitated at a pass, considering a fork in the well used trail. A low moaning from the hillside foliage distracted him from his decision. Tossing back his sweaty mane of brown hair with a nervous flip of his head, Cadeyrn listened intently with one hand upon the sword hilt under his draping cloak.

The sound was faint, but definite. The scarred brush of the hillside led his curious gaze to the author of the sounds. It was a girl-child, no more than nine or ten years old. Her blue *leine* was soiled and torn, and she lay sprawled in the underbrush like a discarded doll.

Cadeyrn swept the area with a wary gaze before he went to the child and snapped the branches that entangled her with brawny hands.

Half conscious, she cringed from him, but he soothed her. "Be at peace, child. I mean you no harm." There was blood on her head where it had struck stone and a raking slash of four claws across her shoulder.

Extricating her from the hillside brush, the man wrapped her in his checkered war cloak and cradled her small form as he passed along the trail.

"You must've fallen and rolled down this cursed hillside," he said, half to himself. "A mountain girl should have more clever feet."

"It chased me," she whispered weakly.

"Whatever chased you is long gone, child" he assured her. "For I have a sense of these things. Rest now."

There was no longer a question of what path to take. Cadeyrn followed the highroad from which she had clearly tumbled. When he surmounted a mountain pass, he found a beautiful valley opening up before him. It was wide, but not too deep. The oak and aspen grew thick throughout, and trails of smoke marked a village in the distance.

Yet, nearer to hand the trail branched toward a solitary hut whose roof peeked through the surrounding woods. It was to this lone abode Cadeyrn carried the child.

As he approached, he heard the sound of wood chopping cease and a powerful-looking man came up the trail to meet him.

"Greetings stranger." The man was bare-chested with shaggy blond hair and beard. He held up his empty right hand, but the axe he'd been chopping with dangled in his left, available if it was needed.

"Greetings." Cadeyrn hefted his limp burden and called out, "I found this child unconscious upon the mountain side. Is she of your village?"

"Aye, Cloti is no stranger to these hills." The man looked with concern at her pale face. "She is the daughter of my brother. I did not even know she'd strayed. I thought she was gathering herbs upon the mountainside. Is she badly hurt?"

"Her wounds are not deep, but she struck her head upon something, and any healer understands what mischief such an injury may cause."

"Then haste to bring her to our sacred grove." The woodsman waved toward a dim trail that pierced the surrounding woods. "Perhaps the gods will grant us the blessing of their aid in her healing."

Cadeyrn eyed the trail with suspicion, but followed the local man to a spreading grove of ancient oaks. Many grim and leering figures were carved and posted throughout the trees of the shadowed grove. Cadeyrn knew that their spirits, if not their sightless eyes, watched over the holy place.

"Come and pray with me," the man urged as they entered the sacred grove. "For the healing of the child."

"Better were that done by one of more pious disposition," Cadeyrn replied, lowering the unconscious girl. "I am a better beast of burden than druid."

"Pity," the man said. "Our village has many laborers, and few druids left." So saying, he took a feathered cloak from where it hung upon a tree and cast it over the still form Cadeyrn had placed upon the sward. "My folk have dwindled these last months through mysterious acts of violence."

Cadeyrn drew back from touching the feathered cloak and asked, "Are you a *gutuatrí*?"

"I speak for the gods," the man affirmed. "We shall seek their aid in her healing."

"Not I," Cadeyrn snapped. "I ask no favors of the gods and offer them no sacrifices."

"Then you should not have entered the holy grove!" the man replied sternly. "Take your heresy and depart. You know it is not lawful for unbelievers to pollute a sacred place."

"Sssssss." An odd shushing vented from the unmoving child. "Balor Mac Nessa, be at peace. This man was invited."

"Cloti?" The man bent down and

spoke to the child.

"Uncle." The girl's eyes fluttered open but they were blind and staring. "Uncle, the world is swathed in darkness and I taste smoke and bitter ashes in my mouth. There is something cold and evil within the grove..."

She sat up suddenly as though she were a puppet tugged by invisible strings. Her uncle flinched back in surprise.

"Do not scold my child from the hallows of this ancient place," the girl's voice croaked as though dry and ancient. "He has been…invited."

"She's a channel?" Cadeyrn demanded as he backed away toward the trail. "A speaker for the gods?"

"Yes," the man told him. "All in our family have the gift——"

"Treacherous bitch!" Cadeyrn snarled as he leveled his spear in the child's direction. "You would use even a fallen child to lead me down your shadowy path? Leave me alone!"

A low rumble of poisoned laughter passed through the girl's lips and her sightless face smiled in a terrible parody of human mirth.

"My most beloved child," her voiced creaked with an eldritch, inhuman wheezing. "Will you or nill you, whether I must push or pull, you *shall* travel wheresoever I wish."

"Leave me alone!" Cadeyrn screamed.

"Most beloved," she wheezed with a hollow, deathly sound that made the endearment seem like a foul blasphemy, "you are never alone." And the child crumpled back to the ground with the *gutuatri's* cloak of many colored feathers settling about her.

"Who are you, stranger," Balor asked, "that the gods speak to you with-

out sacrifice or ceremony?"

Cadeyrn gave the silent snarl of a trapped beast. It was as though every shadow within the grove held a lurking enemy.

"Leave me alone!" he roared again then whirled and ran down the trail toward the village.

It was a jog of no more than half a mile before he reached a knot of warriors barring the road.

They were big men, perfect of body and clear of eye. They carried wall-shields painted with bright animals and entwining patterns, long slashing swords, and spears with sculpted, iron heads. Their bright clothing was woven of many colors in checks and patterns. Likewise their necks were encircled with figured torcs masterfully cast of silver, electrum, and gold. Trimmed beards and waxed moustaches decorated the faces of all but their leader. He, the most resplendent among them, wore a beard only. The ancient mark of a king.

Cadeyrn halted and awaited their challenge.

"Welcome, stranger," their leader drove his spear into the earth and held out an empty right hand. "I am Áed Mac Dowell, king of the mountain pass."

"Hail Áed, King of the mountain pass." Cadeyrn drove his own spear into the earth, shifted his gladius behind his hip, and raised his own right hand. "I am Cadeyrn Mac Ansa, of the valley Sennons."

"Even so far to the east, we know the valor of the Sennons," Áed replied with a nod. "How fares King Brennus?"

"Mighty and hale as a stripling youth, though there is growing some frost in his beard."

"Verily, time is an enemy which shall undo us all," King Áed replied. "So then, we must make merry as we are able, eh? Come visit my hall Cadeyrn Mac Ansa. There is roast boar, fresh from the morning's hunt, newly baked bread, Greek wine, and sweet mead. Then you may tell us a tale of your travels while we sit close-by the guarding hearthfire. For this land has fallen under a curse and it is certain death to wander the forest after the sun sets."

As they walked through Áed's silent guards, one of the men commented upon the shield Cadeyrn bore slung over his back.

"Your shield is covered, Cadeyrn Mac Ansa."

"Do not insult our guest with questions before he has even eaten, Macari," the king cautioned the warrior.

But Cadeyrn was not insulted and replied with a shrug, "I am traveling far from home and on a mission of peace. I would not offend the many good folk I visit by parading tokens of war."

The answer seemed to satisfy the warriors and no one else commented upon the linen covering that wrapped the shield.

The hall of the king was much like any other. Built of hewed logs, with a peaked roof and a trough lined with stones in the center to contain the fire. Oil lamps trailed dark smoke up to sooty rafters and smudged thatch, and Áed's warriors sat upon the ground around long, low tables.

Smoking slabs of meat were tossed upon trenchers and tempered wine was served to all by comely women in long *leines* of various, colorful weaves. It seemed to Cadeyrn to be a prosperous village.

Yet, it was a curious thing that no *bard* sang songs or recited the deed of heroes at the banquet. Instead, the king

himself related the tale of their woes. It was this lack that piqued Cadeyrn's notice and made him realize that he saw no representative of the druidic cast at the feast at all.

"Our curse came with the spring thaw," Áed related to Cadeyrn. "People started disappearing in the woods at night. We found many corpses out in the trees, torn as though by wild beasts. Warriors and dogs who dared to track this monster were never seen again. Now I sit as a prisoner within my own hall and my people live in such fear of this monster that we hide, clinging to the blessings and protection of hearth and home."

"And what do the *gutuatri* say?" Cadeyrn asked. "What word from the gods?"

"They say it is a demon," the king told him. "But what sort of demon can kill our mightiest warriors? We have made blood-sacrifice and yet the gods have not revealed its name." He shrugged and took another drink of his wine. "At least we did while there were still *gutuatri* to ask."

"It began by killing off the druids," one of the other warriors told Cadeyrn. "The *bards*, the *gutuatri*, the *vates*. We shrugged and told ourselves, it is only the druids and there are many of them, but now even groups of armed warriors disappear."

The warmth of wine pulsed through Cadeyrn's veins and he looked at the haunted faces in the hall about him. They honestly didn't know.

"I can claim little of the wisdom of the druids, yet I know something of demons," he told the crowd. "If you would know your own, I can reveal it to you."

King Áed laughed loudly and urged him with a motion. "Show us then good Cadeyrn. Share with us how you will divine this demon which baffles our mystics and defies our mightiest warriors."

"As you command, good king." Cadeyrn stood and told the warriors, "All should follow me outside into the night. Bring no weapons, but shields and torches only."

Grumbling among themselves, the assemblage did as they were bid. Cadeyrn pulled the baldric of his gladius over his head and dropped it to the floor, then took up his shield and went out with them.

The full moon was just peeping over the mountains to bathe the huts of the village with its cold light and Cadeyrn hazed all the warriors into a murmuring circle.

"Well?" Áed asked as Cadeyrn stood in the center of the circle. "We are outside the blessings and protection of the hall, what is this demon that afflicts my people?"

"Panonnia is a land of many *keltoi* tribes," Cadeyrn told the men. "But our laws are few.

"Arrogant and foolish warriors!" Cadeyrn's accusing finger swept the crowding circle. "Do you think that force of arms is the only power in the world?

"The speakers of the law and keepers of the stories of the past are the first to be taken, and you are surprised that you cannot ferret out this demon without their wisdom? The warriors are the guardians of the people! Are the druids and farmers worth less than you?

"From the first drop of blood drawn of your tribe, the warriors should've been mad for battle and rested for not a moment until this demon was killed. Now this fiend has grown too great for the hand of man to withstand.

"Recite to me the law of the land." He looked at the blank faces in the circle of torchlight. "That the king *is* the land!"

He stabbed an accusing finger at King Áed. "What king would allow his folk to be taken while he sat, safe in his hall?"

"You accuse——me?" Áed tossed down his torch and stepped into the circle to confront his accuser.

In answer, Cadeyrn grounded his shield and ripped the sleeve from his right arm. The act revealed a blackened, puckering scar across his right bicep in the perfect form of a fluttering raven.

"I'll show you mine, if you show me yours, monster."

The king laughed coldly and cast aside his shield. "A scarred warrior? Simply another foolish mortal to feed my growing power." The king ripped down his bright *leine* to display a mighty chest, but scarred with the mark of some unearthly beast's teeth. All men knew that the laws of the *keltoi* demanded a king be perfect in body and mind. The scarred or infirm were forbidden to rule.

"Murderer!" Macari screamed and leaped at his smirking king. But Áed easily caught the man's head in his hands and forced him to his knees. "I am *tar-rákokintu-lung*," the possessed king declared and broke the struggling warrior's neck with a negligent twist. "I am the fearsome hunger which slumbers within the souls of all mankind.

"And you," Áed told Cadeyrn with a gloating laugh, "have led all the warriors of the village outside the protection of hearth and home, under the full moon, and without sword or spear.

"I thank you Cadeyrn Mac Ansa. You have delivered them all into my hands."

The king was visibly swelling as his power waxed under the light of the moon. His hands became claws, his eyes bulged to sickly yellow orbs, and his teeth sharpened like a cat's.

"Stand behind your shields, men," Cadeyrn ordered the wavering circle. "As you value your lives and families, do not allow the beast to escape until its power fades!"

"A wall of shields cannot hold me!" The possessed king roared, his clawing hands flexing in anticipation of wholesale murder.

And Cadeyrn replied, "I did not bring these men to hold *you*."

He yanked the covering from his great shield. Moonlight and torchlight shone upon the scarlet surface. Its face was painted with the grim form of twin descending ravens in black.

Like the hollow cry of a morning loon, the demon's whisper echoed in the eerie night, "You dare to bare tokens of *Cathbodua?*"

"You are merely a demon," Cadeyrn hissed between labored breaths. "*I* am the child of *Death*."

Cadeyrn could already feel his muscles writhing uncontrollably under his skin as the unearthly fire of the *riastradh* took him.

The demon screamed in a hideous fashion and Cadeyrn replied with a bellowing war cry of insane fury. His mind clouded with a frenzied lust for blood, but he managed to retain enough of his senses to meet the demon's raking claws with his shield. Layers of laminated wood splintered under the attack, but Cadeyrn replied with a swinging fist that would've snapped the neck of an ox.

The demon flinched at the bone crushing power of the warrior, but

Cadeyrn felt no elation. He felt only the raging conflagration of poisoned fire that roared through his veins, the surging of raw, physical power, and the smoldering ember of hatred for all living things that burned in his clouded brain.

The monsters hammered and tore at each other in an orgy of rampant violence. The warriors surrounding them desperately lapped shields to keep the combatants from bursting through the shieldwall in their inhuman fury.

Their battle lasted longer than mortal thews could have stood the strain. Even when Cadeyrn's shield finally splintered under the demon's attack, the exhausted king found that he had not the power to injure the warrior. As the ancient legends told, neither sword, nor spear, nor tooth, nor claw could injure a man when wracked by the horrible warp-spasm of *Cathbodua's* battle madness.

When the combating monsters locked in a grapple, it was Cadeyrn who crushed the breath out of the possessed king, and it was Cadeyrn who ripped the wilting man's throat out with his teeth.

Then, with all life in the circle extinguished, the victor turned upon the surrounding shieldwall.

He raved and smote upon linden shields with thunderous blows, but those shields were lapped so that each attack was met by no less than three stout warriors, desperately holding the wall against his fury.

Cadeyrn roared his defiance and bellowed threats of blood and murder, debase and foul to hear. But the warriors knew what would happen if their courage failed. They stoutly held their ground against his mindless, battering assault.

Finally, as the moon sunk low in the sky, the battle-madness faded, leaving Cadeyrn exhausted and sitting in the center of the circle.

When the shaken warriors released him, Cadeyrn returned to the fallen king's hall and took up his weapons.

Musing, he fingered the ivory hilt of his Roman gladius, the cursed weapon he'd stolen from *Cathbodua's* votive lake more than a decade before.

Eternal victory in battle she had promised him. Little had he guessed the curse that eternal victory portended.

He left the village un-thanked, for the terrified people scattered and hid in their cabins, sitting close to the hearth fires and praying to their many gods for protection from the monsters and demons of the night.

"Cadeyrn Mac *Cathbodua*," a young voice called from near the trail as he passed out of the village. "You have forgotten something."

The small figure of Cloti stepped out onto the light of the fading moon. She held out a shield that was nearly as tall as she was, and his checkered cloak.

"The nights are cold in the mountains and there are sometimes violent men. You will need these."

"I died as a man dies when I was but a few years older than you," he told her as he took the cloak. "I am not troubled by the cold of the world, but I thank you for the sentiment."

He looked at the shield. It was painted green with yellow lions in its corners.

"It belonged to Macari," she told him. "You killed the demon who murdered him. It is now yours."

"It's luck I did not slaughter your whole village," Cadeyrn told her.

"There was no luck behind you ordering all the weapons to be left inside the king's hall when you challenged the demon. That was cleaver planning. Had you sword and spear to assault the shield-wall when *Cathbodua's* madness took you, you would have overborne our warriors. And without weapons to battle against you, they could only hold the shieldwall until the madness within you faded. You fought as a monster, but you planned as a man."

"Though she may strip away my will in battle and twist me to her bloody purposes," Cadeyrn told the girl. "Yet I *am* a man!"

Cloti gave the shield over to him and asked, "Why did the pitiless goddess of war and death send you to help us?"

"You are the *gutuatri*," he replied sourly. "You speak for the gods."

"We do not speak for the goddess of war and death of our own accord, nor do we ask for the curse of her foul blessings."

"That is wise," he commended her. He considered the question for a long moment before he answered.

"Understand then, that gods and demons are jealous of their power upon the mortal plain and fight their petty battles through the corruptible hands of men. Perhaps *Cathbodua* felt that this hungry demon was gaining too much power.

"Yet I should not trust to her aid. She knew I would kill the demon, but doubtless she meant for me to murder the people of your village also."

"And what will you do now that you have slain this demon for us?" Cloti asked. "Do you have a purpose?"

"I'm for the sea," he replied. "Word has reached king Brennus that there is war between Carthage and Rome. He sent me to gather warriors of the coastal tribes to support the enemies of Rome lest the Imperial pestilence of the legions devours all the world."

"You, by yourself?" she asked.

He shrugged and told her, "When the greatest nations of the world summon up their armies to join in battle, who else should meet them but death?"

The battle done, the demon crushed, and Death he marched away
To join with men in foreign wars, and kill another day.
~ from the Celtic Tale of Death

Rob Mancebo, former Soldier, Security Technician, and Guard, is now up in the Pacific Northwest working in an emergency care clinic as a Medical/X-ray Tech. He's had a variety of horror, fantasy, and fiction stories published over the years and is awaiting the release of his first western novel. He also edits books for Cyberwizard Productions.

THE FURNACE

by Sandro G. Franco

Coin-sized snowflakes dropped from the lacework of branches overhead. The knight's breath steamed silver wisps in the broken rays of moonlight, vanishing in the cold night air. Sword drawn, Brompst glanced about and listened for the sound of the witch's footsteps. Only the soft pitter-patter of snow against the floor of rotting leaves made any noise.

The crunch of his boots pierced the hushed night with each step he took. Brompst spotted a fern with snow brushed from the tips of its leaves. Beside it, he found the faint footprints of his deadly quarry. The falling snow buried the tracks even as he followed them around a broad oak, long ago hollowed by lightning, and up a rock-strewn hillside.

At the top of the hill stood an arch of woven branches. Runes carved into the wood twinkled like starlight. A warm breeze flowed from the archway; outside on the hilltop, the ground was sodden with snowmelt. Inside the arch's frame stretched a long, dark hallway. Ensconced torches cast intermittent rings of yellow-orange light against the rounded walls of the tunnel.

Lore told of the ancient portals leading to distant lands—some even to other worlds. Had Ravenel stumbled upon this one? And had she passed through it, or did she mean to mislead him? Such portals did not always allow return passage.

The lords of Harkelo Hall had charged him to hunt Ravenel. Brompst had witnessed her crime; indeed, he would not easily forget the image of Malden the Red—terror gripping his face, blood spilling from the cavity that once held his heart and spreading on the snowy alley in a crimson pool.

He had known Malden since his first days in Harkelo Hall, had listened to his songs as a child. Still, nothing could be done for the old bard now, and to hunt the witch into some unknown, distant land seemed folly. For a moment, Brompst considered destroying the arch, trapping Ravenel on the other side. But he knew what the lords of Harkelo Hall would tell him if he returned without her head: the witch's fate should not have been left to chance. She would kill again. And they would demand that he find her and avenge Malden.

Unslinging his shield, Brompst stepped through the arch.

97

A warm draft met him, a sharp contrast to the chill of the Wildwoods. The forest had vanished behind him; in its place stood a wall of granite bricks. The arch on this side, a rounded frame of copper flush against the stone, was dormant. Brompst looked down the dark hallway. He had nowhere to go but forward.

Sheathing his sword, Brompst examined the floor. His fingers broke a small puddle in the shape of a footprint. The water, still cold, glistened in the torchlight. Ravenel couldn't be far.

From the distance came the faint sound of screams. Brompst rose and hurried through the tunnel, knowing the shadow witch was quick to kill anyone who stood in her way. The steady clip-clop of his boots echoed on the stone floor.

To his right, a short side tunnel trickled the pallid glow of moonlight against the walls. He had little time to ponder where the portal had taken him. Beyond the wrought iron gate at the end of the tunnel, he saw the source of the screams.

Through the gate's iron bars, the wind howled, whipping sleet and snow in spinning eddies. Men and women ran across city streets, fleeing from winged demons that fluttered between buildings. The creatures swooped and clawed at the city folk with hooked talons. Ruddy, leathery skin hung loose on their dog-like frames. Horns curled from their brow, and long, pointed snouts sprouted from their heads like stilettos.

Dozens of corpses lay sprawled on the cobbled avenues, their faces blanched and withered like dried fruit, the blood drained from their bodies.

A woman draped in a woolen cloak crawled on hands and knees as a demon sank its snout into her back. She fell flat, quivering and whimpering as her skin went pale and shriveled. When her struggling stopped, the engorged demon hopped from her body and took flight.

So much death! Not since childhood had he seen such slaughter. Brompst shook the iron gate and tried to pry the bars, but it held firm. Powerless to help, he watched a man in furs overtaken by two demons. Memories of Lynoch's civil war flashed through his mind.

In streets littered with corpses and the husks of burnt buildings, three militiamen towered over him; a band of orphans, barefoot and dressed in tatters, cowered behind him. The militiamen, hunger and lust in their eyes, grinned like wolves in a field of mice.

With a carving knife, he fought them back, adding three more to the pile of bodies lining the streets. As war brought the village to ruins, he led the forgotten youth through the bordering forest to the safety of Harkelo Hall.

He could save these people as well, if only he could find a way outside.

A bestial growl resonated through the tunnel. The distant sound, like the moan of a rabid dog, sent a shiver through his spine. Drawing his sword, Brompst backed away from the gate and retraced his steps to the intersection.

The passage was long and winding, and gently sloped downward. Brompst raised his shield as the walls opened to a wide room, lit by a bronze brazier burning with red and gold flames.

Blood dripped from the walls and glistened in the grooves of the stone floor. Soldiers in drake-horn armor lay dead, their flesh desiccated like those on the streets outside. Carcasses of demons lay strewn amongst them, as well as discarded swords, spears and axes.

Brompst knelt to a soldier leaning

against the wall. The man's lips were cracked, and though he had seen no more than twenty winters, his skin was like wrinkled parchment. Blood seeped from a single puncture in his neck.

The soldier's eyes snapped open. He lurched forward, gasping for air.

Brompst held the man steady. "Be at ease. You are safe now."

The dying soldier shook his head. "The furnace—send it back!"

"Send what back?"

"The Hotthgote, the lord of these—" Frantic, the soldier scanned the room. He began to shake. Blood spouted from his wound. The man's eyes closed and his head slumped back. "Always more—the Hotthgote's minions—"

An icy chill prickled the back of Brompst's neck. The brazier's flames flickered and went dim. He cursed under his breath for lowering his guard and sprang to his feet.

Ravenel's black, wild eyes went wide as she entered the room from the opposite hallway. The swishing flutter of wings, like a swarm of bats, came from behind her.

"They're—they're here!" the soldier cried.

Brompst raised his sword.

Ravenel bit her lip and glanced over her shoulder as she moved farther into the chamber. Her dark eyes darted to him. "Attack me now, and we both die."

From the hallway, the flurry of beating wings grew louder.

Ravenel lifted her arms. Tendrils of black magic arced across her fingertips. A spinning bolt of black energy hissed past Brompst, an icy wind trailing in its wake.

A demon tumbled into the room, head over tail. Its blood hissed on the brazier's coals as it slammed into the opposite wall.

"Behind you!" she warned.

Brompst readied his shield and spun. The pitch black of the hallway wavered and roiled. The Hotthgote's minions poured into the room. The first slammed into Brompst's shield and bounced back into the throng of flapping wings. The next fell as his sword punched through its chest.

A dark wave of energy rippled into the monsters. The demons screeched and died, yet twice their number took their place. They circled in a current of wings, beaks and claws.

One of the monsters latched to his back, its talons sinking into his neck. Brompst twisted, trying to pull the demon free while keeping the others at bay. He brought his shield arm up, grasping the thing's probing snout. Tugging its head forward, he growled and bit through the needle-like beak.

Steaming, putrid breath burned his mouth. He spat out the rubbery flesh and gripped the monster by its leathery hide, launching it into its kin.

A spear of darkness shot past him, impaling a pair of the creatures. Behind him, Ravenel screamed. A demon, upside down, clung to her robes, wings flapping awkwardly as it buried its snout under her arm.

Without hesitating, Brompst hurled his sword at the creature. The blade twirled in the air and slammed into the demon's chest. The force of the blow wrenched it from her robes.

Weaponless, Brompst punched out with his fist, batting away the nearest beast. He raised his shield and pushed through the throng of flying demons.

Claws hooked into his leather gambeson and the edges of his breastplate. Snouts poked at his armor and tapped against his helm, seeking an opening to his flesh.

Brompst dived forward into a roll. He seized a fallen short sword as his hands reached the ground. His tumble crushed one of the monsters beneath his armored shoulder and knocked the others from their grasp. Back on his feet, the knight stood at Ravenel's side.

"Keep them from me," she ordered, and lowered her head. He shivered as the shadows gathered around them.

Brompst worked the shorter blade in a spinning frenzy—hewing, cleaving, smiting. Despite the cold of the witch's magic, his face dripped with sweat. His arms burned from exertion. The Hotthgote's slain minions piled around his legs.

Ravenel's arms went wide, sending a wave of eldritch energy across the room. The ice-cold magic took his breath and swept the creatures aside like leaves in a storm. Limbs and wings flailed as the shadowy force pressed the demons into the wall. Smoke-like arms tipped with talons leapt from the stones, clawing and hacking. The room resounded with sounds of tearing hides and whistling screams and the crunch of bones.

As the last lifeless corpse of the Hotthgote's minions slid from the wall, Brompst turned to the witch. Fighting to steady his breathing, he brought his sword to her neck.

The witch's legs buckled and she fell to her knees. She glared up at him. "I saved you, and now you would kill me?" Her hair framed a pale and youthful face, and spilled over her shoulders like waves of ink.

Brompst had not expected her to be so young, nor so pretty. She had surprised him; the lords of Harkelo Hall had convinced him the witch was merciless, and had taken pleasure in killing Malden.

Yet she had fought valiantly at his side. "You murdered the bard—why?"

"Ah, Malden the Red," she replied. "Perhaps now he will be known as Malden the Dead." She tucked a stray lock of black hair behind her ear. "You would not believe me if I told you."

"Try me."

"Very well. He asked me to kill him."

Brompst thought back to the nights in Harkelo Hall, listening to the bard's stories. Malden was a knave, but he had a passion and spirit for life. "You're right," he said. "I don't believe you."

"It was not a direct request, you see, but—"

"Stop," Brompst said. "The lords of Harkelo Hall want your head—they sent me for you. And you make light of it?"

"Make light of it?" She scowled. "I killed him for the same reason you hunt me. Justice. Vengeance. Whatever you wish to call it."

"There is a difference between justice and vengeance."

Ravenel's dark eyes flashed. "Not for Malden."

"What could he possibly have done to you?" The warnings of the lords of Harkelo Hall rang through his head—the witch was a liar. "If Malden had somehow wronged you, why didn't you seek the Hall's watch?"

"Because I do not trust them," she snapped.

The sound of fluttering wings came from behind him. A single demon appeared from the hallway. Ravenel hissed through her teeth. With a wave of her hand, a shard of black energy leapt from her fingers and tore into the beast. The demon fell and skidded along the floor.

Ravenel winced. The torn end of a demon's snout jutted from under her arm, dripping with blood that soaked into the thick, black robes concealing her figure.

"You're injured," Brompst said. *Prudence be damned. If I take her life after she has fought so valiantly, I'll never forgive myself.* He tucked the short sword beneath his belt and knelt to examine her wound.

Ravenel flinched as she looked under her arm. Her hand groped around her back.

"Here, let me." Brompst pulled the stiff, needle-like snout free. It went limp and wriggled in his hand like a maggot. He tossed it across the room. "Better?" He held her arms as they rose.

She leaned against him. "Give me a moment," she sighed.

Brompst stiffened at the feel of Ravenel's body against his. Her hair had the pleasant scent of winter lilies. Whatever her offense, these demons—and their master—were a far greater danger. He glanced about the chamber, scattered with corpses, and recalled the butchery that the Hotthgote's minions had wrought on the city folk above. If they weren't stopped, they would spread like a plague. Such was the way of demons. "Stay here," he told her as he held her by the elbows. "Rest. When I return, we will discuss your crimes."

"No. I'm coming with you." Determination gleamed in her eyes.

Brompst shook his head. "If I don't make it back, you will be free. Why would you want to join me?"

"Don't you listen?" she asked. "These demons—they have asked me to kill them." She grinned at him. "Do not argue with me. You need me to defeat them."

Though he hated to admit it, she was right. Alone, the swarm of demons would have overwhelmed him. But fighting side by side, they had prevailed

where a score of men had fallen.

Brompst glanced to the dying soldier, who had fallen over during the battle. When he lifted the man's head up, dull, lifeless eyes gazed back at him.

The Hotthgote's brutish growl moaned in the distance.

"We shouldn't linger here," Ravenel said.

Brompst found his sword and pressed his boot against the demon's chest to pull it free. He sheathed the blade and took a torch from the wall. "All right, let's go."

Together, they made their way through the dark corridor. Brompst led the way, holding the torch before him. A tepid, dry air blew against them; it grew warmer the deeper they delved.

Flapping wings echoed in the hallway. From the darkness flickered the shape of two demons.

Brompst dropped the torch and drew his sword. He stepped forward to meet the monsters. Pivoting, he swung his sword in an arc. His shield smashed into the first. The sword sliced across the other's side, splitting its belly open. It tumbled past him as the first demon bounced against the wall and leapt at him.

Wings beating angrily, the creature clutched the edge of his shield with its claws. The stench of sulfur overwhelmed him as its spade-shaped head reared, its flute-like snout whistling. With a backhanded swipe, he lopped off the demon's head. Its limp remains slid from his shield. Behind him, the hiss of Ravenel's magic silenced the other beast.

"Foul creatures," she sneered.

Brompst recovered the torch. They continued down the passage. It twisted and sloped, finally ending in a descending stairwell. In the silence of the tunnel, the clink of his steel boots against the spiraling steps seemed unbearably loud. At the bottom of the stairs, Brompst paused. A faint sound thrummed in the distance.

"What is it?" Ravenel asked.

"Listen."

As they stood, Brompst could make out a humming cadence—a chaotic tune over a steady, resonating bass. The faint music reminded him of something, though he couldn't place it.

"Like the pipes of Lynoch," Ravenel said.

Yes, she was right. He recalled the summer fairs of Lynoch, before war had ravaged the village. A band of brightly dressed pipers would parade through the streets.

Brompst turned to Ravenel as he registered the implication behind her words. "What do you know of Lynoch?"

"It was my home, long ago," she replied. Her brow furled. "You cannot be—" Her mouth dropped open and snapped shut. She scanned the floor, searching for a memory. "Yes, it is you. Brompst."

Of the orphans who followed him, there was one...a pretty girl, quiet and shy, who never spoke her name. Her skin was white as cream, her eyes like the midnight sky.

He stared back at those same dark eyes. "Why did you leave Harkelo Hall?" he asked at last.

"You wanted to know why I killed Malden?" She pulled the heavy robes from her shoulders.

"Wait—" Brompst gave a fleeting look behind him, making sure none of the Hotthgote's minions approached.

"No," she said. "I will show you." Her robes folded in a black pool around her skinny legs. Under the arm where the demon had stabbed her, blood clung to her white chemise. Ravenel lifted its frayed ends up over her belly. "Shortly after you brought us to Harkelo Hall, he did this to me."

Ravenel's silvery skin shone in the torchlight's orange glow. Brompst wondered if it would be cool to the touch like her magic. His musings died at the sight of a jagged scar under her ribs, left from a wound that should have killed her.

"Do you believe me now?" she whispered.

He frowned. "Malden did this?"

"The wretch tried to have me. I refused him, and he cut me open, threw me into the Lualin River." Ravenel's features went dark. "The fool left me for dead. He deserved to die for that mistake, if nothing else."

The Laulin River. Its current ran south, to the home of the shadow witches. There, Brompst realized, Ravenel had learned to cast away fear and replace it with something else. It seethed in her eyes now.

"You said we would be safe in Harkelo Hall." She glared at him. "I would have been safer in Lynoch."

He shook his head. "No, there was nothing left there, nothing but death."

"Think of it," she continued. "If you had left me in Lynoch, you would now be in your precious Hall, listening to Malden's songs—"

"Ravenel, I didn't know. How could I—"

"—instead of trying to kill me in these cursed tunnels," she finished.

Brompst knelt at her feet and gathered the robes, her words sinking in. He'd led her to Malden. Despite his intentions, he'd played a part in what she had become. And his lords had wanted her dead. The order seemed absurd now.

He gently wrapped the robes over

her shoulders. "When we are finished here, come back with me to Harkelo Hall. Together, we will tell your tale. We'll bring the truth of Malden to light."

"Too much has changed."

When he gazed into her eyes, he no longer saw a murdering witch, but the young girl he had known as a child. *Can I guide her back from the dark path she has taken?* He knew what his masters would tell him—that he would be a fool to even try. "I haven't changed," he said.

Her eyes narrowed. "No, but I have."

In the glimmer of Ravenel's past, Brompst saw hope that she could change again. Somehow, he would persuade her to abandon the darkness and shadows of her magic. "Trust me," he said, offering her his hand.

"I was nearly killed the last time I trusted you." She glanced at his hand. "And now you expect me to follow you again?" The witch brushed past him. Brompst felt as if he had been slapped.

Farther ahead, she stopped. A smile curled her scarlet lips when she turned to him. "Come along."

The tunnel led to a massive, sloping cavern ill-lit by the green-blue glow of faerie moss that blanketed its rock face and hanging stalactites. They scurried behind a broken wall and peered over its edge.

A colossal demon—tall as twenty men and with a bladder pipe long as an elder pine under an arm—danced around a well boiling with flames. A skirt of fire whisked about its potbelly. With each step of its cloven hoofs, the ground shook; the buildings near the well had been trampled to rubble. Serrated horns curved from its bobbing head. Unfolded wings, too small to bear its weight, fluttered behind it as it turned on inverted knees.

A stream of the Hotthgote's minions sprang from the well's flames. They buzzed about the cavern like a cloud of deerflies. Red and gold runes shimmered on the well's edge. It was another portal—one to a land of fire and ash.

"So the Hotthgote summons its spawn with the music," Brompst said.

"Who would have opened such a portal?" Ravenel asked. "And why?"

Brompst recalled the soldier's words. *The furnace—send it back!* "To fight off the winter cold," he answered grimly.

"The beast's flames will foil my magic."

Brompst wasn't sure his blades would prove any more effective, even if he could reach the monster before its minions surrounded them. He shook away his trepidation, knowing in his heart that the Hotthgote was a scourge on the land. It was his duty to destroy it. "I'll take the Hotthgote. Try to keep its spawn off me."

"I can bring you to the beast more quickly." The witch's teeth gleamed white in the eerie light of the faerie moss. "Let me give you the gift of the shadows."

Brompst blinked at her suggestion. His lords had told him the consequences of embracing the shadows. Its cold darkness corrupted those who submitted to its influence, rendered the heart callous and cruel. "No, I cannot—"

"You ask me to trust you." She placed her hand over his chest. "Yet you would not do the same for me?"

Brompst enfolded her hand in his. Her fingers were so small, so delicate. *If I take her offer, perhaps she will accept my own and return with me to Harkelo Hall.* Looking to the giant demon, he knew he would need any advantage he could get. *Yes. I will accept her dark magic in order to guide her to the light.* "Do it."

Ravenel brought her arms around his neck. She whispered arcane words into one ear and then the other. He surrendered to the magic. A cold shudder ran down his back with each foreign syllable of the ritual. As her words trailed off, he felt empty and hollow, like an old tree succumbed to rot.

For a moment, he wondered why he was about to confront the Hotthgote at all. *The people of this city don't know me; they care nothing for me. Why should I care for them?*

Brompst gazed into Ravenel's eyes. He wanted nothing more than to be away from the demon and its tunnels, with her at his side. He wrapped his arms around her slender waist. "Let us leave this place. Perhaps the city above deserves its fate for opening such a portal."

"No Brompst," Ravenel whispered. Her fingertips glided from his neck. "Remember what the beast has done to me. To us."

The Hotthgote paused its tune and plucked a handful of blood-gorged minions from the air. Brompst's jaw clenched. *Its spawn tried to kill me; they wounded Ravenel.* Juices dribbled from its pointed chin as it stuffed the creatures into a puckered mouth lined with curved teeth. *It dared to attack us for no other reason than wanton hunger. Are we nothing more than crumbs to it?* The notion insulted him. A cloak of darkness swirled around him. *The Hotthgote should learn to revere us. It will come to fear us before it dies.*

"The beast should be punished." Ravenel need not have said the words.

It blew into its pipe, and more minions, dripping fire, leapt forth from the red-hot well.

Brompst took Ravenel by the shoulders. "Fall back if the demon spawn overwhelm you. Use the tunnels to limit their numbers."

"Focus on your task," she replied. "And don't worry for me."

Unfurling wings of shadow, Brompst soared through the cavern. The furnace's hot, stifling air burned his lungs. It only inflamed his anger. Ahead, the Hotthgote stopped its music and turned. Brompst raised his sword.

The demon's hourglass-shaped pupils went wide as the knight flew straight into its face.

With a cry of rage, Brompst rammed his sword into one of the Hotthgote's eyes. Jelly spilled from its socket. The demon screamed, spitting cinders and ash from its round mouth. It dropped its pipe and reached for its wounded eye.

Pulling the sword free, Brompst twisted and slashed, taking one of the demon's fingers. The Hotthgote's roar shook the cavern, the flames around its waist jumping and crackling. In the blistering radiance, the witch's magic wings tattered and vanished.

Sliding down the demon's face, Brompst stabbed again, burying his sword deep into the Hotthgote's flat muzzle. His legs dangled far above the cavern floor.

Around him, sheets of black magic streaked across the cavern like a hailstorm. The demon's minions screamed and plummeted.

The Hotthgote slapped at Brompst. Steam sprayed from the slits of its nose.

Grunting, his armor rattling, the knight held on. As the beast's hand came at him again, he tugged the short sword free of his belt and wildly swung—taking off another monstrous finger.

The Hotthgote's palm smacked against Brompst, breaking his grip on the sword planted in its snout. Wind whistled in his ears as he fell toward the cavern floor.

The demon's pipe blew a quick, shrill note as he landed, feet first, on the inflated bladder. Without considering his luck, he flipped the short sword in his hand and slashed it into the thick membrane. The fleshy bag belched noxious air as he slid from the sinking bladder skin. Demon spawn crashed to the ground around him, torn and eviscerated from bursts of dark magic.

With an echoing bark, the Hotthgote raised a leg and smashed a cloven hoof down on him.

Snarling, Brompst leapt aside and spun. The Hotthgote's foot cracked the cavern floor. As he turned, the knight swung the short sword high overhead, above the demon's hoof. The blade bit into the demon's tough flesh. He sent the sword across the other way, cutting through tendon and muscle.

The Hotthgote lurched and crashed into the stone edge of the well. Howling, it pulled itself over the rim as the portal boiled and bubbled flames. Vines of pink drool swung from the Hotthgote's round mouth as it looked over its shoulder.

The demon's bleeding eye fixed on Brompst as it bent its leg back. The knight raised his shield. A cloven hoof slammed into him. The jarring impact sent him flying back, into the wall of a ruined building.

Rock rumbled against rock. As dust kicked up around him, the Hotthgote crawled into the well and disappeared. The remaining minions followed its master, headfirst into the flames. A brick smashed into Brompst's helm, knocking his head to the side. He tried to lift his shield but his shattered arm refused to respond.

With a thundering crash, the wall toppled over him.

Darkness. Silence. And then, the subtle shift of rubble. Brompst coughed as the weight of rock and stone lifted.

Ravenel straddled him. Her splayed fingers swirled with wisps of shadow magic.

Brompst's heart thumped in his chest. *Does she betray me?* He tried to move his sword arm, but his weapon was gone, lost in the stones. He had trusted her before, but now, at the witch's mercy, doubt crawled through him like worms through dirt. The image of Malden, the gaping hole in his chest trickling blood, blazed in his mind. Ravenel studied him with her black eyes.

Was this what Malden saw before the witch murdered him?

She reached down and pulled the helm from his head. Her breath was sweet and cool against his face, like rain after a summer drought. "Fear not," she said. "I will save you, as you had saved me."

The cold darkness enclosed the knight and lifted him into Ravenel's arms.

Sandro G. Franco is a librarian living in the Pacific Northwest. His hobbies have included various martial arts, and he now practices fencing. "The Furnace," his first published story, is a prelude to a novel he is currently writing.

THE FIRST LEAGUE OUT FROM LAND

by Brian Dolton

Schiava only began to relax when the wind, spilling around the headland, filled the sails of the *Campo Del Mar* and sent the caravel riding over the waves. Though she did not care for the way the ship pitched and rolled, she was far happier with the salt-crusted deck under her feet than the paving-stones of Alim Grayne.

Not that there was anything wrong with the paving-stones themselves. She liked paving-stones; they were solid and implacable. But equally solid and implacable, and far less likeable, were the Magistro's guardian ogres. Anywhere on land, they could reach her, and tear her to bloody ruin. Only out here on the water was she safe.

She felt the pouch tucked inside her shirt. Through the leather, she could feel the power of the Venstone. She hated the feel of it, so close to her skin. In other circumstances, she would have cast it into the depths of the ocean in which—so it was said—it had been made, hewn by an ancient race of demons.

But circumstances were as they were. A Venstone would sell for a thousand tolari—maybe more—in the lawless markets of Taracco. And a thousand tolari; well, that would be enough to buy her family out of the slavery that she had escaped from.

I am not proud of being a thief. Not even a damned good one. But needs must—

A hand came down on her shoulder, and she started.

"Nervous?" Barto asked, his voice rough, but with gentleness beneath it.

"You startled me, is all." Schiava pushed herself up off the rail, and turned to face the captain. Barto was a big man, but the hand that now let go of Schiava's shoulder was the only one he had. His right arm ended in a stump, just below the elbow. Schiava had heard any number of stories as to how the captain had lost it. Bitten off by a sandshark in the Southern Skerries, some said; hacked off by the Emir of Castano as a punishment for piracy, others claimed.

One drunken night on the way to Alim Grayne, Barto had told her it had been severed during a duel with the Boltroni brothers, supposedly notorious men of Taracco, though Schiava had never heard of them. She suspected that all three stories were lies, and that the truth was nothing more than a simple shipboard accident. But the stories enhanced the captain's reputation, in certain ways. And captains needed their reputation in these waters.

"We'll be clear of the headland soon. Wind's set fair. Eight days and we'll be back in Taracco, free and clear."

"Eight days." It had taken twice that to reach Alim Grayne, against the wind and current. But it still seemed a terribly long time. To stern, the towers of the port city showed, clustered together, hung with their banners. "Are you sure? It looks like we're barely moving."

"First league out from land is always the worst," Barto said, with a grin that showed exactly how many teeth he had left.

"The first league out from land," Schiava repeated. Something was poking the back of her brain. She'd forgotten something, missed something. Something important.

There was a flash of pain in her chest. No; not in her chest. *On* her chest. The Venstone. She clutched the leather bag instinctively, and could feel the heat of it. The power of it.

It was the Magistro's doing, she was sure of it. A locator spell, perhaps. One did not steal from a wizard and expect to go undiscovered for long. But she was asea, and the Magistro was ashore, with all his magic attuned to the earth. She was free and clear. She told herself that, and wondered why she didn't believe it.

She found out, all too soon. "Captain!" a voice shouted, in clear alarm, and another shout: "To port, boys! Shift her to port!" Schiava pushed herself off the rail and ran toward the bow. Only yards ahead of the ship, impossibly, an island was rising out of the ocean. Water sluiced off it in a thousand brief waterfalls, and around its base the sea roiled in anger.

The Magistro could not touch her on the water. But he had poured his power into the seabed, and it was rising under the *Campo Del Mar*. Even as the ship heeled about, tilting treacherous under her feet, there was the crack and groan of timber that told everyone on board the ship was running aground.

She had only one hope; to get into the water, somehow, before the Magistro's ogres rose from the very rock of the new island, tore her limb from limb, and returned the Venstone to its owner. Heedless of the sailors panicking around her, she raced toward the stern of the ship and, without even looking, dove over the rail.

Her hopes died even as she splashed into the water; for the water was barely a yard deep, and she found herself bruised and battered, and lifted by the rising, groaning rock beneath her.

She pushed herself to her feet. There was pain in her chest, again; this time, her own, and not the Venstone's. She was not sure if her ribs were cracked. Every breath made her wince.

She was facing north, back to the towers of Alim Grayne around the harbor. She could see the Magistro's tower, shaped all from stone; could imagine the old man, his eyes brilliant with anger, standing there in the cupola of his tower, pouring his magics out to one purpose and one purpose alone.

Reflexively, she clutched at the leather pouch that hung around her neck. The painful warmth had ebbed; the locator spell no longer needed, now that she was stranded on this temporary island. For a moment, she thought of tossing the Venstone away. But without it, she had nothing save the Magistro's implacable enmity; for no one had ever spoken of the Magistro as a forgiving man.

The grinding of rock had ceased; the island had been formed sufficiently to the Magistro's purpose. Schiava gulped in painful breaths. Around her, uncomprehending fish flapped and gasped on the slick stone.

"Thief," the voice of an earthquake said.

The ogre was twice her height, three times her breadth, and was covered in a skin like gravel. It stood splay-footed and sure on the new-made land. Schiava, looking up at it, knew she was dead. There was no way to defeat such a creature without magical assistance; and she had used her few tricks in stealing the Venstone in the first place...

The Venstone. Even as she turned and ran, hoping that she could buy some time by keeping out of the ogre's reach, she realized that she did have magic. Powerful magic. Wild magic. Unpredictable magic.

It might kill her. But, as gravel feet crunched their way over the rocks behind her, she realized her choice was between the Venstone's chance and the ogre's certainty. She scrambled up over sharp rocks, tearing her hands as she did so, and turned, balancing precariously on a spur of damp rock.

The ogre stood beneath her.

"Return what you stole and die swiftly," it intoned—the Magistro's words, she realized, the ogre no more than a mindless mouthpiece. "Resist, and your death will be unthinkable."

She believed the Magistro. She had heard of what had happened to Tarkis of Near Bentray. He had been three months dying, and it was said that no-one in earshot of the Magistro's tower had slept for the horror of the screams.

Schiava lifted her hand to her throat, and tore the leather pouch open with desperate fingers. Somehow, the Venstone slipped from her grasp, onto the rock below. She stared at it, appalled; her last hope had betrayed her. The ogre was stretching upwards, its rock body hideously malleable under the Magistro's control. It would be on her in a moment...

She dived. Her head cracked against one rock, her shoulder against another. Her ribs seemed to clench around her chest. But her left hand; her left hand was all that mattered. Her palm came down square on the Venstone, there where it lay.

She felt the demonic power of it in an instant. It shot through her body like carmine fire, like sapphire ice. It wreathed her in its wild strength; she could feel it consuming her. The ogre's hand came down on her shoulder, all raw stone and massive weight. She reacted instantly. The power in her rose to her will, flaring out of her. Stone transformed into smoke; the very rock of the ogre boiling off where it touched her, wreathing Schiava in rancid clouds that made her cough, each spasm sending agony through her ribs. She dropped to her knees, pressing her clenched left fist down against the rock of the island, gritting her teeth as she set her will, and the power of the Venstone, against the Magistro's power. Stone cracked and split and hissed and retreated from her.

Despite all the pain, she laughed, her voice nothing against the roar of breaking stone, the war of wild magics. If she had only known what power the Venstone held...the stories were nothing. She could feel the magics under the skin of the world, feel veins and lodes of power. It was glorious. She stood, and rolled her will out, and the island smoked and sublimated under her desire. She could feel, somehow, the Magistro's impotent rage, palpable through the boiling stone.

That was not all she could feel. She looked down at her hand and stared in utter horror. She was no longer holding the Venstone; it had burrowed into her flesh. She could feel it, worming its way between sinew and bone, making itself a part of her.

She pushed herself to her feet. The caravel lay, tilted but intact, in a cusp of rock; she could see some of Barto's crew, dim figures in the choking clouds. She took a step towards the ship.

It was like wading through the swamps of Far Bentray. The air seemed to have thickened around her. The water around her feet was black and cold and seemed to welcome her. For a moment, she thought it was some last trick of the Magistro's. But then she realized. She had been wrong. The Venstone was not making itself a part of her. No; it was making her a part of itself. This was no symbiosis; this was possession.

Schiava staggered toward the ship, her arm out in front of her, as if she could delay the Venstone from crawling its way through hers body to her brain, where it would surely hollow her out and make her its puppet, slave to its unknowable will.

Schiava had no intention of being a slave again. She screwed up her eyes against the stinging air, and screwed up her will, adamant that the Venstone would not master her.

She could feel cold, demonic laughter dismissing her presumption. She could feel fragments of memories, horribly alien. There were stories, told in hushed whispers in the dark nights, of the demons that had shaped the Venstones, had poured into them all their power, and all their knowledge, and all their hatred. Schiava had always been a skeptic, but now, faced with the sensation of the Venstone crawling into her, she was a believer.

"Help me!" she gasped.

The crew of the *Campo Del Mar* paid her little heed. They swarmed over the ship, inside and out, trying to ensure that it righted itself as the island evanesced. Schiava groped forward, felt the damp wood of the hull against her fingers. Some horrible memory, not her own, slithered into her brain; damp wood, and flayed skin, and the taste of raw flesh in her mouth. She vomited, every spasm sending another explosion of pain through her chest. All the while, the Venstone crawled slowly into her, scraping past the bones of her wrist, and pushing veins and arteries aside in its relentless pursuit of her skull.

There was water around her hands and knees. The island was almost gone, now; the Magistro's power futile against the counter-magic of the Venstone. The ship's timbers groaned in protest as its weight shifted back from land to ocean.

"Grab hold," a rough voice said, as a damp rope fell across her shoulders. Schiava clutched at it, gritting her teeth. *It would be easy to just let go, to lie back in the water, to accept the waves of the harbor as the waves of pain. Easy to yield, and fail, and die...*

The Venstone wanted her to; wanted to recreate its ancient maker, wanted to hollow her out and make her something utterly inhuman.

No. She hauled on the rope, hand over pained hand, banging her shoulder against the flank of the ship as she climbed those few, terrible feet to the sanctuary of the deck. Over the rail, she lay on the strakes, gasping like a gaffed fish.

The Venstone's power hissed and roiled and burned the very air around her.

"Help...me..." she begged again. "Kill...me..."

She saw Barto step toward her, a heavy axe in his one hand. She did not want to die. But she would not live as some small and huddled thing, some cache of memories in whatever the Venstone reshaped her into, powerless and rueful. That was worse than any slavery.

The Venstone had no intention of letting her die. The power flicked out of her, without a thought on her part, and Barto hissed a curse and dropped the axe as if it was red-hot.

"Master it!" he shouted. "I can't help you unless you master it!"

He asked the impossible. Hot tears stung her eyes. In her veins, her blood was turning into something else, something cold and deep. Through the tears, she could see her hand, flexing of its own volition. It appeared to have developed scales, and some kind of web between the stiffened fingers.

She closed her eyes and drew in one long breath, bringing herself under what control she could. She would never be anyone's slave again. And her family...they had no hope, if not for her.

The demon laughed in her mind, dismissing her absurd presumption. She poured her anger at it, all her rage and all her independence and everything that was hers, every scrap of will that she could muster, to drive it back out of her mind. *You are mine*, she told it. *I am not yours. You are mine.*

It slithered around her anger, trying to clutch hold, here and there and everywhere at once, like a squid. She screwed up her courage and beat at it with everything that was a part of her. She threw every horrible memory at it, to spur herself on, to maintain her defenses. Her eyes were closed; she had no sensation, now, of anything outside herself. The world was gone. There was only her and the Venstone, at war with one another in the vast plains of her soul.

And then there was only one. There was one bright flash, a jagged thunderbolt of terrible agony, and the war was abruptly over. She opened her eyes.

Barto stood there, a bloody axe in his hand. There was something lying on the deck of the ship. It took her a moment to realize that, under the covering of scales, it was her own left arm, severed at the elbow.

She slumped back against the rail, the clean agony of what Barto had done washing through her, purifying her like fire. She let her head tip back, looking away from the ruinous place where her arm ended; the torn flesh and broken bones and gouts of bright blood. Barto, the axe dropped onto the deck, knelt beside her, fumbling with some kind of tourniquet.

"I had to do that," he said. "I'm sorry."

"I thought...I don't know. I thought you were going to kill me." She remembered asking him to. Pain washed through her again, and she wanted to yield to it. But there was one more question she had to ask.

"How...how did you know what to do?"

He gave her a gap-toothed grin that blurred its way through her tears.

"I know more than I care to about Venstones, girl. How do you think I really lost my arm?"

Brian Dolton was born in England, and has visited thirty countries across five continents. He's played volleyball on a sandbar in the Pacific, watched the sun set over the Sahara from the back of a camel, and stayed in a Buddhist monastery on a sacred mountain in Japan. He currently lives in New Mexico, where he is owned by two cats, and his blog may be found at www.tchernabyelo.livejournal.com.

THE SACRIFICE

by Jason Irrgang

They made their stand in the throne room.

The braziers on the walls had dimmed, their light choked off by the very presence of the unclean host that battered at their holy barrier. The myriad shrieked and cursed, throwing themselves against the holy symbols etched into the stones outside, dying by droves as they probed for a weakness. Hyperion's sigil was all that stood between the horde and the three men bottled up inside.

Guntram stood in the center of the room, looking up through the thick, stained glass dome. Its ancient grandeur depicted the many battles of the paladins against their traditional enemy, bright figures locked in eternal combat with dark minions of ruin. The bald man's face was severe beneath his goatee, his eyes narrowed sternly at the malevolent creatures outside. His armor was a dented, worn testament to his long years fighting against the encroaching shadows.

"It won't be long now," he announced.

Jakob shifted, rising from his seat against one of the hall's pillars. He was Guntram's opposite in almost every way. Where Guntram was thickly built and bald, Jakob was all sharp angles, with a head full of blond hair and a clean-shaven, almost boyish face despite his middle years. "Are we sure about this? Guntram, Sigmund?"

Sigmund did not respond, so deep was he in the midst of prayer. He was the youngest of the three by far, a farm boy called to Hyperion's Order before he'd passed his tenth summer. He clutched the amulet that hung from his neck with one hand, almost desperately so, while the other gripped the hilt of his sword. He spoke his prayer in a murmur, so as not to disturb his brothers' conversation. "Keep me in your gentle care," he said, "and give me the will to face the challenges that lay ahead with honor, dignity, and above all courage."

Guntram eyed his brother critically, growling, "We are well past the time for discussion, brother, and we do Sigmund no favors by undermining the council's decision. Asmodai will be upon us soon."

Something scrabbled against the hall's imposing, iron-shod doors, found purchase, and began to tear at it, gibbering and howling as it did. Above them, another of the myriad threw itself against the barrier, cracking the glass dome. Shards rained down, clinking like wind chimes as they fell against the stony floor.

There was no uniformity amongst the surging horde; one could look upon them for hours and not see two creatures alike. The maddening, chaotic throng came with a thousand different faces; in sizes from smaller than a cat to those that dwarfed a horse; with wings, some like those of bats, others of oily feathers; with teeth like needles, or tusks, or great sharp canines. They shared only one trait between them—a maddening desire to tear down man and all of his works.

Today, it seemed, was the first step toward the victory they had so long been denied.

Guntram gathered up his bastard sword, habitually running his thumb along the edge and smiling. "We have a few moments, at best."

Jakob gave the old warrior a sidelong glance. "Try not to sound too excited, Guntram. Or are you in a hurry to be eaten?"

Guntram's smile turned into a grin then. "Hyperion, no! I intend to cut such a swath through the disgusting little bastards that they'll be whispering my name in hell for all time. They'll tremble and look to their demonlings, telling them, 'Behave or Guntram will leap out of the shadows and get you!'"

Sigmund couldn't help but laugh at that. He rose from his knees, freeing his sword from its scabbard as he did so. He took his place at his brothers' sides, his eyes hard and flat. As the hall's doors continued to crumble and the dome above gave way, Jakob spoke to him quietly.

"Are you ready, Sigmund?"

Grim-faced, the youth nodded.

"Hyperion be with you, brothers, and I will see you on the other side. Asmodai will regret his arrogance today," Jakob's face became a cruel smile. "For the rest of his miserable existence."

The doors failed, and the horde surged in.

Sigmund met them unflinchingly, leaping into the myriad's embrace as eagerly as he might a lover's. He struck to and fro with his sword and shield, but allowed the crush to crawl over him, biting, clawing, tearing, seeking to tear his flesh free from his bones. "If I am your loyal servant," he beseeched, "then bless me with your righteous flames."

Beneath the myriad a clean, blue-white fire burst into life, a thing that clung to Sigmund like a cloak and turned his attackers into dust, or sent them wheeling away, screaming for mercy. Sigmund redoubled his efforts, hurling himself again and again into the thickest knots of the demons, hacking, hewing, and stabbing. In his heart, Sigmund knew that this is what he'd been born to do, to throw himself against the enemies of man and see them destroyed, burned away in Hyperion's cleansing flame.

The glass dome above finally shattered. Slivers of glass and winged abominations rained upon the three companions. Guntram turned to face them, calling up a great fist of Hyperion's holy fire which he hurled against the myriad. The enemy's excited squeals turned to pained shrieks in but a moment.

It was but a moment, yet the dome's collapse distracted Sigmund long enough for one of the myriad's champions to rise up out of the throng. Black-skinned, four-armed, with a head like a snarling dog's, Sigmund did not see it until it struck. The force of its blow made Sigmund strike himself in the chest with his own shield and lifted him from his feet, hurling him half a dozen paces. A pillar halted his impromptu flight and scattered his wits, leaving him dazed as the hulking monstrosity closed the distance.

Sigmund shook his head, trying to clear the haze of pain and struggle to his feet at the same time. The brute clenched its fists and reared, preparing to strike. Mercifully, Jakob appeared, his broadsword licking across the creature's face and his off-hand dagger slamming between its ribs. The monster howled and twisted to face Jakob, ready to hammer the senior paladin down.

The distracted beast did not see Sigmund's recovery. The young warrior brought his sword up in a wicked arc. The holy blade wreathed in Hyperion's flame took the brute's left arms off at shoulder and elbow. Sigmund then drew his weapon back and thrust forward, hoping the beast had some black heart hidden in its chest. The point of his blade stabbed through its back and erupted from its chest, startling Jakob, who had drawn back for another strike.

As the beast fell to dust, Guntram roared laughter from somewhere on the other side of the seething enemy. "Well done, brothers!"

The battle with the myriad lasted only minutes, but it seemed an eternity of howling beasts, gnashing teeth and glinting claws. Inexorably, sheer numbers forced the battle brothers back, though each new surge of beasts had to climb over the charred remains of their fallen brethren to bring the fight. Each attack took its toll, bringing new wounds, and robbing the brothers of strength and will.

But then, like the tide, the creatures ebbed, chittering and gibbering plaintively as they retreated. Encircled by the dead, the three struggled for breath, gripping their swords in desperate, white-knuckled fists, looking to one another for assurance that each still stood. Outside, the myriad's cries grew fainter and fainter. It was in their nature to flee in the face of creatures greater than they, and Asmodai was more than a match for the lot of them. Perhaps more than a match for three tired and wounded brothers of the Order.

"He's close," Sigmund mused. "I did not think it would take him this long to come."

The shadows stretched like things alive, spreading out from the darkened corners and into the light, slinking up the walls toward the braziers and torches. Outside the throne room, the lights winked out one by one, inexorable, dreadful. Animated and willful, the tendrils leapt out and smothered every source of light, leaving only the moon and Hyperion's flame to guide the brothers through the darkness.

He emerged from the blackness, formless and indistinct at first, slowly taking on the features of a man. Asmodai, the demon lord who had plagued the order since its inception by forever stealing mortal skin to walk among mankind wreaking despair and pain. This time the demonic master had taken Duke Gregor's skin, patron of their order. The Duke had been a handsome man and Asmodai's vanity would allow nothing else from his host. Dark-haired, sharp-featured, he sneered instead of smiling, and the stolen eyes flickered with barely contained fires of Tartarus.

"Good sons of Hyperion," Asmodai's voice reverberated through the stones. "I commend your courage, but your struggle is in vain. I have already visited the council chambers, your elders are dead, your order reduced to naught but a shadow of what it once was."

Sigmund's brow furrowed and he glanced to Jakob and Guntram, but Guntram merely spat in response and bared his teeth. "The oath binds us to our last breath and beyond, devil. Do you think you can cow us with the murder of our brothers? For all your centuries spent battling us, you still cannot fathom the heart of a paladin."

Asmodai scowled, and stabbed a finger at them. "Little fools—"

"No more talk!" Jakob cried, charging forward.

Asmodai willed a wall of inky blackness into existence to shield himself from Jakob's furious strikes. The fiery blade left smoking furrows in its wake; in response a score of thick black tentacles billowed out, bobbing and striking like snakes. Sigmund took a step, meaning to defend his brother, when Guntram pushed him away and took up a place at Jakob's side, bellowing as he did. "Do it, Sigmund, now!"

Reminded of his duty, Sigmund sprung the trap. He raised his fist in the air and spoke the necessary holy words to bring Hyperion's might to bear. The faces of the stones blazed to life, revealing scores of hidden symbols carved into the throne room's walls, marks of binding that the order often used against the forces of the underworld. Singularly, Asmodai would have brushed them aside, but massed as they were it was impossible for the demon to overcome them.

Asmodai howled and clawed at his eyes. The great shroud of blackness that had fallen over the room faltered and shrunk, pulling back within itself. Diminished so in the face of Hyperion's symbol, it was all the demon lord could do to keep Guntram and Jakob at bay. His summoned tendrils lashed out wildly, cracking stones and shaking the entire throne room with the force of the blows.

Bolstered by their enemy's sudden weakness, Jakob and Guntram lashed out. Weakened, but not defeated, Asmodai retaliated. Jakob threw himself behind a pillar to avoid the demon's tendrils while Guntram gamely battered another away with his shield.

All the while, the demon lord raved. "Worms! Do you think that your tricks will contain me? When I am done grinding your bones to dust I will bring this entire fortress down with my hands!"

"Speak no more, devil." Jakob returned to the attack and struck Asmodai with the hilt of his sword squarely between the eyes. Asmodai staggered, spat, and lashed out with his fists. Jakob could not dance away quickly enough and absorbed a bone-rattling blow that took him off his feet entirely. He crashed to the throne room floor in a heap of armor and limbs.

Guntram replaced him, bringing his bastard sword down in a low arc, white-blue flames trailing it. The blade bit into the back of Asmodai's knee, taking the leg off cleanly and sending him down to the cold stone floor. While the demon lord struggled to a sitting position, Guntram hacked downward again, separating Asmodai's arm from his body. Jakob rose to his feet, lending aid to his brother's grisly work, until the demon lord was a brutalized mess.

Asmodai thrashed and howled, his power dwindling further as his host's life blood spilled onto the floor. Still he screamed defiance. "Finish it then, and free me so that I might return to Tartarus." His face twisted into a leer, his teeth bared. "I have all the time in the world, while you will turn to dust. Your order is broken and when I return, there will be no one left to oppose my will."

Sigmund, gritting his teeth from the continuing strain of holding the barrier, stepped forward. "You've underestimated us gravely, Asmodai, and for the last time."

Guntram and Jakob looked to Sigmund, both their faces growing sullen. It was Guntram who spoke first, breaking the momentary silence. "Are you ready, brother?"

"I am." Sigmund replied, staring at Asmodai with contempt.

The demon lord's brow knitted, his eyes narrowed. "What new foolishness have you brought?"

"An old thing," Jakob said, producing a dagger from his belt. "A secret rite that the order has ever refused to make use of." He held the dagger up, a wicked thing etched with terrible runes.

Guntram slipped behind one of the throne room's pillars where he recovered a length of thick chain, made of white metal, adorned with the flickering blue runes of Hyperion. With the chains, he bound Sigmund, ever watchful of the demon lord's broken form. Asmodai's gaze remained fixed on the kneeling, bound paladin until Jakob loomed over him, dagger in hand.

"You know this one? You should, it was Erik's dagger. He thought to bind you with it when he defeated you."

"And failed. Will you repeat such a tired trick?"

"Aye, it's true. It didn't take you long to break its bonds."

Guntram, ensuring Sigmund was well and truly bound, then took Asmodai in his grip, exposing his chest to Jakob. The demon lord struggled in vain. "You'll not escape this time, Asmodai. You overcame the dagger's binding once, but it needs only hold you for a few moments, that we might direct you into our brother's body. We will see how you contend with a paladin's will."

Asmodai's countenance twisted with fear at Jakob's words. He thrashed and struggled, gnashing his teeth and spitting curses. Jakob gripped Asmodai's throat and plunged the dagger into his chest, once, twice, three times, until the blade finally kissed the demon's heart. He leaned forward, whispering in the demon's ear as the light faded from his stolen eyes. "You cannot break us, demon. Our brother will bind you for eternity. I bid you farewell."

Jakob withdrew the dagger, slick with blood, runes now alive and dancing along its surfaces. He turned back to Sigmund, placing one hand on the boy's shoulder, readying to strike the fateful blow. "Forgive me for not being strong enough to be in your stead, brother."

Sigmund looked up, smiling gently. "We do only what Hyperion calls upon us to do, Jakob. Guntram." He nodded. "I will not fail you, brothers, nor the order."

Guntram nodded in return. Jakob, holding Sigmund close, hesitated for the briefest of moments. "It is we who must not fail you, brother." Jakob drove the blade into Sigmund's chest; one clean, quick strike that rent the boy's breastplate with ease. Sigmund stiffened and sucked one last breath between his teeth, then slumped to the floor.

The brothers stood in silence for a long time, looking down on the body that had become the prison for the order's greatest enemy. Then, wordlessly, they gathered up Sigmund's body and made their way deeper into the keep's bowels. They snaked through winding, forgotten passages until they came upon a pair of silver doors, great things etched with further binding symbols, shared by those that held Sigmund's body fast. Beyond the open doors waited a simple cell with loops in the floor.

Reverently, they placed Sigmund's body in the room's center, lashing him to the stone floor with more lengths of the engraved chain. Guntram and Jakob gazed into Sigmund's empty eyes and knew that the battle had already been joined. Their brother's soul would become a ravaged battlefield, hopefully for all time. And though they both wished fervently that they could have gone in the boy's place, in their hearts they knew that they would not have had the will to condemn themselves to an eternity of torture.

Together they exited, pulling the cell doors shut as they did so. Their shoulders sagged, though not from wounds or exhaustion.

"He deserved a better end than we asked of him." Jakob set his back against the wall, allowing a moment's respite.

Guntram cleaned his blade, then slid it back into its scabbard. "Sigmund did what had to be done. Come, we must go to the new council and tell them of our victory here."

"Do you truly count this a victory, brother?"

To that, Guntram had no answer.

Jason Irrgang *is a student at Lane Community College majoring in Literature and Language. "The Sacrifice" is his first published story. Writing this section in the third person makes him feel extremely pompous, but he's okay with that. He runs a LiveJournal called Titan's Musings at http://savage-jason.livejournal.com/, which he doesn't mind people visiting.*

SON OF THE ROCK

by Laura J. Underwood

A demon slept within the fist-sized stone. Michan O'Brannach could feel its dark presence scratching against magic-sensitive nerves as he stood on the road in front of the gates of the abandoned farmstead on the borders of Tamnagh. Curious, he pushed mage senses at the stone to determine what manner of demon it was.

A trapped one, he quickly concluded. Must have been one of the lesser kind for he detected no immediate hint of rational intelligence in the thing. Only insane anger and frustration over being unable to feed. Hunger wanting fulfillment that did not readily come, and the taint of blood grown old.

Leave it be, Michan told himself as he continued to stare at the farm stretched beyond those broken walls.

But curiosity battled within him all the same.

Why would someone trap a demon in a stone and leave it outside the gate of an abandoned farmstead that looked like it had once served as a keep?

"Feels a wee bit bogie, this place," Conor Manahan said.

"Yes, it does," Michan agreed and cast a half smile back over his shoulder at his tall Keltoran companion. Death did permeate this place, giving it a grim, unnatural taint. Then again, death was often the air of war. Its odor saturated battlefields and villages and townships alike. The kingdoms of Tamnagh, Cinnoch and Elenthorn had been devastated under its grasp since the Hound of the Blackthorn led his armies of Haxon barbarians and demonic monsters to overrun Ard-Taebh. Oh, there were pockets of humanity left here and there, but they huddled as frightened survivors who would never see magic or mageborn with the same innocent eyes again. The Hound—*Damn his wretched soul!*—and his bloodmagic had seen to that. Even with the High King's militia pushing the borders of the invaders back to their mountainous realms with the aid of battlemages like Michan, the ordinary folk kept suspicion of magic in their hearts.

119

With a sigh, Michan stepped forward to release the anger his thoughts briefly aroused. He heard the creak of leather as Conor dismounted and tethered the horses so he could accompany Michan. The Keltoran was a good man to have at one's back, and Michan was always grateful when the fire-haired youth he'd come to know as a friend would volunteer to accompany the battlemage on these scouting forays. Though young, Conor showed no sign of the unease most men felt in a mageborn's presence; but then, Conor had been raised in the very kingdom where the last of the Old Ones once dwelled, and the Council of Mageborn still kept its headquarters.

The gates were stone, and felt cold to Michan's touch when he removed his gauntlet to brush them with more sensitive fingers. Spell craft left its faint patina here. Dark patterns in the stone spoke of warding glyphs older than the war. Michan frowned, testing them with his mage senses once more, and recoiled almost immediately when the blood taint assailed him. Blood magic had made these marks. Yet there were other marks as well, more recent scratches in the stone not made by an Ard-Taebhean hand. Haxon runes.

"Well?" Conor said quietly, knowing Michan would hear even if he whispered. "Have we a reason to go around this place, or can we use it for a camp?"

Michan squinted, brushing pale blond hair from his eyes. "There's magic here, but it feels quite old."

"Old," Conor repeated and scratched his nose. "Then why do I feel like ants are crawling up me kilt."

"When did you last bathe?" Michan quipped.

A growled epithet about Michan's state of mind answered him, making him grin. Michan gestured to the runes. "Have you ever seen these before?"

Conor moved closer, squinting. "Can't say as I have."

"The Haxons wrote this," Michan said, brushing the marks with his fingers.

"I thought the Haxons didn't write things down," Conor insisted.

"Not these days that we're aware of," Michan said. Scribes and scholars among the barbarians were rare. "But theory is that they came from the Ice Plains beyond the Great Range, driven into Carn-Dubh when the Great Cataclysm tore the world apart and turned their realm into nothing but ice and snow. But your own countrymen have always told tales of a race of men who raided Keltora's shores back before the Great Cataclysm, and they supposedly came from this land of ice. And we know that some of the Haxons did end up in Ross-Mhor where they intermingled with the Ross-Mhorians."

"And they laugh at us for blethering about the old days," Conor said.

Michan smiled. "Actually, if it hadn't been for Keltoran storytellers, mageborn would never have been curious enough to seek the truth. Years ago, based on those same tales, mageborn scholars made a foray into that realm and found evidence of a civilization that fell when the ice descended on their land. The scholars carefully recorded the writings these people left, and from what they found, they concluded the folk were Haxons, though bits of their culture resembled those found dwelling in Curraghduff and Ross-mhor."

The very culture believed to have birthed Cudreaighean Moran, Hound of the Blackthorn, against whom the militia of Ard-Taebh fought. No wonder the

Haxon's followed his mad conquest.

"So the Haxons can write," Conor said with a hint of impatience. "What do the runes say, or can you read them?"

Michan made a face. In his youth, training his mageborn powers, he had learned to read a number of writings that no longer mattered to ordinary folk. "They read," he said, "'This is the place of a madman of dark powers. Beware.'"

"Cudraeighean must have slept here," Conor quipped. "And here I thought the barbarians liked their Hound because he was as mad as they."

"Let's go in and check it out," Michan said. The sooner they looked around, the sooner they could return and report what sort of place they had come across, and leave it up to the Baron of Dun Ferlie to choose which path this front-line militia would take.

The gate tunnel was long and low. Conor boldly strode its length, one hand on his sword hilt. Michan took a more cautious pace, but like Conor, he kept a hand on his weapon. Being a battlemage, Michan knew there were times that steel was more useful than his other "skills," just as there were certain creatures left by the Hound's dark ravaging that had no respect for either.

The tunnel emerged in a shamble of a courtyard. This place had suffered from a raid, for signs of burning and pillaging were present. Weeds choked what had once been a small garden behind a low stone wall against one side of the farmhouse.

"Gentry farmers," Conor said with a glance around.

Michan nodded. Tamnagh had been full of gentry folk who thought their station in life alone would protect them. But Haxon barbarians knew nothing of class differences since they lived a *kill-or-be-killed* way of life. Gentry died as easily as peasants. Blood was blood, no matter how fine. It soaked the ground just as dark.

The stone keep that once served as a main house lie open. Conor was first to peer into a lower hall that would have housed livestock and farm hands in the winter. Now it wore a thick blanket of detritus, cobwebs, broken bits of wood and old straw. Ravens called the rafters home, and their eerie *qworking* echoed from above. Michan heard the skittering of mice beneath the straw and in the walls.

The men ascended a set of stairs at the far end that took them into the main house. The large hall filled most of this level, though Michan could see chambers off to the sides and a gallery overhead. Here, the faint echo of life was barely perceptible, enough to make Michan want to withdraw, for it held a taint that burned his nerve endings.

A sense of magic and blood.

"Looks deserted enough," Conor said, and his voice thundered back at him. "Howt awa. MacTalla!"

"Who?" Michan said, and his voice repeated itself in the expanse as he reached for his blade in expectation.

"Son of the rock," Conor said. "The echo. My auld nurse used to tell me that an echo was the taran of a child who died without blessing. Ah well, enough men and pallets will stop the sound."

Michan shivered, his thoughts running back to the demon in stone out by the gate. *Son of the rock echoing hunger and rage. Not a pleasant thought to creep in just now. Damn Conor and his bogie tales.* Sometimes Michan suspected Conor was a bard in his soul, for the Keltoran knew a wondrous bounty of what he called granny lore, and blessed little of it was cheerful.

"I'm not so sure this place will be safe," Michan responded, lowering his voice to reduce the echo. "There's an air of occupation I can't quite put a finger on."

"Stoats and ravens," Conor suggested, but he wore a grim look that said otherwise.

"Not unless they move on two legs," Michan said and pointed toward the dusty floor. Footprints started from a central point, as though the owner had simply appeared there. They headed toward a set of circular stone stairs in one corner that led to the gallery above.

"Shall we follow?" Conor asked.

Michan nodded, though a small part of him wanted to retreat. No telling what or who hid up there.

Son of the rock? Or the soul of the mad blood mage who had sought to claim Ard-Taebh and started this bloody war.

Conor was first to make the stairs with practiced ease and a courage Michan could not help but envy. *I too would possess such confidence if I were tall as a tree and young as he.* Michan was obliged to recall that his skill had gained him this post, and not his heart. He would have been happier serving back with the High King's main militia, safe among mageborn he had known as friends for nearly twice Conor's lifetime. The blood that made Michan mageborn also slowed his age, making him look and feel not much older than his tall companion, and his sensitivity to blood magic's taint was what made him an ideal front militia battle mage. He felt the spoor of magic often before he knew of an enemy's physical presence ...like now.

Their ascent took them into a gallery. Conor moved like a panther stalking prey. A quiet killer who had seen more death than Michan considered healthy. But that was the way of war, stealing a man's innocence. What amazed Michan was, for all the blood and death witnessed, Conor remained affable and calm. Whatever gave him that stalwart nature, Michan envied it as well. *You could be a captain, commanding these men, were it not for your stubborn Keltoran pride, and your insistence that such posts belong to older, wiser heads.*

The footprints led across the gallery to a broken door. Conor and Michan peered through a gap revealing more stairs. A watchtower, Michan decided. Even farmers needed defenses.

Again, Conor took the lead. He stayed close to the outer curve of the wall, mindful of the crumbling stones at his feet. The footprints followed the spiral up three and a half full turns. At the top, they found a landing and another door. This one was closed, and cleaner than Michan would have expected, having seen the rest of the keep.

Michan motioned for Conor to stand still, and sent mage senses stretching into the wood. Marks revealed themselves to Michan, glyphs and wards more akin to those his own kind would have used to guard a gate or pathway. Slowly, Michan let his senses trace them so he could know their full nature and the danger they might present. A trickle of sweat rolled between his shoulder blades, leaving an icy trail across his skin.

One by one, he unmade the glyphs, always aware of the fact that he left himself open to magical attacks in the process. At the edge of his awareness, there seethed the sense that something was not pleased with his interference. Yet nothing attacked him from those peripheral shadows. No demon sprang for his throat.

No spirit stirred in wrath. Not even a blood mage emerged to cast spells of doom and destruction on the pair. Only the essence of anger and hate echoed around Michan.

At last he unsealed the final ward; he felt it dissipate under his persistence. The door became no more than an ordinary barrier to them now.

He opened his eyes and nodded. Conor needed no instruction. He put a cautious hand to the latch and discovered it was locked by more ordinary means from within. Frowning, the Keltoran raised his heel and firmly applied a boot to the stubborn wood.

Age had weakened the lock, just as Michan had weakened the wards, and the door splintered under Conor's well-applied kick like matchwood. It fell open, slamming against the wall. Michan shouted, "*Solus!*" and sent a large ball of mage light rolling into the semi-dark. They rushed in together, Conor only slightly ahead to keep from catching them both in the doorframe.

What greeted them was a circular room with four narrow slits at cardinal points for windows. Michan was swift to recognize the tools of magical work. Books gathering cobwebs and dust. Shelves crammed with vials and jars of herbs and unidentifiable bits of animal anatomy. Death reeked from the walls, and was stronger still in the center of the chamber where there rose an arcane circle of stone like a small dais.

The footprints led to the edge and disappeared.

"Howt awa," Conor muttered softly.

Michan knew all too well what caused the Keltoran's unease. Bones littered the floor of the conjuring room. Most of them were heaped in a discarded pile off to one side, but some were still scattered across the center of the circle. Michan carefully made his way up to the edge, willing his mage light brighter. The bones looked as though they had been broken open and deprived of their marrow.

Frowning, he touched the circle with mage senses. It was inactive, so it was safe for Michan to step across the edge. He made his way to the pile of bones that looked fresher than the rest. Squatting, he fetched one for closer examination.

Teeth marks greeted his gaze—humanoid teeth marks on human bones. *But why?* He stretched mage senses again to touch the splintered white material, and felt its untimely death overwhelm his thoughts. He felt the fear that bubbled forth as cries for mercy were ignored. Felt a hand close about his throat, pressing him to the ground, as a knife reared over him. Steel slashed into tender flesh, and Michan cried out with the memory of another's painful death. And all around him, voices whispered, echoing agony and grief. Little *tarans* of children at the moment of unwanted death.

Then it was gone, the images, the sense of terror. Fading like sunlight in the gloaming, gliding away from his nerves. But not the whispers. They continued to grieve around him.

Michan bowed his head, unable to stop sobs of sorrow breaking free from deep inside him. His whole frame convulsed as he crouched on the floor. Then a hand gently settled warm weight on his shoulder, and a voice called to him. "Michan?"

"They were children, Conor," Michan groaned. "Mere children. And he killed them."

"Who? Cudraeighean? Why?"

"I don't know if it was him," Michan said, "but whoever it was, killed them for power. *Tienm laeda.* To gnaw the marrow, to gain knowledge and power through their deaths."

"But for what purpose?"

"To summon demons," Michan said, raising his head. He stretched mage senses around himself, wishing he were away from this terrible place.

"To serve the Hound?" Conor said.

Michan shrugged, wiping tears on his sleeve and forcing himself upright. He took a deep breath, pushing grief back to replace it with resolve born of practice. "I don't know," he said more somberly. "The image was terrifying, and I still hear their cries." Whispers of pain. Pleas for mercy. They raked at him, begging for mercy, stealing his calm. "By the horns of Cernunnos, I still hear them. Can't you?"

"No, Michan," Conor said. "But then, I'm not one of the mageborn, remember."

"But, they're here!" Michan insisted, anger now replacing dismay. He flailed his arms to gesture to the chamber. "They're all around us!"

Conor's grip tightened on Michan's shoulder, and the pain drove through Michan's muddled senses like a beacon of truth.

"Michan," Conor said steadily. "I don't know what ye hear, but I do sense that something is not right about this place. I think we'd best leave and report what we've found to the Baron."

Michan nodded. To leave had every appeal. To escape the dark images of death swirling around him like translucent leaves in the corners of his thoughts. They had died horribly, these poor children. So suddenly, and he knew recently as well, for he would not have felt the death of those bones he touched so strongly unless...

He frowned. *Why do I feel them at all?* The essence of the dying child still cried from the past. Had the spell finished, and the essence traded for the knowledge it would bring, there would have been no echo of death within those bones.

He was interrupted. Whoever he was, he was stopped before he could summon the demon and feed it the essence.

But that wasn't right. The demon was in the stone...

So what had *happened here?*

"Conor, I can't leave yet," Michan said.

"What?" Conor looked astonished at the announcement.

"I have to find out the truth of what happened here."

"Why?"

"Because something is wrong," Michan said. "Something was not finished, and I must know what and why before I can give my recommendation to the Baron."

Conor rubbed his stubbled jaw with a gauntlet-wrapped hand. His green eyes narrowed in thought. "All right," he said slowly, "but ye'd best be quick about it. 'Twill be dark in less than an hour, and I'd just as soon not be larking about these woods without the sunlight. Haxon scouts are right fond of the gloaming, ye ken."

Michan nodded. "It won't take long, I promise. But I must have silence, and I must not be disturbed. Do you understand?"

With a nod, Conor stepped back.

Michan returned to the center of the dais, and though his hand trembled, he brushed the bones aside, clearing a central place. There, he seated himself and opened the satchel he always carried off one hip. Within, he found the bit of silvered scrying glass wrapped in a patch of black velvet. He spread the cloth before him, laying his little mirror in its center.

"Do you see any candles?" he asked quietly.

Conor said nothing. He merely moved around the room, stopping at one or two points to collect small stubs of candles that sat on shelves and in window ledges. These he brought to Michan, stepping boldly into the circle as though it were no more than a clearing in the woods. Michan hid a smile. He doubted any other man he knew, save a mage-born, would cross the circle without flinching or making some warding sign.

Michan took the candles and arranged them around him as Conor went back to his place by the door. Whispering "*Loisg*," Michan lit the wick of one with magic, then used it to ignite the rest. He closed his eyes, seeking the stillness within as he drew essence from the world around him to feed his spell. Then opening his eyes, he stared at the small oval of mirror while stretching mage senses to touch the footprints at the circle's edge

Darkness sprang up around him so that the world was invisible for moments. He felt detached from his physical self, afloat on the ebon stream. Then, like players on a stage, figures swelled into his view. A man, old and decrepit, and somewhat reptilian in nature was standing on the very spot where Michan sat holding his breath. The old one clutched a bone in his hands, stripped of flesh and cracked open. At Michan's feet lay the pile he had touched, but now they appeared fresh and glazed with blood.

At the edge of the circle stood the figure of a man who seemed young and ancient at the same time. White haired, tall, and dressed in black armor, he stared at the old man with amber eyes that burned like twin embers in the shadows surrounding his face. Cold fear iced every inch of Michan's being, for he had no doubt that this was the Hound himself, the dreaded Cudraeighean Moran, blood mage and self-proclaimed king of the Haxon barbarians.

"This will not do," a voice whispered. "You have managed to frighten my armies with your fiendish ways. If you will not agree to serve me, then you are against me."

"I serve no man!" the ancient one snapped back. "Mage or otherwise! I earned my freedom from a Shadow Lord's bonds long ago, and I shall not relinquish it now!"

"But you are not a man," the Hound said with a malicious grin. "And if you will not serve me as others of your kind do, then you will not be allowed the freedom to stand against me."

Cudraeighean stretched forth his hand, and fire raced from the fingers. The old one snapped like a dog gone mad, batting the flames from his face. He dropped the bone clutched in his hands, and only then did Michan realize that the creature had blood staining his mouth.

You are the one! Michan screamed in his head. *You are the dreaded devourer of these innocents.*

"MacTalla, I consign thee to an eternity of entrapment," Cudraeighean said in the mage tongue, filling the air with the gale force of pure raw magic of a like Michan had never known. "You will wear stone until stone wears away!"

The old man writhed, shrinking until he was nothing more than a fist-sized rock. The Hound smiled and stretched fingers toward the stone, and it flew willingly into his hand. With a laugh, he tossed it toward one of the window slits, sent it careening to the ground outside, and though Michan could not see where it landed, he sensed that it fell by the gate.

The demon in the stone! MacTalla! Son of the rock. The old mage was some manner of greater demon!

A shout rang through the tower, and Michan felt himself thrown to the floor by a heavy force, jerking his ethereal self back into solid form with a blinding flash. He opened his eyes to find Conor had seized him and hauled him to one side. For moments, Michan was confused as the sudden act of leaving his otherworld vision so quickly sent shards of agony slashing along his nerves. He could not focus, and the only thing that managed to penetrate the haze of pain was the angry shouts of the Keltoran.

"Horns, Michan!" Conor's voice raged. "Snap out of it, or we are both dead men!"

Angry shouts were filling the chamber. Michan fought against the pain as Conor released him and leapt to his feet again. Michan staggered to get his own legs to support him, and in moments, he realized they were not alone. That the rabble of voices filling the chamber belonged to the angry Haxons who were rushing up the stairs. One of them had fired his bow at Michan, and the arrow had embedded itself in the shelves far to his back. The man nocked another even as Michan shook his head and focused. Swearing, the battlemage stretched forth his hand, and though the effort cost him, he jerked essence from the world around him to feed his spell. "*Gath saighead buail!*" The small bright bolt of magic shot at the Haxon and smacked him in the face. He cried out and fell, clutching

his head. His bow shot off to one side, and the arrow went astray, slamming into the calf of the Haxon warrior who had been in the act of rushing past the archer.

Conor's voice was raised in a Keltoran battlecry. Michan glanced briefly at the tall youth whose blade scythed through the throat of one Haxon, then into the heart of another. A third shifted his battleaxe to swing at Conor.

Michan shouted and jerked his own sword free. Magic was too costly on his nerves and essence just now. He would have to muster himself against the enemy with steel. He dove at the Haxon and thrust his blade deep into a muscled back. The Haxon screamed and turned, lashing at Michan with the ax, and for once the battlemage felt grateful that his height was lacking. The ax cleaved the air, leaving an opening to stab through again.

Michan's steel skittered off a rib then found its way between them. The Haxon died clutching his heart, teeth gritted.

Conor shouted again, and Michan was pulled out of harm's way as the Keltoran's longsword sliced into the throat of the remaining Haxon. Then silence filled the room, and even the whispering voices Michan had first perceived here were gone. He took a deep breath, feeling his knees wobble beneath him, and sank unceremoniously to the floor. The stench of copper and warm, unwashed men cankered the air in his nose, but he was too tired at the moment to care.

Conor quickly head for the door and peered down the stairs to see if others were about.

"They're gone," Michan said.

"You're sure?" Conor asked, returning to kneel at the battlemage's side.

Michan nodded, and though it was still an effort, he stretched mage senses to test the world around him, just to reassure himself.

"What were you doing anyway?" Conor insisted.

"Looking into the past," Michan said.

"And what did ye see?"

"MacTalla," Michan replied.

"Aye?" Conor looked confused, and Michan could not stop himself from grinning.

"It's a long tale, and I'll gladly share it with you once we get back to the rest of the militia."

"And what are we to tell the Baron about this place?"

"We'll tell him it isn't safe," Michan said. "That's all he'll really want to know."

Conor nodded. "Just who was this MacTalla?"

"Son of the rock," Michan said. "He was a demon captured by the Hound."

"Come again?" Conor insisted.

Michan shook his head. "Later," he said.

Outside, he sensed MacTalla writhing in his prison of stone, no longer a threat to innocents, thanks to the wretched Hound.

Laura J. Underwood *is an East Tennessee librarian, a former fencing champion, and an occasional harpist. She has authored over 200 short works in the fields of fantasy, dark fantasy and horror, as well as several novels, novellas and short story collections. More information on Laura and her work can be found at www.sff.net/people/keltora.*

INTO SHARDS

by Murray J.D. Leeder

King Vorthe rose from his feather bed, his skin crawling with gooseflesh. Despite his age his senses were acute, his intuition finely honed, and he knew something was there in the darkness. Something terrible stalked the halls of his castle, had even penetrated his bedchamber, and for all of his experience he had no name for it.

Vorthe rolled from the bed silently, leaving his young wife Tanista sleeping angelically. Not delaying to put on clothes, he grabbed the club mounted on the wall. Of all the weapons with which he was proficient—having wielded them in war since he came to the throne of Malakar—none felt more comfortable to his hand than his very first. Solid and weighty, the club felt like an extension of himself. He stepped out into the darkness.

The silence crashed and crescendoed in his ears. He caught no glimpse of an intruder, but he knew one to be present all the same. How he did not know, but it was there for him. It posed no threat to anyone else in the castle.

Vorthe moved through the still hallways of his castle, past his elegant tapestries and paintings, his furnishings gilded with gold. How far removed he was from his origins, from animal skins and wooden weapons. But now, a crude club in his hand, naked flesh bristling from the chilly air, he felt himself the same barbarian hunter he had been all those decades ago.

The first traces of daylight began to creep through the window slits facing east, and Vorthe thought that he would soon see his opponent…unless it was invisible, a spirit of some kind. He caught a glimpse of something, a flash, glinting in the fresh light. His gray hair stood on end and excitement flushed his features. It was corporeal, it was real. He could fight and kill it.

He took slow, measured steps through the hallway toward it. His knuckles turned white on the handle of his club.

Then something moved in the corner of his eye and he reacted, bringing his weapon to bear. But all that stood before him was a full-length mirror, patches of it illuminated by the shards of light that cut through the air.

It took him a moment to realize what was amiss. Then he gasped. It was a mirror he gazed into, but he did not see himself reflected in its polished glass.

A sharp prick cut into his cheek, setting a line of blood drooling down his face.

He spun to face his attacker and found himself looking into himself. A familiar face hovered before him, lined with a thousand cracks but youthful and beautiful, with cold white skin and flaming red hair. It was him…and it was not him. Both. A frozen image of a time long past, a person he once was.

Vorthe peered deeper into the image, his club at the ready.

It was flat. Flat as glass. Indeed, it was glass, and glass riddled with fractures as if it had once been broken and pieced together again. It caught the light from the windows and shimmered, giving the figure movement of its own.

The eyes abruptly fixed on Vorthe's. Its flat lips twisted into a sickening smile, though one in which Vorthe recognized himself. He swung his club but it never struck. The glass specter disintegrated, breaking into hundreds of flying shards that separated to avoid the path of his club. Vorthe raised an arm before his face and spun away, the flurry of flashes and glints enough to overwhelm his senses, but not before he watched them vanish into the looking glass.

He blinked his sight clear, and saw himself in the mirror. His real self. Nude, he saw clearly every wrinkle upon his body, every steel gray hair that clung to

his flesh. His arms slumped at his sides, and he swore that the club in his hand had never seemed heavier.

As proficient as his many royal advisors were in most respects, Vorthe knew they could not be consulted about this. So he slipped from his castle and his capital and into the Wastron Wood, to the remote hut of Yaja Lalaarin, the Glad Witch. Hers was a cramped dwelling that stank of unnamable substances, where pots always bubbled with thick and viscous potions. The atmosphere made Vorthe uneasy, though in some ways he felt more comfortable with Yaja's brand of esoteric, mysterious magic than the regimented, reasoned magic his court wizards practiced.

"The king of the land," Yaja said as she welcomed him. "A rare guest." She never seemed terrifically impressed by his title, and Vorthe was happy for that. She was unimpressed by rank and responded to deeds over titles, so this made Vorthe doubly proud that she was as loyal as any of his subjects.

The witch Yaja was stout and hunched, and she favored robes of subdued earth tones. Her magic had marked her flesh a patchwork of shades of mottled green, though her hair was an incongruous cascade of lustrous black curls. She had a ready smile and eyes that swam with blue mists.

Many whispered, and perhaps not unjustly, that Yaja approached madness as her years advanced, but Vorthe regarded her as a faithful—albeit unconventional—advisor,. There were matters he could bring to her that he could not take to any others in the kingdom of

Malakar.

"I need advice," he said. "Advice on a matter most esoteric."

"Then you have come to the right place," said Yaja, her cracked lips smiling. "Tell me what is the matter."

Vorthe explained what had happened. He gestured at his wound to prove it, a thin red slash upon his cheek. Throughout his tale, Yaja leaned on her elbows and peered at the king with rapt attention.

"Hmm," she said as he concluded. "A most strange tale."

"Is that all you have to say, Glad Witch?"

She chuckled. "I have known you a long time, Vorthe. I remember the figure you cut when you first came to these lands, the barbarian of the wilds. People rallied around you when they heard you speak plainly and nobly, so much of a contrast to the doublespeak and empty rhetoric that they were used to hearing from the King's Castle.

"But all the more, they respected you, loved you when they saw your visage. A strong chin, chiseled cheeks, open and honest features; these things convinced them to march behind you against the Old King, to enthrone you in his place." Yaja leaned a little closer, jutting a black-nailed finger against the side of her temple. "I recall well your face in those days. I hold it here."

"Yes," said Vorthe with a touch of sadness. "I remember it too."

"When did you first see it?" asked Yaja. "Think back and think well. How did you first come to know yourself?"

Vorthe stroked his gray-stubbled chin and searched his memory. "My people had no mirrors," Vorthe said. "If we even knew that they existed, they were dismissed as a token of civilized vanity."

"Not wrongly," Yaja said, her hands toying with her glossy hair.

"One can see one's reflection in water, or in steel, but never so perfectly as in glass." Something suddenly crossed Vorthe's face, and his voice grew more fateful. "I went wandering, away from my people for the first time, seeking to find my true self in solitude. I traveled through the Steel Mountains in winter. A band of mountain men attacked me, strange hairy creatures that live among the peaks, raiders and bandits, ancient foes to my kind. They sought to kill me, but I won the day. I gave them chase, tracking them to their burrow deep under the mountain.

"True to form, and being the young fool that I was—" Yaja smiled at this "—I set upon the whole tribe with my weapons and fists, smashing their skulls, grinding them to nothing. Their warriors dead, I slaughtered the women and children as well. I found their nursery and crushed their babies under my club."

Yaja's smile vanished.

Vorthe raised his shoulders slightly. "This is the act of a barbarian, and do not forget, I am a barbarian. Many things I am not proud of. With the mountain men dead, their treasury was mine. Most of it was probably raided from caravans. Among the piles of gold I found an astonishing object, the like of which I had never seen before.

"It was a sheet of ice, or so I though, set into a gold frame. When I looked into it, imagine my shock to see a face looking back at me. The face of an enemy, or so I thought. Perhaps of a monster, a demon. Eventually I realized that the face was my own. I shuddered with the horror of it. With my barbarian superstition, I thought that some force of magic had taken my image and placed it within that cold surface.

"But I held it up before my face and kept it there for hours. I made every expression I could. Smiled, frowned, howled in anger, in ecstasy. I thought I had seen them all before, but then I realized that I was seeing my parents and my brothers in myself. My image terrified me, excited me. But what scared me most was how seductive the image was. I grew to hate this, despise it. In the end, my face still held in the glass, I smashed the mirror against the rock.

"I watched very carefully as my face, my very own face, shattered into a million pieces. I screamed, even though I felt no pain; my howl echoed through the caverns." Vorthe smiled faintly and looked up at Yaja. "I can still hear it today."

"And it was that same face that you saw in your hallway," Yaja surmised.

Vorthe nodded. "I had forgotten all about that mirror till this day. It is hard to think that I was ever so naïve."

"Perhaps you were at your wisest then," said Yaja, "before you lived in a den of luxury. Mirrors are normal when you see them every day, but to see your first mirror, that is another story." She stood and plucked a small, gauzy mirror from her mantelpiece, held it up to her face and frowned at her bizarre visage.

"Or to look into a mirror and not see your reflection," Vorthe said. "Is this not the case with the vampires?"

"Those blood drinkers are but a trace of the life they once lived. Put simply, they are and are not, both at once," Yaja said, holding the mirror up so that Vorthe could see his reflection. "We look into mirrors to remind ourselves that we are still alive. To look into one's absence...this is to observe one's own death."

A chill raced up Vorthe's spine. He snatched Yaja's mirror and peered at his reflection. "A very worried king stares back at me," he said.

"What is on the other side of the mirror?" asked Yaja. "What is a reflection made of? Mirrors are cruel things. You are not the young man you once were, Vorthe."

Anger flared in the king's breast, but then sank into sadness. "I know."

"Does not your young bride, the Princess of Arekan, help keep you young?" asked the witch.

"I fear that she makes me feel all the older," said Vorthe. He thought of Tanista's vital warmth and the taste of her kisses. He felt her young tenderness of skin against his old wrinkled flesh. How he loved the feel of his hands on her lithe form, but thought of how his flesh so often failed to respond. He feared that no heir could come of their union, though the production of an heir was the only thing in it for her.

Yaja grabbed her mirror out of Vorthe's hand and turned it back on herself. She looked worriedly into it. "Mirrors are our enemies, I think. It is in mirrors that we see ourselves dying." With that, she pulled her black wig off her head. Vorthe gasped at the revelation of naked greenish flesh, patches of unkempt white hair clinging on.

A tear crept down Yaja's cheek.

"You were not wrong, Vorthe," she said. "Mirrors are magical. I speak not only of the scrying mirrors that figure in the stories we tell children—all mirrors are magical, or at very least, they are windows on a world that is. A demon world, a place of inversion and unknowability, inhabited by creatures that mix the familiar and the strange. And you opened a hole into it."

"Through that mirror I shattered?"

Yaja nodded. "Something came through then. They are known in the writings of man, though few have ever seen them. It is called a *shardling*. More than that—it is *your* shardling. It is a demon that resides inside mirrors, or, if you prefer, on the other side of mirrors. The place where we all end up sooner or later."

"The other side of the mirror," repeated Vorthe. He knew the name of the place. "Death."

"Few know it," Yaja said. "We who do are careful with the secret. To think, a demon domain so close to us. As close as any mirror, as close as still water or the blade of a knife. We waste half our lives gazing into death. If the world knew of it, the world would die screaming in its own madness. You have freed an inhabitant of that realm, Vorthe. It knows you, is tied to you. You gave it your face, and it has kept it for all these years."

"Why is it back now?" asked Vorthe. "All those years, I never saw it, never sensed it. Then suddenly it is here now. Why?"

"Isn't the answer obvious?" asked the witch, carefully replacing her wig.

Vorthe's heart turned cold. A raw aching dread vexed his limbs.

"Perhaps you should count yourself lucky," said Yaja. "Few people get any warning about their death."

Color drained from Vorthe's face. "What good is a warning if there's nothing one can do about it?" he asked. "What can we do?"

A strange sadness surfaced in Yaja's misty eyes. "Only one thing I can think of," she said.

All of the mirrors in the royal castle were brought to the same room, lined up around its edges. After this, all persons were ordered away from the castle until further notice. This included the queen. Vorthe tried to give a reason to Tanista, but he could not bring himself to explain it all. "It is a husband's will," he finally said, and she left in a huff.

The small room was an eternity of glass, and wherever Vorthe and Yaja looked, they found their own faces staring back. Where mirrors faced mirrors, images redoubled into eternity.

Vorthe's club lay on the floor, a moment's reach away from the king. Every time he moved in this strange chamber they had constructed, a flurry of motion fluttered around him. It set off his warrior instincts, and each time he was close to snatching up his club and turning the room into a sea of shards.

He watched Yaja sit in a corner, gazing into her own sea of reflections. She obsessively stroked her false black hair, her expression wavering between delight and despair. She was drunk on her own vanity and loathing her own flesh at the same time, Vorthe decided. He could believe the whispers that said her brain was addled by her pursuits. *Too much exposure to chaotic magicks*, one of his court wizards had said. He knew she was getting worse. She was always eccentric—it suited a witch to be so—but now it was beyond that. Her emotions were getting the better of her.

Now he suspected that it was not contact with her potions and spells that made her the way she was, but contact with strange ideas. The information, for instance, that a world of death lurked in every mirror sat very uneasily with Vorthe. It was the sort of knowledge that would drive men mad. And who knew how many such strange and torturous facts lurked in the mind of this unfortunate woman?

Vorthe ran a finger over the slight scar on his cheek. "Why do you think the shardling slashed me like this?" he asked.

"Why don't you tell me?" asked Yaja, distracted from her image. "You claim to have had a sense of its motivations. Rightly so…it is you, or at least a frozen moment of you."

"At first I thought it meant to kill me but didn't get the chance," Vorthe said. "But now I think otherwise. It marked me."

"Why would it bother?" asked Yaja.

"You say it is me as I was then? Then it does as I would have done. You do not know what sort of a man Vorthe was in those days."

"I know enough," said Yaja. "That he slaughtered infants for no other reason than that they were of a tribe other than this own."

She wore her disgust plainly, and so did Vorthe. "With a glad smile on his face," he added grimly. "It is my own guilt that chases me now. Why should I try to avoid it?" He looked around him, his image staring at him from every surface. "The man that I was would be disgusted by me now. An old man wrapped in this cage of reflection, trying vainly to preserve his life against the inevitable."

"Our young selves would all hate us, true," said Yaja. She gazed into her infinity of reflections. "Who would know better than I?"

The hairs upon Vorthe's body bristled, his senses sounding warning. "It wastes no time," he said, in barely more than a whisper. He gripped his club, though he wondered what good it would do him.

Yaja jumped to alertness, reaching into her burlap sack to produce what she needed. "If you could choose your death," she asked Vorthe, "what death would you favor?"

"I am a barbarian," Vorthe told her. "I would choose death in battle."

"And an afterlife of the same?" asked Yaja.

A faraway smile crossed Vorthe's face. "If the gods would be so kind, yes. Not as the cruel youth I was, but as the man I am today. Battle unto eternity, rage spilling from my senses, would be a glad fate, for certain."

Yaja smiled. Then she let out a gasp of fright as Vorthe disappeared, winking out of her frame of vision with no warning. It took her a few anguished seconds to realize that it wasn't him who vanished, but his reflection. His *reflections*, the countless images glittering all around the room.

The genuine Vorthe felt a chill descend over his body as he witnessed his vanishing. His stomach roiled and his skin felt as a cold as glass.

And death came stalking.

The demon stepped from the mirrors—from all of them—a thousand whirring shards. In a blink's time it coalesced into the flat shape Vorthe remembered, his own face of old. Red hair flamed instead of Vorthe's gray.

Facing down the old man, the shardling's glass lips twisted into a disgusted smile. Vorthe knew that, this time, there would be no warning. He raised his club, and in a warrior's stance prepared to face his last battle.

Yaja pulled a handful of powder from her sack and tossed it into the air. It burst with a flash and swirled about the room, draping it in streams of black and brown. Boundaries blurred. The surfaces of the hundred mirrors bent and warped, yawning open before twisting back to flatness. Flesh and bone did the same. Rigid opposites merged and melted and swam into one.

The effect ended, leaving no trace but a brown dusting over the floor. Yaja was alone.

Vorthe's club hit the floor. It wasn't of any use where he went.

Yaja trained her gaze at one of the mirrors. All she saw was her own green-tinged face staring back, but she knew she looked into another world. She closed her eyes and envisioned the battle taking place there, Vorthe and his shardling locked in combat. Now and forever.

She rested her fingers on the smooth glass. The surface was hard, but she felt the infinity beneath it. The king was so close, yet an eternity away as well.

Yaja wondered how long it would take King Vorthe to realize there was no way of returning. But then, was there actually time in the demon universe across the mirrors? How would Vorthe perceive the passage of time in a place where the rules of existence were inverted? She had no idea. There was no way to understand the place without first going there, and no one who had ever returned.

Nor was there any way to envision it, she realized. A world of negation. Not only no life, but no dimensions, no bodies as they were conventionally conceived. The thought boggled her mind, made it shriek in revulsion.

The shardling's home, the land across the mirror, was *Incomprehensibility*, plain and simple.

The Glad Witch had done the right thing, she knew. She had protected her king, the man she had quietly loved for so long, from death. He would never die.

There was only one thing left to do.

She pulled off her black wig and let it drop to the floor. Then she snapped up the club, so heavy that she could hardly handle it, and smashed each mirror in turn. As the room filled with shattered glass, she let each hold her face first—indeed, all the many versions of it reflected within mirrors reflected upon more mirrors. *What an army of shardlings I must be conjuring!*

The woman she looked upon, as she shattered her image again and again, was Yaja the Glad Witch in all her hideous glory.

The High Judge of Malakar could not sentence Yaja to death for the crime of murder, for there was no murder to speak of. King Vorthe left no body, but simply vanished. No investigation, magical or mundane, yielded any trace of him. Yaja refused to say where he went, but said only that he was not dead, that he was where he wanted to be, where age and time could not touch him. Any more knowledge made public would threaten the very sanity of the people.

In lieu of the death sentence, Yaja was commanded to live out her natural life in her cottage in the Wastron Wood, stripped of all her magical possessions and the means to create more. When the court wizards came to make sure this ruling was enforced properly, they searched the place thoroughly and hauled away many potent objects and substances, but they left one potent item of magic, not recognizing its true significance.

A small gauzy mirror, sitting on her mantelpiece.

Yaja sat for many hours each day staring into it. She never wore her wig any longer. She had no need for vanity, or the affectations of youth, for she never studied her reflection any more. She looked right past it, to a world behind it, thinking about lost King Vorthe and awaiting the day when death would come to her, with her own face and a body of shards.

Murray Leeder
is an academic and writer living in Ottawa. He is the author of Plague of Ice *and* Son of Thunder *as well as more than twenty short stories. Additionally he has been published in the* Canadian Journal of Film Studies, *the* Journal of Popular Film and Television, Popular Music and Society, *and* Early Popular Visual Culture.

THROUGH THE DARK

by Darla J. Bowen

The bell tolled. Eclipsea sat in the center of the room with her legs crossed and her hands, palms up, resting on her knees, holding her sword. The bell tolled again. She opened her eyes, red orbs in the black void of the room. It was not morning. She listened as the bell tolled again, recognizing the tone. This was her bell. The guards were calling her.

With a sigh, she stood. She returned her sword to its sheath at her belt, then quickly plaited her waist-length, white hair. Fastening her black cape at the neck, she made sure to pull the hood forward to conceal her face. If anyone was out, which was unlikely, she knew they did not want to see her. No one wanted to see her. Not unless they needed her to deal with the Shades.

She locked the door of her room, and headed downstairs. At least Gregory tolerated her presence, though with her there, little would bother him. She entered the darkened street just outside The Jolly Rover. Though a few lanterns lined the road, no one was out. Everyone knew the Law: the Living were to remain indoors once the sun set. Everyone in the town of Scaeduburg knew that the Shades came out at night.

Eyes followed her as she made her way down the street. Some watched from cracked windows while others watched from the shadows; all knew whose bell rang.

Eclipsea entered the guard tower without knocking. Two guards confronted her as she closed the door behind her. A fire burned brightly in the hearth. A man seated before it stared into the flames.

"What is it this time?" She threw back the hood of her cape. The guards took a step back. She smiled. "It has been well over a month. I almost thought this place would not need me anymore."

The guard closest to her indicated the man seated by the fire. "An outsider came to town today with his daughter. They were not indoors before sunset."

Eclipsea felt a knot in her stomach. "Weren't they told the Law when they entered?"

"Yes. They were told." He swallowed hard. "I was the one that told him."

"I didn't understand." The man staring into the fire whispered, his voice barely heard above the crackling of the fire. "No one said why. We had been detained. We were making our way to an inn for the night." He clasped his large, calloused hands together. "She saw something in the dark and ran toward it. I should have grabbed her. I should have reached for her faster. She was gone. A heavy darkness was where she had been. She was just gone."

The man slumped forward. He buried his head in his hands, disheveling his mane of honey blond hair.

"How long ago?" When no answer came from the man, she turned to the guards. "How long has the girl been gone?"

"At least an hour."

"Much longer and the trail would be cold." She approached the man, standing at his back. "Where were you when she went missing?"

The man was silent.

Eclipsea rested a hand on his shoulder. "If you do not help me, I cannot help you."

The man turned to her, then jerked away. Fear and anger filled his eyes.

"Do not fear me. I am not going to hurt you." She stood patiently while the man appraised her. She knew that the fire light only enhanced her unnatural appearance. No human had skin as pale as hers, nor eyes that shone red. No human had horns on their forehead. Yet while she was not human, she was not Shade either, for she had substance in the Living realm. "I will help you, if you will trust me. But we must go now."

"What are you?" The man regained some composure, but still kept his distance.

"Does it matter?" Eclipsea turned.

She pulled her hood back up. "I am called Eclipsea. If you want to get your daughter back, follow me."

There was a brief hesitation, then the man was beside her. "I will do whatever is necessary to get Aran back."

"Good." She led him from the guard tower. She could hear the guards talking inside, but ignored it, turning to the man. "What is your name?"

"I am Cesare. We are heading north to my wife's people." He looked away. "She died last spring, and I wanted a better life for Aran. If I had known…"

"You are an outsider and do not know the ways of this place. There is not time to explain it all, but know that here in this town, the Shades do walk among the Living. There has been an uneasy peace of sorts, an understanding that has become Law. As long as the Living stay indoors once night has fallen, the Shades stay to their shadows."

"But why did they take Aran?"

"Because you broke the Law." Eclipsea shook her head. "You and your daughter were out at night, and thus the Shades had the right to deal with you as they saw fit."

"But she's only a child."

"All the more reason for the Shades to choose her. Her life is more vibrant, it warms them more. Her energy is stronger."

Cesare stared at her. "What will they do to my daughter?"

"Consume her energy. Then when she is drained, they will either dispose of her, or have her join them, making her a being of the shadows." Eclipsea clasped the man on the shoulder. "Cesare, show me where Aran disappeared. I will do all I can to return her to you."

Nodding, Cesare looked around the dark street. He gathered his bearings, then began to lead her. Their passing was watched. He led her to an intersection near the market, beside a blacksmith shop and a weaver shop. They stood in the light of the lamp as he pointed to the darkness beside the weaver shop. "She vanished there."

Eclipsea knew the area well. She hated the memories that came flooding back, of angry shouts and accusations, as though a child had a choice in the way she was born. Her father, sworn to slaying demons, had killed himself with his own sword upon learning he had fathered such an abomination. She recalled the fleeting embrace of her mother, just before she fled to the shadows, abandoning her unnatural child to the mob. Gregory, the tavern keeper, had taken pity on her, providing a haven, if not affection. Eclipsea took a cleansing breath, and grasped the hilt of her father's sword. It was the sword that grounded her, focusing her emotions.

"Put this on." She pulled an amulet off her belt, handing it to Cesare. "It will help shield you while we are in the Shadows. You will need it."

"What will you use?" He pulled it over his head, inspecting the design: two crescent moons back-to-back over a full moon.

Snorting, she pulled her cape aside to reveal her sword. "This is all I need. It can kill a demon, if the need arises, and the Shades know that."

"Come." She walked alongside the weaver shop and closed her eyes. She spoke words her mother had once spoken, pulling apart the fabric that divided the realms of the Living and the Shadows. Without looking back, she grabbed Cesare by the hand and pulled him with her through the portal.

The air was heavier here. She opened her eyes to the various shades of grey and black that swirled around them. "I will warn you now. The Shades appear as dark figures in the realm of the Living, but here they take on different appearances. You might be frightened, but whatever you do, do not leave me until we return, or you will be lost here." She released Cesare. He stayed at her side.

Eclipsea felt a slight vibration to the air. It must have been left when Aran was brought through; the amulet she had given Cesare masked his own energy imprint here. The energy trail went north. The Shadows resembled a dark, blurred water-color rendering of the Living realm. Buildings still stood, but they appeared more as shadows than as physical objects. Eclispsea followed the vibration in the air down the street, then turned back toward what would have been the guard tower.

Cesare gasped. Eclipsea glared at him.

She returned her attention to the tower, which in the Shadows stood like a stone tree of obsidian. Seated on its jutting branches were various, hideous beats. Most were massive in size, and vaguely human in appearance. Some had thick hair covering their bodies and horns on their heads, while others were but bones wearing armor. At least thirty Shades were present, and all stared at the light pulsing at the base of the tower. A girl of about eight years lay there.

"That is Aran." Ceseare breathed. "Is she alright?"

Eclipsea crouched down. Cesare followed her example. "They are watching her, perhaps savoring her energy much like a human enjoys the warmth of the sun after a long winter. They have not harmed her, yet." She pulled her sword from its sheathe. "I don't intend to give them the opportunity." She turned to him. Respect, rather than disgust, shone in his eyes. "Stay here. I will try to draw them away. When I do, get your daughter. If I fall, run back to where we came in at." She slid her thumb along the blade piercing the flesh. Blood welled up. She grabbed his hand and smeared her blood into his palm. "Rub this on the wall where we entered and the portal should return. Go through. Run to the guard tower. Do not look back."

"But how are you—"

Before she could hear more, she moved forward on all fours, lithe as a panther on the prowl. There was not much to use as cover, but she managed to move from one shadowy doorway to the next. She gripped her sword. She paused in the door nearest the tower, the last place to hide until she decided what to do. She could try to sneak in and get the girl unseen, cause a diversion, or attack them head on. While the Shades knew her and feared her blade, she had never confronted so many at once.

The demons chanted. It was a low, guttural sound, resembling the roll of distant thunder. She turned her attention to the girl again. Closer now, she could see that Aran was asleep.

Eclipsea was about to make her away around to the side of the tower to see if there was a way to climb up unseen, when Aran stirred. The girl stretched. Her movement roused the Shades who grew silent and leaned forward as though anticipating her fear. The girl opened her eyes to find demons perched.

Heart pounding in her chest, Eclipsea looked back to Cesare, who knelt beside the building, ready to spring forward. The girl looked up at the tower and the creatures in it. She sat up, her mouth opened wide, caught in a silent scream.

The Shades sat back and laughed at the girl's terror.

The Shade sitting on the lowest branch leaped down to stand in front of the girl. It was a vicious looking beast with a horned skull with fiery eyes. Its armor was black, and emblazoned with faces distorted in terror. Eclipsea knew that those images might be all that was left of his actual victims. He raised his face to call to his companions, then drew his large sword, bringing it above his head.

She sensed Cesare stir and knew he was about to risk his life to save his daughter. She had to do something. Years of frustration, fear, and anger coiled like a nest of snakes within her. A cry escaped her that shook the tower and reverberated on the very air. Stepping forward, she revealed herself to the Shades. She held her sword aloft in challenge. The Shades stared at her. The girl looked from the beasts to her, then backed up against the tower, wrapping her arms around her knees, crying and shaking.

"What is this? The half-breed?" The horn-skulled Shade stared at Eclipsea. "You dare come here? We do not fear you, half-breed. There are too many of us."

Eclipsea stood her ground. "Perhaps." She felt her muscles tense, her face warm. Realization hit her: this may be the time she knew would one day come in which she would not return to the Living realm. "But it will be fun to find out for sure." She lunged forward, taking him in the side. As he tried to swing his massive sword, she leapt in the air and lopped off his head. As the headless body collapsed to the ground, the Shades from the tree launched themselves upon her.

There was no time to think. Claws and swords swiped at her. They lunged for her and growled their challenges. She blocked, then swung her blade. It whizzed through the air and bit into flesh. She whirled and ducked, slashed and struck. Each attack and parry moved the horde away from the tower. She could not see Aran, nor if Cesare had yet reached her, but she continued the dance. The longer she could keep them occupied, the more time they would have to escape.

Her attackers became a blur of bone and fur, of steel and hide. She entered a trance, letting her mind control her motions. She could taste their sweat, hear their feet scuff the ground, feel them move around her, and smell their fear. Though they outnumbered her, they still feared her. They could not comprehend her willingness to die. In that moment, Eclipsea knew it to be true. She was willing to die to free the girl and her father. Her existence had purpose.

At least ten bodies lay strewn upon the ground when she finally managed to steal a glance back to the base of the tower. Aran was not there. She did not see Cesare. There was no time to look further as she felt the Shades press in on her. She swung again, then leapt in the air to avoid a blow from a battle axe. She clasped her sword in both hands and swung down in an arch, taking out another Shade.

There was movement beside her. She stepped back and began to block an approaching blow, when a black fletched arrow struck her in the chest. It flung her backward, her sword flying from her hands, but she managed to stay on her feet. She stood motionless, staring at the bolt that protruded from her chest just above her left breast. The Shades stopped their attack, mesmerized that she had finally been injured. Warmth began to flow from the wound.

"Forgive me," Cesare whispered from behind her.

She thought to ask *For what?* when she felt cold steel pierce her back. She gasped as the bloodied end of her sword appeared just below the bolt. Intense pain engulfed her. She could not even cry out. Her legs buckled, and as she fell, something inside her very being tore. A blinding light flashed and everything closed in upon her. It felt as though she was drowning within a pool of fire. She could not breathe. She could not move. There was nothing but the pain. All that existed was this moment.

Then like the renting of cloth, Eclipsea felt herself pulled back.

A massive fire burned at the base of the tower. She saw herself, a white-haired, black-caped demon, lying on the ground. She watched as Cesare pulled her from the horde.

She could hardly breathe, but they urged her to run. She moved her legs, though she did not feel them. Cesare half carried her down the street, with Aran running beside them. They came to where the portal had been.

Cesare smeared Eclipsea's blood on the wall, and the shifting shadowy doorway appeared. Grabbing Eclipsea by the waist and Aran by the hand, he flung them all through the portal. They collapsed together in the Living realm, the doorway vanishing behind them.

The bell of Scaeduburg tolled for the coming morning. Eclipsea did not hear it. She lay on the cold ground and listened to her own heartbeat instead. She rested a hand across her forehead. It was odd that she did not feel her horns. She opened her eyes to the pink sky of the sunrise. A ray of light touched her hand. It did not hurt; there was no burning skin. Pushing herself up on her elbow, she gasped for air and found the black fletched bolt still protruding from her chest. It was her only wound.

Cesare sat beside her, supporting her weight. "I am sorry. I did not know what else to do. I had to try."

"What did you do?" Eclipsea looked into his eyes. He had a kind face with lines in the corners of his dark brown eyes. His brow was pursed in concern.

"You said that the sword killed demons. I heard them call you half-breed, so I figured you were part human and part demon." Cesare shrugged. "I couldn't leave you like that. I decided that either the sword would kill your demon half, or it would kill you. Either way, they would not be able to torment you."

Aran crouched at her father's side, holding to him, tears streaming down her cheeks. "Thank you."

Eclipsea let herself lean against Cesare. She breathed slowly, trying to ignore the pain in her chest. For the first time in her life, a peace settled over her. She felt around on the ground and found her sword. She wiped one side off on her cape, then held it up to see her reflection in the blade. There were no horns on her forehead, just smooth, pale skin. It was a warm pale peach, rather than an ashen grey. Her eyes no longer shined red, but were rather an icy blue. She watched as a tear fell. She felt the dampness trickle down her cheek, but felt like she was watching someone else.

"No. Don't thank me. You gave me a purpose. You allowed me to find myself." She let the sword fall from her hand. She welcomed the warmth of Cesare's embrace and the kiss of the sun on her face. She heard the bell of Scaeduburg toll for the coming morning—and smiled.

Darla J. Bowen lives in Cincinnati, Ohio. When not working, busy with things at home, and writing, she finds enjoyment in hiking in the woods with her fiancé and their son. Faith provides her strength and reassurance. In 1999, she graduated from the School for Creative and Performing Arts, with a focus in Creative Writing. She has a B.A. in History, with a minor in Written Communications, and a Graduate Certificate in Women's Studies. Her stories have appeared in Lorelei Signal, Flash Scribe, MindFlights, Silver Blade, Bards and Sages Quarterly, *and* Emerald Tales.

JOENNA'S AX

by Elaine Isaak

Killing a demon was almost as difficult as being a man Joenna reflected as she jerked free her ax from the corpse. Crouching in its vast shadow, she scanned the battlefield, hoping to spot her captain or the banner of their company. The darting figures of men could be seen between the hulking figures of the demons. *There!* She saw the crimson banner held aloft, its bearer defended by three soldiers. A demon towered over them, smacking the feeble standard down before it struck the bearer in two.

Joenna cried out, then cursed herself as a group of demons broke off from the mass and sprang to the attack, their tattered leather wings darkening her view.

Gritting her teeth against the throb of muscles too long abused, she fended off the first sword. With the backswing, she hacked a leg off the next demon. The huge creatures blocked each other in their eagerness for blood.

Momentum swung her around to face a third, the reek of its breath staggering her as she ducked its poisoned blade. With a sweep of ragged wings, the demon sprang into the sky. It howled and a chorus of replies answered.

Joenna stumbled back from the waves of sound, both hands flying to cover her ears. The ax-haft she still gripped gave her a nasty knock. "Blue Lady smother me for a fool!"

Across the ruined field, warriors dropped to their knees, hands pressed to their ears. Like her captain, Joenna had stuffed hers with wads of wool, but the sound came on, rattling her teeth and aching her bones.

"Shut up, shut up," she chanted through clenched teeth. As she swung wildly, she scanned the corpses and stones, searching for her company and hoping they fared better than the poor sots tossed on the points of demons swords. She had been doing this too long now to feel sick any more, or even to feel much sympathy.

Distantly a horn-blast called her back. The demon's weak wings gave out and it dropped heavily, slamming to the earth in her path. The others shifted away, leaving her to face the shrieker. Its knobbed face split into the parody of a grin, the blood-spattered skin more red than brown.

143

Snarling, Joenna raised her ax and roared. She roared as if she were giving birth and this monster was the bastard who'd got her there.

For a moment, the beast hesitated, its dripping jaws gaping, and Joenna charged, swinging the ax for all that she was worth and more. Short and quick, she ducked the demon blade and carved into its belly.

The creature gave a horrid scream, and Joenna said a prayer of thanksgiving for the wool which cut the sound. Dark viscera spilled out as the demon struggled backward and fell.

"Come on! Joseph, come!" shouted a hurrying figure.

Thank the Lady, the captain! Propping the ax on her shoulder, Joenna leapt the thrashing of the demon's tail to join the retreat. Grabbing wounded comrades and stumbling over the dead, the scattered army fled. They flung themselves over the ridge of stone, a barrage of flaming arrows fending off the demons in pursuit, granting the soldiers time to burrow into tunnels too small for demons to follow.

Men straggled by twos and threes into the cavern where they had their camp. Joenna bent over, hands on knees, catching her breath.

Beside her, the captain stopped to clap her on the shoulder. "Good work, Joseph—if we had a few more like you, we'd rout those bastards, eh?"

Despite her exhaustion, Joenna snorted her laughter. "There aren't no more like me, Gavin. You've got the original." She plucked the wool from her ears and wiggled her jaw to clear out that stuffed-up feeling.

He laughed back, pushing the red shag of hair from his face, leaving it red with blood. "Aye, well, if more men were inspired…" He trailed off, his excitement fading. "Gods, I'm sorry, Joseph. I don't mean…"

She straightened and nodded once. "Aye, Gavin, I know. If only every man who lost a son joined battle with us today."

He lowered his gaze. In a softer voice, he asked, "Have you made your mark yet?"

Grunting, Joenna lifted the ax once more and stroked the smooth wood of its handle. A dozen years ago, she taught her boy to hew logs with this very ax, the weapon now used to avenge him. The head had none of the fancy work some smiths were prone to, but it kept a good edge and was not so large that a boy, or a woman, would have trouble wielding it. Just below that head, twelve notches chinked the wood. She wiped away the new sheen of blood already turning the notches to the dark, aged brown of the rest of the wood. Slipping a knife from her belt, Joenna hesitated. "Two for sure…and a leg wound." Raising an eyebrow at Gavin she offered a smile. "To be honest, the morning's a bit of a blur, isn't it?"

"I saw you take one by the river, early on, then we were hard-pressed for a while. I lost track of you." He sighed. "We're down four men today—that's only six of us from the troop remaining." Again, he scrubbed a hand over his face. More red streaked his ruddy cheeks and trailed down into his beard.

Joenna frowned, then turned back to her ax. "Makes three, then." Carefully, she cut three new notches. *Fifteen. Seven more to go to make the total of his years, my son's life cut short in this damnable war.* "That your own blood, Cap'n?" The urge to care for his wound prodded at her conscience but four months of playing her role kept her still.

Gavin stared into his hand. "Aye, it may be. I keep wiping it off, but I feel only the dirtier for it." He stiffened, his glance sharpening. "Oh, Gods." He turned abruptly, striding away.

Tracking his gaze, Joenna found a small party approaching. Dressed in the dull camouflage of scouts, they walked stooped over, black hair sticking out in tufts from misshapen heads. Heavy swords almost as tall as her were strapped across their backs. Her stomach knotted when she saw them, but she merely nodded acknowledgement, seeing the slant of exhaustion in their long limbs.

The leader stopped and blinked at her, then gave a queer grin, wide open to show his snagged teeth. "Don't you run with your captain when the orcs come calling?" His guttural voice grated on her ears, but she stood her ground.

When the orcs come calling. Joenna shuddered and swallowed hard, her eyes dropping for a moment, then she shook her head. "Your mother was no orc, was she?"

"Doesn't matter to your kind, does it?"

Growling, his two companions trotted off, their long arms dangling dangerous fists.

Joenna gave them a sidelong glance, then faced the half-orc before her. "What's your name, then?"

"Are we playing at questions?" He shook back his hair, longer than her own, and more comely since she had hacked hers off without a thought to appearance. The face revealed, once he closed his mouth, looked nearly human. To be sure, his nose was over-large and flat, and his eyes a curious dull black, like two cauldrons freshly scrubbed.

Now that she stood still, the aches returned with full ferocity and Joenna groaned, dropping the ax to put her hands at her back. She was too old for this. "Get on with you—if you can't have a civil conversation, I've done with it."

The half-orc's fingers twitched and his big nostrils flared as if he smelled magic. His eyes narrowed, then widened over another grin. "Valanor, like the hero of old. My mother read the classics." He hissed the last word, drawing it out. His mother was a lady, then, and if he had been another son, he would have been a knight riding with the king's men rather than a scout derided by the very men he served.

Joenna nodded her understanding. "Mine's Joseph. You know a lad named Loref?"

Pulling himself up almost straight and a good deal taller than she, Valanor replied, "Aye. He rode with the ones who went after the dragon, and died there, I'm told."

"He was a friend of mine."

Valanor regarded her, his black eyes unblinking, then he tossed back his head and laughed, the sound raucous and brutal in its bitterness. "Cor—I didn't think you full-bloods could turn your spite so subtle. A friend of yours? What's that make me, your brother?" His cackling broke off and he spat on the ground at her feet. With a snarl low in his throat, he spun away and caught up with his kin in long, loping strides.

"What'd they have to say to you, eh? Nothing good, I'll warrant," Gavin rumbled, returning with a fresh bandage wrapped around his forehead.

Joenna opened her mouth to answer from her anger and exhaustion, then clamped it shut again when the general stomped up. She dropped a short bow, gasping against the confines of the breastplate which held her too tightly. *Breastplate—now there's an irony!*

"Captain, Joseph." The general nodded to each in turn. "Good work out there."

"Thank you, sir," Gavin replied, then hesitated until the general prompted.

"What is it?"

"Had a thought just now, sir." He looked off where the half-orcs had gone, a little enclave surrounding a grubby pond where they set about their compulsive bathing. "Demons don't care for that sort any more than we do, do they?"

The general gave a noncommittal *whuff* through his graying mustache.

"Well, what if we put them in a vanguard attack, get the demons so bent on ripping them up that we might get an edge on them?"

"You can't do that," Joenna blurted, drawing the officers' keen eyes to her. She floundered, then finally said, "They're our scouts, sir. Without their noses, we'd not know where the demons are."

The general snapped, "But we know where the damn things are—" he thrust his arm toward the roof "—they're at our very doorstep!"

"Just so!" Gavin matched the general's fervor.

"And we need a change of tactics. This may be the very thing. Good thinking, Gavin." He gave the captain an approving smile, tight-lipped and regal, then ruffled his mustache, staring toward the scouts and nodding to himself.

Across the room, Valanor hitched a thumb in their direction, gesturing to his comrades as he told his tale, the new joke some full-blood had tried on him. Joenna, despite her age and uniform, felt her cheeks flush. She gritted her teeth, then said, "Sir?"

"Mmm?" A gray eyebrow arched at her.

She took a deep breath. "These half-breeds—they'll need a leader, someone brighter than they are to bring this thing off."

"Mmm." The general frowned, flicking his glance to Gavin, then around the cavern to the other commanders minding the battered remnants of the army.

Joenna, too, looked to Gavin, noting the sudden pallor of his wounded face. "I was thinking, sir, that you'll not like to waste a good officer on this, and I know I'm no officer at all and not like to be—" she chuckled, hoping to strike a note of humor, and failing, she plunged ahead "—but I'll do it, sir, if that's your will." For her son's sake she stood firm.

"Joseph," Gavin muttered, "it's suicide," as the general focused down his long nose at her, mustaches bristling.

"You raise a point," he mused. "You do raise a point."

"Please, sir," she glanced toward the scouts. "What better way to avenge my son?"

"Yes, yes." He looked her up and down, frowning at the top of her head, but nodding at the heft of her ax. "Good lad, your boy. Keep the rabble together, eh, Joseph, and if you win through, there might be a commission in it for you." He slapped her shoulder and she hid her wince. "Meantime," he drawled, "get some rest, we'll work out the details. Come, Captain."

She bowed again as they drew away, Gavin looking back at her for a moment. The general leaned to him and whispered, "What was his son's name?" as they left.

At last, Joenna flopped on her aching buttocks and loosened the breastplate.

Her breasts underneath seemed to protest their freedom almost as much as they had protested the close-quarters. She drew a long, shaky breath and lay back, pillowing her head on her sack of worthless belongings. They'd tell her the plan some time, and probably tell her troops when they kicked them out of bed for the assault. *Why bother to warn the rabble?*

Her mouth tasted sour, and the backs of her eyes throbbed to the pulse of her heart. Tomorrow, she would lead the half-orcs in a feint against the demons, hoping to kill her seven, even if she never again notched her ax. Tomorrow, she would die.

The thought was still in her mind as Gavin introduced her to the company that she would lead, the general looking down his nose at the lot of them. The half-orcs, awakened early to this news, glared at her from their kettle-black eyes. They squatted on their haunches, long arms dangling, long fingers working into fists and back again as if they sought a throat to close over.

"And if we don't?" said Valanor. "If we refuse to follow *that*—" a sharp gesture at Joenna "—to this slaughter?"

"You shall be ignoring a direct order and I shall have you slaughtered by your own army. They may be only too happy to comply. Have I made myself clear?" the general said, the three feathers of his golden helmet bobbing over his shoulders. "I am giving you the unprecedented opportunity to die with an honor you do not deserve, and to see that our forces win out." He pivoted on his heel to give Joenna the benefit of his regard. "This charge shall be known as Joseph's Charge. Best of luck. We'll be an hour behind you." He gave a stiff nod and left.

"You're a brave man, and a good soldier," Gavin murmured close to her ear. "Lady be with you."

Straightening, Joenna found thirty glaring half-orcs shifting before her. A few glanced toward the archers whose job it was to be sure they followed orders, then back to her, baring their sharp teeth.

"What's it to be, frontal assault? Shall we bother with swords, or will that only make it harder for the demons to rip us to shreds?" Valanor loomed over her.

Joenna hefted her ax and propped it on her shoulder. "Blue Lady, there's got to be a way through this," she muttered.

"Yeah," cried a harsh voice, "kill the general!"

The dark mass stilled as the archers drew their bows, searching for the joker. "Who said it?" called a sergeant. "Point him out, or we'll open on the lot of you."

"Not if we get you first," snarled one of the crowd, and the half-orcs drew together as the archers advanced. Beyond them the mass of the army, sharpening swords and checking the buckles on their armor, paused to watch. Even so few half-orcs, with their agility and strength, could make good that threat, tearing into the army until all thirty were dead.

Bowstrings drew taut, arrows nocked, and the soldiers behind stood at the ready as the half-orcs fingered their swords, weighing the odds.

At their head, Valanor kept himself still, addressing his comrades. "Think, would you—better to die on the field than in this cave."

The dark group swayed as if they weren't so sure.

A crew pushed through the army, carrying the barrel of rotten meat they used to keep the scouts in line. Its stink preceded them, and the half-orcs recoiled, giving ground before the archers.

"Enough!" Joenna shouted. "Enough. We've a job to do." She sharpened her glance toward the archer-sergeant who offered a curt nod and swung his men away, providing an opening for the company to move out of the cavern. The fetid barrel encouraged the half-breeds through the tunnels, and they gulped at the breeze carrying the less foul stench of war across the caves. They scrambled up the steep slope toward their death.

The reek of fire and blood, and the unmistakable sickly stench of demons not far off greeted them. At her back, the half-orcs retched and gasped for breath. Thirty young men, the age of her own boy, marred by the hideous orc features. Their knuckles whitened on their sword-hilts just like any other men. "There's got to be a way."

Close by, Valanor snorted. "Don't fool yourself, full-blood. We face the one army or the other and you get the glory when we're dead—twice as much for volunteering to serve with us. As appealing as it sounds, killing the general would only confuse the issue."

"Aye, killing the general. Pity we can't kill theirs."

"You know how they fight, better than we do, I'll warrant. They're like insects, one leader dies and another takes its place with a damnable shriek. They don't wear feathered hats to tell us who's in charge." He tossed his shaggy head, growling low in his throat.

As they started the long trudge up the slope, the archers taking their places, Joenna turned over in her mind the events of the previous day. She had cut down one demon, and another came, leaping up with that shriek. "But they can't all fly," she mumbled to herself.

"They've all got bloody wings, but can't none of them fly more than a few feet straight up."

"Those're the ones that shriek, though," she said, hesitating, looking to the field. Dawn's light began to creep over the shapes of the dead. Somewhere across the field, the enemy hunched down, waiting. "The shriekers are the leaders, I think, not just one of them, but any one of them. We kill one, another takes his place and they fight on like nothing's happened."

"You're talking nonsense," Valanor snapped. "And it doesn't matter anyhow to a company of the dead."

But the idea took form, and Joenna waved away his despair. "Do they smell different?"

"What?"

"The ones that can fly, do they smell different?"

"They all reek like a week-old murder."

"Come on," she tipped her head toward the battlefield, then faced her surly crew. "You lot stay a minute, and keep low. Come on," she urged Valanor again.

With a shrug that rolled from one shoulder to the other, he followed, crouching among the rubble as they shifted their way through the corpses and scorched trees. In moments, they came to the site of yesterday's stand, where Joenna slew the shrieking demon. "This one," she pointed. "Does it smell different than the others?"

Losing his grin, Valanor glanced at the wreck of the demon, and his face in the vague light looked pale. She, too, looked down where the flood of fluids and intestines clogged the path. To her, the thing smelled much the same as a live one, it hadn't had enough time to rot in the short hours they had been sleeping. Catching Valanor's eye, she grimaced. "Sorry. Hard to imagine what it's like for you, with that sensitive nose and all."

His eyes narrowed and he bent over the demon's head, then over that of her first victim. Immediately, he rose again, his throat working as if he fought down bile.

She set a hand on his arm. "Gods, I am sorry, mate."

Snarling, he shook her away, then leaned in close, taking a sniff of her and baring his teeth. "You're a lying, stinking bastard like the rest of them—woman."

Joenna jerked back from him, catching her breath.

Valanor advanced and she dare not move again, dare not reveal them before they were ready. "Aye, this sack of stink smells different. Rotten, with a hint of evil a little sharper than the rest. He does, but so do you." He shot out a long finger, the claw scratching her breastplate. "You smell like baby-making and kitchen-cooking and stitching on a pillow. Paugh! Somewhat funny about you I thought yesterday." He tapped his blunt nose with a hooked nail. "Just the sweat, or the blood, or what, but now I see it, you bloody liar. What if I go back in and tell your man? Your Gavin, is he the reason you're here? No, I'll take it to the general—if he'd hear me." A cackle passed his curled lips. "Maybe that'd give us time to get out of here without all of us losing our necks." He rose away from her, still hunched, and started to turn.

Lunging forward, Joenna caught his arm and yanked him down. Both landed hard on the slimy stones. Valanor knocked her away, sweeping the sword from his back, his teeth bared as he crouched over her. Joenna flipped up her ax, catching his blade and turning it, a new and unintended chink appearing through the stain.

Hooking her feet on a stone she yanked herself downward and out from under, ramming aside his sword with the flat of her ax. Despite his strength, the half-orc was a scout, not a soldier, and Joenna smiled.

With a heave, he flung her off again, propelling himself back toward the line.

Joenna dove, the ax ahead of her, catching his ankle and toppling him even as their archers took aim.

She pushed herself up beside him, proving her conquest to the rearguard as she faced him. "Watch yourself, you bloody bastard!"

His cauldron eyes glinted fire as his lips twisted. "Will I be the next notch on your ax, oh mighty woman? You do your captain proud."

She lowered her weapon, arms shaking with the rush of fighting. Mastering herself, she whispered, "It's not Gavin I'm fighting for—it's my son. Don't you see?" She wiped back her hair, matching his fierce expression.

His face, inches from hers, looked more wrong than ever, the heavy single brow furrowing down in his disgust. "Oh, aye, nobility, honor, sacrifice. I know all about that from those accursed stories my mammy tossed aside. I think she died from the shame of it, or maybe from the sight of me, as if it were my fault the orcs took her, my fault what they did to her." His fist rapped against his narrow chest as his voice moved into a hushed wail of unanswered pain.

Joenna snatched his fist, the hairy strength of it captured by her two small

- Elaine Isaak -

hands. "What they did to me," she said. "To me."

After a moment, Valanor let out a breath through flaring nostrils. He swallowed, his shaking fist twisting in her grasp, but not yet applying his strength to freedom.

"The orcs came to my house, too. I never seen a brute so awful, not until this war. That raiding party, they broke and beat and took what they would." She gave a short, nasty laugh. "Look at me, Valanor. I make a better man than a woman—I'm so ugly, no man would take me to wife. But I was good enough for orc-bedding, wasn't I? My parents cast me out. And there I was with child—this gangly, screaming little baby."

Dropping his hand, she scrubbed tears from her face. "And I thought two things as ugly as us, we might as well love each other." Her chin rapped against her breastplate as she wept, her ragged hair flopping around her face. Cursing herself, she fought the tears, drawing long breaths, snorting like an ass.

Nearby, Valanor breathed in little gasps. After a long time, he said, "Loref. He was your son."

"Aye."

"He's the reason you fight, the reason you've got those notches in your ax."

More calmly, the tears trickling away at last. "Aye."

"He was like me." His voice became a hot breath across her damp face.

Joenna faced him fully. "Aye," she said. "Like you."

They sat beneath the growing light surrounded by demon filth, and Valanor stared at her from his dull-black eyes, so like her son's. "You've got a plan, haven't you? You've thought of something."

"I don't think it'll save us, but it may cause confusion enough that the others can win. Valanor—" she took a deep breath and expelled it, along with the grief she could not afford "—it may be enough to show those bastards you're not to be spat on."

A grin started at the corner of his thin lips. "I doubt it."

She sighed. "Me, too, but at least we'll know we did our best. We'll have to convince the company."

"That we will." He cocked his head at her. "What's your name, Loref's mother?"

"Joenna."

"So, Joenna's Charge."

"Naw." She touched the head of her ax. "Better to call it, Half-orc's Revenge."

The troop had few complaints— any plan was better than what they'd been ordered—and they fanned out around Joenna and Valanor. Quickly, closely, they began their advance. They rippled over the stones and bodies like a shadow not yet dispelled by the feeble light of day. It felt like miles, jogging over the rough ground when the demons rose up, shrieking before them.

The vile wind of their voices slapped back the attackers, but the troop shifted and swirled around her. Instead of attacking, Valanor and Joenna threw themselves under the first swords. They dodged and sprinted and Valanor sniffed. Wherever he pointed, there they struck.

The company plunged in with them, knocking aside the demons as best they could, crying out to block the sound of demon shrieking. One demon leapt up, flapping, over and over, its voice howling out the commands. Three of hers went down in the first strike and Joenna set her jaw against the dread.

Rather than driving straight on,

150

Joenna's force moved as if at random, following the whims of Valanor's nose. The shrieking filled her ears and echoed inside her aching skull. Grimly she followed where the half-orc led.

Joenna's ax defended him, cleaving the arm from this demon, slicing the leg off another, until he could finger a shrieker—and the company set-to and brought it down.

The half-orcs swirled around them, slaying the marked ones, themselves falling beneath the poison blades, this one hacked in two, that one crushed by taloned arms. The gray of the scouts vanished beneath a wash of red. The distant sound of horns announced the army's coming—if any of hers would be alive to see.

A great demon sprang up before them, outspread wings heaving to get it off the ground as it shrieked. Its lashing tail caught Joenna broadside and she tumbled over the ground, sprawling with her ax underneath. "Blue Lady," she cried, as the demon thudded down again.

The demon leapt away, a wail of pain escaping it. Demon blood spattered Joenna's face as she rolled and snatched up her ax.

Bellowing, it stretched toward Valanor, slapping aside his sword at the cost of its own fingers. It lunged again, the half-orc scrambling across the ground.

Matching its bellow, Joenna buried her ax in the demon's side. She slammed to earth as it spun around, and its sword bit into her shoulder.

The demon's head filled her vision, its fangs dripping as it gaped over its prize. The head reared back for another shriek and dove toward her.

With her off-hand, Joenna whipped free her knife and rammed it home into a smoldering eye.

Blood spurted, obscuring her vision, then the breath *whoofed* from her lungs as the demon collapsed on top of her.

For a long time, the world went silent. Joenna thanked the Lady for this reprieve, promising to visit Her temples the first chance she got. She struggled against the pressing corpse to drag air into her lungs .

Thunk! Thunk! The sound penetrated her fog, and Joenna cracked open her eyes. *Thunk!* The steady sound of an ax into wood. "Loref?" she croaked.

The weight bearing down on her fell aside and he stood over her, ax in hand, shoving the severed demon from her chest.

Letting the ax-head rest beside hers, Valanor bent down. Agile, hairy fingers stroked the blood from her eyes. "Praise the Gods, you're alive!"

"You, too," she managed, sucking in great breaths. "Like to smother me, that beast." She moved to rise, but Valanor plucked the wool from her ears.

"Listen!" He shouted.

"Can't hear a damn thing." Joenna slapped her ear with her right hand. The left hand only twitched numbly.

"No shrieking! They're retreating from us, a bunch of half-breeds, before the damned army even got here!" His laughter sparkled with hope, echoing the horns which drew the army past. Valanor leaned in closer. "You're wounded. Joenna, I'll get you to the surgeons." He bent to gather her up.

Slapping his hand she rattled, "Don't. They'll know."

"Aye. They'll send you home to get over all this, you fool woman."

She shook her head. "How many?" she asked.

"How many what?"

"Demons I killed."

Tilting back his head, Valanor considered. "Five."

"Then I'm not through yet." She shoved herself into a sitting position, his arm hovering near her. "Don't haul me from here like a fragile woman. If you want to be useful, raise me up like a man."

"But you're wounded! Surely this battle is honor enough."

Joenna shook her head again. "I've two more notches to carve, my friend." Then she grinned at him. "Valanor, hand me my ax."

Elaine Isaak
dropped out of art school to found Curious Characters, designing original stuffed animals and small-scale sculptures, and to follow her bliss: writing. She is the author of The Singer's Crown *(Eos, 2005), and sequels* The Eunuch's Heir *(Eos, 2006), and* The Bastard Queen *(Swimming Kangaroo, 2010). A mother of two, Elaine also enjoys rock climbing, weaving and exotic cooking—when she can scrape the time together. Visit www.ElaineIsaak.com to read sample chapters and find out why you do not want to be her hero. Further adventures in Joenna's realm are also available at AnthologyBuilder.com.*

THE LESSER: A SWORDS OF THE DAEMOR TALE

by Patrick Thomas

"Why do these things keep happening to me?" I said, waving my sword back and forth in frustration.

I stopped once I noticed the blood flinging about the dungeon. I didn't want any of it spattering into the spell circle. I wasn't sure if that would free the demon, but that was one chance I wasn't about to take.

"Just lucky, I suppose," said the grinning crimson demon. "Your own fault really."

"How the hells do you figure that?"

The demon's smile widened at my choice of words. "You didn't have to kill Kaldon. You could have wounded him. Or at least attacked from the front. Very unsporting of you."

The last thing I wanted was to get in a debate with a thing from the Pit, but until I figured out what to do with what was very obviously a him, I didn't have any better ideas. "I suppose he was summoning you to get a report on the weather."

"Bright and bloody, with a hundred percent chance of slaughter," said the demon. "Of course, I can tell you if your fellow Daemor will take the castle or die in the attempt. Not all of them were able to fly above it to sneak in like yourself."

"We'll win," I said, dragging the mage's corpse to the far end of the chamber before I wiped the blood from my sword on his robe.

"Ah, confidence. Very inspiring and believable coming from such a lovely lass," he said in what I imagined was his bedroom voice. If I closed my eyes, I might be able to consider it sexy, but with my eyes open I had trouble getting past the scales and horns. Not that scales and horns are bad in and of themselves, just when attached to a demon.

It was my turn to laugh. My half ogre parentage made sure I didn't receive many sincere compliments on my beauty.

"You find your beauty amusing?" he asked, leaning forward in the same manner a certain kind of man does in a pub when trying to convince a woman he is something he's not.

"No, but it is hard to believe in your sincerity after that phony piece of flattery," I said, looking around the room and seeing nothing of use. I guess it was too much to hope for a manual on how to send this thing back to Hell.

"Insecurities, at such a delicate age."

"Hey, I'm fifteen," I snapped and instantly regretted it. I'm one of the youngest Daemor and it's a touchy subject. For an ogre, this would be my first year as an adult. For my pixie half, it would be my fifth.

"You are a very mature lady for such few years. And beautiful, although it is sad that you cannot see what is so obvious to me," he said, pushing his lips together and moving his head side to side in a slow and calculated motion.

"Perhaps you need glasses," I said.

The demon's eyebrows rose at that. "You've spent time on Earth."

"No, but some of the other Daemor have," I said as I flipped through papers piled on a stone table.

"They left beautiful Faerie? Not something I'd do."

"Faerie is in the midst of a bloody war in case you haven't noticed," I said.

"I am quite aware, which is exactly my point, although I suppose beauty is in the eye of the beholder. From my perspective, you are beautiful, especially those wings. They look sharp enough to decapitate."

They were, but it was none of his business so I kept looking for a way to get rid of him.

"You won't find anything. Kaldon was meticulous, memorized everything."

"You'll understand if I don't take your word for it," I said, turning the table on its side in hope of finding some hidden instruction.

"Suit yourself. I'm not going any-where."

"We'll see about that," I said, but it seemed hopeless. Magic helped people in Faerie speak and understand each other, but it didn't work the same for the printed word. I couldn't make horns or wings of the papers I was riffling through. I was good at fighting and breaking things. I certainly wasn't a mage. All I knew about demon summoning was to avoid it. Sadly, that wasn't an option.

"What is your name?" the demon asked.

It's Terrorbelle, but I wasn't dumb enough to tell him that. I shot him a look instead. "What's yours?"

"Very nice, but you can't blame a guy for trying. This doesn't have to be a losing situation for you," said the demon.

"Really?" I said, not bothering to disguise the sarcasm in my voice.

"Kaldon has already completed the binding. I'm at your mercy. I am bound to perform whatever task is set before me."

"Sorry, I'm not ready to part with my soul," I said.

More laughter. I guess I should consider giving up the front lines to entertain the troops. If Hornhead here was any judge, I was hilarious. "That is one price. Life and blood is another."

"I'm not willing to offer up innocents to you either," I said.

"Who said anything about them having to be innocents? Send me to do your bidding, kill your enemies for you. Their lives, their blood could suffice as payment. As long as you offer at least one up to me of your own accord," he said. "Isn't there anyone you'd like to see dead?"

I stopped my searching. There was. More than just one. It must have shown on my face.

The demon wrinkled his brow. "Let us see who a gentlewoman like yourself would want slain. Your fellow warriors, who steal your glory?" The demon rested his pointed chin on the back of his scaled hand. "No, glory does not attract you. But you do have issues with physical attractiveness. I could make you beautiful."

It was my turn to laugh. "I thought I was already beautiful."

Hornhead smiled and nodded approvingly. "Very good. You are to others, but not to yourself, so in your mind you are not attractive. I could change that."

"By messing with my mind?" I said, tossing through shelves full of books.

"No, just your body," said the demon.

"You're not going near my body. I've never been that desperate," I said.

"You wound me and I've been nothing but nice to you, Daemor," pouted Hornhead.

"I'm not exactly in the mood to apologize," I replied as I reached up and pulled down the bookcase. There was nothing behind it but wall.

"Nor should you be. I wouldn't have to touch you to make you the most attractive woman on the face of Faerie," he said.

"I could save up and buy a glamour. What do I need you for?" I said, though I've had my fill of glamours.

"A glamour merely changes what others perceive and they are hardly foolproof," said Hornhead. I couldn't argue with him on that point. "What I offer is to change you and perhaps then you could begin to change yourself."

"I have enough trouble dealing with Mab's mind healers. I don't need more problems from you," I said, patting down the stones in the walls in hopes of finding some secret chamber.

"We will forget about beauty then. What of power? I could make you the rebel queen instead of Mab. You could lead the troops, make the crucial calls, save the day," said the demon, rubbing his hands together.

"No thanks. Too much work," I said. Besides it was way too much responsibility.

"How about physical power? I could make you indestructible and stronger than any foe," promised Hornhead.

I was already pretty strong, although it would be nice to not have to worry about getting killed. "Nah, life would be pretty boring then."

"Then a mystic weapon. A magic sword or shield perhaps?"

"Probably wouldn't match my outfit," I said.

Hornhead chuckled. "I see I am getting closer."

"You get close to me, buster, and I'll beat you down," I said, getting on hands and knees to search the floor.

"There is no need to bow to worship me, not that I'm not flattered," said Hornhead.

"Dream on," I said.

"I'll have you know that there are succubi who beg for me," said Hornhead, pushing his pelvis forward so his demonhood was made more prominent.

"To what? Leave them alone?" I said. I sat near the pile of books and started flipping through pages.

"Mortal and gentry women have been known to scream my name."

"What, during nightmares?" I asked, tossing another book aside. My comments seemed to annoy Hornhead.

"Don't strain your eyes. Light another candle," said the demon. The only light in the room was coming from a lone black candle on the front tip of the spell circle that was keeping him trapped.

"I'm good," I said. "I can see well in the dark."

Hornhead seemed disappointed by my answer. "I have something else you might be interested in. Love."

"You're not my type," I said, picking up another book.

A masculine giggle came from the demon's mouth. "Not me. The most handsome man in the world could be made to fall in love with you. And you with him, if you like."

Hornhead was playing dirty. Like any girl I dreamed of finding my true love, but how I looked made that more challenging. "So you would enthrall some gorgeous guy to fall in love with me?"

"In essence. You could do no wrong. He would protect you with his very life and fill your nights with passion," said Hornhead.

But it would never be real, only a spell. "No thanks."

"Wealth and treasure?"

"Wouldn't have enough time to spend it," I countered.

"You are a challenge, aren't you? I need to look deeper to find your price. Everyone has theirs, you know," said the demon, staring at me in silence. It was far more uncomfortable than his trying to tempt me. "I've got it. I will deliver to you those men who slaughtered your mother and did horrible, unspeakable things to you when you were but a child."

"Get out of my head," I demanded, barely stopping myself from flinging a book at him. Crossing a spell circle was a bad thing, especially with a demon on the other side.

"Not that it isn't a wonderful place to visit, I'm sure, but I have other methods of getting information. You have yet to find all of your attackers and avenge yourself. I could gather them for you, even if another has stolen your chance at

vengeance by killing them first. We could place their heads on spikes surrounding your mother's resting place in tribute to her."

"No thanks. Ma always liked flowers and jewelry," I said. Not that she was above wearing skulls for a belt, but they were from animals, not people. Still, there was no denying the temptation, but how to do it while avoiding the damnation was beyond me.

"Then what of Thandau?" That stopped me short and I rose to face the demon. "That got your attention, didn't it? The despot you and your fellow women warriors are toiling so hard to defeat. The creature your attackers were in service to. I could destroy him for you. You only need ask and grant me some small favor."

"Which is?"

"Break the spell circle. Obliterate some small portion of it and grant me freedom."

"And trade one tyrant for another? I think not," I said.

"I would of course grant you my personal protection in perpetuity."

"Just how would I be able to enforce that if you changed your mind?" I said.

"Standard contract. Spell out what it is you want and sign in blood," said Hornhead.

"I am not letting a demon lose," I said.

"Ah, but you are not rejecting the deal outright are you?" he said.

The chance to destroy the enslaver and slaughterer of Faerie? Entire cities have been slain by his forces. I've seen corpses piled to the sky. What would it be worth to stop that? My voice was barely a whisper when I answered, "No."

"Excellent. I can work with that," said Hornhead, but I noticed him staring out of the corner of his crimson eyes at the black candle. It was burnt down to a nub. "I can understand your position. You're not a bad person and you don't want to be responsible for the killings of innocents. And that is exactly what I would end up doing too. So we put a clause in that I cannot kill without your express permission."

"What about maiming?" I asked.

The demon shook his head. "Not going to let me have any fun, are you? We can put that in there too. Shouldn't you be writing this down?" The demon was again trying to not look at the black candle. "There is blank parchment and quills on the table."

I walked over and picked it up. "Just because I'm writing this down, doesn't mean we have a deal yet."

"Of course not. It becomes binding once your blood is on the parchment," said Hornhead.

"And what would be expected of me?" I asked.

"Allow me one kill a year. The victim would be of your choosing. You may pick the most evil and heinous people and I will eliminate them for you, starting with the tyrant."

"What if I refuse to give you a target one year?" I said.

"It would be most unfortunate. I would have to take your life. And soul. But that need never happen," said the demon.

"Why not?" I asked.

"Because there are so many wicked in the world, you will never run out of people deserving of death," said the demon.

"And what do you get out of it?" I said.

"Oh that. Not much. I get to stay in Faerie and not return to Hell. That's enough motivation, trust me," said Horn-

head.

"I don't, Hornhead," I said.

"I don't see why you had to go to name calling. You don't see me referring to you as Razorwings, do you? But you don't have to trust me; you just have to spell everything out in that contract. You can also have me kill in between if you like. I don't mind and I get bored easily."

"That's good to know. What happens if I die?" I asked.

"Won't happen. I won't let it, because when you go, I go. So do we have a deal?"

I held the paper out in front of me, reading what I wrote. "I don't know. I have to think about this." It wasn't like I hadn't killed before, but it was always someone trying to kill me. Even this mage Kaldon. Sure I snuck up on him, but had he loosed this demon, Hornhead would have slaughtered myself and the rest of the Daemor as we attacked this castle.

The black candle started to flicker and Hornhead started to panic. "Please sign. I'll even put in a clause allowing you a onetime renegotiation before the second victim."

"That's awful generous of you. Too generous," I said, my suspicions growing.

Hornhead started to scream and his entire body swelled up to an enormous size. Flames filled the spell circle and focused into a tiny beam that shot out onto the tip of my left index finger.

"Ow," I said. The tip of my finger was dripping blood. "What are you doing? I thought a demon couldn't harm anyone outside of a spell circle?"

Hornhead had collapsed to the floor and was gasping for breath. He was now half the size he had started at. "Normally, we can't. There is a tiny defect in Kaldon's circle. Not enough for me to gain freedom, but enough for me to affect the world outside if I am willing to spend the power."

"Why do it?" I asked.

"Hell is not a place most want to be, not even demons. I don't want to go back. Please, press your finger on the paper and seal the pact with your blood." The black candle flickered again. The wick was almost burned through.

"I'm still not sure," I said.

"We haven't time to waste," said Hornhead. "You know very well that Mab would want you to do this. In fact, she would order you to."

I put the paper done at my side. "Be that as it may, I'm not going to be pressured into this."

Hornhead wouldn't even look at me. He had eyes only for the dying flame on the shrinking wick. "Okay, take your time, but you will have to call me back."

"I have no idea how to do that," I said.

"It's simple. Kaldon already did the hard work. Simply soak a wick in a drop of your blood and reuse this very wax to make another candle. Light it and say my name three times to summon me. Use the same spell circle if it would make you feel safer."

"I don't know your name," I said.

Hornhead must really have been desperate, because he told me what it was. "I am Ghordon. Don't forget. Please, don't forget…"

Then the candle went out and Ghordon screamed. I drew my sword, ready to defend myself, but there was no need. The demon was actually gone and I was left standing next to a pile of wicks on Kaldon's work bench with a bleeding finger.

As I listened to the screams of the dying and wounded outside, I was left to decide which was the lesser of two evils—and what I was going to do about it.

Patrick Thomas is the author of 150+ short stories & 20 books including 8 in the popular fantasy humor series Murphy's Lore; 3 in the Mystic Investigators series–including Bullets & Brimstone with John French and Once More Upon a Time with Diane Raetz; Fairy with a Gun; Dead to Rites. He writes the syndicated satirical advice column "Dear Cthulhu" and two collections of columns–Have a Dark Day and Good Advice for Bad People–are out for those searching for the meaning of life or a good laugh. He co-edited Hear Them Roar and New Blood. His Hell's Detective is crossing over to comics in Ghostman. Drop by his website www.patthomas.net.

WHEN THE DARKNESS GROWS

by Frederick Tor

The tides had receded from the gritty shoreline of Skovolis like water separating from dirty lamp oil. The sand was a gray-black and coarse underfoot. Rocks and boulders piled here and there, belligerent to the churning surf. On this particular portion of dusky shore, below the walls that jutted five spear-lengths tall and angled outward—a defense against seaward raiders and the lash of the always angry Maltose Sea—two men stood over a large lump of fishnetting heavy with seaweed and other churned waste.

"A shame," said the gray-armored Talon Sergeant named Norvis Kavellum. Both superiors and inferiors called him Sergia Brand-Eye: Sergia due to his position in the Skovolis city guard, and as a ten-year standing member as the only Talon Sergeant to last that long; Brand-Eye due to his left eye which had been ruined by a fanatic Phantos acolyte many years ago. His mesh-gloved left hand rested upon the ebon hilt of his sword. His right hand, stub of an index finger lost to the knuckle, rubbed at his bristled chin. He stared at the sea-bound mass with his good eye.

His partner, dressed in a thin fleece and leather vest, brown breeks and black Talon-issued boots, drew a dagger sheathed at his waist and squatted before the ocean refuse-encrusted pile. He began sawing at the thick hemp netting, trying not to inhale too much of the foul air which rose from the thing.

"Ashamed of what? That the sea won't hold her dead, or that the Fangs won't touch an issue that is actually theirs?" The honed blade cut through the coarse threading as if through soft flesh.

The Sergia exhaled sharply, turned his head in a vain attempt for fresh air, crossed his arms across his broad chest as he watched the knife work, and replied, "You know the Fangs are bred and trained a superstitious lot, Kaimer. If the sea gods don't want the bloated carcass, then them salty bastards ain't going to lay an eye, even less a finger on it. You'd be prodding at your very godhead by fishing—no pun intended—around more on the subject."

"Not a religious man," Kaimer said matter-of-factly as the blade abruptly cut through the remaining strands.

159

The netting had been entwined with many layers of seaweed and refuge it had snared in its float about the dirty shores of the Maltose and the cityscape which pressed at her banks. Under knife, the thing split open like a slashed gut-bag and its internal components unfurled and oozed like the rot squeezed from a large over-ripened fruit.

Brand-Eye took a step back and gripped the hilt of his sword as the foul odor and even fouler contents caught his senses. So strong was it that he looked ready to draw his weapon and fight the empty air.

Kaimer coughed, the initial stench burning his nostrils and throat. He bent his head forward and pulled the flap of his leather vest up as a thick filter while he studied the now-exposed contents of the torn netting.

"Someone you know, Sergia?" Kaimer asked. The broad-chested Talon stepped close again and took a look.

Like a hog amidst a great garnished dinner platter, a dead body lay in the netted quagmire of sea scum and litter. It was void of clothing; male by genitalia; skin bloated and gray from too long a-soak in the Maltose. The broken shafts of black-bodied arrows stuck deep into the soft flesh. The right leg lasted until it met the knee; the muscles of the left leg were bared and pulled from the bone between knee and ankle. A great many burn marks blotted the upper body, some deep in the skin so as to make small black, puckered craters.

The head had been bald, the left side a mottle of bumps and deep gashes, obviously beaten by some form of blunt object until the flesh tore. An eye was gone. The mouth lay open in an eternal black-tongued scream. The arms of the victim were still tied behind his back, and on the lumpy flesh of the right shoulder was a still perceivable tattoo of a burning brazier encircled by a thick red line and four six-pointed stars.

"I know the markings, not the man," the sergeant commented, recognizing the symbol to be the sign of a High Priest of Phantos. The undercity of Skovolis, where the Phantos—Guul cultists—thrived, was more vast than the city above. Norvis 'Brand-Eye' Kavellum had many dealings with the Phantos Mercenti, and knew of many of its brethren and upper leaders. The tortured dead man at his feet, even if the face hadn't been so disfigured, however, did not strike a discernible name in his head.

Kaimer knew the sigil too. He wiped his wet blade on a brown patch of beach grass and grit, dusted the bits of sand off, and sheathed the dagger as he stood. "A leader-follower discharged from the sect?"

"They tend not to go to these extremes even when a member is excommunicated or blasphemes their godhead, though they are a tad sensitive when an outsider casts such words..." The Sergia scratched at his ruined eye with the stub of his index finger. "We'll probably not understand the endeavors that led this soul to its seaside resting place. My only concern is the fact this is the fifteenth victim found torn to ribbons like this."

Kaimer looked at the Sergia with a raised brow.

"Yes, yes. I am afraid this isn't just another casualty caught within the foul grasp of our dark metropolis," Brand-Eye said licking dry lips. "Don't ask. We have no leads, and our dear Third Ward commander Clacius—where all the killings have taken place—has no interest in pouring manpower into the issue. It's been all members from the Phantos guild, and he figures they can deal with their own problems. Wouldn't be the first time I suppose."

"All I have is a collection of items from the deceased," the Sergia continued. "Trinkets and baubles, some Guul religious items—ghastly pendants and such. My wee ones enjoy playing with the oddities their old man brings home. In the meantime, we haven't gotten a scrap of anything that really tells us who the killer or killers are."

A breeze stirred from the Maltose and tousled Kaimer's long reddish hair. He was done here, meeting his Sergia friend outside the city walls for payment on a previous job accomplished for the Talon. The small but heavy bag of silver coin hanging at his belt reminded him he had a meeting later that day with Avener Krumtin who tended a fine forge and had recently crafted an impressive—and costly—blackened steel blade. The discovery of the washed-ashore body had been a surprise and distraction to both he and the Talon Sergeant. The information of the multiple murders, however, was news to Kaimer. It did concern him, though he rarely stuck his nose too deep into the various guild or Talon stink piles. It concerned him that he hadn't known.

The Sergia, recognizing the end of their meeting, adjusted a burnished steel forearm guard and turned his eye to an open arch in the city wall. Thick timber doors, black with dried tar, were set within the arch and one stood open. "Well, be on your way. My men will take care of this malodorous carcass. Perhaps some of his ilk may alight and brighten with response when we toss him their way," he said with a hoarse chuckle, trying for a bit of amusement regarding the Phantos Mercenti's obsession with vision and

luminosity.

Kaimer didn't respond and the Sergia thought he'd offended his friend somehow. Knowing the man's dark moods, the Talon Sergeant turned and strode toward the archway.

Kaimer hadn't heard the Sergia's last statement. His attention had been caught by a glimmer in the refuse under the tortured man's destroyed right leg. He squatted again, reached out with tough, weathered fingers, and pinched the object from under the mangled appendage. As he lifted what looked to be a palm-sized medallion of pressed copper, he noticed something peculiar about the halved leg. Where the thing ended just above the knee, it looked as if something had bitten clean through the limb. Stranger yet, the flesh at the stump was blackened and closed, as if cauterized by flame. He leaned closer to inspect what he had originally spied as a piece of bone sticking from the flesh of the stub.

"What foul creature?" Kaimer breathed as he grasped the object, slowly extracted it like unsheathing a long curved dagger, found it akin to the fang of a viper though one of quite substantial thickness. Lifting it at arm's length before him, he surmised the "tooth" was easily the length of one of his own killing blades.

He snapped upright, and cast a hard eye upon the frothing gray-black sea. He backed away slowly, studying the curving fang and the reaching waves behind it.

This victim hadn't come from a simple falling out of his sect. There was a pre-meditated purpose to the damage the body had taken. That, and a mighty large beastie that somebody had been keeping under wraps.

Kaimer peered at the medallion,

not fathoming the arcane symbols and disturbing image on its face. He did not believe in any city religion, finding most lead by men who simply twisted and conformed witless followers to their own self-serving biddings. He had seen the many pendants and insignia of the upper and under sects within the city, of those who followed this or that god or goddess. Yet the embellishment on this copper disk was not familiar to him.

A chill prickled at the base of his skull as he pondered the imagery. A giant tooth was one thing, for if whatever owned it could lose it, it could also bleed; an unknown or new god however, was something different. He knew someone who might have a knowledge of such things, and perhaps even bring answers regarding the corpse and its grisly death.

Shoving the massive fang into his waistband, Kaimer was sure he really didn't want to know those answers. He was just as sure he had to know them, for they would be of import to Skovolis. He was not a man detoured by adventure and mystery, and nothing—animal or god—interfered in his own battle with the City of Thrones.

With purposeful strides and sure-footed steps, Kaimer descended into the bowels of the undercity. He took a well-traveled path through leaning tenements which kept him for the most part in gloomy shadows. Here and there braziers of dying fires or dimming coals weakly lit the narrow corridors. There were no true names for the paths Kaimer traversed. The undercity was an ever-changing entity, alive in its twisting and moving and settling. From time to time

the earth itself rumbled and shook, as if disapproving of what sat upon its upper crust and in the pock-marked scars of its millennia-old flesh. The weight of the city topside, building heaped upon building, pilings stressed to creaking and cracking limits, caused entire dank neighborhoods and throughways to shift and change. An entire section of the east warren of Skovolis, Miregardt, had collapsed into a sinkhole less than a year ago; new structures and their squatters had already begun to settle the still-trembling area.

Kaimer knew his course.

He also knew that he was followed.

Turning into a narrow alleyway, he took five heavy steps then stepped onto the ledge of a doorway, letting the blackness of the entry and the monstrous shadowy loom of the buildings obscure him. This section of the undercity he had entered, Bolborus, was mostly void of life except for narcotics-addicts and a frighteningly huge population of rodents that fed off the nearby garbage dump. It was the shortest route to his destination, and the lack of human interaction—pushy vendors, drunken and drug-induced revelers, street thugs wanting to test their muscle, ankle-grabbing beggars, honest and law-abiding Talon troops who wanted to know all comings and goings, corrupt Talon troops who wanted payment to allow all comings and goings—would not interrupt his travels.

He waited out of torchlight, dagger in his right hand, listening for the footsteps of the figure that had been following him for the last quarter mile. No footfalls came nor sound at all, except for the squeal of a rat from afar.

Kaimer blinked and in that instant a dark form whipped around the corner. He hardly had time to lift his blade as a flash of steel angled down at his chest. His attacker was fast and silent, and if not for Kaimer's lightning reflexes, his long dagger would not have met the other blade mid-stroke and kept it from driving into his heart.

With blades locked, Kaimer turned upon his assailant and grabbed the wrist holding the weapon. It was a man's face he met, though the eyes were covered with a thick strip of dark cloth tied around the shaved head. At first he thought the person black of skin, but the flesh had a sheen to it and reeked of grease paint.

"You are not a common street thug," Kaimer snarled behind clenched teeth. Though the man was smaller in stature than he, there was power behind the weapon arm. "What guild do you hail from?"

Painted and eye-draped thugs came from many of the thieves' guilds in the undercity, though he had never known of any who slinked about both blind and black. He winced at the thought of a power play afoot, or a merger of guilds he had yet to hear of, angry at being in the dark for the second time in one day.

The thrum of a loosed bowstring sounded behind him and he jerked toward the brick frame of the doorway. Something tore at his left shoulder, splitting the cloth down to his flesh. He twisted in the same instant the arrow dropped and clattered off the alleyway floor, driving the man in his iron grasp to that same hard-packed surface. He kicked at the attacker's weapon arm, sending the blade out of his hand. He thought he heard hissing laughter from the downed man.

Kaimer didn't wait for another arrow or for his foe to regain his feet. He ran back into the open corridor and zig-zagged down the empty street.

He turned right, heading into another alleyway shadowed by the lean of dilapidated buildings. Footfalls scuffed above him and he glanced up as he ran, counting three dark forms leaping across the angled rooftops. All three gripped bows.

Kaimer wondered at the unwanted attention as he came upon a four-way intersection and took a sharp left. He saw the three figures pass overhead, going straight. His predicament was nothing new to him, except usually he knew why he was being pursued and often had a fairly good idea who his pursuers were.

Following the alleyway, he cut through a collapsed building and sent a small horde of rats skittering every which way. He squeezed through a series of vertical pipes that ran up through the levels and into one of the private communities of wealthier homes in the upper city. Today the pipes were but warm to the touch, the constant fires of the Vaul Mercenti who worked in their smoke-choked underburrows deep in the bowels of Skovolis stoked. Fortunately it wasn't the dead of snowfall, else the very air about them would have seared his skin.

He teetered along planks which connected buildings or spanned deep cracks or sinkholes. He climbed rusted fire escapes, crawled through shattered windows, and took stairways three steps at a time all the while keeping attune to his surroundings.

Kaimer reached the western portion of the undercity without further interruption. The Plaza of Voices was somewhat of an artisan's area where one could find almost anything that could be manufactured by hand or tool. It was also home to many secretive alchemists, fortune-tellers, soothsayers and oracles—the latter who sometimes annoyed yet often humored Kaimer with their ranting and ravings of being touched by divine entities. He considered them simply ones who had taken too many raps to the head by cudgel or fist, or who had too excessively imbibed upon the drugs that devoured their sanity.

Though surrounded by the multitudes of Plaza dwellers, Kaimer kept to himself and close to the buildings, avoiding any conversations with stranger or shopkeeper, and the small squads of Gray Talons who walked the streets.

He arrived at a small building with five plain wood doors, peeling of paint, along its front. Knocking on the center door, he waited. There came the sound of shuffling, then a small square panel slid open.

Knowing the routine, Kaimer slipped two fingers into the bag of coin at his hip as a crone's voice emitted from the door. "Is there a reason you bother an old woman and reason why I shouldn't skewer you where you stand?"

A rattle from below caused him to eye another small door that had silently opened about crotch level. The blackened tip of a poisoned blade hovered a hand from his groin.

Kaimer flashed three silver solidi, and replied, "More of this for some information and interesting items for your review."

"Four, and you get to keep your other jewel bag," was the raspy response.

"I'm good for it, Lorelei."

The blade retracted and both door panels slapped shut. A series of deadbolts slid from their stanchions, and the door to Kaimer's left opened.

With a backward glance over his shoulder—still feeling the sting of the arrow graze—Kaimer entered the building.

The woman who sat before Kaimer, though gravelly and ancient-sounding of voice, was not anywhere near ancient of body or actual age. Long golden locks draped over the gentle shoulders of Lorelei Lonewand and framed a sharp oval face. She wore a blue brocade doublet, burgundy linens and blue velvet shoes—normal artisan ware for the Plaza.

"It's an unholy medallion of the Secret World, specifically of Larcae also known as Thazg Black Veil." She lifted her head to look at Kaimer. "More commonly known as Larcae the Blind Sephiroth King." Lorelei returned to studying at the copper medallion—though Kaimer noticed not too closely. She avoided direct contact with the object by putting on a thick smithy's glove to take it from Kaimer. "He is one of seven Death Lords."

Upon entering the narrow store interior, it looked like a common metalworkers shop. In this sector of the undercity, *Lonewand Ornates and Ironworks* was well known for fine metal sculptures and jewelry. Walls and shelves were lined with interesting trinkets of steel and tin, copper, brass and bronze. It was the backroom of her shop that was the most interesting.

Slightly vexing and surely unnerving too. For the right price, and if a close working relationship had been struck and proven trustworthy, one could enter this rear room lined with shelves of ancient tomes, texts and scrolls. There were also other oddities kept here—painted skulls etched with strange black sigils, pelts of queer beasts from far off lands, crystal spheres where wisps of ghostly images seemed to flit and flicker.

Kaimer often felt on edge when in the woman's presence. Though she was only twenty-six winter's old, she possessed great knowledge of all things concerned with metallurgy and the arcane.

"Why would this be found on a corpse?" He watched as Lorelei swiveled upon her stool and pulled a red-bound text from a bookshelf behind her.

"I haven't seen or heard of the Cult of Larcae since my travels far east with my father many years ago," Lorelei said setting the large book before them and opening it near its center. She flipped heavy pages, yellowed with age, and peered at sketched pictures of horrific-looking creatures and appalling visages.

She turned the page to a rabble of undecipherable writing—at least in Kaimer's eyes—and a dark line drawing of a blind-folded creature. Severed limbs and mangled heads hung from its grisly maw. The page was heavy with dripping and flowing gore. Kaimer leaned over and studied the illustration, feeling a cold chill wriggle down his spine at the over-extended jaw of the masked being. Long, dagger-like fangs filled its mouth. He clearly recalled drawing the large bloody tooth from the torn-asunder priest of Phantos.

Lorelei shook her head as she set the medallion on the page next to the ghastly image. "It doesn't surprise me that they've finally come."

"Who?" Kaimer questioned.

"The Cult of Larcae. Skovolis is such a breeding ground, more like a feeding ground, for death," the woman said, handing the medallion back to Kaimer and looking just a bit nervous when he simply took it in hand.

"A violent lot needing to murder to spread their chaos and appease their god-

head?" Kaimer asked, knowing something of the annoying acolytes of dead gods. He couldn't count how often he'd run across zealots who preached spiritual greatness, peace and tranquility, and simply used it as an evil disguise to gain power and intimidate others. The City of Thrones was a place of many religions trying to procure a bloody handhold in the mire of the dying metropolis.

"No," Lorelei replied, running a finger along the arcane text below the beastly image. "They only do sacrifice when their god, the Blind Sephiroth King, walks among man. He is said to feed on chosen ones brought to him. *The Blind God will come and sup upon sixteen and one who have been chosen by his ebon-clad apprentices...or so it says.*"

The room in which they sat was dimly lit by a corner brazier, but Kaimer suddenly noticed the woman's face grow white as her eyes followed more of the text on the ancient page.

"You must leave from here immediately." Lorelei surged to her feet and looked ready to draw the blade at her side. "Your session is free. Be gone, Kaimer, and I wish the fortunes upon you."

Kaimer rose, the copper medallion still in hand. A look of confusion and slight annoyance hung on his face. "What is it?" he asked, not knowing what startled her.

The woman snatched up a flask of gray-tinted powder and shook it over the spot where Kaimer had sat. She also doused the table and the red tome set upon it. She turned the open flask toward him.

"The ones who hold the copper badges, the sacred pendants of Larcae, are the poor dredges who are to be the living god's meals," Lorelei Lonewand exclaimed. Her panic was evident as she moved toward Kaimer, not touching him but obviously prepared to empty the gray power over him. Unsure of its sorcerous powers, he backed away. She gestured violently, repeatedly threatening him with the flask as she sprinkled it over his retreating steps.

He found himself back in the street shortly, the door to *Lonewand Ornates and Ironworks* slammed and bolted with speed and much commotion.

"Damn these superstitious fools," Kaimer grumbled under his breath. "Living demonspawn gods, my arse, and their motley followers causing such a ruckus."

But then his thoughts went to something the woman had said. *Sixteen and one who have been chosen*...and *the ones who hold the copper badges*...the copper medallions.

"Sergia Kavellum!"

A black-fletched arrow rattled off the cobbles, missing Kaimer as he side-stepped the dark blade of an ebon-clad acolyte of the Blind God. He growled as one of his drawn short swords deflected the downward swing of his attacker. Though his adversary was smaller in stature, his strike was like that from a giant's fist. Kaimer felt it through his entire sword arm, and it numbed his fingers, but he did not yield his weapon. He continued twisting to his left, avoiding the second black swordsman's overhead chop.

It had taken Kaimer nearly an hour to reach the Third Ward where Sergia Norvis Kavellum and his family lived.

The area was not considered a part of the undercity though it was in the shadows of the bigger metropolis that slowly crept over and around it like the drawing of a massive dark blanket. Many of the Talon upper echelon were quartered here. It had seemed a secure place as there were guards and patrols everywhere.

Nothing stopped the path of the Blind Sephiroth King and his disciples however. The Death Lord had obviously imbued his followers with some form of unnatural power, for Kaimer had come across a score of savagely slaughtered Talon guards, their bodies filled with arrows, gutted and hacked to pieces. He had briefly sought to find a downed Talon with a *chifre deaviso*, a warning horn, to call other soldiers and Talon superiors. Finding none and his primary concern the Sergia and his family, Kaimer had continued to the man's home.

The two black-clothed swordsmen weaved about Kaimer. They were quick but Kaimer had been a warrior and survivor since his early youth. Even with dire thoughts of his friend wafting through his mind, his outward focus lay in the battle at hand and the skill in which he brought his steel and strength against his aggressors.

Another arrow *thunked* into a wood bench beside Kaimer. He rocked off the fixture as his attackers stabbed and hacked with wicked abandon. They weren't sloppy fighters, just intent on the kill.

The foe in front of him stabbed forward and Kaimer twisted to the right, letting the acolyte's momentum bring him close. With the speed of a striking adder, Kaimer brought a steely-muscled arm around the man's ebon-shrouded neck and twisted in one fluid and abrupt jerk.

Neck broken, one follower of the blind demon-king dropped to the ground and did not rise.

"You will feel a hundred lashes before my lord tears out your entrails and devours you alive," the second swordsman hissed behind his dark mask.

The disciple swung his blade round in an underarm thrust as Kaimer came up with his own weapons. No steel met but Kaimer's dual short swords punched through the black-cloth wrappings, emerging out the lower back of the acolyte as the acolyte's single ebony blade punched through his right side.

Both men collapsed atop each other and lay still.

Nothing moved in the death-slicked courtyard of Sergia Kavellum until the black-garbed archer slipped from his perch in a tall maple beside the slate-colored brick-and-mortar home. He stepped gingerly along the path of dead and hewn Talon guards until he was upon his comrades and their downed adversary, another chosen sacrifice for his demon lord.

The copper medallion lay in a pool of blood beside the dead men. The archer snapped his bow across his back, drew the black garb from his freehand and leaned to snatch up the item.

Eyes obscured behind a dark cloth mask bulged and breath burst from exhausted lungs as a boot rose hard into the archer's crotch.

The black archer fell backward clutching his groin as Kaimer surged upright. He brushed away the sword that stuck from the right side of his leather vest and let it clatter to the ground, simultaneously pulling his dual blades from the dead man he'd fallen upon.

Standing above the huffing acolyte, Kaimer snarled, "Let us see how you enjoy the torture."

Crimson-stained swords snapped down and drew across from left to right, then right to left—once, twice, thrice. The man screamed as the weapons bit deep, through fabric, flesh, muscles and tendons, effectively crippling him.

Leaving the screeching acolyte and all caution behind, Kaimer ran into the Sergia's house.

He bolted through the front door, calling to his old friend. Hearing what sounded like a scuffle from the upper floor, he took the stairs three-at-a-time. He stopped at the top, his breath leaving him as his eyes partook of the carnage in the hallway before him. The Sergia had a wife of nearly fifteen years and two older children, a boy and a girl. The ravaged bodies of all three lay in almost indiscernible piles upon the red-stained flooring.

"Brand-Eye, where are you!" Kaimer called, peering at the open doorways up and down the hallway.

A groan and a heavy thump came down the hallway from the upper floor study.

"My...my friend..." Kaimer heard as he approached the room with weapons at the ready. Entering, he found the Sergia, his broad back toward Kaimer, standing over the remains of another black-clad figure, the face of this one wrapped in an elaborate ebon scarf—and a large battleaxe embedded in its chest. Kaimer studied them, noting the arms, legs, and head hewn from the body.

"Are you injured?" Kaimer asked, stepping closer.

Sergia's right hand waved Kaimer off, stopping him from approaching further. For a second, Kaimer thought he saw a bloody index finger dripping with gore, but the Sergia, who had momentarily glanced over his shoulder, pulled it back around.

"I live, and think I have brought the end to this mortal form of Larcae, or a follower disguised as him," the Sergia replied, his voice low and slightly stunted as if he spoke through clenched teeth. He shuddered and seemed ready to pitch forward. "And he has butchered my family. I—"

Kaimer put a hand to the man's shoulder and turned him around. He choked back the bile that suddenly rose in his throat as he gazed upon the Sergia's destroyed face. Deep gash marks crossed just above the bridge of his nose and across both eyes. The wrecked branded eye and what had been his good right eye were ruined bloody sockets. Kaimer was surprised the man was not crumpled upon the floor with such horrendous wounds.

"I will go and sound the cry for more Talon, and fetch a practitioner to see to your wounds," Kaimer said sheathing his swords and turning from the gore-filled room.

"Aye. Do that, my…friend," the Sergia said. Then, in afterthought, "Do you have the last pendant of the Sephiroth King?"

Kaimer stopped halfway out the door, averting his eyes from the carnage in the hallway. "I do not. One of the cultists found it with what he thought was my dead body. He took it, and my boot in his groin and steel across his flesh. I let him keep the foul medallion. He may still be alive in the courtyard."

"Very…good." The Sergia's big shoulders rose and fell, as if a great weight had been relieved of them. "It is said the last medallion decides if the Death Lord stays or departs the realm of man."

Though his heart was grief-stricken for his friend, Kaimer had to chuckle, surprised at the Sergia's superstition-influenced words. "Only if you believe in such refuse."

"Not a…religious man," Sergia said, more statement than question.

"That is I," Kaimer replied, hands on his sheathed weapons, moving down the death-filled hallway.

The black-clad acolyte of Larcae the Blind Sephiroth King lay groaning on the pavement, his arms and legs useless. He struggled to keep from falling into the fathomless abyss of unconsciousness.

Footsteps came to him and he craned his head back, peering through the dark but sheer fabric of the cloth mask he still wore. He saw the old Talon Sergeant, the one his God-Made-Flesh had directed him and his fallen comrades to attack. The second-to-last sacrifice to sate the hungry demon god. A great helm hid the upper portion of the man's face, but blood flowed from beneath the visor, painting his face a dark crimson.

The Sergia knelt by his side and felt along his body and arms, finding the hand that clutched the medallion. He screamed as the big Talon officer tore it from his fingers. The dying disciple watched the man raise it to his bloody face and press it momentarily to his lips. A sigh—more like a dry rattle—escaped his lips, then a smile spread across his face—a smile that grew larger and wider, deforming the lower jaw until long sharp teeth set close together appeared.

The acolyte, realizing he lay before

the Blind God of Chaos, cried out. "My Lord, please assist me. I have always been your loyal servant. Give me strength to fight at your side and spread pain, fear and death in this dying city."

"Thank you," said Larcae the Sephiroth King, now in the body and guise of Sergia Brand-Eye, sniffing at the man's bloody wounds. "I have decided to stay here, where the sheep are fat and easy to slaughter. I thank you for bringing me forth to this dark metropolis. What fun I will have."

The acolyte nervously watched the dark demon god's black tongue slither through its lips and over his torn appendages.

"My—my Lord! What—what about me?" he said before his pleading words turned into a shrill shriek as the Blind God opened its obscenely extended jaws of long, razor-sharp fangs and fed upon the last sacrifice.

Frederick Tor
was born with a pen in one hand and a falchion in the other. One dripped blood, and the other—the other!—ran black with ink. Fred entered this world with one purpose: to write tales of high adventure for Rogue Blades Entertainment. With him came the sprawling city of Skovolis, the cosmopolitan metropolis that dwarfed Constantinople in breadth and Nineveh in depth. Skovolis. The City of Thrones. Home to the best civilized humanity could offer—in all its decadent glory and savage decay. Home also to Kaimer, the barbaric street warrior who knew the byways of her lowest levels as well as the corridors of her highest power mongers. A man—and a city—of many stories. Visit the www.roguebladesentertainment.com/kaimer/ for more of his exciting tales.

DEMON HEART

by Bryan Lindenberger

Sir Ritehart fired his sling, and the hare that bounded across the grassy heath leaped only once before it fell still. A hound retrieved the animal, and Ritehart turned to the scholar, Priestess Risa Melicles. "How much time passed?" he asked.

Risa examined her hourglass. "Sixteen minutes," she said and the other hunters applauded. Two hares and a pheasant had fallen to Sir Ritehart's bullets. Ritehart had won the hunt every year as far back as memory served, and none expected this year to be any different. The wizard Set stepped forward.

"Celebrating so soon?" he hissed, lips twisting across his embittered face. A crow sat upon his shoulder as it had now for days. The bird grasped a bit of cloth in its beak and pulled Set's hood down so that his bald head glistened in the sun.

"No one has forgotten your turn," Risa told the wizard

"As well they should not!" Set huffed. He closed his eyes, and the crow lifted from his shoulder into the sky. Sir Ritehart watched with fascination as the bird circled overhead before diving into a nearby grove. Without opening his eyes, Set released his first bullet. And then, another.

And another.

Ritehart and the others stood incredulous as two hares, a pheasant, and even a fox fell victim to his mark. For no reason than to flaunt his skill, Set downed a sparrow that took flight, and the little bird fell with a plop at Sir Ritehart's feet.

"Need I ask the time?" Set scowled as he opened his eyes again. "Or should I collect my prize now?"

The hunters stood dumbfounded. Ritehart was the first to congratulate the wizard. "Impressive work!" he said. "How do you manage such a feat?"

"I see what the crow sees," Set replied. "We are *familiar*, yes? So I can take only half the credit."

"Then you should receive only half the prize," Risa Melicles said, resetting the hourglass. Her face, as beautiful as it was, showed no pleasure. Yet Sir Ritehart knew he'd lost fairly and he patted the wizard's arm——forgetting how much Set reviled being touched.

171

Near the grove, one of the other hunters shouted a warning. He pointed across the hillside, but Sir Ritehart saw nothing. A foreboding wind fell from the north, and a shadow spread across the heath. Ritehart squinted at a whirl of dust and leaves in the distance. The hounds barked wildly.

"What is that?" one of the hunters asked, but Sir Ritehart had never seen anything like it. Horror gripped him as the whirlwind swept hungrily toward the hunter. He tried to run, but the thing moved faster than any man or beast. It fell upon the hunter—a blur of gray claws and yellow fangs and shredded the man before he could scream. Ritehart and his fellow hunters fired at the creature. Neither bullet nor arrow could penetrate its hide.

"Demon!" the Priestess Risa Melicles cried. Sir Ritehart had drawn his sword, and she pulled him by the arm. "No! Flee to the city gates!"

The hounds howled and ran, and Ritehart called his men to retreat. Set was already on his way up the hillside toward the gates of Uenden. A sharp-eyed gatekeeper gave the cry, and the doors opened. Ritehart already felt the demon's breath hot at his back, and the smell of the foul creature was like a sulfur pool. When Set stumbled and fell, Ritehart gathered him over his shoulder and leaped through the city gate.

"Drop the portcullis!" Ritehart cried, and a thousand pounds of spiked iron crashed upon the demon. The thing screamed from many mouths, a dozen claws lashing in every direction. Sir Ritehart set the wizard on his feet. He wiped sweat from his eyes, certain the demon had met its fate. Yet the winds rose again. Lightning flashed, and a swirl of a million colors restored the hellish beast outside the gate. The city walls shook. Archers gathered to fire from battlements and loopholes. It seemed nothing could kill the thing.

"Invincible," Risa said, chest heaving beneath her vestments.

"No creature is invincible!" Ritehart declared. The wooden walls of the city trembled. Splinters whizzed through the air. Set, with the crow upon to his shoulder, agreed with the priestess.

"We must retreat to the castle," he said, out of breath but strangely calm. "The stone curtain should hold him."

The people of Uenden poured from their homes and shops. Some of them cried and fell upon their knees as the city walls shuddered. Others gathered weapons, but Sir Ritehart commanded all of them to retreat to the castle. Men gathered their horses to spread the word. Others collected provisions, and a wave of citizens fled up the grassy motte to the castle gates. Finding his white steed, Sir Ritehart ushered as many townspeople as he could find. Over two thousand men, women, and children found salvation behind the stone curtain just as the city walls burst inward. The demon leaped into the city.

"We must go now!" Risa declared.

Ritehart pulled her up behind him. He galloped his horse across the bridge and over the festering moat. He heard the screams of Uenden's as the creature tore open rooftops and ripped apart flesh, but no time remained to save those good people. Fleeing, the knight never felt so helpless.

"There must be a way to kill it. Everything has its weakness—even the gods!"

The sky was cloudless, the moon full. On cool nights such as these, the people of Uenden usually built fires outside of town. They'd eat good food, dance, and sing. But tonight the multitude made no sound. They clung to each other in the courtyard, and even the terrified remained silent as the demon flung itself against the stone castle curtain. Dust rose and mortar strained. The rumbling was terrible, and the beast seemed as tireless as it was cruel. The stone shield held fast for now.

King Urides arrived from the keep. He hoped desperately to offer some solution and suggested that his men sally forward. Risa Melicles argued against it. Countless archers had fired flaming arrows into the demon without effect. Others poured boiling pitch over its shapeless body, and the demon replied with a vengeance by spewing poison clouds from its dozen mouths. Some warriors succumbed to the poison instantly and fell from the battlements. Others remained blinded for hours. The king retreated to his castle.

"It's a Kliton," Risa told Sir Ritehart. They sat together with several others in an area of the bailey clear of grass. Set stood over them with his arms crossed. Risa's face appeared yellow and grim in the flickering light of a small fire. "A Kliton is a demon of Inos...or, somewhere," she said.

"Somewhere?" Set mocked. He scowled down at the priestess. "For all your scholarship and learning, somewhere is the best you can do?"

His crow chuckled in his ear, and Risa glared back at them. "You have offered no advice, wizard!"

"What about our brave knight here, then? Isn't it his job to slay errant beasts? Yes, I believe that's how the folk stories go."

"The demon wants something. There's no other reason for it to appear now."

"Perhaps he wants your knowledge, priestess. How sadly disappointed he will find himself!"

Ritehart listened to the two bicker in vain. The priestess had taken his hand in hers. She held on and squeezed, but no comfort could ease the sickness in his heart. When he'd heard enough, he pushed her hand away in frustration.

"The wizard is right," he said. "I can hear the whispers of our people. I can read their eyes. They expect me to do something."

"To do what?" Risa sighed.

"To save them!" Sir Ritehart shouted, and he saw that his anger had hurt her. "Risa, please understand. What good am I to be a hero abroad when I cannot save my people at home? What use the greatest hunter who cannot kill this monster?"

"Second greatest," the wizard Set muttered.

"What?"

Set shook his head. "He is the *second* greatest hunter. Earlier today I——"

Risa Melicles kicked. Her heel struck Set's shin, and his bird squawked and flapped its wings. "I'm through with you!" she said, standing to dust herself off as the castle curtain thundered from a fresh strike. She turned to Sir Ritehart. "I'm going to the library. Promise me you'll wait here."

"It would seem I have little choice."

"I'm glad you understand," Risa said, and she started through the crowd toward the keep. The guards all knew her.

They snapped at attention and threw open the doors. Ritehart watched her disappear, then cocked his head.

"Do you hear that?"

"What?" Set replied, rubbing his shin. "I hear nothing."

"Exactly," Ritehart said. "The demon...he has quieted."

"Perhaps he needs a nap. That witch of a priestess could use one as well."

The knight frowned. He strained to listen, but all he heard were the whimpers of frightened children. "Anything that needs rest can be killed," he said. "Send up your crow."

"Why?"

"You can see through his eyes, can you not? I want to know what the Kliton is doing."

The wizard Set got up and spat at Ritehart's feet. "A sore loser, are you?"

"What do you mean?"

"All my life, I stood in your shadow. You can't stand that someone actually beat you at your own game. Now you want the demon to kill my crow. Well, I'll not fall for your tricks!"

"For the love of——!"

"I'm going to my quarters," Set sneered down at him "You know, adjacent to the king. Where is it that you sleep, heroic knight?"

"The barracks," Sir Ritehart replied, and Set raised a bony finger at him.

"Aha! And let you not forget it!"

Some things never changed. Set was one of them. He retreated to the castle keep, and Sir Ritehart curled upon the ground. He watched the moon. The castle walls thundered again before dawn, and the knight could only hope that his presence helped calm the people. There was little else he could do.

When the sun rose, so did the smell of food. Ritehart opened his eyes from a slumber, and a child of no more than seven brought him a bowl of spiced porridge. The girl stood far back out of respect, and her blue eyes were wide behind her dirty face. Sir Ritehart smiled and beckoned her near. The girl set down the porridge and scampered away, shouting to her friends that she'd met Uenden's most famous man.

"You see," Risa Melicles said. She approached from the castle, and her eyes were dark from lack of sleep. She carried a bound book of leaves. "You still inspire our people."

"If only I could help them," Ritehart replied.

"You will," Risa said. "And I know how."

She showed him the book and read the important parts to him. The priestess was right. The demon was a Kliton, and his earthly form was strong—but not invincible. To the north a great wall of fire masked a vast underground sea. Beyond both stood a temple door, sealed by magic, the Life of the Kliton hidden inside.

"It is his heart," Risa explained. "His soul. If you destroy it, the Kliton dies."

Sir Ritehart took things one step at a time, and so concerned himself first with the fiery wall. Nothing could extinguish it, but a hero could pass through unharmed if he wore the proper armor. Only a suit woven from the silk of the yulan worm would do. Such worms dwelled in the burning embers of the sacred willow tree, and King Urides had once received such trees as a gift. One of them was immediately chopped down and set to burn.

Second, Sir Ritehart needed a Hand of Glory to penetrate the magic seal of the temple doors. Such an item could only be made from the hand of a hanged thief. The castle dungeon was not lacking for such criminals, and the martyr King Urides chose seemed almost cheerful to pay back his people in such a manner. Risa chopped off his hand and prepared the rites personally. That left only the underground sea to contend with.

The priestess acknowledged that this was the most difficult part of the task. It stretched for miles, she said, with no place to rise for air. The gill of the copper lancefish offered the only known solution. "You must apply its gill to your mouth," Risa explained. "It will allow you to breathe for very long periods underwater."

"Where do I find this fish?"

"At Black Lake," she told him. "We're already sending someone."

"No! I must go myself!"

Risa smiled. "We can't risk your life. Not if you are going to acquire the heart and soul of the demon."

But Sir Ritehart, foolishly perhaps, ignored her warning. Few soldiers knew the way to Black Lake. They were too young to remember, but Ritehart had campaigned near there. He set out alone that very night with only a blade, a strong net, and a steady heart. A postern at the back of the castle led him outside.

He sallied forth, hugging the shadows of the night. The demon, so busy hammering the walls and spewing poison, did not see him sneak away. Nor did it see him return six days later. Ritehart saw that the mortar curtain had cracked badly beneath the Kliton's relentless blows, and stone had crumbled. The wall would only last a few more days.

Sir Ritehart found his people equally shaken and broken down. Some had gone mad. Others stared at the ground in front of them, awaiting their doom. Still, there was hope. The castle's finest seamstresses had gathered enough yulan silk to weave a suit of fire resistant armor. The Hand of Glory was sufficiently blackened, and its fingers curled like a dead spider to hold the magic within. Ritehart produced the copper lancefish, and Risa sliced it to remove the gills.

"When you enter the sea," she demonstrated, "you must hold these gills between your lips and teeth. Breathe through them, not your nose."

"It's hopeless," the wizard Set grumbled from nearby. "All this effort will produce nothing. This foolish knight got out through the postern and back again. That's what we should do!"

"And how many have died trying?" Risa snapped at him. She looked back at Sir Ritehart and sighed. "So many, in fact, that I feared they would spoil your chances for return. Here. Let me help you with that yulan armor." The suit was heavy, yellow and orange threads glistening. Risa couldn't help but smile to see him in it.

"Rather ornate, eh?" the knight said, allowing himself a grin.

"More than what I'm used to!" Risa replied, but her mirth soon faded. "You need only wisdom and bravery now. You have everything else that you need."

"All but one thing," Ritehart said.

In an act that would have brought him to the gallows on any day but this, the bold knight leaned in his glistening armor and kissed the priestess. Without waiting for a reaction, he turned and mounted his white stallion.

"Sir Ritehart," Risa said.

"Yes, m'lady?"

She smiled up at him. "When you return—and I am sure you will—make certain that never happens again."

"I'll cherish the memory," the knight replied before setting off into the night.

The map Risa had given Ritehart led through low-lying swamps to the east and mountains in the north. He found the ravine marked on it, and followed a stream into its depths until he came to a fissure in the rock wall. Larger than a man, this crevice blazed with smoke and fire so hot it caused the stream to boil. Sir Ritehart's horse whinnied at the unnatural heat and fiery roar, and the knight knew that he stood before the wall of fire.

He dismounted and tethered his beast in the shade near the water, promising to return soon. He pulled the coif of his worm-spun mail over his face, and gripped its over-long sleeves about his hands. With every part of him covered, he blindly approached the source of heat. The roar of the blazing wall grew into a horrendous bellow, and his skin blistered even through the protection of his armor. The knight held his breath and hurried through.

Heat and noise vanished, and Sir Ritehart emerged on the other side, surprised to be alive. He uncovered his eyes and found himself in a small grotto enclosed by rock. A small pool of water at its center mirrored the blue sky above. He stripped down to his tunic and breeches, and stuffed the gills of the lancefish into his mouth. He took a hesitant breath, then descended into the pool until the water closed above his head.

The gills proved effective, though they did nothing to help him see. The knight felt his way through the slippery dark, following the meandering cavern for what seemed like miles without any need for air.

At last, the watery passage arched and rose toward daylight.

Ritehart crawled into the open air. Cold and dripping wet, he found himself in a place unlike any other. A green valley stretched to unseen distances. There were white deer and brightly colored flowers with petals that twirled on their stems. He saw vines with fruit as big as sheep, and trees that dripped golden honey from their stems. Perhaps this was the legendary Land of Promise, but he had no time to ponder. The object of his quest lay before him: a temple of stone with massive pillars and stairs that led to a high, golden door.

He ran to the door, but found that it would not budge. Taking the blackened Hand of Glory from inside his tunic, Ritehart tapped the door with it while saying:

Heed the call
Of the hanged thief's fall!
Open lock
To the dead man's knock!

The fingers of the dead hand opened, as did the door itself. Heartened, the knight tossed the expended hand aside. He dashed inside the temple and raced to the stone altar. Risa had told him that the heart of the demon-soul could be anything—a pebble, even some small animal—but that he would recognize it at once. Ritehart found nothing of the sort.

Upon the altar stood the statue of a man. The man had seven arms, and in one of them he held a wicker cage. The cage door was open, and there was nothing inside.

Sir Ritehart fell to his knees. The demon's heart—whatever it was—had already been taken. His people were in danger, and this foolish quest had only wasted time. Nearly weeping, he shook his fist at the cage.

A bird's cage.

Just big enough for—

"A crow," Ritehart said. His chest seethed with anger. He shouted again, but not at the cage this time. He cursed the wizard Set, and now he understood why the demon had appeared so suddenly. He wanted his soul back, now in the form of that infernal crow.

Dashing from the altar, Sir Ritehart stuffed the gills into his mouth and swam back through the watery cavern. He emerged in the grotto at nightfall, but his worm-spun armor was not there. He searched frantically, confused and afraid that he'd swam in the wrong direction.

"Is this what you are looking for?" said a voice.

Ritehart looked up. He saw Set, a black silhouette against the great wall of fire. "Bring me my armor!"

The wizard chuckled. Ritehart had always hated that laugh. Now he had reason to.

"But I like your armor," Set told him. "Of course I have my own, and I spent months sewing it. Still the royal seamstresses do much finer work."

"Give it to me!" Sir Ritehart commanded.

"No."

Cautiously, the knight moved toward Set. He wanted to kill the wizard, but the man stepped back quickly toward the fire. "Why, Set?" Ritehart cried. "What do you want?"

"Want? I want the things that come so easily to you. I want to win the hunt. I want the admiration of my people. I want

Risa. Mostly, Sir Ritehart, I want to be rid of you."

"For that, you'll see our city destroyed?" Ritehart shouted in disbelief.

"Even I'm not that cruel. No, I'll destroy the demon when he breaks through the walls. You can be assured of that, former hero."

With that, the foul wizard turned and started through the fiery wall. Ritehart had no choice. He would not let it end this way. He dove into the inferno.

The fire chewed at Ritehart. It bit through his flesh and tore into his lungs. Yet he had hold of the wizard now, and no amount of agony could make him let go. The struggle itself was brief. Sir Ritehart pulled Set back into the grotto and grabbed both sets of armor.

"You won't leave me here!"

"Enjoy eternity," Ritehart said and marched through the flames.

Despite his horrible injuries, Sir Ritehart rode hard to the castle keep. He entered the postern as the curtain began to fall. Risa wept at the sight of him. All of his hair had burned off, and blackened flesh peeled from his arms. Every breath brought forth bitter pain and blood. She started toward him, but he wasted no time in hurrying up the tower and into Set's room.

Ritehart found the crow and snatched it from its cage. The bird squawked and pecked at his scabs as Ritehart took it outside. The sun was rising. The air was still. The demon flung itself into the wall one last time.

Stone crumbled and dust rose. The

people ran screaming as the demon spat venom and charged. Sir Ritehart stumbled toward the creature, the crow held forward in both hands. He twisted its body.

The demon froze. Then its multitude of eyes grew wide, and it screamed with all the fury of the heavens from all its mouths.

Sir Ritehart tore a wing from the crow. The demon's limbs snapped. He tore off the bird's beak, and the creature's fangs shattered into dust. Soon a convulsing heap of flesh and gristle was all that remained of the demon.

When Ritehart snapped the crow's neck, both it and the demon's remains burst into flame. The knight dropped the corpse and staggered back. Smoke rose into the blue sky, the fire quickly reducing the horror to a pile of ash.

Ritehart collapsed to the earth. Risa Melicles ran to him, but it was too late. The knight's flesh had been all but burned away, and his blood boiled like broth in his veins. The priestess applied ointments and balms to soothe his remaining hours, though she knew Sir Ritehart felt little pain. She had seen the gleam in his eyes and knew that he saw only the eternal green valley with the white deer. She prayed that he already tasted the honey upon his scorched lips.

Bryan Lindenberger currently researches and writes market research and business plans for entrepreneurs. His love is still reading and writing fiction. He has recently had work accepted for publication by 69 Flavors of Paranoia *and* Mirror Dance Magazine. *He was also editor and publisher of* Symphonie's Gift, *a kitchen-sink press 'zine which he plans to revive online.*

AZIERAN: RACKED UPON THE ALTAR OF EEYUU

by Christopher Heath

Weakened from days of hunger, thirst, and excruciating torture, Brom struggled in vain as over a half-dozen priests of the demonic patron Eeyuu wrestled him prone to the circular altar face. His bare back scraped against coarse granite carved to form a strange tableau of three eaglets in a nest. The weights of his captors pressed hard to restrain his massive, bruised limbs, denying him leverage while he writhed in futility.

Barely cognizant, Brom felt hard, iron shackles clamped tightly upon his wrists and ankles. Chains led outward in all four directions, threaded through squat, thick basalt obelisks carved in ancient symbols—their meanings forgotten by all save the clan mystics. The chains continued to the base of each obelisk, then wrapped upon an iron wheel meant to be turned as an instrument of torture.

Further exhausted from the struggle, Brom's head fell sideways. He tasted the metal tang of blood in his mouth, could barely see through swollen eye sockets. In his delirium, he managed to glimpse down the steep, rough-hewn steps on the slope of the Axehead Mountains to where many thousands of the Eagle Clan waited for his blood to be shed. The wide shelf below, nearly a mile in expanse on a scarcely forested plain, hosted bonfires around which clansmen screamed and danced in their ceremonial feather dresses to the rhythmic pounding of primal drum beats. These were the most savage of all Fohktouhl's barbarians.

The high priest led the dance with a slim obsidian dagger in hand, its edges chipped to razor-edged perfection. His face was covered with mock beak and feather mask, its long headdress extending to his calves. He danced up the stairs, intent on shedding Brom's blood in offering to Eeyuu, the Eagle Lord. His eyes were bright and piercing in their sinister stare.

Upon reaching the plateau where the altar stood, the shaman turned and bowed before his clan-king, Akkos. The barbaric noble—rail thin and adorned in buckskin with armbands sprouting white and brown feathers—sat overseeing the procession. His scepter likewise conformed to the feather motif, its apex ringed with eagle beaks.

The king of the Eagle Clan occasionally scanned the skies, a glazed look upon his face. His attempt to remain stoic was betrayed by a lurking fear in his eyes. Not even Akkos was exempt of the awesome wrath of Eeyuu should the demon beast materialize from the deepest pits of the Abyss and find displeasure with the ceremony.

The clan-king reached for a ruby encrusted goblet on the armrest of his wicker throne, and ritualistically upturned it over the high priest, pouring blood and staining costume feathers crimson.

Brom lingered on the edge of consciousness, his mind struggling to recall…to recall something…important. The drums silenced; all was still, and even the keening winds which blew harsh along the steep walls of the Axehead Mountains seemed to cease. Thousands of the Eagle Clan waited in anticipation for their bloodlusts to be quelled.

Utanak, the high priest, turned and approached the sacrificial victim. Beneath his mask a sly grin formed as he stared at the colossal brute. His priests had been fortunate indeed to discover the warrior defiling their temple.

The desecrater had surrendered with little struggle after making a wrong turn down a hall that ended in a cul-de-sac; upon realizing he was trapped, he offered little resistance. Fortunate again, the Cult of Eeyuu, to take this massive prize alive——and then discover it was Brom himself, King of Ar'uuk, the Bear Clan, to which the Wolf and Elk Clans swore fealty. No greater offering to Eeyuu could the high priest imagine. This would be the ultimate sacrifice, and the legacy Utanak would leave to his people. All the savages of The Broken Kingdom would know the might of the Eagle Clan, and the fall of King Brom would begin a new age, where the shadow of a united Fohktouhl would not threaten his clan's way of life.

Suddenly Utanak screeched and threw his hands into the air, waving the obsidian dagger in wide, deliberate arcs that ushered in the grinding of stone on stone, the creaking of chain. Brom felt his bonds grow taut and the shackles cut against his skin. His thick limbs fortified by muscle strained against the chains, and he felt those muscles painfully stretched to their limits. Teetering on the edge of consciousness, Brom managed a subtle groan.

The great circular dais upon which he lay slid apart to form two halves, grating the skin from his back and forcing him to cry out, nearly vomiting what little remained in his battered stomach. Now his body hung over a yawning portal encased within the walls of the altar. The clan-king twisted his bruised and battered neck and glanced sideways to see that just beneath him, now revealed by the opening of the altar face, rested what appeared to be a sculpture of stone. This sculpture mirrored the tableau on the altar face. A petrified nest housing three fossilized giant eaglets the size of large hounds gleamed as if brushed with lacquer, and Brom smelt the stench of sorcery long entombed. It jolted him to reality; now he remembered—now he knew why he was here.

"Let us see what fortune brings," the aged shaman Oktuun had warned as he spread the rubbing across a stone table. Only the center had survived the fire, its burned edges even now crumbling away.

Brom studied it intently, wishing his clansmen had brought the priest of Eeyuu to meet with him personally, rather than shooting the man on sight and then burning the corpse out of spite. The priest must have been outcast from his clan, and seeking haven. This parchment was perhaps some offering or payment, surely. It seemed to have spiritual significance, illustrating human sacrifice, though only the torso of the victim could be seen, anything above burned away.

Both Brom and Oktuun had heard the tales of the Altar of Eeyuu and knew the horrors said to transpire there. Whether true or myth, the two could not say for certain. Brom eyed the bottom of the parchment, the lower half charred to a dark smudge. He strained to see faint outlines. "There is script upon it." He picked up the page and passed it to Oktuun.

The old man scoured the document, nodding.

"The writings may yet be read; they are in the old tongue of Bjorsek," informed the shaman, continuing to eye it closely. He arose stiffly, leaning hard on his twisted staff, and moved slowly toward the back of his cave. He returned shortly, placing a small clay pot on the table. Removing the lid to reveal an azure powder, he then dipped a horsehair brush into the contents and spread it over the script.

"Ah, yes. Here it is. 'The lamb that becomes the lion and slays the high eagle shall gain fealty from the Eagle Clan.'"

"Intriguing," Brom stated, his thoughts turned inward at the opportunity presenting itself. At length he continued. "The high eagle?"

"It may be what they call their high priest, their lead shaman."

"Ah."

"I know what you are thinking, my king…and it is a risky plan."

"Yes. So are all paths to glory, it seems."

"Well said. But how will you survive being racked upon the Altar of Eeyuu, and then slay their high priest with no ally, and chained with no weapon."

Brom fingered the bear totem hanging around his neck, the totem instilled with the partial essence of Barshakk, the eldest of all bears. "Let strength be my ally, the chains with which they rack me become my weapon."

The clan-king thought some more. "But where shall I hide the bear totem."

Oktuun looked to Brom's thick, jet black mane for the answer. There his locks were braided fourteen times over, a bat skull dusted with ash entwined upon each—each one signifying that Brom had slain a dracul, a fiend akin to the vampire. "Ah, if we clump several skulls together, and braid the totem in beneath, it will be hidden from view, undiscovered unless they seek to untangle your locks."

"Nay," Brom frowned. "They will leave the bat skulls in place; the priests will wish to display the strength and status of their sacrifice to the Eagle Clan."

"And what if their warriors merely slay you on sight, as our warriors slew their priest?"

Brom pondered the point, thankful that his wise man had considered this possibility. "I will sneak into the Temple of Eeyuu, and be captured by the priests. Surely, even in such excitement they will have the wits to take me alive and offer me as sacrifice."

Oktuun nodded in contemplation as a smile surfaced on his face. "As you say."

Brom did not share in this grim mirth, but instead contemplated leaving the comfort of his wife Arula and his son Brahm.

Brom bucked against the clutching arm and sweet breath of the high priest of Eeyuu. He tried to twist away from the man's knife, but the rigid chains suspending him above the frozen eaglets resisted. The nerves in his back exploded in pain when the obsidian blade ripped through his flesh. He cried out in agony, and in his rage turned his thoughts inward to call upon the strength of the bear totem hidden within his heavy mane, beneath the bat skulls dusted in ash.

With inhuman might he thrashed against his bonds, thick limbs slamming against the edge of the altar's face on each side, shattering it into large, heavy fragments. The chains holding his legs creaked but for a split second before bursting, and as his legs dropped, the brute found himself standing amid chirping eaglets, now alive and hungry as his dripping blood dispelled the gramarye which had transmogrified them to stone.

Utanak lashed out with the obsidian dagger, the stroke stopped short as a chain burst and Brom caught the high priest's wrist and with supernatural strength rent the limb asunder, the dagger falling to the altar face. The priest's scream was drowned out by the chirping of eaglets, now eagerly tearing into the flesh of Brom's legs.

With a fierce push, the clan-king sent Utanak sprawling to the ground, the high priest clutching at the thick shard of bone jutting from his shoulder. The other priests, now gathering their wits, rushed the altar. Brom reached his free left hand as far up the opposite chain as he could, pulling hard and breaking a link; he now possessed a thick, heavy chain whip several feet in length.

The eaglets changed their cacophonous song from one of voracious greed fueled by hunger to one of horror and dismay, for Brom's blood had long ago through sorcerous pact been tainted by that of the Serpentine Witch. It was no longer fit for the demonic offspring of Eeyuu, the eagle god, but instead served as a poison to the chicks, and so they retreated from what they could not understand, but knew was ill-suited for sustenance as it burned in their gullets.

Brom turned against the attacking priests, catching one on the temple with the whirling chain and sending him into instant oblivion. The enraged clan-king caught another priest across the chest, robbing him of air, while a third closed with dagger in hand. An eaglet lunged forth and cut into its erstwhile guardian's side, dragging him down into the nest where he was quickly dissected, intestines dined upon like worms as they slopped forth in grotesque display. The chicks slurped his blood and meat with inhuman fervor in vain attempt to sooth their flaming guts.

The other priests retreated upon witnessing the fates of their brothers, and Brom took the opportunity to turn his links upon the hatchlings. The heavy chain lashed out thrice over with immeasurable strength, each strike leaving a smear of crimson and cloud of downy feather.

As Brom stood reveling in destruction and death, drunk on power gifted to him by totem essence, a shadow fell upon him and with but that scarcely detectable warning his instincts for survival became an irresistible tyrant. In a split second he fell prone, narrowly avoiding the mammoth talons that sought to clutch his shoulders and carry him away to certain doom.

Brom's blood chilled as he gazed overhead to see the sun blotted from the sky. A massive form with seventy-foot wingspan glided on the winds in horrific majesty; Eeyuu the demonic eagle come to rescue its distressed chicks—moments too late. The clan-king knew its anger would be unquenchable, and that his peril had just escalated ten-fold. Brom noticed that the entire Eagle Clan lay bowing low, groveling on the rocks, fear overwhelming them all.

As he watched the great eagle circle around, Brom, too, felt fear. He sought and found solace in the strength of the bear totem and the hard steel in his hand. His back yet burned from the incision made by the ceremonial obsidian dagger, and his eyes sought eagerly for the instrument of that cut; quickly he found the blade. Although not the quality of a steel edge, it felt good as it shared a place in his grip with the chain. He eyed its precise point; he felt ready to wage war.

Mighty Eeyuu was no mere bird of prey. It circled again, made a pass on high to survey the altar, knowing its offspring were all dead. Brom surmised it had also sensed the essence of Barshakk coursing through him and would perceive that he was no ordinary foe; yet the eagle remained undeterred. It banked and loosed a demonic screech that froze the blood of all hearing its paralyzing sorcery—all save Brom, spared by the grace of the witch-blood.

Eeyuu dove at a steep angle, ready to snatch the man and avenge its eaglets. Brom squatted beneath the low walls of the altar and hid his battle preparations. A sorcerous wave of Eeyuu's arrogance hammered at him, its confidence in its domination and carelessness of his threat simply the first assault. Both knew the reach of its talons were formidable and the outcome seemed inevitable. The demon-bird would have its revenge. It would feast on the entrails meant for its offspring.

But the proud clan-king did not hide in fear, and sprang forth in the last instant to face this ultimate challenge. Brom launched himself onto the narrow lip of the curved altar wall, and stood defiant, chain in hands, its trailing end hidden behind the wall.

The large, golden eyes of Eeyuu blazed as twin suns into its quarry, burning with desire to inflict well-deserved punishment. But Brom did not wilt beneath that gaze, as a lesser man surely would; he accepted the challenge, and for the pride of the Bear Clan he yearned for victory.

Eeyuu closed in as Brom steadied himself for the clash. The great eagle adjusted its attack to lead with its beak, and the clan-king heaved upon the chain with the demonic strength lent by Barshakk, twirling its links in one tight loop before paying out its length with deceptive speed. The heavy mass arced high over head, then fell upon Eeyuu, its end wrapped around one of the heavy chunks of the granite altar face that Brom had cracked free when he thrashed like a tiger in water to break his chains.

For all of Eeyuu's potency in the shadow realm and its demonic lineage, the creature was still hollow boned. The mass of granite that pounded into its head with phenomenal strength crushed the eagle senseless and sent it crashing downward to explode against the altar wall. Its fall shook the edifice violently and sent stones tumbling from the mountainside.

Brom maintained his balance upon the narrow altar ledge, and stared down at the gargantuan carcass that had once been the fabulously insidious Eeyuu. He surveyed the wreckage amid a storm of feathers. The head was a rough hemisphere of beak, blood, bone, and brain; its neck had compacted and contorted, vertebrae shattered. Its two eyes lay sprawled, revealing their overtly massive sizes, now free of skull. They were punctured sacs oozing jelly, thick cords hanging limp and trailing off, disconnected from the brain. The wings were disjointed, sprawled at odd, unnatural angles. He considered the demonic bird of prey with solemn awe, and was humbled by its majesty even in mutilated death.

Mere seconds ago the demon had been the likely harbinger of his doom. Now it was a trophy, vindication that none should defy the Bear Clan, and that the Eagle Clan should join the confederation of Bear, Wolf, and Elk in obeisance to Brom. He would ensure they followed his rule.

A cloud of ensanguined feathers covered the plateau, left all onlookers stunned; none moved save a slim man with crooked staff who chanted low ritual prayer as he ascended the steep, rough hewn steps toward the mountain shelf.

Brom set upon the once-potent high priest, who clenched his ruptured arm and whimpered in pain. The clan-king bared his teeth in fierce rictus and allowed Utanak a quick look at the instrument of his demise—the obsidian, sacrificial dagger. "It seems your demonic liege no longer requires your services," he snarled. A single stab and the high priest breathed no more.

The king's guards remained crouched as Brom approached the throne, and the Eagle Clan-king himself merely accepted his fate, remaining motionless and slack-jawed on his wicker chair, eyes fixed to the lifeless feathered fiend he had worshipped and revered for so long. The sacrificial dagger plunged deep into his chest and snapped.

Brom shrugged off any guilt over these killings, for he knew if the Eagle Clan was to loyally serve his confederation, new authority from within would be needed. It was the only way. As with all the barbaric clans of Fohktouhl, internecine fighting was a means of life. Within this clan, there would be sympathizers who understood the value and necessity of uniting all the clans for the great war to come. The priest that had died bringing the parchment rubbing to the Bear Clan must have been one of them. They would be put to good use.

At a sound behind him, Brom spun to greet the cloaked figure mumbling ritual prayers above the carcass of Eeyuu, only to be ignored. He watched the man fall upon the gargantuan bird, and with his own ceremonial dagger cut a talon free. An owl flew down to rest on the man's shoulder.

"You have served your clan well," the man stated.

"With your guidance, as always, Oktuun," King Brom replied.

He turned west to face the falling sun, staring out over the larger plateau beneath him and the hills beyond. Grimacing from the pain of the gash along his back and the lacerations caused by the beaks of Eeyuu's offspring, he let out a bellow of triumph that echoed across the landscape. His work was done.

Far below, the Eagle Clan remained on their knees, many thousands bowed in submission. Feathers drifted light as snow upon them as Brom's clansmen filed in, standing among the already docile, recently freed children of Eeyuu.

Brom and Oktuun comprised a fifth of the expedition led by a guide with glowstone. Delving deep into the Axehead Mountains, where relics of the Eagle Clan were hidden in ancient tombs of kings, they hoped to find the origin of the rubbing that had led Brom to place himself on the Altar of Eeyuu. It was learned that the priest who discovered the relic confided only in his brother, and then left that very next night to seek out King Brom for reasons unknown. None had journeyed to this vault since. At Oktuun's pressing for spiritual knowledge, Brom agreed to seek out the original.

It took many hours of wandering with several trackers of the Wolf Clan before they eventually found the secret portal from which led a long narrow hall. It ended in two gilded doors inscribed with an eagle's head and scripture from the old tongue which Oktuun assured condemned and blasphemed the demon. Beyond, a vast chamber housed a monolithic representation of Eeyuu, of life-sized stature in minute detail, and below the sculpture was the etching from which the rubbing had been made.

Brom frowned as he gazed upon it, seeing for the first time features that had been burnt from the rubbing. The sacrifice was now fully illustrated—clearly depicting fourteen bat skulls above the victims head in two semi-circles of seven, attached by thin lines construed as braids. Of all the clans, Brom alone sported fourteen bat skulls, and as such was heralded throughout The Broken Kingdom. The priest who first discovered the prophecy must have certainly known this, and so determined to deliver it to the Bear Clan.

King Brom immediately realized the implications. He had not made use of superstition and legend to impose his will upon the Eagle Clan; they were not even aware of this long forgotten prophecy. The prophecy had ordained that he would come and slay Eeyuu, and so he had. He felt smaller then, as when The Serpentine Witch had imposed her will upon him in exchange for his virility.

Were my deeds not heroic? Did I not squelch my own fears to savor the victory of courage and reap spoils for my clan and all the clans of Fohktouhl? Or was I merely moved as a game piece by the gods, pulled by the strings of their whims, pushed by the folly of their desires?

Brom's soul railed against a sudden weight of despair as he swore and solemnly ordered the chamber sealed for all time. Though this was done, the men that knew him well noted a taint that persisted upon his spirit for many years. Some would call it a burden, some a shadow, some a curse—but none would dispute its presence.

The Bear, Wolf, Elk, and Eagle

Clans were now united, and all acknowledged Brom's successes. Only Oktuun
truly understood the great personal toll
uniting them had exacted upon the one
they called their king.

Christopher Heath
lives in Indiana and has been writing fantasy for over a decade, either as a
role-playing game designer under the official Dungeons and Dragons logo or
producing short stories and novels for his Azieran fantasy world. These works
have seen publication in over thirty venues, including professional pay rate
sales to Kenzer and Company, Fantasist Enterprises, and Pitch-Black Books.

BORN WARRIORS

by TW Williams

The demon's eyes glowed as it circled the tiny chamber, stirring the pale fog. Like a miniature cyclone of impotent rage, it careened around the crystal prison, swirling the milky essence, finding no release.

Its hatred was a thin, bitter draught, one that the demon had steeped in for an eternity—or a moment. Time, bereft of freedom, had no meaning.

Humans have ever been my *playthings*, it sulked. *Yet here I am, in thrall, treated not even as a pet. Pets and draft animals might be coddled or beaten. Even a battle-demon was despised and feared. None were simply* ignored. That thought sent the creature into a fresh paroxysm of rage that sent sheets of light spinning and flashing from its prison.

Narrowing its cats' eyes, the demon extended its senses beyond the transparent walls. Jostled as it was in the cask on the Hairy Man's back, the task was one that demanded concentration. The demon's scaly brow furrowed with effort—and salvation came, unheeding, unsummoned, stubbornly fighting its way across the rolling plains, a tiny clot of strangers, alone in a vast land. So few, but brimming with iron will and cold determination.

If a spectator I must be, the demon chortled, *at least I will be entertained.*

Recoiling at the touch of the magic-infused crystal, the demon redoubled its attempt and a thin sheen of evil intelligence penetrated the adamantine surface like a flake of mold on bread. A thumbnail's breadth, the patch represented almost all of the demon's will. From it, one slender thread of malicious energy extended, wafting on the storm-laden air.

There! Well hidden, almost buried. That's the lure!

The demon pulled delicately on the tiny thread of hope, reeling in its catch. At the same time, it tickled the mind of its cloddish master, pointing out the foe.

187

The storm boomed overhead and with it the sound of the screams increased. Waves of Hairy Men, by the dozens and scores, swept up the low rise. Kyr Kingslayer pivoted left, feinted farther left and brought his curved tulwar around to slice deep through the scaly hide into the gut of a bellowing demon.

That wouldn't finish it, Kyr knew. He thrust upward, his blade seeking the battle-demon's heart. A steaming gush of red-black blood signaled that he had found his mark.

One of his marks. Slashing down and to the left, the tulwar's tip found the creature's secondary heart, and the demon finally died.

Kyr spun, face to face with a screaming Hairy Man, and stabbed viciously. The man's howl rose an octave then ended abruptly as he fell into the muck, vainly trying to hold in the gush of intestines.

Kyr stepped back into the line of his men and planted his feet wide as two more Hairy Men charged. He took a breath, coolly devising his next move, knowing he had time to check the men of his Pentiad—all fifty where they should be: shoulder to shoulder, two deep and five across, then, angling, five again and again until the pentagon was formed. The kneeling front rank bore shields and swords—as First, he alone stood. Spearmen whose shields overlapped their kneeling comrades stood in the second rank.

The roar of thunder and a hissing scythe of rain and hail should have deadened the battle's sounds but the enemy's shrieks of rage and wailing pain instead intensified as the Hairy Men crashed against the shield wall. Dozens fell, maimed and dying, but sheer numbers caved in the pentagon, and the battle disintegrated into knots of men wreaking havoc and hell.

Coolly, Kyr ducked a wildly aimed axe cut as two warriors lunged toward him. He shouldered the first man backward, then brought hilt and mailed fists up to ruin the second man's face. Dropping to a knee, he hamstrung the reeling fighter and spun, chopping the axeman's left leg off at the knee.

A stab to the throat dispatched the lamed man; a cut to the shoulder finished his one-legged comrade.

Kyr parried a blow, killed another Hairy Man with a slash of his tulwar. Out of the corner of his eye, he caught a glimmer of light where there should have been none, and turned that direction. A huge foeman, all leather and iron with a wolf pelt across his shoulders, fended off Kyr's darting warriors. He was almost as big as the battle-demon, Kyr thought, and wielded a two-handed axe like it was a mere twig.

A crystal cask about the size of a fire log was slung on his back, and that vessel swam with milky radiance—the mysterious light Kyr had noticed.

"None can best Aegus Wolfclaw!" the big man roared, his deep voice rumbling beneath the scream of the storm. "I am demon-blessed! Yield to me!"

Kyr dashed water out of his eyes and sidled closer, like a panther in human form, the blow that would part the loud man's ribs already imprinted in his mind. Coiling his muscles, he sprang—just as the axe-man pivoted. Twisting in mid-leap, Kyr avoided the axe blow. His own slash went wide, slicing the harness that secured the cask and sending it tumbling to the muddy ground.

A flash of lightning and roar of thunder dazzled Kyr for a moment, and he furiously blinked sight back into his eyes. The big man fled, screaming, and the rest of the Hairy Men were retreating too—stumbling over one another in their haste.

No Hairy Men were left nearby and Kyr was struck with faint surprise, as always at such times: The battle was over, and he lived.

Kyr nudged the fallen cask with an iron-shod foot. Curious to bring such a thing into battle. There would be time to examine it later—priorities must be observed.

A glance left, then right, counting heads. No hurry; the Hairy Men were in full flight. *Stinking fools. They still outnumber us at least three to one.*

His grim tally was quick: A dozen missing out of his Pentiad. Slender, serious swordsman Ular; brawny spearman Avun, his wild red hair a rarity among the People, Tinglu, Gorl…he knew each face, each name. Bile rose in Kyr's throat and he swallowed harshly.

What is the point in staining my life with emotion? You are; you do. Then, at some point, you are not.

Thirty-eight still standing—not bad, Kyr told himself, then remembered that they were alone, lost deep in enemy territory—so not good, either.

The People's Army, ten-score Pentiads, had moved east into these steppes, an exploration of conquest. His fifty men had been sent out to scout to the north as the army ground ever eastward, seeking cities and ports, trade routes and mines.

Kyr had found Hairy Men, and lost his way. He was the leader, so the blame was his—as was the shame.

He spared a cold glance at the fallen enemy. Still, not bad. There must be at least four dozens of Hairy Men dead on the battlefield, and perhaps that many

more wounded, who, in moments, would join their comrades in death.

Thankfully, there had been only one battle-demon, a creature Kyr had heard of, but never before encountered. The thing, he knew, had agreed to fight on the Hairy Men's side in exchange for reaper's rights—the opportunity to harvest the souls of the dead, both friend and foe. The demon had gambled that it could fight on this plane, where it was mortal, and had lost that bet.

The storm's sound thundered onward, even louder now that the battle was over. *Over? Suspended for now, perhaps. Battle was never over.*

Kyr remembered the cask and walked briskly to it, careful to keep his posture erect, careful to show his men that he remained strong.

The cask began whispering.

Something peered from the squat cylinder. *Well met,* a voice spoke in his head. *And well-played.*

Kyr started, almost dropping his sword. Swearing silently at his lack of control, he squatted, examining the cask and the eyes studying him.

So, a demon. Yet not a battle-demon, nothing like the scarlet-befanged, seven-foot ebon monstrosity he had just killed. This was something small and puny, and, most telling, captive, and therefore weak.

Eyes with black irises around red, cat-like pupils met his with malevolent intelligence.

The container, bound with silver bands, was filled with a swirling, milky light. One end flared to a short neck stopped by a ruby the size of a plum. The demon's face, grotesquely distorted by the cask, pressed against the glass, tongue lolling.

Not distorted—grotesque by its

very nature, Kyr decided.

My apologies for scaring *you,* the whisper said: the faint sneer threaded among the soft words. Kyr flushed angrily. Mustering pride, he thought his reply.

I am Kyr, First of a Pentiad of the People, and it takes more than a demon stuffed in a bucket to scare me.

"And what truck do the People have with demons?"

Kyr looked up into the face of Trem, his near-cousin and Second. No kin-love there, Kyr knew, just duty: A Second was expected to question his First privately, obey him unquestioning in public, for no single man was unflawed.

The demon's eyes shifted between the two officers.

"It whispers…" Kyr hesitated. What *was* it whispering? "It promises… " He stopped again. The creature hadn't promised anything.

Turning his back on the cask, Kyr laughed harshly to convince Trem—to convince himself, too, he admitted. "It speaks of immortality and, as all such creatures, foul and twisted, its words have no spine. They are shadows, ill dreams, lies!"

He clenched a blood-stained fist and waved it in the Second's face. "*This* is our immortality. Our legacy lives in our enemy's pain, their missing limbs, their daughters taken, their sons enslaved, their fathers missing from hearth and table!"

The storm roared, nature's fury collapsing under its own weight, falling in on itself, doubling in size. Thunder and lightning crashed and flared around him. Kyr staggered in the storm's din. He sheathed his sword and covered his ears with his hands.

As his battle-drained men staggered and fell, the fury of the storm drove Kyr to his knees, and his greaves crunched against the ribs of the last man he had slain. He knelt there, in the ruin of his enemy, bowing his head before the onslaught of the storm, as the demon's whispers cut through the torrent in sharp, bitter bursts.

Trem shouted, his words lost in the chaos.

And the Hairy Men came again, wave upon wave. Screaming, red-eyed, furious.

Kyr whipped out his sword, burying it quickly in a spearman's groin. "Is this demon-crafted or nature-spawned?" he muttered, slashing again. It all came down to the same, either way: The storm simply *was.* And thus, it must be endured.

The second attack was fierce yet short, with the same result: The Hairy Men fled, leaving a fresh dozen bodies sprawled on the battlefield.

Belatedly, Kyr realized the cask and its unwholesome occupant were gone as well. He shuddered a sigh—the most he would allow himself to vent his frustration.

Four more men gone. Only four? That surprised him—it seemed that the whole purpose of the attack had been to retrieve the demon. *Let the Hairy Men dabble in slimy magic and hot rage. The People will depend, as they always do, on hard muscle and cold steel*

An echo whispered in his mind: *You're down to thirty-four.*

The demon's cunning hints twisted through Kyr's mind.

Root. Twine. Grow, grow, grow until there is no chance to dislodge them.

The best lies were born in truth.

Kyr chose himself as scout.

"Not your role, First," Trem said. "And we have no need to stay here. We need to keep moving."

Kyr shrugged. "A leader is as capable as any of his men, *has* to be that and more, and I must see with my own eyes, must understand. And we've been moving for a month. Tonight we stay here."

Trem glowered, thrusting out his lip—a familiar pose since their boyhood games. "You spoke truth before the last attack. That demon's words are worms, wriggling, helpless, shriveling in the hot sun, and…"

"Put the men in a defensive position and feed them—full rations," Kyr interrupted. "They deserve it after two battles." And with sixteen less mouths to feed than when they broke their fast this morning, he thought bitterly, full rations might last a week longer.

He turned without a backward glance, feeling his Second's gaze on his back, knowing his orders would be obeyed.

Kyr found the rhythm of a steady trot, the beginnings of a new storm raking the back of his neck, static electricity crackling in his dark, shaggy hair and the chill of the demon's hiss dancing along his spine.

A short time later, he crested the next in an endless series of rolling ridges. Dim light and deep shadow painted the night as the moon and thick clouds played a restless game of hide-and-seek. A ruddy smear painted the sky ahead, and Kyr dropped to his belly.

An arrogant man, Kyr thought, or a fool, to light a campfire as a beacon to enemy eyes.

He moved cautiously toward the crimson light and smelled horses and sweat and roasted meat. Crawling on his belly to the top of the next ridge, he realized that the contours of the land and some trick of perspective had hidden part of the glow: Not a foolish scout's campfire, but the enemy camp, dozens upon dozens of tents pitched in haphazard and slovenly fashion.

Not arrogance, nor even foolishness, he realized—just numbers. Hundreds of Hairy Men.

Kyr edged closer. His gaze was drawn to the largest of the tents, a gaudy affair, red and white silks shimmering and billowing. A wolf's skull, fringed by dozens of gilded claws, was mounted on a staff at the tent's entrance. A half-dozen wolf's tails, the tips also gold-dipped, dangled from the shaft.

If he could slay the leader—and the big tent with its decorations bespoke a chieftain—then the hordes of Hairy Men might lose heart and wander off. He had seen it happen before.

That's what the People do, Kyr told himself. Seize advantage where none existed; change long odds to certain victory through persistence.

The fools, bloated and careless by their numbers, had spread sentries too far apart, or perhaps Kyr had found a gap where a sentinel had fallen down drunk or left his post for a piss or a jug.

He breathed a mix of relief and scorn—even if he commanded ten times his number of men, he wouldn't be so neglectful of their lives. Kyr worked his way to the left for long seconds, until a rustle signaled the next guard.

The man's spear was leaning against a tree; he was leaning against another, trying to stay awake by humming some atonal tune that, against all Kyr's training, still managed to grate against his nerves. *Nah-nah-nah naaaaaaah. Nah-nah, nah-nah.* It would be satisfying to end that droning chant.

Kyr slid through the darkness, footfalls muted by a carpet of pine needles. Finally behind the humming man, he drew his dagger, and the blade flashed left to right then back again. The hum died in a gurgle; the iron tang of blood and the stench of released bowels fouling the fresh, sharp aroma of the pines.

The gap between sentries was more than enough for him to sneak through. Kyr grimaced: More than enough to slip his entire Pentiad through.

Pentiad no longer. Thirty-four, now sitting, exposed, a few hours from here.

A feeling of suffocation rose in Kyr's throat; he forced it away.

Kyr darted between shadows until he crouched outside the big tent. He paused, feeling the weight of scrutiny, and strained his ears. Far-off sounds of drunken singing—no prettier than the sentry's tune—the clash of cooking pots, coarse jokes, mock swordplay. Closer still, footsteps, then the hiss of urine as someone emptied his bladder against the side of a tent. A groan of relief, then steps stumbling away into the darkness.

No one raised an alarm. *No guards at the leader's tent?* Kyr wondered at that, counting a score of heartbeats, then another, then a third. As he slipped inside the tent, the rumble of thunder rolled across the camp.

It was dim inside, the tent lit by a single wick guttering in a bowl of oil atop a chest. Kyr could make out the bulky shape of a man snoring soundly on a mound of furs. Emptied leather flasks and stone bottles lay about the tent like slaughtered soldiers. He inched closer, eyes adjusting to the faint light.

He recognized the sleeping man—it *was* the same bellowing fool who had carried the demon into battle.

Aegus Wolfclaw shifted in his sleep. Kyr froze, but the snoring didn't change. Silently, he drew his blade and prepared to slash the chieftain's throat. He paused as he saw the man was cradling the cask against his chest.

The demon-cask would explain the lack of bodyguards, Kyr realized. *Superstitious fools!*

He raised his dagger.

The sleeping man snorted and hiccoughed and Kyr sprang away, blade poised. After ten long breaths, the Hairy Man settled back in, clenching the bottle tighter.

Against all training, Kyr crept closer, looking into the flask. The demon's blood-red serpent's tongue flickered across blackened lips that stretched into mockery of a smile.

Once-met is chance, the mind-whisper said. *Twice-met is destiny.* Its tone became softer in Kyr's mind, servile, fawning. Kyr thought he detected the faintest laughter in the shadow of the whisper. *Your so-called "People" must be strong indeed, it hissed, to have spawned such a mighty warrior.* Scorn drenched the words.

We are warriors born, Kyr replied, pride flaring. *You would never find us trapped in a glass barrel to do a Hairy Man's bidding.*

The thing laughed at him.

Kyr shook himself. Why was he chatting with a demon? He knew himself; taunting an inferior didn't make him stronger. Trem was right—he didn't need the demon's trickery at all. He had a mission to accomplish, and it had nothing to do with demons. He raised his blade.

Wait! The whisperer begged, almost whining. *If you kill Aegus Wolfclaw where does that leave me?*

Stuck in your bucket.

He shifted to get a clear angle at the sleeping man's neck. Every second brought a chance for interruption. It was time to end this now. Outside the tent, the thunder rumbled and Kyr could hear the wind picking up. His escape would be easier if timed to the storm's first lash.

Wait, please wait, the demon whispered in his mind. *If you leave me trapped here, the next pelt-covered poltroon will simply keep me as a charm or talisman. Furry dolts! They think that having a demon is the same as using a demon. You are wiser.*

My powers can help a cunning warrior, the mind-voice gushed. *A warrior like you. A born warrior.* The red-black lips simpered within the crystal and the tongue flickered once, then again.

Kyr hesitated, flattered despite his feelings of distrust and revulsion, and then thrust the thought away. The People didn't need demons. Discipline, duty and steel were enough. Still…

I can grant your wish, the demon promised. *I know your wish; I see it in your heart—your puny band huddled in the dark. So few. What if you could live forever? That would not only get you back to your precious army, but make you a general. A lord! An emperor, with your band of immortals around you!*

All I ask in return is that, after you kill this hairy king-thing, you pluck the stopper from this cask. We'll go our separate ways.

"I can go my separate way without releasing you," Kyr replied, aloud. Still, he shrugged, there was nothing to lose with the asking. This night would end with a dead Hairy Man chieftain and him safely away, whether the demon spoke truth or not.

Matching actions to thoughts, Kyr snatched up the cask and slung it over his shoulder. His sword swept down, and a spray of blood drenched the furs.

"Their chieftain is dead," Kyr told Trem. "Likely that means disarray, and buys time for us to move away. We leave at dawn. This time we won't stop until we find the People's Army." Under his Second's gaze, he couldn't bring himself to say "retreat."

Trem didn't seem to hear. He stared at the crystal cask. "And this ill-spawn? What of it?"

"Listen!" Kyr said. Shaking the cask, he hissed. "My terms."

I know. I hope immortality serves you well. Kill many, many Hairy Men. The demon's laugh was cruel mockery of all things joyous.

Kyr rested his hand on the ruby knob, listening coldly and carefully as the thing swore its oath. For good measure, he made the creature repeat it.

"See, Second? No harm done, and perhaps some good."

Kyr pulled the ruby stopper, then tossed container and ruby at Trem's feet. The Second frowned as the milky essence wafted from the container and shredded on the winds.

Kyr thought of the scores of tents he had seen. Telling Trem to wake him an hour before dawn, he fell asleep in a few heartbeats and dreamt of long iron swords and heavy axes whittling the Pentiad like a knife carves pine kindling.

The winds across the steppes shrilled a demon's laugh as they marched south and east. They made good time before the storms and Hairy Men caught up with them.

The leader's death had emboldened the Hairy Men, not discouraged them.

His strategy had been mistaken and the demon had lied.

Breck dead, as was old Turlan, and, even more irreplaceable, his kinsman Trem, his Second, as well as six others.

My Pentiad is at half strength, and the demon had lied.

Trem, who had been overdue for his own Pentiad, if ever they should regain the main army. Kyr swore. *When* they regained the main army.

Of those still standing, none were without cuts and bruises and a few were worse—Chemyu looked like he might lose an eye, Mekim, the Pentiad's Third, held his shield arm at an odd angle. Dislocated, maybe broken, Kyr thought, and, as their eyes met, he raised his sword in salute, the blood fast cooling in the rain, washed away before it could dry as it ran down the blade and across his clenched grip.

Mekim, eyes devoid of expression, raised an equally gory sword and returned the gesture. He was Second now, and if that thought pleased him, the emotion didn't reach his face any more than did the pain from his wounded arm—duty first, always.

The demon had lied.

Kyr let his shield drop, flicked raindrops out of eyes with his free hand. Mekim deserved a few words to settle him in the new role and Kyr found them.

"It is the same each time we face this enemy," he said, drawing near.

"Defenders fill the air with their screams, while the Pentiads of the People stand firm. The foes' rage runs red-hot, yet shatters always against the People's will. Just like their blades shatter against the steel of the People's armor. And of the People's will."

Nine men lost, where there should have been none. Kyr reproached himself for indulging in disappointment, yet was angrier still that he had been deceived, and angriest because he had dared hope.

"And what truck do the People have with demons?" Trem's words echoed in his mind.

None, cousin. None at all.

Kyr raised his head and peered across the battlefield. In the gloaming, the plains before him were like an overturned chest from the heart of the Eleven Hells. Broken spears, swords, shields. Broken bodies, indecent in a hundred postures of death, jawbones ripped from faces, revealing grins that none could have smiled in life.

The moon was coming up, nearly full, bright in the sky. Instead of masking the carnage, it seemed to accent it, turning the blood black, the bones incandescent.

Amid the devastation, there was a faint milky-red swirl, where none should have been.

He ordered campfires to be lit, and went alone to investigate. A small boy stood in the center of the pale ruby glow, naked, smooth skin shining in the ruddy light. Two years at the most, Kyr estimated. As he watched, the glow seemed to dissolve into the last swaths of the sunset, yet a familiar *something* clung to the boy.

The tiny lad's dark eyes were studying him from beneath shaggy bangs, as quiet and expressionless as one of the People.

Kyr hawked battle grit from his throat, spitting rust-colored phlegm. "Who are you, lad, and how come you here?"

The boy turned, wobbling on colt's legs to the far side of the battleground, stopping before a mound of Hairy Men bodies. Slipping, he climbed to the top and pointed into the heap.

Trem's neck had been cut almost through, but his face seemed undamaged, at peace. The boy peered at Kyr, then stuck out his lower lip, a pout both eerily familiar and yet misplaced on the chubby face.

Two dozen shouts interrupted Kyr's thoughts as pale crimson clouds eddied and swirled across the battleground. So it was not just today's dead, but yesterday's as well.

Immortality! Damn the demon for keeping its promise!

The final shreds of the storm were mumbling in the distance. Kyr stared at the clouds, rippling here and there with milky flashes of heat lightning, thinking. Toddlers in a day, full-grown again in a week. Ready for battle.

With sudden insight, he realized that, when grown, they would be killed only to be born again, all for a demon's amusement and bloodlust. And the Pentiad would take baby steps toward the People's Army, yet never draw nearer.

Kyr's howl was a mixture of defiance and despair.

His curses woke the babies, and they began to cry.

TW Williams lives in suburban Chicago and whines more than he should about the weather and traffic. His fantasy and science fiction stories have appeared in numerous anthologies and magazines and you can learn more about them at http://sites.google.com/site/twfiction/. He and his precious wife Lynne have five interesting and intelligent children and a cat that is both amusing and annoying.

MISTAKEN IDENTITY

by Robert J. Santa

Mauriel blasted the demon with energy. She held the jade ball with both hands, and it fought her as it poured out its power.

The demon howled and threw its limbs about. Twice its flailing arms contacted its body, and the demon's sharp claws tore ugly gashes in its hip and chest. Its tail thrashed and beat the ground, chunks of stone flying away.

Arms before its face, the demon tried to lunge away from the torrent of magical fire. Mauriel's binding held its feet firmly on the exposed bedrock, aided by the strength of the holy site. The Priests of Xo were no more, yet it was forever a testament to their abilities that their ritual circles continued without them.

Mauriel felt her heart racing. With each breath, her lungs ached more and more, as if she were leaning over a blacksmith's forge and inhaling the smoke of the melting iron. She knew she had only moments left before the portal she had opened consumed her life-force. She asked the jade ball for more energy, and it obliged with no more complaint than a simple jerking attempt to free itself.

The fires turned from emerald green to starry-night blue. The demon's painful howling also changed, to a wail of terrified agony. It dropped to its knees and dug at the ground. Bits of its claws broke off in the scars on the stone until it stopped scratching and clutched the earth. Its shoulders buckled, and its back trembled. A heartbeat later, its tail stilled, and the demon lowered its head until it touched the ground.

Mauriel silenced the jade ball and stumbled, tripping over her scabbard until she collapsed beside the demon. She lay heavily on her side, her head resting on her shoulder. Her eyelids lowered like a sunset, and she lost consciousness.

The hold on the demon's feet broke. It fell forward onto its chest, its palms and face flat against the stone. It tried to rise several times, failing with every attempt. It crawled the distance separating it and Mauriel. The demon stretched out its hand and placed its claws on her belly.

"Mauriel," said the demon weakly. It shook her, and her eyelids fluttered.

"Mauriel," the demon repeated. This time her eyes opened, though with little light behind them.

"Tomas." She blinked and trained her eyes on the demon's face. "Oh, darling, I'm sorry."

Tomas stretched out on his side, facing her. His hand stayed on her belly.

"You tried your best," he said.

"I thought the jade ball would be the key."

"As did I."

Mauriel's gaze wandered down Tomas' torso.

"Oh," she gasped. "You're hurt."

"Think nothing of it; the wound is not serious. In any event, it will be healed by nightfall. If there is a bright side to all this, it would have to be this body's recuperative abilities."

Mauriel leaned her head in and kissed him on the jaw. Tomas nuzzled her, unable to kiss back without lips.

"Can you stand?" Tomas asked.

"Let me rest some more," she replied.

"As you wish, my love. Go ahead and sleep."

And she did.

When Mauriel awoke, it was within the glowing radiance of a shallow fire pit. She saw that it was dug out of the bare rock, and the timber in the flames was a shattered stump. She smiled and stood.

The world spun. Mauriel took a half step that failed to restore her balance. The edges of her vision blurred down to a single spot: the fire pit that rushed at her as she fell.

Tomas' arm wrapped around her

middle, and it was as if Mauriel fell against a stone balcony.

"I have you," he said. Mauriel smiled again and let herself be carried away from the fire. Tomas set her down with her back against one of the standing stones of the site.

"Thank you," she said when he crouched down beside her.

"Did I hurt you?"

Mauriel reached down and touched the front of her robe. There was a small rip tinged with crimson.

"Only slightly," she replied.

Tomas drove his fist into the standing stone, leaving a fair-sized crater. Then he flexed his hand.

"These damn fingers!" he said. "I'm still not used to their arrangement. I'm so sorry."

"It's a scratch."

"I'm sick to death of not being able to use my hands."

"Darling," Mauriel said with a smile stretching her face, "you would think not being able to use your hands would be the least of your worries." She glanced down at the demon's sexless front, and it was Tomas' turn to smile, though without any lips it came across as an open-mouthed exposing of too many sharp teeth.

"I'm not the only one of us who doesn't get the opportunity to use it, my sweet."

"Touché." Mauriel blinked her eyes that were suddenly heavy. "I guess I'm weaker than I thought."

"That was a powerful casting."

"Not powerful enough." Mauriel stroked the side of the demonic face, the cheeks being the only part not studded with bony protrusions. Tomas closed his eyes and let the caress soak into him.

"I was certain the jade ball would

have enough energy." Tomas lifted it and held it out to Mauriel. She balanced it in her palm. A novice would have been able to tell it was drained, for it rested in her hand like any other stone. She willed the jade ball to release itself, and it did nothing.

"If not the jade ball," Mauriel said, "then what?"

"I know not." Tomas squatted and propped himself on his tail. He put his elbows on his knees and rested his chin in his hands. They sat quietly for a moment and thought.

"Does the Sultan of Qaam-ru still have his scepter?" asked Mauriel after a long while.

"He might," Tomas replied. "There was some ugliness with that duo. You recall them? The big one and the little one?"

"Yes, yes. From down south."

"That's the pair. There was a rumor going around last year that they stole many of the Sultan's most prized possessions, including a daughter, if I'm not mistaken."

"How scandalous. The scepter was among those possessions?"

"I don't know for certain. It's not as if the Sultan published a list of the stolen items."

"Maybe we should head that way," suggested Mauriel.

The demon rolled his red eyes.

"That's a long way, just to see," he said, "bearing in mind that there's no guarantee the Sultan would let us use the scepter even if it were there."

"I can be very persuasive when I try," she replied, and the demon smiled, another ugly baring of fangs.

"It is one of the many reasons why I love you so," said Tomas. He leaned in to nuzzle her again.

"Get back, demon!"

Tomas whirled at the same time Mauriel stood. From the corner of his eye, he saw her reach a hand out to the stone for support before fainting forward. Tomas tried to catch her, but the voice shouted again.

"Stand fast!"

The demon looked at the approaching figure. He was powerfully-built, with wide shoulders centered by a neck as thick as a normal man's thigh. He wore a sleeveless, leather jerkin, and the arms that held a bared sword bore mounds of hard muscle. His jet black hair was tied in a simple braid bound by strips of leather. His pants were buckskin, and were it not for the remarkable sword, Tomas would have thought the man no more than a primitive.

The blade fairly shimmered. It was more than the fact that it was held in those powerful arms. It was more than the cleanliness of the sword, without so much as a speck of dust tarnishing the metal where the man himself was covered from head to toe with the grime of travel. And it was more than the ease with which the man held the sword, effortlessly, the way a girl would hold a freshly-picked dandelion.

The sword was an instrument of death. The man knew it, and so secure was his knowledge that Tomas couldn't help but know it as well.

Tomas glanced back down at Mauriel. She had struck the ground hard, and the naked rock had cut her upper lip. Blood trickled out of her open mouth.

"Get away from the girl!" commanded the man. "By One-Eyed Jorl, don't make me say it again. Engage with me, demon, and meet your end at Na-Arak's hand."

"You don't understand," Tomas said,

and the barbarian reacted with stunned surprise.

"You speak." Na-Arak shifted the sword slightly but continued to advance until he was no more than six long strides away.

"Of course. I am not a demon but a man merely in its form."

"Cease your trickery, demon. I warned you that I did not wish to speak again of your position. Decide now whether you will move by your will or mine."

Tomas sighed. He stepped straight away from Mauriel and allowed the swordsman to approach her. With eyes still on Tomas, Na-Arak dropped one of his hands and lifted Mauriel under the arms with as little apparent difficulty as he held the sword. He carried her backward to a block of stone and laid her comfortably upon it, her scabbard angled across her legs.

"Do you feel better now?" asked Tomas.

"The girl is safe. I am contented by this."

"If Mauriel heard you call her a 'girl,' I assure you that you would be anything but contented."

"Is Mauriel your master, demon?"

"No," Tomas said, though his exasperation came out as a hiss. "She is my future bride."

"Such an unholy bond! I cannot permit this abomination."

Na-Arak pounced like a great cat, his arms lifting the sword high over his head. He landed not two steps from Tomas and swung the sword straight down as if splitting firewood.

Tomas leapt to the left. The sword came so close to him that he heard the whining complaint of the air being cut. The blade contacted none of Tomas'

body and smashed into the bedrock. Sharp wedges of stone flew away, and the barbarian raised the sword to attack again. Tomas noticed that the metal wasn't so much as nicked.

"This is a mistake," said Tomas, but he threw himself backward as Na-Arak cut across his body. The sword's tip caught Tomas' forearm and opened a small slice. A spray of arterial blue jetted out. Tomas clamped his hand over the wound.

The swordsman pressed his attack, swinging the blade over his shoulder in a diagonal arc. Tomas ducked as the sword sailed past, but Na-Arak shifted his hand position at the bottom of the arc and swung backhanded. The lightning-quick return stroke connected with Tomas' head, shearing two of the bony horns from his right side. Pain blinded him for an instant, and when he recovered, he saw the barbarian spinning around with the sword extended.

Tomas stepped into the cut so that the Na-Arak's arms were all that touched his side. Tomas lowered his hands to push his attacker back and found Na-Arak falling away while clutching at Tomas' wrist. The barbarian dropped and pressed one foot against Tomas' middle. Tomas lost all balance and was flipped over Na-Arak who regained a crouch even before Tomas hit the ground. Tomas spun around and was battered back by the barbarian's charge. His shoulder caught Tomas below the ribs. Tomas was knocked to the ground, and he rolled aside as Na-Arak's sword took another chunk out of the rock.

Tomas flung out his tail and swept the man from his feet. He scrambled away and turned around when he heard Na-Arak rise.

"Please," Tomas cried, holding his

hands out. "Please stop."

"I will not be distracted by your false begging," the barbarian said as he cautiously shuffled closer.

"My name is Tomas, and just so we get something settled, I'm not begging. I just want to talk."

"You tell me your name, demon?" The tip of the sword lowered a finger's length. "Odd that you would sacrifice this security. But it is obvious I am no master of the sorcerous arts and have no way of using your name."

"Blast it all! Just listen to me. My name is Tomas. Mauriel and I were adventuring through the Shiri Pass when we were set upon by a witch and her goblin horde. Before the battle was over, the witch bespelled me in a way that was unfamiliar to Mauriel, who is, incidentally, a master of the sorcerous arts. For months my body changed into this demon form you see. We have spent the last year looking for the way to transform me back."

"An interesting story," said the man, "though I can hardly trust the word of a demon."

"He speaks the truth," said Mauriel. They turned to see her slowly sit up upon the stone block. She wiped her bloody mouth with the back of her hand. "Put away your sword. He will not harm you."

"We may continue to speak," said the swordsman, "but I will not put away my sword."

"As you wish."

"Why a demon?" asked Na-Arak. He side-stepped so that he could see both Mauriel and Tomas without moving more than his eyes.

"I suspect she meant to transform him into something more harmless." Mauriel wiped the flowing blood from her chin with the back of her hand again.

"I interrupted her."

Na-Arak grunted in a way that indicated doubt.

Mauriel gagged and spat upon the stone. The instant her bloody spittle struck the block, it sizzled as if frying in a pan.

The sky darkened in only a few heartbeats, transformed from a bright blue to a black and gray carpet of clouds that rushed in from all horizons. They swirled overhead as if filthy bathwater draining out of a cracked basin.

"This does not bode well," Tomas said as he looked up. In his peripheral vision, he saw the barbarian ready his sword.

"More trickery!" Na-Arak shouted through clenched teeth. "I should have pressed the attack."

"Mauriel?" Tomas said, lifting his voice above the rising wind.

"Looks like something's coming through," she said. She wiped the boiling blood off the block with her palm, but it had no effect on the whirling clouds. "Something big."

Centered over the site of standing stones, the clouds continued to race in tightening spirals. A black void formed at their center, crackling at the edges with electric blue. Dozens of monstrous hands clawed at the rim, as if they were climbing out of a pit

Suddenly a massive set of fists pounded at the smaller hands and arms, driving them back into the void. The screaming of hundreds of demonic voices wailed anger and sadness, but the giant fists continued to beat everything else back. Then they gripped the edge of the void, and the demon that owned the fists jumped out. The void immediately closed behind it and disappeared. The clouds, too, stopped their motion, but all three figures on the ground took no notice as the demon landed among them.

It was five times Tomas' size, who was already three times the size of a man, and stood among them like two logging horses fused into one body. It was disproportioned, so that its giant chest and arms were supported by stunted legs. It had no neck, its head merely sloping up from shoulders as wide apart as two men lying down. Like Tomas, it was covered in bony protrusions, running in straight lines down its arched back and arms. Unlike Tomas, however, it had nothing resembling a human face: no nose, no chin, no symmetry. A wide, frog's mouth studded with teeth like stone chips split its head in half. Seven eyes were as scattered as thrown dice, and varied in size from that of a robin's egg to that of an ale cask. Fur covered its belly. A stubby tail topped its rear. Fat talons spread out like ferns at the end of its legs.

Slobber fell from the demon's mouth as it looked first from Mauriel then to Na-Arak and finally to Tomas.

"Well met, little brother," it said. It looked again at the barbarian. "How good of you to bring me both food," and its gaze lingered on Mauriel, "and pleasure." A forearm's length of flesh stirred beneath the demon's fur. Mauriel moved away from the stone and centered herself.

"Not today," she said, and threw her arms forward. Her thumbs and two fingers formed a triangle. Bright purple light blazed out of the created shape and landed on the demon's combined head and chest. It splashed over the creature, obscuring it. Tomas had seen this casting before. It had laid waste to the witch's goblin army, blasting hundreds of them into dust.

Yet when Mauriel opened her hands and the light faded, the demon stood there unharmed.

"Ah," it said, opening its mouth in what could have been a smile, "I see we will have some sport first."

"Sport with this!" Na-Arak cried as he bounded forward, his radiant sword held with both hands.

"Allow me to show you what that casting is supposed to look like," the demon said. It turned its hand over and opened its palm toward the onrushing swordsman. Where Mauriel's fires had been clearly purple, the demon's were solid white. The casting flashed then disappeared. The demon curled its hand again and rested on its knuckles. Blinding afterimages lingered over Tomas' vision, but when he blinked them clear, he saw that not so much as a handful of ash remained of the barbarian. His beautiful blade was reduced to a puddle of slag.

"The woman is mine," Tomas hissed. The demon looked down at Tomas' front and let loose a choking laugh.

"What could you possibly do with her?" chortled the demon. "Whereas you can see I could clearly find a use." A pink obscenity jutted well out of the demon.

Tomas launched himself at the demon, claws extended. The demon lifted one of its massive arms and swatted him away without so much as twitching another muscle of its body. Tomas flew across the site and smashed into one of the standing stones. He dropped to the ground and shook his head.

The demon raised both its arms and gripped the air, pulling down as if it were tearing a tapestry from a wall. Twin bolts of lightning streaked down and contacted Tomas. They pinned him to the earth. Unable to lift himself, Tomas could barely manage to writhe beneath the onslaught. He opened his mouth to scream, and nothing came out but bile.

A third lightning bolt joined the others. The glare hid Tomas. The demon laughed its alien laugh and silenced the storm.

Tomas lay naked on the stone, pink skin touched here and there by scorch marks, brown hair singed, but otherwise unharmed. Gone were the tail, the horns, the mottled hide. He was every bit human, looking small beside the massive demon.

It stared at him as he lifted his head. Then it laughed clearly and forcefully.

"So," it said when it recovered some composure, "little brother is not little brother after all. That was a powerful curse on you. I meant to strip away your resistance. Instead, I am rewarded with a replacement for the food I so hastily removed earlier. You say the woman is yours. Well, then look upon me and know she is mine."

"I said 'not today.'" Mauriel thrust forward, and her sword pierced the demon's back. It shifted at the pain, preventing the blade from penetrating any vital organs. The demon made another swiping motion. Mauriel was struck and lifted into the air. She landed ten paces away in a motionless heap.

Tomas rose and sprinted forward. The demon turned at his approach, and Tomas ducked under its arm and gripped the sword's hilt. He drew the blade out of the demon as if from a scabbard, and turned, chopping down. His blow struck the demon on the hip and bit deep, but Tomas didn't wait for a reaction. He drew the blade back to gain more cutting advantage then spun as the swordsman had. The extended claymore caught the demon under the arm and sliced through to the ribcage, halted by the unearthly bones.

The demon howled and drove its fist backward. Tomas was already gone, pulling the blade free and cutting again at the demon's leg. His powerful stroke amputated the demon's tiny leg above the knee, and Tomas let the momentum of his swing carry the blade over his shoulder. He brought it down after it reached the top of its arc and attacked the creature's head.

Screaming with pain, hobbled by the loss of its leg, the demon did nothing as Tomas brought all the strength of his shoulders and arms to bear on that last cut. The middle of his blade touched the top of the demon's head and split it down to the breastbone as if only a melon. The demon's screaming quieted instantly, and it fell to the ground in a pile of useless meat and bones.

Tomas wrestled the wedged sword free.

"That," he said to the demon's carcass, "is why the witch went after me and not Mauriel." Tomas ran to Mauriel and couched her head on his leg. She was breathing without weakness. As he brushed the hair from her face, she opened her eyes.

Mauriel blinked and stared at Tomas. Her eyes watered, and the corners of her mouth lifted.

"I missed that face," she said.

"Are you well?"

"I have broken bones in my chest, but I will live."

Tomas leaned down and set a lingering kiss upon her mouth.

"Lips," Mauriel said when they broke contact. "That is not all I missed about you, Tomas."

"Recover your strength, my sweet. Then we can search for that swordsman's belongings. With any luck, there will be something in the way of clothing among them. When you are strong enough, we can make for Qaam-ru."

"Why should we need to?"

"Um, darling, the transformation was not complete."

Mauriel turned her head in Tomas' lap and stared.

Her laughter echoed over the site for a very long while.

Robert J. Santa
has been writing speculative fiction for more than twenty-five years.
He lives in Rhode Island, USA with his beautiful wife and two equally
beautiful daughters. Robert is the editor-in-chief of Ricasso Press.

BOX
OF
BONES

by Jonathan Moeller

Maraeus awoke to see a naked woman standing before his bed, her skin illumed in the moonlight pouring through the window.

"My lord," she said, her voice a soft purr.

He stared at her for a moment.

"Nika?" he said, recognizing her at last. She had caught his eye a few years past, when she started working in his father's kitchens. But his father had strong feelings against the highborn dallying with commoners, and Maraeus had spoken to her maybe a dozen times in the last two years. Besides, his lifestyle did not lend itself to romantic encounters.

So why on earth is she naked in my bedroom?

"My lord," whispered Nika, shivering, her eyes sparkling. "Let me join you. Let me warm myself in your arms."

Maraeus sat up, staring at her. How he wanted to pull her close, to feel the heat of her naked flesh against his skin. Yet something was wrong. Something was terribly wrong.

She glided toward him, smiling.

"Wait," said Maraeus, licking his dry lips. "Wait. You're betrothed, aren't you? To Dmitri, one of the grooms." In fact, he had seen them kissing in the stables.

"A lowborn dog, my lord," said Nika. "He is nothing. Let me join you."

Maraeus looked away, trying to clear his mind. A suspicion took shape, followed by a flood of fear. Nika had been a shy, timid woman. *What could cause such a change?*

Nothing good.

"Do me a favor," Maraeus said, "and you can join me here."

A smile spread over her lips. "I'll do anything for you, my lord. Anything at all."

"That box, on the table by the door," said Maraeus. He pointed. "Bring it to me."

"As you wish."

She turned on one heel, dark hair swinging over the shifting contours of her white back. Maraeus wrenched his eyes from the tantalizing sight and picked up one of the bottles on his nightstand.

"This box?" said Nika, pointing.

"Yes," said Maraeus, "that one. Bring it to me."

Nika smiled, her fingers curling around the box.

The silver box.

There was a sizzling noise, wisps of black smoke rising from her hands. Nika screamed and arched her back, shuddering. She leapt away from the box, moving with inhuman speed, and clung to the wall like a spider. Maraeus wrenched his way free from his blankets, still clutching the bottle from his nightstand. There was one force that could give a slender woman like Nika the ability to move with inhuman speed and strength.

A demon had taken up residence inside her skull.

"Mortal fleshbag," spat Nika. Her voice had become a growl, rock rasping against rock. "I shall tear the skin from your carcass and feed it to you inch by inch."

Maraeus hefted the bottle and waited.

She came at him even faster than he expected, her body flowing, rippling, additional limbs sprouting from her sides, talons bursting from her fingers, her mouth twisting into a fang-filled pit. Something like a freakish hybrid of an insect and a wolf leapt at Maraeus, eyes blazing with hellfire.

He hurled the bottle at her. It exploded, spraying her with clear water. Nika wrenched backward with a scream, her skin sizzling, white flames dancing over her chest and arms. She beat herself against the wall, trying to rub the water away.

Demons could not endure the touch of silver, or of water blessed by priests of the Threefold King. But neither silver nor consecrated water would expel the demon from Nika's body. Maraeus ran to the windows and threw open the shutters. An iron spike had been driven into the stone, and a coiled rope lay upon the sill.

Maraeus had learned the value of preparation long ago.

He flung the rope into the night, vaulted over the sill, and descended as Nika thrashed and howled. His bedroom was on the fourth story of his father's mansion, and the wind tugged and pushed at him. By the time he reached the third story the screams came to a sudden stop. Maraeus looked around in sudden panic, kicked off the wall, and flung himself onto a nearby balcony. Maraeus ducked beneath the marble rail, peering through the balustrades.

An instant later Nika sprang over the windowsill, coming down the wall like some monstrous spider. Maraeus watched her vanish into the streets below. He counted to sixty, took a deep breath, and pushed open the balcony door. It opened into one of the mansion's many guest bedrooms, the furniture covered with heavy sheets. He crossed to the empty wardrobe, opened it, reached inside, and removed the false back panel.

Steel and silver reflected the moonlight.

Ever since his mother's death he had hunted demons, and he had indeed learned the value of preparation. Consequently he had caches of weapons and armor hidden throughout his father's house. Maraeus pulled on a leather coat studded with steel plates, followed by a belt of silver-plated knives. A crossbow went over his shoulder, and a quiver stuffed with both silver and steel-tipped quarrels onto his belt, along with several flasks of consecrated water.

He hurried into the hallway. The gods alone knew what the demon might do if it roamed free.

Maraeus needed a horse, the faster the better. The demon could outrun him, but he doubted the demon could match a good horse. He slipped through the kitchens, exited into the yard, and headed toward the stables.

The noise stopped him in his tracks.

Cacophony came from the stables. He heard the horses neighing and stamping, the walls trembling as they banged against their stalls. The horses sounded as if they had gone mad. Maraeus knew a few things that could frighten a horse like that, and he doubted that someone had dropped poisonous snakes into every last stall.

He pulled one of the flasks of consecrated water from his belt and entered the stables.

"Nika?"

A man's voice, surprised. Maraeus stopped, listening.

"Nika, what are you doing here? Cover yourself!"

"Dmitri, my love," said Nika, her voice purring. "How have I missed you. Come to me."

"But...but here?" Poor Dmitri sounded flummoxed. "In the stables? In another week we shall be wed..."

"I cannot wait for you, my love," said Nika. "Come to me. Come to me now."

Maraeus gritted his teeth.

The demon might have been sent to kill him, but it would kill Dmitri just for the fun of it.

Maraeus stepped around the corner, saw Dmitri standing in the aisle between the stalls, his hair tousled from sleep, a lantern in his hand. Nika glided toward him, opening her arms for him, her naked body glimmering in the lantern's glow.

Her face twisted in hatred as she saw Maraeus.

"Nika?" said Dmitri, turning in confusion. He saw Maraeus and his eyes widened. "My lord? It's...I don't understand..."

"Down!" roared Maraeus, pulling the stopper from the flask.

Nika's body rippled, extra limbs bursting from her side, talons sprouting from her fingers. The horses went mad, screaming and kicking at the walls. Dmitri saw Nika's grotesque transformation and shouted in terrified surprise. Maraeus shoved him out of the way and flung the flask at Nika. She shrieked as the consecrated water splashed over her naked flesh, white flames dancing over her skin. In her rage she smashed through a wooden gate as if it were no more than paper. The horse within the stall screamed in terror, trying to pull away from her.

"My lord," said Dmitri, scrambling to his feet, "my lord, my lord, I don't understand, what's happening..."

"Shut up," said Maraeus, wrenching open another stall door, "and help me saddle this damn horse."

There was a ghastly ripping sound from Nika's direction. A jet of red blood spattered across the aisle, followed by the severed head of a horse, the eyes wide and terrified. Maraeus turned, pulled his crossbow free, and slammed a steel-tipped bolt into place.

"What…what are you doing?" said Dmitri.

"Saddle the horse," said Maraeus.

"You're going to shoot her?" said Dmitri. "But you'll kill her!"

"Saddle the damned horse," said Maraeus, raising the bow. "And this isn't going to kill her. It won't even scratch her. It's just going to annoy her a bit."

An instant later Nika whipped around the corner, smeared with the dead horse's blood. Maraeus squeezed the trigger a heartbeat before her claws would have buried themselves in his throat. The quarrel slammed into her chest, the force of the impact throwing her off her feet and into the wall. Nika dropped to the floor, stunned, and Maraeus took the opportunity to dump another flask of consecrated water over her. Again the water erupted into white fire, Nika thrashing and howling.

The quarrel lay intact and undamaged next to her. It hadn't even broken her skin.

"My lord!" shouted Dmitri, gazing in horror at his betrothed.

Maraeus ran to the trembling horse and swung into the saddle. "Get behind me." Dmitri scrambled after him. A bare instant later Maraeus dug his heels into the horse's flanks. The terrified beast lurched forward, which also had the salutary effect of knocking Nika back to the ground. Maraeus yanked the reins to the left, and the horse galloped out into the night.

Nika raced after them, running on all fours like a wolf, but the horse soon outpaced her.

"My lord?" said Dmitri.

They had been galloping for some time. Maraeus had a destination in mind, and he had steered the horse away from the city's mansions and toward the docks. He saw no trace of Nika, but he had no doubt that the demon was in pursuit.

"What is happening, my lord?" said Dmitri. "What happened to my Nika?"

Maraeus hesitated, wondering how much to reveal. He decided to dell Dmitri everything. The man deserved to know.

Besides, they both might die before dawn.

"Nika has been possessed," said Maraeus. "A demon, a fallen angel. One of the lesser orders, but still dangerous. It makes her faster, stronger, impervious to steel weapons, along with other powers."

"Possessed? My Nika?" said Dmitri, bewildered. "Why?"

"A sorcerer could do it, or one of the magi," said Maraeus. "That kind of demon can't escape from hell on its own. They have to be summoned. Once they're here, they'll claim a body for their own and go out to make trouble."

"But why, my lord?" said Dmitri. "Why take Nika? She is a good woman…when I saw her naked in the stable I thought she had gone mad. She'd never do anything like that. Why would the demon take someone like her?"

Maraeus sighed. "It probably took her to get at me."

"You, my lord?" said Dmitri. He sounded shocked. "A sorcerer sent a demon to kill you? But you're just…you're…"

Maraeus glanced back at him. "The fourth son of a lord? A drunk?" He smiled. "A useless idler?"

Dmitri blinked. "It's…it's not my place to criticize my lord's sons, my lord."

"That means yes," said Maraeus. "I hunt demons, Dmitri. My father doesn't know. He wouldn't believe. People either don't believe in demons or are too frightened to pay attention. So I hunt them. Someone has to." He sighed. "It's my fault Nika has been dragged into this. The demon possessed her to get at me."

"Is there a way to save her?" said Dmitri, voice quiet.

"Maybe," said Maraeus. "If I can find the sorcerer who called up the demon, I can force him to end the spell. Or if I kill him, the spell breaks, and the demon goes back to hell. Either way frees Nika."

"Will you try to save her, my lord?" said Dmitri.

"Yes," said Maraeus.

If he could.

He did not tell Dmitri that killing Nika would also expel the demon from her body. The demon might have the ability to repel steel weapons, but its powers were not proof against silver daggers or silver-tipped crossbow quarrels. And the sorcerer who had conjured the demon might be too strong to kill. Maraeus might have no choice but to kill Nika before the demon in her head killed him

He had done it before.

"I will try to save her," said Maraeus at last. "If I can. But you have to understand. You've seen how fast and strong the demon makes her. If it catches us off guard it will kill us both before we can react."

"I'll do anything," said Dmitri. "I'll do anything to save my Nika. I'll help you, my lord. I'll do whatever you say."

"Good," said Maraeus. "Then tie up the horse. We're here."

He reined in before a dilapidated house of brick and clay-fired tiles. Dmitri tied the horse to the rail, while Maraeus took a quick look around. He saw no trace of the demon, but it was clever enough to hide when necessary.

"Who lives here, my lord?" said Dmitri.

"Help," said Maraeus. He crossed to the door and knocked. "A priest of the Threefold King."

"The Threefold King?" said Dmitri. He looked uneasy. "What good can a priest of a foreign cult do us?"

"You'd be surprised," said Maraeus, still knocking. "That water I threw on her? A priest of the Threefold King blessed it."

The door groaned open. A middle-aged man in a ragged gray robe leaned against the doorframe, peering out at them. He blinked a few times, and then smiled. "Maraeus."

"Abban," said Maraeus. "There's trouble."

"Of course there is," said Abban. "Why else would you pound upon my door in the middle of the night?" He peered over Maraeus's shoulder. "Who is this?"

"This is Dmitri, a groom in my father's house," said Maraeus. "His betrothed has been possessed."

Abban looked grim. "You'd better come inside."

Maraeus and Dmitri followed the priest into the house. The main room was empty, save for a few benches. Here the worshippers of the Threefold King gathered to worship and pray, free from harassment from the authorities. Abban handed them both stone cups of wine, and they sat on the benches.

"Tell me what happened," said Abban.

Maraeus took a long drink and started talking, with Dmitri adding details.

"I thought something like this might happen," said Abban. "Yesterday a whore's newborn child was stolen from her. The guards didn't care. I told the followers of the way to remain watchful, but no one has seen anything."

"That is sad," said Dmitri, "but what has that to do with Nika?"

"Because," said Maraeus. "The blood of an innocent is necessary for the spell to conjure up a demon. An infant under a week old would do nicely."

Dmitri looked sick.

"It seems clear that the child was slain, and his blood used to summon the demon," said Abban.

"But who?" said Maraeus. "As far as we know, there are no magi in the city who have dealings with the demons."

"That we know of," said Abban. "You of all men know how easily magi are turned to dark sorcery."

"What about Volestro?" said Maraeus.

"I have heard that name," said Dmitri. "Your lord father was talking about him. He was…one of the master magi, I think. He disappeared last month."

"Yes," said Maraeus, "disappeared."

Dmitri blinked, looked at the daggers hanging from Maraeus's belt, and swallowed.

"That missing child?" said Maraeus. "Volestro did that at least a dozen times. That we even know about. He'd become addicted to it. The demons would give him arcane power in exchange for lives,

for murder. He had to be stopped." Maraeus thought for a moment, and said, "Could this be one of Volestro's demons?"

"I don't see how," said Abban. "You killed him. Any summoning spell should have ended after his death."

"He was a master magus," said Maraeus. "Maybe he could have bound a demon here."

"Did he have any students?" said Dmitri.

Maraeus and Abban looked at him.

Dmitri shrugged. "Well…don't sorcerers usually have apprentices?"

"They do," said Maraeus, looking at Abban.

"Volestro had three," said Abban. "Two of them left the city to take different masters after you killed Volestro. I think the third is still in the city."

"Where is he?" said Maraeus.

"His name is Harwulf," said Abban. "An outlander, an Arthag barbarian. He's living in Volestro's old house."

"Good enough," said Maraeus. He rose. "We'll have a talk. Come on, Dmitri."

"Are you sure you should involve him?" said Abban.

"She is my betrothed!" said Dmitri.

"Demons are incredibly dangerous," said Abban. "If you don't know how to fight one, you'll probably get killed."

Maraeus shrugged. "Like he said, she's his betrothed."

Volestro's house stood grim and silent, looming over one of the city's wealthier streets. Maraeus crossed the street and slid a silver-tipped bolt into the crossbow. Dmitri tied up the horse, giving the silent house nervous looks.

"What do we do now?" said Dmitri.

"We find Harwulf, and if he gives us any trouble, we kill him," said Maraeus.

"And if Nika shows up?" said Dmitri.

"Then we definitely kill Harwulf," said Maraeus. "If the demon shows up to defend him, then it's a good sign that he summoned it. Also, look for a wooden box, carved with sigils upon the lid and sides."

"What is that?"

"It will contain the materials he used in the spell, to keep control over the demon," said Maraeus. "If we can destroy it, the demon will go back to hell. If we're lucky, it might even turn on Harwulf first. Follow me."

He had broken the lock on the front door during his confrontation with Volestro, and it hadn't been repaired. Maraeus walked inside, crossbow ready. Inside the house smelled of old blood and rotting meat. Maraeus crossed to the dining hall. All the furniture had been removed from the room, and strange symbols and runes had been carved into the floor and walls. Here Volestro had used innocent blood to conjure up demons, sending them to kill his enemies.

A man in a ragged brown robe sat in the corner. He had a wild mane of fire-colored hair, and a greasy red beard. His eyes glittered in sunken sockets, and fixed upon Maraeus.

"Welcome," said the man, his voice a whispering rasp. "I thought you might find your way here."

"You are Harwulf?" said Maraeus.

"Yes," said Harwulf. "You slew my master."

"Your master had it coming," said Maraeus. "How many people did he kill?"

"The great dark ones did the killing," said Harwulf. "The great dark ones will rule the earth. The day will soon come, and the mortal races will be as cattle to them. Save for those who have served them well."

"So, you summoned up the demon to kill me?" said Maraeus.

"Yes," said Harwulf. "If my demon slays you, the great dark ones shall be pleased, and they will reward me." His eyes flicked to Dmitri. "Who is this? Your protector?"

"Your demon possessed his betrothed," said Maraeus.

Harwulf burst out laughing, and Dmitri's hands curled into fists. "Did it? How delightful. The great dark ones are pleased by cruelty. Yes. His own beloved shall rip his heart from his chest."

Maraeus leveled the crossbow. "Nothing of the sort shall happen."

Harwulf's smile didn't waver. "Will it?"

He glanced toward the ceiling.

And Maraeus realized that he had made a mistake. He squeezed the trigger just as Nika dropped from the ceiling, talons erupting from her fingers. She crashed into him just as the crossbow released, the bolt missing Harwulf by a few inches.

Maraeus rolled across the floor as the demon slashed and clawed at him, the talons skidding off the steel plates of his jacket. He yanked a dagger from its sheath, but the demon's hand closed about his wrist and wrenched the blade free. Maraeus clawed at his belt with his other hand and pulled free a flask. Consecrated water spilled out, splashing over both Maraeus and Nika. The demon reared back with a scream, white flames spilling from Nika's flesh, and shook itself like a dog. Maraeus scrambled back to his feet, yanking out a silver-plated dagger, while Dmitri fled from the room.

Maraeus couldn't blame him.

"Kill him slowly, my pet," crooned Harwulf. "Make him scream. I want to see blood. Lots and lots of blood."

A hiss came from the demon. It circled toward him, talons extended, and Maraeus circled in the other direction, hoping to get a clear shot at Harwulf. But the demon skittered sideways, keeping itself interposed between Maraeus and Harwulf. It lunged, and Maraeus lashed out with the dagger. Nika danced away, and Maraeus followed up by flinging the dagger. The demon snarled and ducked, and Maraeus lunged for his fallen crossbow. He slammed a silver-tipped quarrel into the bow and pulled back the lever.

He'd prefer to shoot Harwulf, but he might have no choice but to kill Nika. He didn't want to. But if he didn't do something soon, Nika would kill him, and then would probably kill Dmitri just for the joy of it.

The demon was fast enough that he'd only get one shot. Maraeus leveled the crossbow, took aim—

"My lord!"

Dmitri ran back into the room, a wooden box under one arm. Maraeus saw runes carved into the box's sides, runes that flickered and glowed with bloody light. Harwulf stood up with an alarmed shout, pointing at the box.

"I found it," said Dmitri, "it was hidden under the bed—"

"Slave!" Harwulf yelled, "kill him, kill him, kill him now."

The demon whirled on Dmitri.

"Dmitri!" said Maraeus. "Drop the box!"

Dmitri dropped the box, backing away. Maraeus took aim and pulled the trigger. The silver-tipped bolt lashed out and buried itself in the box's side. The glowing runes flickered and sputtered. The demon came to a sudden halt, Nika's face twisting in agony. Maraeus threw aside his bow, lunged for the box, and ripped open the lid. Tiny bones filled the box, white and polished, no doubt the bones of the murdered infant. Maraeus saw his own name written upon a piece of parchment threaded through a tiny skull.

He seized the box and flung the contents across the room. Small bones rained across the floor. The box shuddered in his hands, the runes flaring, and crumbled into ash. The demon went perfectly still, Nika's eyes closed.

"Kill them both!" squealed Harwulf, "kill them both now—"

The demon sprang across the room in a single bound, and plunged its claws into Harwulf's throat. The red-hair man sagged to his knees, eyes bulging, blood spilling across his robes as he died. The demon shuddered, once, and stepped back.

And then it was gone.

Nika stood in its place, blinking in horrified confusion at the carnage.

"My lord?" she whispered at Maraeus. "What...what—"

"Nika!" said Dmitri. "You are all right!"

"Dmitri?" said Nika, trying to cover herself all at once. "What...what happened to my clothes?"

The next morning Maraeus felt battered, bruised, and sore, but he staggered out of bed and made his way to the breakfast table.

"Look who has deigned to join us," said his father. "A long night?"

"It was," said Maraeus, reaching for the wine.

His father scowled in disapproval. "A wastrel lifestyle."

Maraeus glanced out the window, and saw Dmitri and Nika walking together by the stables.

"It has its compensations."

Jonathan Moeller wrote the novel Demonsouled *published by Gale/Five Star in 2005, so it's only appropriate that his story appears in* Demons: A Clash of Steel. *His short fiction has also appeared in Marion Zimmer Bradley's* Sword & Sorceress *anthologies 22, 23, 24 and 25,* Apex Digest, Lilith Unbound, AlienSkin, *and* MindFlights. *Visit his website at www.jonathanmoeller.wordpress.com.*

BY HELLISH MEANS

by Bill Ward

Yrisa slashed at the pack of shadeforms that surrounded her, swinging her dwimmerblade in tight, lateral arcs to keep the things at bay. One demon, braver than its fellows, lunged at her with outstretched talons, and Yrisa took one of its arms off at the elbow, relishing the fiend's resultant howl. The pack had surprised her as she picked her way slowly through the dead city, coming upon her unexpectedly at twilight; six fell beasts of shadow-flesh and smoke, all but invisible to human eyes. But Yrisa, as the pack was finding out, was no mere human.

The injury to one of their number galvanized the pack, and they rushed her. Yrisa pivoted to intercept a pair charging her from behind, and both demons vanished in a blast of acrid smoke as the dwimmerblade flicked out to find their secret hearts—the soulcages within every hell spawn that enabled them to cross over onto the physical plane. Without pause, Yrisa followed the line of her second thrust with a lunge that took her beyond the tightening circle of her attackers. She was close to the ruined temple where she had intended to camp that night, and she ran toward it through the empty city with the snarling pack at her heels.

She had come in out of the wastes scant hours ago, and already the place was proving livelier than expected. Yrisa reached the lowest stair of the temple and launched herself upward, taking the crumbling steps two at a time. The four remaining shadeforms bounded after her, gibbering and shrieking like a pack of carnivorous baboons.

The dying sun of her world was low in the west, casting Yrisa in its blood-red radiance as she ascended the high marble stair and left the shadowed blackness of the street behind. She had been the youngest of her order but circumstances had aged her beyond her years, and her once smooth features showed the cracks of worry and pain, and strands of premature silver glinted from within her night-black fringe of hair. In this age of sorrow her beauty—for all the Brides had been beautiful—was now of a different sort. Men had once said of her that she possessed the face of an angel; she did still, but it was now an angel of the avenging kind.

Yrisa vaulted the last step and arrived at a landing before the temple's colonnaded entrance. She spun to confront her pursuers; blade held easily before her, limbs poised in readiness as she had been taught. The first of the shadowy beasts to lope to the top of the stair was the one she had maimed, a demon driven mad with rage. She dispatched it quickly, plunging the dwimmerblade hilt deep into its chest and ripping outward as the thing's body dissolved into hissing mist. The remaining three were more careful, and looked at her now with keen appraisal. No mortal could have done what she just had, and some measure of comprehension dawned on the demons. They checked their headlong, rolling charge and instead advanced in cautious unison.

Yrisa felt the stirring within her that battle always engendered, the force she could not allow to the surface, that thing to which she was wedded. She was the last of her order on this overrun world, this Hell on earth, and she had only survived because the stolen power within her was greater than that of any Bride who had ever dared tryst with the sons of Hell.

To fight Hell, Mother Superior had said, *one must use hellish means.*

The shadeforms tore heavy paving stones from the stair and flung them at Yrisa, before clattering up the escarpment in a unified assault. The dwimmerblade blurred before her in defense, gonging a rich bass note with each deflected rock. Yrisa sang her own song, sweet and high, a song of ritual battles and warrior-women, of sacrifice and of death. The demons closed upon her—

——and were blown back into the stuff of smoke and night with three swift strokes of the enchanted weapon.

Alone, atop the temple steps, with the tomb-hush of evening settled upon the lands and the last knife-edge of red in the west to illuminate the world, Yrisa looked out over the dead city of Arghoz Lok that sprawled ruinously beneath her and wept.

Survival had been hard.

In a land littered with the putrescent corpses of beasts of the air and of the field, where wells ran dry or yielded up only a thick slurry tainted with hellpower, where even the ground blistered and ran with toxic scum like the lymph from a leper's sores, survival had been hard. Hunted, alone, and sick within her soul, even Yrisa had lived but a breath away from death and damnation all these long years.

But she had power and, when the shock and anguish that had poisoned her will had run their course, Yrisa too found that she had motive to survive. Revenge.

She found pockets of survivors, Geometers and Lawseekers, and even common men and women of rare fortitude. Communities here and there, hiding, nursing their wounds, knitting together new kinships while they discovered ways to live again in a world gone mad. She had been most welcome among them, though the demands on her had proven a test she had not expected. A test she had risen to as the last representative of her kind. All had known her immediately for what she was, a Bride, the sole remainder of an order at the forefront of the war against Hell's minions.

For five hundred years the Brides

had fought the incursions that erupted periodically from the Hellmouth, and for five hundred years they had kept the world safe. And then, in Yrisa's youth, had come their greatest triumph. Ilania Tashrl, champion of their order and vessel of the Archfiend Reaniax, one of the most powerful demons ever harnessed to a mortal's will, had found a way to end the war forever, to seal the putrid maw of the Hellmouth and sunder the world of men from that of demons for all time. Yrisa had been at the ceremony, she had tasted the tears and the triumph of Tashrl's plan, and had bid the champion farewell as she rode away from the monastery on her world-changing task.

For Ilania Tashrl had sealed the Hellmouth from within. From the other side, from the tortured landscape of the Abyss itself.

But it had not worked, Yrisa reflected bitterly as she lay in her bedroll in one of the ruined temple's anterooms. Tashrl's sacrifice—the greatest sacrifice that ever mortal was to make—had afforded the world but a short-lived peace. And what emerged from the Hellmouth a decade later was the strongest force Hell had ever assembled for war upon the world.

Her order had been at the forefront of the fight. Tashrl's act of sealing had not caused them to give up their art, far from it. For the Brides were a powerful force for good in the world, and much did they accomplish in uniting the quarreling kingdoms of mankind once the demonic threat was countered. The Brides continued to take within themselves their greatest foes, summoning them from the other side, offering them willing and pliant vessels—vessels that turned out to be traps, for the Brides' art was the art of ensnarement and domination, and any demon unfortunate enough to find itself entering such a host was harnessed to a will of iron.

She could feel the demon within her now, unquiet, restless, hungry. She could not say what level of awareness the bond-charge possessed, whether or not it knew its kind had won. She tested it now, alone in the quiet dark, teased it with a mocking touch, meeting it soul to soul. She felt its hatred and returned it ten-fold, and the beast within her trembled at her wrath.

Yrisa, last of her kind, was also the greatest, having managed a feat of binding never before witnessed by the order. It was small comfort. She wondered, not for the first time, if it would be enough.

Her quest had brought her here, to Arghoz Lok, a city a thousand-years dead. Long researches by the Geometers of Sul had unearthed rumor that within the city existed a fell book, the Liber Malefactum, the text of the dwimmer-caster Eglan Glassera. The book, so the Geometers believed, contained rites of the vilest kind, those of summoning and possession, of sacrifice and defilement. But also, scant hope maintained, of banishment and binding.

And one rite in particular it was said to posses, a weapon of ultimate power against the enemy. The rite of dissolution, an instrument for the utter destruction of demonkind both in this world, and in Hell itself.

Senses attuned to the faintest stirrings around her, Yrisa slid into fitful sleep. Tomorrow she would have the book. Tomorrow she would know revenge.

Tomorrow.

Arghoz Lok was indeed livelier than she had anticipated.

They were called Venoments, Doomcriers, the heralds and scouts of Hell's minions. Yrisa had them now, fixing them in her mind, an easier kind of hell spawn for her kind to track than those shadeforms; for the Venoments were of the formal hierarchy of Hell, and each had within itself a piece of the power of the Dukes of the Abyss. Easy to find and keep fixed within one's mind once detected, and easy to avoid for one such as she.

Yrisa stole through the quiet predawn streets with a stealth honed by years of survival in the wasted landscapes of her distant homeland. She knew which ways to turn, which paths to steer clear of, which lanes were safe and which watched over by one of Hell's black crows, the misshapen and broadwinged humanoids that were the outriders of its armies. Twice, when presented with no other option, she tapped the stolen strength within herself to blind the eyes of a watching Venoment and slipped past its perch unseen. Often she stopped in the dark of an empty building or within the shade of a heap of rubble as the heat of day seeped into the dry desert air, and consulted her map of the city. Arghoz Lok was a city reengineered by a madman, a mazy winding of switchbacks and blocked-over alleys, crooked avenues and constructions that followed no earthly logic, and several times Yrisa had to double back to retrace her steps and find a new path.

Even with a map, such a sprawl would have been un-navigable without her own demonic eyes to guide her. As she crept through the stillness of the long-empty streets, Yrisa sent her hellish senses outward on wings of ethereal force, questing for those other, more deadly spawn she knew must lurk somewhere within the city—for Hell would not send its Venoment watchers if Arghoz Lok had been, as she had originally hoped, overlooked by its legions.

She wondered again just who it was that led those legions. The commander of the invasion had never been discovered. The King of the Abyss, Zuul Karanaxarax, had been absent from his realm for nearly a decade, this fact Yrisa knew all too well, but which of his rebellious underlings had possessed the skill to breech the Hellmouth seal? Which had shown such genius on the field of battle that the entirety of her order had been wiped out in but three successive engagements, alongside the golemantic armies of the Geometers and the proud forces of a hundred principalities and free cities? Yrisa shuddered to recall her nagging suspicion that one of the Dukes, Ylaghat Vileskin most likely, or the hateful, many-headed Sheel, had made prisoner of Tashrl and torn from her the secrets of the order.

And the thought never left Yrisa that, if that had indeed been Tashrl's fate, then Yrisa was not alone, not the last of the Brides of Hell. The greatest champion of her order would still be alive, enduring the inconceivable tortures of the damned, alone on the other side.

But the book might hold the key to bringing her back.

After hours of slow maneuvering through the city, Yrisa caught the first glimpse of her destination. Above the crumbling tops of a wall of tenements the green stone of the great amphitheater of Arghoz Lok flashed in the midday sun. It was the last resting place of the Liber Malefactum and a place of great evil, and as Yrisa moved closer the sheer size of the construction became evident. Tier upon tier of tinted crystone rose in heavy courses above the city, dominating the nearby buildings. A series of eroded friezes depicting the agonies of Hell circled it, and Yrisa scanned each one until they were lost behind the curve of the structure. Despite its height, the amphitheater exuded a weighty presence, and seemed almost squat and earthbound, like the crouching form of some broad beast of the land.

Upon its flanks the green stone was stained and tarred with what Yrisa knew to be the blood of countless sacrifices.

In the twilight years of Arghoz Lok, Eglan Glassera had held court within the amphitheater, often demanding the attendance of the entire, diminished populace of the city he was slowly poisoning with exposure to the netherworld. There he would summon spawn and work dark miracles, and spread the taint of Hell to all in attendance. And it was in the amphitheater that he attempted, with the aid of his unholy book, to become a Prince of Hell himself, offering his city and people as sacrifice. But his spell met with failure, and the great dwimmercaster instead succumbed to a terrible, transformative surge of hellpower.

The Geometers said that Eglan Glassera still lived, there within the amphitheater, changed beyond recognition and insane with despair, ever-guarding his dread book.

Yrisa loosened the dwimmerblade in its scabbard, attenuated her senses, and approached the yawning chasm of blackness that was the building's open front gate.

There was no sign of the Venoments, nor of any other spawn, but Yrisa nevertheless felt something foul lurking within that cursed place. A presence both like and unlike the familiar taste of the demonic; a soul tainted by Hell, but also apart from it. An ancient evil of almost rarefied subtlety, a sensation she may have missed if she had not been told to watch for it. She moved through the gate, into the dark.

Absolute dark proved less a strain on her vision than twilight—for twilight was the middle ground, the meeting place between mortal and demon where neither set of senses operated at full capacity. But within the amphitheater vestibule was a thick, unbroken darkness, and the demon within her saw through it with a crystalline clarity. It relished, too, the tormented and frozen forms of the hundreds of corpses that filled the place.

Caught in their last agony, mummified by long years in the desert air and by the blast of hellpower that must have slain them, the dead surrounded Yrisa, screaming silent screams. Many of them, impossibly, still stood, withered limbs rooted to the spot, clothing and flesh fused into a tough skin of mottled black. Most lay in heaps upon the ground, a tangled and undifferentiated mass of contorted bodies. After the shock of discovery Yrisa averted her eyes, and moved past those memories of pain with their outstretched limbs and frozen expressions without a second glance. The beast within her seemed to stir, and she tasted a trace of its amusement or arousal before she clamped it down.

All corridors within the amphitheater led ultimately to her destination, and Yrisa selected one at random and moved purposefully along it. Broad enough for thirty men to walk abreast from wall to wall, and slanting slightly upward even as it curved to the left, the hallway was one of the main arteries of the place. Yrisa, stepping over the corpses that littered the way, imagined the crowds that once thronged here in better times, before the dwimmercaster's mad rule—before the structure had been turned into a vast sacrificial altar.

The way ahead lightened, the air grew fresher, and, almost without transition, Yrisa again found herself under the blinding desert sun.

Her eyes adjusted in discreet stages, and Yrisa blinked beneath the dazzling glare. First the shape of the place came to her; the enormous, dark bowl of the theater sweeping away from her and curving sharply downward before swooping up into a shadowed wall opposite where she stood. She was but a third of the structure's height above the ground floor, and the arena stage was close by beneath her, and Yrisa could feel the solid mass of the stands rising behind her, step upon step. Everything had a soft edge to it, an irregularity of form that, for the few seconds it took for her to see clearly, gave her the sense of being within some enormous natural formation, an ancient crater or the long dead caldera of a cold volcano.

Yrisa's momentary confusion was banished in a flash as her vision sharpened, and she saw just why the edges of the stands had been so subtly, organically irregular. For occupying the benches was a veritable army of the dead, fifty thousand corpses transfixed by the powers that had been unleashed here a thousand years ago, preserved as a testament to atrocity. The horror of it, the enormity of the crime, nearly stole Yrisa's breath as she surveyed the scene—but the clarion of her own warning senses ripped her back to alertness.

Yrisa dropped prone upon the steps as a gout of venom overshot her in a stinging blast. She rolled behind a stone bench, pushing aside tough mummified limbs like tree roots in an effort to find cover. Another hissing strike, and an acrid stink assaulted her, filling her throat with its harsh steam as the bodies around her dissolved. She vaulted the forward bench and its row of corpses, and ran from the cloud of stinging mist that rose from the pool of venom that had impacted not an arm's length from where she had sought refuge. Catching site of her towering adversary stalking the arena floor, Yrisa moved unerringly toward it, bounding from bench to bench, scattering the dead like leaves in the wake of a summer storm.

She sang as she charged, the dwimmerblade ringing in her outstretched hand.

Her foe was ten man-heights of writhing, chaotic flesh. Its hunched and asymmetrical torso was ringed by dozens of mismatched limbs; an array of claws, hands, hooves, and tentacles upon which it moved in a rapid but unsteady manner. A funnel-like proboscis, drooling steaming bile, tracked her dead-on as she sped toward the fiend.

Yrisa reached the lip of the retaining wall that separated the stands from the arena floor far below just as the creature spat another reeking missile. She dove forward, under the venom's arc, and out into empty space.

Such a fall would kill a normal man, but Yrisa hit the ground easily with a roll and sprang to her feet, blade at the ready. But the creature was swiftly upon her, crashing a spiked and chitinous appendage into the earth where she had landed, and scything a rubbery, suckered tentacle along the ground in a raking attack at her flank.

Faster than the human eye could follow, Yrisa severed the crustacean-like spike in a backhand blow, snicking clean through its armor with one sweep of her dwimmerblade, before hurdling the tentacle in a tumbling vault. The beast listed past her, carried by the momentum of its slashing tentacle and badly unbalanced by its severed limb. It crashed forward, and Yrisa darted close-in to strike again—and was smote such a blow as to send her flying across the arena and into the retaining wall.

The thing had not collapsed when it lost its balance. Arrayed as it was, like a starfish, with limbs radiating from all points around it, it had instead rolled nimbly forward in a grotesque cartwheel. Yrisa, crumpled against the wall and momentarily stunned by the impact, barely got to her feet in time to avoid another blast of acidic venom from the beast's nozzle-launcher.

She had some distance between her and the creature now, but she had lost her blade. Yrisa maintained a light, loping run around the exterior of the floor, keeping an eye on the thing's proboscis as it tracked her. Now she spotted the shadowy arched entrance where the beast must have lurked in concealment when she first entered the amphitheater and from which, in times past, chariot teams and acting troupes had filed out to entertain the populace. The floor area itself was scorched and blasted as if by fire and, as she ran, Yrisa in places kicked through ankle-deep ash. A raised dais stood directly in the center of the arena, topped with a grim altar and the shredded remnants of a pavilion. This she made for.

The creature lumbered after, launching the occasional spurt of venomous sputum which Yrisa easily dodged. She could see the beast clearly now, could make out within the jumbled array of flesh—patches of black insectile fur, iridescent fish scales, and more humanlike

skin—the features of a man. High up upon the beast's torso a ruined face peered insanely out upon the world, seemingly more a bubo or canker upon the broad expanse of the monster than the seat of its governing intellect. If, indeed, the shattered remains of Eglan Glassera could be said to govern the great mass to which it found itself locked in bonds of fleshy damnation.

Yrisa surged up the steps of the dais as Glassera trundled at her from the other side. At the top, she quickly made search of the place, poking into the corners of the ruined pavilion, running her fingers through the centuries-hardened muck atop the altar. All in vain, for there was no sign of the book.

The impact of a glob of venom upon the remnants of the pavilion forced Yrisa to abandon her search. Cursing, she started to run back toward the direction of her lost blade, but something upon her attacker's body caught her eye.

There, not far from the tortured head of the transformed dwimmercaster, was one of Glassera's withered arms. And in the arm, clutched tightly to a furry section of its chest, was the Liber Malefactum.

The shock of recognition exploded into a jolt of pain as Yrisa found herself hoisted into the air, imprisoned by a reptilian fist at the end of a long, sinuous arm. Again Glassera had surprised her, striking her before she could react, and Yrisa fought back her confusion and searched for an answer. Something subtle was at work, something that killed her stolen senses in a way unfamiliar to her. Despite the crushing force of Glassera's fist, Yrisa concentrated on opening all her senses, to feeling the city and its surroundings as she did before.

Nothing, no Venoments, no anything. Only Glassera. At once faint and overpowering, the abomination's presence was like that of a delicate perfume that, once noticed, blotted out all other scents.

Yrisa let out a short, sharp cry as she brought her doubled fists down upon the joint of the reptilian hand that clutched her. Glassera was bringing her closer. A wet, uneven slit opened toothlessly in the creature's flank like the vent-maw of some deep-sea creature. Yrisa struck again, and again, and within her welled the dangerous presence of her imprisoned demon lending her its unholy strength.

Her body throbbed, her head swam with visions of abyssal landscapes…

The demon was close now, a snake under the skin, a tickle at the back of the neck, a scratching beneath the temples aching for release.

With a cry Yrisa dealt a final strike with all the demonic strength she could muster, and bone thick as a tree-trunk shattered beneath her fists and she tumbled out of Glassera's grasp.

She hit the ground rolling, running toward her blade, dodging a chaos of limbs—a tumescent flipper, a sticky length of feeler like that of a giant fly, an improbable pincer arm of human flesh, its skin pale and maiden-smooth. Venom steamed in the air around her, and the high keening of her pursuer reverberated through the stands so that it seemed to Yrisa, in a grim reflection of her own black mood, that the withered multitude of dead that ringed the scene cheered and screamed for more.

Yrisa reached the dwimmerblade and scooped it up at a run. The hilt fit her hand perfectly, reassuringly. Carved from the single thighbone of a fallen angel, the weapon was of the rarest and most potent kind, and had once been in the sole possession of the champion of her order. It had been Tasrl's blade, that worthiest of Brides, and had been left behind for the one that would succeed her.

Yrisa stopped running.

She turned and raised the blade.

Glassera was upon her in an instant, a roaring wave of tortured flesh.

Once attuned to its subtle, cloying aura, she could not be blindsided by Glassera again. She hewed and dodged, deftly choosing her targets, dealing deep wounds or else completely severing whole limbs. The fiend's high-pitched wail turned into a bellow as she weaved amongst its scything arms and avoided its gobs of venom, her gore-splattered form a blur, her war-song hanging in the air like the brazen note of a funeral gong.

The beast within her grew hot. Diving from beneath a stomping hoof, Yrisa sprang up with a vicious pirouette to hack it off at its hairy ankle. Glassera stumbled. It was the opening she needed, and she leaped upon the heavily furred leg as it jerked upward in pain. Sheathing her blade as she clung to the rising appendage one-handed, she prepared to leap again.

She rose swiftly; a cliff of flesh blurred past, a jumble of ill-matched textures and types. Yrisa flung herself toward the chaotic mess of Glassera's torso just as the rising leg found its highest point. She landed heavily against a flank of leathern scales and, finding ample handholds, scrambled higher.

Glassera plucked at her in vain, clawing and digging at itself. Yrisa drew the dwimmerblade for a vicious stab at the vulnerable flesh beneath her. The weapon bit to the hilt, and Glassera bucked and trembled. She stabbed again, and ripped out and down, spewing a geyser of jet-black ichor from the wound.

The demon within her laughed, and Yrisa bit back her own echoing laughter and an icy blade of fear crept up her spine. The bond-charged demon wrapped around her soul was dangerously close to breaking out. She imagined it emerging in one great blast that would destroy her utterly—a discarded chrysalis for a demonic butterfly.

She moved and smote again and again, a flea with a deadly bite upon the hide of a giant. Glassera slowed, and she could feel its own fear now—but more than fear, a longing. A longing to be done with this existence.

The flame of mercy kindled within her, and her demonic passenger receded with a howl.

Yrisa stabbed again, precisely this time, surgically. Mercifully. The beast shuddered, sucked in a rasping breath, and collapsed. She rode the body down to an impact like the breaking of a mountain.

Exhausted, crawling over the quivering flesh of the damned dwimmercaster, Yrisa found what she wanted. Blood-spattered, nestled in a clump of insectile fur, the withered human arm of Eglan Glassera still clutched the unholy tome tightly to his body.

With a single stroke she parted arm from body, and bent to retrieve the Liber Malefactum.

But something gave her pause. Glassera's glamour was gone, the strange aura that pervaded her senses, and she discovered with a shock that she was not alone. She looked in horror at the ruined face of the dwimmercaster there above his severed arm, recognized in his dying gaze the reflection of a presence she never suspected here...

"It is fitting that it should be you, dear Yrisa, that would find the book. You are a worthy successor," said a voice Yrisa had never thought to hear again.

They surrounded her, had moved upon her undetected while she battled the fiend, the great Dukes and Princes of Hell in all their majesty. They stood gigantically in the stands, massive Formgr towering like a stone pillar, Sheel and her thousand heads like beads of water on a slug-like body, Zimrc Maw greedily scooping brown corpses into his mouth, deformed Gashrag and the hag-demon Neh Lehen locked in sickening, passionate embrace, Lord Baaj surrounded by a halo of flame, burning everything around him to cinders, and pestilent Ylaghat Vileskin, his rotting flesh sloughing from the bone.

But in all that assembled might, one figure among them held Yrisa's gaze, one impossible, human figure.

"Had you thought me dead?" Ilania Tashrl, one-time champion of the Brides of Hell, asked in feigned surprise.

Yrisa stared. Tashrl looked the same as she had a decade ago, but felt different. A figure loomed behind her—Archfiend Reaniax, her one time bond-charge. Within him, and within all the host, Yrisa's demonic vision detected the soulcages that allowed hell spawn to exist upon her world indefinitely, pulsing with dark energy. Her own demon surged to life at the sight, thrashing beneath the surface of her consciousness in frenzied awareness, and Yrisa clenched her teeth to keep from crying out.

"I had hoped you were dead...sister," Yrisa said haltingly.

Tashrl smiled sweetly. "How compassionate. But I am, as you see, very much *alive*." As she spoke Reaniax caressed her lasciviously with bestial, claw-tipped fingers.

Yrisa, clutching the book to her chest, futilely scanned the arena for a means of escape, but the unholy court ringed her on all sides.

"Alive, and awake for the first time, Yrisa. We Brides were foolish in our half-measures, foolish in our support of the weak cattle of this world. We had every power at our fingertips—a partnership could have been ours, a true marriage of our kind and theirs. A pity."

Yrisa shook her head, fighting back sudden tears. "Hell has poisoned you, whom once I loved." She could think of only one escape from this, and the demon within her writhed in excitement as it detected her thoughts.

"Hell has poisoned me? I *rule* Hell! And I rule this world and, with the Liber Malefactum," Tashrl gestured at the tome clutched tightly in Yrisa's arms, "an infinity of other worlds shall feel my yoke, shall bend before me and call me mistress."

Yrisa trembled with the force of the demon boiling within her, straining for release. She would let it out, let it out in one, final apocalypse that would send the court and Tashrl back to Hell. Her own bond-charge, lacking a soulcage, would exist but a short time before it, too, dissipated back into the Abyss.

But it would take Yrisa's soul with it.

"Place book and blade at my feet, Yrisa, and I will give you a clean death." Tashrl smiled the lying smile of a predator as she said this, and Yrisa shuddered.

"And what of Zuul Karanaxarax? What of the King of the Abyss?" Yrisa asked, her whole frame shaking as if to explode.

Around her the demons brayed laugher, the Dukes and Princes of Hell filling the arena with malicious hyena-shrieks of amusement. Tashrl joined in, as much a monster as the rest.

"Gone, flown. Fled his realm in the midst of a losing war against certain rebellious princes, and none have heard tale of him since. There is no longer a King of Hell, Yrisa. I rule there now, as is only fitting. I, the finest champion of our order, bound mistress to the greatest demon ever wedded a Bride—I now am Queen." Reaniax bared his black teeth as he played with Tashrl's hair, and Hell's new ruler smiled at Yrisa, and held out an imperious hand.

Yrisa, with her last shred of control, spoke. "Second greatest, sister," she returned Tashrl's smile and noted the dawning realization in the ex-champion's eyes. "Second."

And with that Yrisa, champion of her order, relinquished control of her bond-charge, and the King of Hell raged forth like a second sun.

Bill Ward's fiction has appeared in numerous magazines and anthologies, including Murky Depths, Every Day Fiction, Morpheus Tales, Kaleidotrope, Dead Souls, Northern Haunts, Return of the Sword, Rage of the Behemoth, *and* Desolate Places. *In addition Bill has written background material and serial fiction for fantasy and science fiction games, is a Contributing Editor for* Black Gate Magazine, *and is co-editor of the* Magic & Mechanica Anthology *from Ricasso Press. He maintains a personal site at www.billwardwriter.com.*

Lightning Source UK Ltd.
Milton Keynes UK
UKOW042241211112

202575UK00002B/49/P